I0649622

IF YOU LIVED HERE,
YOU'D BE HOME ALREADY

IF YOU LIVED HERE, YOU'D BE HOME ALREADY

a novel of rural life in the 1980s

CORDELL STRUG

RESOURCE *Publications* · Eugene, Oregon

This is a work of fiction. The characters, locations, and events are figments of the author's imagination. Resemblance to anyone, living or dead, is purely coincidental.

Resource Publications
A division of Wipf and Stock Publishers
199 W 8th Ave, Suite 3
Eugene, OR 97401

If You Lived Here, You'd Be Home Already
By Strug, Cordell
Copyright©2017 by Strug, Cordell
ISBN 13: 978-1-5326-8848-5
Publication date 4/12/2019
Previously published by Ytterli Press, 2017

Part titles are taken from the hymn "For All the Saints," verses 1, 2, 4, 6, 7.

For all children and parents at war with each other, and all the country children who grew up to love cities.

Our hearts are restless until they rest in you.

—Augustine

The heart has its reasons which reason does not know.

—Pascal

PART ONE
before the world

Chapter One

On a bright April day in 1984, when Ronald Reagan was president and, by presidential decree, it was Morning in America, James McGrath entered a morning that would change his life.

He ordinarily awoke to an environment that cared for him. His senses were stirred gently to awareness by the classical harmonies of the Minnesota Public Radio morning broadcast, rarely straying into the twentieth century and therefore soothing to the mind. His bedroom was as warm as he needed or wished. It was kept so by no effort of his, nor could it have been, since he lacked both the knowledge and the skill for maintenance work. But his rent helped support the apartment building's custodian, who silently provided the raw materials for James' comfort. The custodian, of course, only acted in concert with the utility companies of Minneapolis, without whom James would have perished and to whom he was only too happy to pay a monthly pittance, for they not only gave him heat, light, and water, but also made possible the radio's playing and the refrigerator's purring, which was the second sound he ordinarily noticed.

As he rose, he would find ready to hand personal and domestic articles for his comfort and convenience, international booty carried home from department stores only a few minutes' travel away: a West German hairbrush, English soap and razor blades, an Italian robe—all carried home by this young, not very wealthy, Midwestern American, at one time or another, in the trunk of his Japanese car. For the hand-ground Colombian coffee that he could buy two doors away at his food co-op, he would boil water in a tea kettle from South Africa, a country which, for all its faults, certainly understood tea kettles. When he drank his second cup, he would smoke a Dutch dry cigar. His morning evacuations and ablutions, as well as anything else he cared to discard, were carried away and disposed of by a dutiful American city.

The streets he would walk out on and drive over had been built and would be maintained and kept clear for him by that same city. That city, in its largesse, also provided men and women who were trained and ready to put out fires that threatened James, protect him from burglars and murderers, carry him to the hospital, and even revive his heart if it should stop. And they would risk their lives to do it.

Anyone, anywhere, who wanted to talk to James could call him on the telephone and hear his voice. Failing that, they could write their message in a letter and civil servants would carry it by hand to James' door, for less than the price of a bar of candy. To his door, the same servants would also bring the journals that debated the intellectual issues that interested James. He could ponder these issues and try to have some effect on them or he could simply ignore them. Others would ponder them for him, and the decisions they made would not be all that bad.

If he wanted access to the accumulated knowledge and creative vision of the human race, he could walk to either the Minneapolis Public Library or the University of Minnesota Library. He could, and did, discuss and debate any issue under the sun with his friends in the restaurants and coffee houses that thrived around him. Book stores, movie theatres, concert halls, art galleries, and night clubs were there for his amusement or spiritual nourishment. And if this had not been enough for him, James could have purchased any stimulant he wanted, from the most docile woman to the most dangerous drug.

This rich, complex, interdependent society hummed beneath him while he was sleeping and he expected to wake in its arms everyday.

It had one more precious gift to give him: the part he played in it, the giving he returned for all his receiving, the activity he contributed to redeem his passivity. James did not have to put out the fires, lay the sewer pipes, bake the bread, brew the beer, or repair the highways. And, because others did, he did not have to slay the animals of the earth and roast them over a handmade fire in a damp cave. James was the organist and choir director at Mount Moriah Lutheran Church.

He liked to be called *Kapellmeister*. It made him think of J.S. Bach.

James, with his music, was a bud that bloomed at the very top of the mature social plant, impossible without that plant and its healthy thriving. This was the last, best gift his world gave him, the final provision for his satisfaction. As it hummed beneath him, he gave it musical expression. He liked to think that was his best gift to it.

Into this orderly, satisfactory, and motherly environment, James ordinarily awoke each day, more or less refreshed, more or less eager for what awaited him. But this was not, would continue to be not, and could by no means turn into an ordinary morning.

James woke with chilly flesh to a silent world. His first thought was that he had gone deaf. Then, no coward at facing facts, he concluded he was dead.

But there was sound. It simply wasn't his own sound. Alien noise, and it had difficulty penetrating his mind. There was a shield just inside his ear, a shield of pain which had its own volume. It was a dull, heavy pain, pulsing, as from a railroad spike being driven into the base of his skull by a sullen worker with sweaty muscles. A few of his next thoughts flirted with the wish to be dead.

He couldn't locate himself in time or space. His senses were obsessed with whatever was crawling over his skin. What was it? Nothing. Creepiness without substance. That, he thought, is probably the effect of the alcohol. This piece of logic, a kind of victory of reason, gave him as much comfort as anything would this morning. It steadied him. He knew who he was: himself.

Like a misty forest touched by dawn, the cacophony in his ears took form. He heard wind, motors, distant voices calling, answering. Human, the voices were human, and happy. And he heard breathing, human as well, a great amount, more than his own, many bodies. It was easy and slow, a house of peace, at rest.

He was naked and in a bed. A sheet covered him. He turned slightly and his stomach rolled with sickness like an angry sea. His left hand brushed another body. Mercifully, it was living.

There had been dancing and much drinking. There had been much noise, wild laughter, and outrageous behavior.

His head was under the sheet. The light was gray. It must be early morning.

The body was a woman's. She was turned away from him, sleeping on her side. Small, soft, flawlessly molded and curved. God had her head on straight when she fashioned a woman's gentle curves. And this shape of beauty was the only proof needed of the femininity of God. Stephanie had taught him that. Stephanie's lovely body. Steph. Lovely.

They had been so drunk. He had started undressing her as they danced. Alcohol and sex: two supreme pleasures of nature and great motors of civilized life. He lay now in the wake of their passage and assented to their supremacy more by deduction than sensation. He felt sick and that was all he felt.

The breathing around him was broken by a comfortable sigh, a guttural groan of unconscious pleasure. But it didn't come from Stephanie. He touched her again to make sure she was alive. At this early stage of agony, he needed the assurance of basic values.

Then he pulled the sheet from over his face. There were two beds in the room. The couple, couples, odd persons, or dormant beasts in the other bed were shifting languorously under a pile of clothing. He thought he recognized Stephanie's blouse amid the pile.

Logic suggested he find the toilet. With any luck, he could vomit away most of his discomfort.

Or was it someone else he undressed last night? A memory of his hands, pulling at the buttons of someone, who?, surprised and pleased, giggling, flashed through his mind. His head hurt. He had ached for Stephanie. But he remembered thinking during the party: I have to get naked with somebody, anybody.

No, this was her. He looked at her body again. The pillow was over her head and he didn't disturb it. She had told him once she always slept with one over her head, then woke with a splitting headache. Eccentricities of the beloved, always charming.

The toilet. Slowly. He rolled his legs off the bed, intending to swing them to the floor. But the floor was apparently two feet higher and much, much harder than he expected. The shock waves of the impact surged up his skeleton and rippled through the marvelously detailed human nervous system he had rarely suspected of being so sensitive. He sank back in disorientation.

It wasn't a bed, only a mattress. Another challenge: he would not only have to leave it but he would have to *rise*. Eventually.

He rolled out, much the simplest thing. His nakedness, which had seemed the night before incandescent and potent, now hung upon his bones and dizzy soul with shameful awkwardness. He wanted clothing. His clothes were not in sight. Next to Stephanie's pillow were a boot, three socks, a necktie, and a slight, powder blue bra. He crawled to the neighboring mattress and its mountain of garments. None of them his. He pulled out some purple sweat pants and an olive drab t-shirt. The shirt had a skull on it and a Marine insignia. It also bore a slogan: mess with the best, die like the rest. It seemed to make a great deal of sense.

The articles he pulled out left a hole in the pile. James peered into it. There was a face with a big toe in its mouth. He saw that there would be little help for him this morning in putting the world back together.

It would probably help to have warmer feet. He crawled back to Stephanie, the only anchor he had found thus far in this gale of confusion, patted her pillow and gathered up some socks.

He found he could sit. Then, dressing, he found he could stand. Walking was not as easy, but walking is a very complex motion, requiring balance, co-ordination, muscle strength and control, the courage at once to defy and to trust gravity, a sense of direction, and a greater sense of purpose. James glimpsed again the absolute and ineffable wonder of life and felt like weeping.

But now he really had to pee, and thus, praise God, was given a purpose, life again springing up from the organs of waste. He shuffled to the only doorway he saw, sick and brittle, placing each foot carefully on the hard wood floor.

As he entered the next, larger room, evidently a mead hall or basketball court or domed football stadium or underwater city built by extraterrestrials, something large and incomprehensible at any rate, as he entered this arena of vast confusion, a human leg barred his path.

He didn't want to risk seeing if it was attached to something. He swayed, tried to step over it, stumbled, ran a few steps, then regained his slow shuffle. Then he sat down. He couldn't go any further without a little more comprehension.

Someone else was stirring. Life was all around him. Life was good.

A body crawling on all fours came into his line of vision. The body stopped and squinted at him. It said, "Oh, wow, I thought you were a dream." It keeled over silently. Then it added, "They don't give parties like this anymore." It paused. "They shouldn't give parties like this anymore." Then it started to throw up.

More motivation. James rose, more easily this time, and continued on. He sustained himself by heroic images: Lewis and Clark, Albert Schweitzer, the deaf Beethoven. One more mile, one more village, one more spirit liberated, one more interplanetary flight, one more metamorphosis. One inch closer to God, one more step to the bathroom.

So where the fuck was it?

All this activity was at least clearing his mind, and this may or may not have been a good thing. He risked a long, thoughtful look at his surroundings.

This could only have been twentieth century America. The images of countless cultures hung about the walls, all of them equally meaningless. He could pick out a head by Lucas Cranach, a torso by Picasso, a reproduction of a page from the Book of Kells, an African mask, a Samurai sword, a baseball cap, pictures of a few movie stars, and, in a curious regression of the artistic spirit, a few scrawled figures of dogs on the plaster, half erased, child-artist height, which recalled the cave drawings at Lascaux. Man-the-Maker was still alive and well. It was simply no longer clear that he knew what he was doing. Or she. His pronouns lost their sensitivity when he was in this shape. He or she or they. Or anybody.

As if, right now, he cared.

More bodies were stirring about him, limbs uncoiling like wary snakes.

Beyond him, he thought he saw a corridor. He followed it and at last found the bathroom. He couldn't, even after several minutes of relatively serious effort, figure out what to do with his sweat pants so he simply removed them. Someone was sleeping with his head hanging over the toilet seat and, although James calculated that, given such a posture and the lack of brain it entailed, he could probably urinate through his ear and have a relatively good chance of having it come out the other side, he decided to use the sink instead.

The drain seemed to be plugged. James filled a good bit of the bowl and made a mental note not to splash his face awake from this source. He smelled like a rotting old man.

His sweat pants were trapped beneath the body of the person who had now slipped off the toilet seat and lay coiled around his feet. This body too seemed warm, living. That was good. Death was still at a distance.

Dimly aware that he was moving in a realm that knew neither shock nor shame, James did not bother to retrieve the sweatpants, not his anyway, and shuffled toward the kitchen. Some sort of morning ritual seemed to have engaged him. Once again in his life, he had cause to give thanks for ritual, habit, tradition, convention, grooves of action and thought, all the things that carried life while reason slept, hesitated, cringed, surrendered, or simply got drunk. And there were actually people who thought such rituals were *flaws*. This was beyond comprehension, at least to James, at least this morning.

The kitchen was empty of human life. More unconscious wisdom: no telling what deadly spores incubated here, brewing biological hazards. Even dazed humans knew enough not to lie here, let alone open the sally-ports of procreation within such a cesspool. No wonder this species had come out on top in the evolutionary struggle.

One look in the refrigerator was almost too much to convince him it contained nothing edible. He would not fight the roaches for the contents of any of the cabinets. People actually lived here, people *that he knew*. He meditated on that thought with all the wonder of a child watching a cut bleed for the first time.

But yes: that was why he was here. He was in a house rented by three medical students, whom he knew not well enough to die or kill or lie for but well enough to party with. He was here along with dozens of other foolish and amoral people, most of whom he did not know, to celebrate their graduation. He hoped the three students were not going into private practice but would be given time to mature by doing menial work in some county hospital, under the firm hand of some wizened and wise old physician.

His mind slid thus from past to future, personal situation to social problem. Like the rolling of his stomach, it was a far from pleasant sensation.

But these facts had anchored him so much more. It had been a wild day, beginning in early afternoon. His niggardly hosts had provided gallons of beer, but no food to go with it. By early evening, those who had begun the party were near raving.

James had wondered if Stephanie would show up. For so long, he had wanted her for so long. But she had. He was in sad shape when she arrived. But she had forgiven him, apparently, and caught up to him, decidedly, high already no doubt on the mere decision to meet him there. She had come. With her husband.

Lord God. It struck him like the executioner's axe, severing brain from body, mind from life and sense. He had slept with her. She was still here. Holy God. She had come with her husband and, the sweet gift of the angels he had wished upon himself, he had slept with her at last.

Between these two facts lay a void he couldn't penetrate. And just now the latter seemed less sweet and supremely sensible than it must have seemed the night before, though he couldn't remember much about the night before. But he had done it. And right now the sadness and stupidity of the post-coital animal descended upon him like a maximum sentence from a merciless judge.

Stephanie and her husband were more or less his superiors. Stephanie and her husband were pastors who shared a call to Mount Moriah Lutheran Church, which appeared now in the stark guise of his sole source of income. Stephanie was still here, naked when last he had seen her, though alive. Her husband was as yet undiscovered. Perhaps he was dead. James disgusted himself by not being able to decide if that would be good or bad. He turned to the sink. A roach scurried along its rim. It was time. He puked.

There would be consequences of this night past, more consequences than a sink full of vomit.

Falling in love with a minister had not been one of his life's greatest challenges. Having done it, having joined the ranks of secretaries, organists, and parishioners who first grew fond of, then obsessed with, and finally slept with the world's clergy, he supposed it had always been easily done. The appearance of female clergy did not affect the logical point. In their tiny worlds, ministers are stars. They're always trying to look their best, constantly courting a demanding audience. They are often talented, articulate, and personable, and they rarely let their hair down in public. They don't snap at waitresses, strike unruly children, or fart at inopportune times—or so, at least, their votaries believe. They are available at odd hours, have flexible schedules, turn up in the strangest places, are easy to buttonhole, work late in lonely environments, feel gratitude for attention, and are as good as or better than anyone else at fooling themselves until it's too late. Like traffic fatalities, the wonder isn't that their love affairs happen but that there are so few.

But that was theoretical knowledge, arrived at by James over the last few weeks, as he travelled a well worn human path.

The particular that both gave life to the theory and seemed to make it irrelevant was Stephanie. To watch her grace from the organ loft as she glided through the service, with delicate gesture and noble bearing, was a rapturous vision. Susannah at her bath, naked before the elders, was not more alluring than Stephanie in her robes, as James looked down on her.

She had a rich and clear chanting voice. It coiled from her throat like a Siren's song, drifting up through the church and lifting him into the heart of music. He had heard her sing, at the Easter Vigil, the great *Exsultet* chant, one unaccompanied voice in the darkened chancel, no lights other than the candles of the congregation and the thick, white Paschal candle standing next to her. She chanted the praise of the candle's light, the work of the bees, and the stirring of new life from the grave. James had needed no hints to comprehend the sexual imagery of the candle's lowering into the baptismal font, wax spilling on the water like hot sperm into the womb of life.

Truthfully, James reflected now, he could have used some hints on the non-sexual aspects of the imagery. Too late.

But this is the way things happen, and now he was stuck with them. He decided to leave it for the moment. Maybe things would look better later. Twenty years or so from now he might be chuckling at this.

He supposed coffee was beyond this house's capabilities. He was gingerly opening up containers when he heard feet shuffling into the kitchen.

Another stranger. That, he thought, was probably easier to take than someone he might conceivably meet again. The stranger was a woman. She was wearing a sweatshirt that might have been the mate of the pants he had left behind, probably not hers either, judging by the size. Its original owner was evidently given more to wit than politics. The sweatshirt bore the words: Nuke the Whales.

The thought of the sweatpants led him to cast a discreet look toward his genitals. The Marine or Marine-fan who owned his shirt was also, luckily, much larger than James. The shirt hung to mid-thigh. He could foresee impending combat between dwarves and giants for the available clothing. He was glad he had awakened so early.

The woman shuffled closer to him. She was holding one hand over her face with the fingers spread wide, as though she were afraid it might slip off her skull any moment, leaving her brain naked. She peered into the sink. Given a few weeks in a healthy environment, she might be attractive.

"Christ," she mumbled. "Isn't there a single sink in this place you can use?" Apparently as an afterthought, she puked in it too.

James tried to think of some urbane thing to say but, standing there with his arms folded next to a retching woman, only two over-sized garments between them, he found himself deserted by his education and background.

Wiping her mouth on her sleeve, she raised her head and squinted at him. "Holy Mother of God," she said. "If I hadn't just puked, I'd think you were a dream. No. I'd know you were a *nightmare*."

This was the second person to make such a remark to him. One was easily dismissed; two were enough to begin mild worry, a low alert-signal for the conscious mind. But all he could think of to say was: "Well, this isn't my shirt."

Sarcasm was evidently a deep and ineradicable part of this woman's character. "Really? That explains everything."

Again he glanced down to check his shirt's length, but the woman wasn't looking down. She was looking up. And now a tiny, undigested memory stirred in him, carrying unpalatable news through reluctant cells to the center of his awareness.

"Nice haircut," she said.

If only time could be stopped, he would accept this kitchen, with its bugs, its stench, and this woman, for his eternal home. They could share hell together and, in a century or two, come to accept it. But, God, he did not want to have to live with what he was beginning to remember.

"It's an especially nice touch," she said, "that it isn't centered. Why follow the crowd?"

He put his hand to the top of his head, knowing already what he would and would not find. "Oh, shit."

"Oh, shit, indeed," she said. Then she laughed, covering her mouth in that polite effort to apologize for ridicule. "I'm sorry. But I knew it wasn't your style. Something about you said 'I am not as strange as I look.' It seemed like a good idea at the time, huh?"

James needed to get to a mirror. He said, not very sincerely, "I hope you feel better. I hope you find a sink."

"You mean you hope I find one to drown in. Listen, man, I didn't cut it, I just pointed it out. And, hey, thanks. I like to start the day with a smile."

God, he thought, don't let it be true. Or if it must be true, then strike me dead.

Locomotion was no problem now. His limbs were oiled and driven by terror. He raced back to the bathroom and, above the sink which still held what his body had rejected, he beheld in the mirror what his body must now accept.

It had seemed like a good idea at the time. It had seemed clever. It had seemed bold and intimate, daring foreplay of an unusually inventive sort. It had seemed a prelude to nakedness together, a kind of preliminary bond of shame, pact of love.

They had been very, very drunk when they thought this up. Paul, Stephanie's husband, had long disappeared. They had been drunk with beer and love and careless transgression.

James now had—in place of his light brown, springy, moderately long hair, neatly parted and carefully sculpted overall—a kind of near Mohawk. The rest of his head wasn't exactly shaved, indeed it was still longish in parts, but more or less harrowed, rudely thatched, in parts ripped out, in parts closely snipped, as though he had been mauled by a careless, myopic, but ultimately merciful Siberian tiger. Somewhat dispassionately, one might say it was the beginning stage of a Mohawk. And yet not quite: for the noble line of short and rigid hair, tracing the warrior's skull from brow to nape, which is the essence and glory of the Mohawk, appeared on James as hardly short or uniform and somewhat to the left of center, as if it were lost inappropriately in thoughts of its own or as if the rest of James were fleeing it. Combing might help.

But he doubted it.

Here was something else to chuckle about in a few decades or so, when he loosened up in the evening with his great-grandchildren, if he ever had any, shortly before his merciful and long awaited death.

How, how, *how* had this ever occurred to them? Never mind the excuse of drunken folly and the perverse inspiration of impending adultery. How could they ever have conceived of this as interesting, exciting, or fun? It was awful. Drunk, insane, or hysterical, how could they have done it? Cutting each other's hair.

And now the catastrophe broadened, oozing outward like the great plagues, disrespectful of station, office, or merit, felling the great and small, the foul and fair, that lay in their paths. They had cut *each other's* hair.

He rushed back to the once beautiful woman he had brought so low.

There were still few signs of life in the house. The strange woman he had encountered in the kitchen was nowhere around. Perhaps she had wandered into the street to spread cheer throughout the city or, more likely, she had shed her mortal disguise and returned to hell to guffaw at his predicament with the Prince of Darkness. Damn all these people and their stupid parties.

Stephanie still lay with the pillow over her head, but on her back now, very still. Not counting utterly spectacular and always gratefully accepted miracles, circumstances were systematically narrowing the possible scope of his prayers.

I'm here, he prayed, I'm still alive, my hair is thus, but, merciful God, let the woman escape, let my memory be faulty at that point, one measly point, what can it cost you? Or let her be dead. We'll bury her discreetly, a closed coffin funeral, the Bishop will preach and I'll play the solemn ceremonial hymns of the great Christian musicians, appropriate to the passing of a minister of the church. She'll live with honor and bittersweet sorrow in the memory of the people.

James sat on the bed, next to the body of his beloved. I'm going out of my fucking mind, he thought. The consequence, as the poets and philosophers of all ages had noted, of love. I don't want her dead.

As if God could take such lunacy seriously.

He lifted the pillow.

The job he had done on her head was, if anything, worse than the job she had done on his. It gave him no pleasure to remember now its furriness stroking his body. Her eyes were wide open and bleak.

"So," she said, her voice a desolate whisper, "I wasn't dreaming."

Everyone was speaking this morning of dreams, as if they were the fount of hope, of redemption, or at the very least of excuse. Don't worry, it's only a dream. It didn't happen, you were dreaming. Hey, if we're lucky, this will turn out to be a dream.

As if nightmares were so easy to take. As if people didn't die in their sleep. As if dreaming hadn't landed him in this miserable predicament to begin with.

"You'd laugh if I told you how many times I've heard that this morning."

She looked away from him. Her face was pale, sick with shame, and undoubtedly too much alcohol. He hoped he wouldn't have to watch this goddess vomit. Not that she looked very alluring right now. She said, "I wouldn't laugh at anything this morning."

"Well, the first look is a shock but it's not—"

She sneered.

"—it's not, well—"

"I've got to look," she said. She raised the sheet and started to rise but her nakedness struck her like a mother's slap, and she pulled the sheet around her and moaned.

James reached awkwardly for her shoulder. He didn't have the easiness of touch for the gesture. Their intimacy had leaped too far ahead of their affection, powered only by fantasy. Consolation wasn't in their vocabulary yet.

Stephanie jerked her shoulder away from his hand and shuddered, as though he were a lizard. She tried to get up again, was defeated again by shame. Then she started to cry.

James' hand hovered above her head, then retreated. "Do you want me to bring you a mirror?"

"How about breakfast in bed? No, I do not want you to bring me a mirror. I do not want you to bring me anything. I want you to leave. Leave me alone so I can get dressed."

He touched her again. "Steph."

Since he needed it said explicitly, she said, "Don't touch me. Leave me alone."

There was a rustling in the other bed. James said, "I can leave, but you won't exactly be alone."

A male bottom, hairy and white, was emerging from the pile of clothing on the other mattress, like a blind slug blundering into a grave. Stephanie put her hand over her eyes. "I have never been so humiliated in my life."

James did not know enough about her life to contradict her. Using his own life as a standard, he thought it more than likely she was right.

Hesitantly, she reached up to explore her butchered skull with one hand. Angry courage and pathetic hope fought in her face, then, as she managed a few touches and a final bold brush, despair won out over both. "Never," she said. She began nodding, like a mad woman in furious interior dialogue, and added: "You did this."

Whether it was satisfied lust, his own despair, or some innate sense of justice risen in self-defense, James began to wake from the love-induced sleep of reason. So he had done this? So he was unmarked? So she was slave, he master, and responsibility a seamless garment that fit only him? "Right. I tied you up. Then I cut mine too, just to make you look worse. Right?"

"You pig."

The slug from the next mattress had metamorphosed into a human and was stumbling toward them. He stopped and blinked at Stephanie. "Nice ass," he muttered. Then he peered more closely. "Oh. It's your head." He yawned. "Well, nice head." He stumbled on.

James could tell Stephanie was on the verge of hysteria. This was a side of her he had not yet had the privilege to see. It seemed to involve a large component of anger, even hatred. He was glad human beings, with all their gifts and clever accessories and complex chemistry, had never acquired teeth filled with venom. Otherwise, as close as he was sitting to her, he wouldn't have lived out the hour. More evidence of a benevolent providence, assuming that living out the hour was good.

She had let the sheet drop from her now as she sat up, looking for her clothes. Her breasts were covered with his teeth marks. He thought again of venom and shrugged. He wondered if Paul would find the marks stimulating, or only be pissed off.

As James could have told her, saving her a little time but perhaps gaining more of her displeasure, her clothes were nowhere around. She might just have to take pot luck, like everyone else. What made her so special?

"Where are my clothes?" She didn't look at him.

"Are you asking me?"

"God! Oh, God, how could I—"

James took a deep breath and tried to calm down. Like Adam and Eve after the Fall, they were raging at each other, as though the disaster would not have to be shared and each could be saved by shifting blame or at least directing hatred at the other. Listening to what was coming out of the small, sweet, and lovely mouth of this woman, James could grasp how the legends arose of snakes and toads leaping from beautiful, cruel lips.

This had been a morning of profound discoveries, a voyage into the fertile and fetid pool from which human nature had sprung. Small wonder we needed clothing of every sort.

Too bad they'd lost theirs.

"Steph," he began, thinking if they could get calm, things could somehow be met, if not mastered. She didn't curse him, sign of hope, so he continued: "Let's take it easy. It's done. We'll calm down and see if we can think of something. What's the rush?"

"What's the *rush*?" She looked at him, and then the horror that came over her face showed that it was just now, at this precise moment, that she herself had indeed realized just what the rush was. She grabbed his shirt with both her hands and shook him. "*What's the rush*? You idiot! It's Sunday! It's Sunday! I've got to get to the service! Oh, shit! It's Sunday!"

"Jesus Christ!"

"You did this to me! You did this to me!"

But patience and justice and pity were no longer issues for James. She had to get to the service? *He* had to get to the fucking service! They could do without her, she could hide at home, her worthless husband could take over, he'd done it before, she'd done it for him, no big deal, common occurrence—lucky bitch!—she had an alibi without knowing it! But he was the organist!

He dashed for the bathroom to find the sweat pants he had left behind. This was no time to be picky about property rights. Let's see: what would his total loss be? He always locked his wallet in his glove compartment when he partied—good. He'd left his keys under the floor mat of the car—good. So he'd be out at most one set of clothes. Maybe Stephanie could use them.

On his way back to the bedroom, hopping into the sweat pants, he thought he passed Stephanie, fully dressed, through some miracle of speed and desperation. He stopped in wonder.

But how had she regrown her hair? Perhaps women did possess strange powers, which they only exhibited in times of utter peril when all else failed. The evolutionary dice were certainly loaded in their favor.

She was sitting on the floor, surrounded by shoes of all shapes, sizes, and sexes, methodically trying them on, one after the other, no matter how absurdly oversized or alien to her they were. James looked on, amazed at her calmness and precision.

But it wasn't Stephanie. It was the woman he had encountered in the kitchen, now wearing Stephanie's clothing. She nodded to him, trying to disguise another laugh.

Well, at least he didn't have to face any miracles this morning. At least the laws of physics were still functioning. Then he realized those were the very things he was up against now: he had to move so much mass at so much acceleration over a certain distance in a certain amount of time. That didn't even begin to factor in traffic lights.

Time!

Obviously, these friends of his weren't civilized enough to own clocks. He had to ask the woman. "Do you know what time it is?"

"I think so."

"*Well?*"

"Morning—Sunday. Yeah, Sunday morning. I mean, judging by the lack of activity."

"What *time* Sunday morning?"

"Any time. Who needs to be specific on Sunday morning? It's a day of rest. You know, like the Sabbath. Do you work or something?"

"Christ! Yes!"

"Well, aren't you a poor soul. Are you a janitor or something? I hope you have an understanding boss. There are some real bastards in that line of work."

For no reason he could think of, James said: "Those clothes don't belong to you."

She smiled dreamily. "I don't think this body does either. That's life, man. Wonderful, isn't it?"

"Well, you ought to find your own."

She arched an eyebrow. "You're wearing them."

"Oh?" Was she lying? Surely, she was lying.

"Trade?"

Now he was certain she was a demon. She'd probably want his soul, too. Fuck it. Time, he was wasting time!

He ran past the bedroom door, heading for a promising looking corridor. Stephanie called out to him, sounding more pliant now: "Don't leave me here! You can't leave me here alone! Please!"

James stopped. Leave me alone—don't leave me alone. What did women want, anyway? Generously, he supposed they had as little idea as anyone else.

She was still in bed, the sheet pulled around her. Bodies were beginning to stir everywhere. If shyness was her problem, she had clearly failed to grasp fortune by the forelock. James hoped a spirit of fairness would prevail as the survivors divided up the available clothing.

He could help her. But her words had stung. Moreover, affection was now at war in him with duty and economics. She'd hate him if he left her. He'd lose his job if he stayed.

Duty and economics won. Besides, someone had to try to cover for both of them. It would have to be him or no one.

"Look, I'll come back. Try to act—I don't know, self-possessed. You'll be fine. I'll explain everything. I'll be back for you. Sorry."

"No! Please!"

If all else failed, she could always donate her body to medical science. Besides, she was married. Her husband could take care of her if he was still willing to speak to her. James, on the other hand, was the organist and choir director at Mount Moriah Lutheran Church. That was all he was, and that or something like that was all he had ever wanted to be.

It was amazing how quickly things had clarified themselves.

Chapter Two

For the first and only time in his life, James wished he were a Central American intellectual, known to be of Marxist leanings, leaving at dawn from a meeting the death squads had under surveillance, striding with pride and dignity toward the black, open mouths of automatic weapons. For the first and only time in his life, the liberty and safety of his beloved country appeared to him as a terrible prison, sentencing him to life and the pursuit of happiness.

Well, he might still be run down by a truck. What other governments do for their people the United States leaves to the discretion of isolated maniacs, the private sector, as it were, of final solutions.

Unless and until that happened, he had to keep going, try something, anything, he had to shape what was happening and what he had done into some kind of sense. *He* had to do it, not God or the government. If this was where the evolution of nature and society had brought us, things were going to get grim indeed for this species that thought itself so clever.

These useless speculations came to James as he ran to his car, found his keys, and drove away from the worst morning of his life. Though hardly *away*: it was still around him like a cloud of poison gas. He was at the mercy of nature, law, space, and time. Fine companions, if you play their game. Lose your step and you're finished.

James hoped he could remember the route to his church. The party had been held in St. Paul. Mount Moriah Lutheran Church was in Jewel Lake, one of the legal fictions that pass for communities on the outskirts of Minneapolis, to which there is no such thing as a short route, and whose boundaries are as meaningless and arbitrary as those of Colonial Africa were.

And as he remembered, he despaired. The streets he had known as pleasant companions, cunningly arranged to facilitate the flow of traffic in all directions, giving all motorists their fair chance, lay before him like a phalanx of enemies, bearing their own implacable demands. Stop. Do not enter. No left turn. One lane ahead. Detour.

Like relatives after the reading of an unfair will, they were the same, but they manifested certain qualities that were often politely overlooked or hidden. One could, with the help of the Interstate Highway System, at least make a reasonable show of rushing *through* an American city. What one could not do was rush between two points *in* an American city. In some cases, it would be easier and faster for two people at either end simply to go to separate airports and meet in Montreal.

There was a digital clock on the dashboard of his car but the battery had died once last winter and he had never bothered to re-set it. He remembered joking to his friends about being above temporal considerations.

This was a morning to learn the true value of cleverness and wit.

Well, he simply had to go as far as he could as quickly as he could.   And so, lifting a prayer he had little hope of having answered, off he went.

As James saw, after what seemed like hours of frantic driving, his exit on I-494 with a barricade across it and a sign that said: exit closed, he wanted to scream. The city that had once made his life so easy was balancing the scales this morning with a cruel thoroughness.

He took the next exit, doubled back laboriously over unmarked county roads sadly in need of the re-paving the Minnesota Department of Transportation claims it is always busy at, and finally Mount Moriah came within sight. He sailed into the parking lot.

It was full of cars, but only a few people were moving toward the church. James did a church professional's calculation: most were inside, but those still outside did not all have children and were not sprinting. Therefore—*therefore*, he had made it!

Praise God from whom all blessings flow! That would be the prelude: variations on *Old 100th*. His own thank-offering.

Now the ridiculousness of his appearance, which he had foolishly imagined he had already fully appreciated, came upon him with new force. Surrounded by vomiting decadents, he had felt silly enough. Venturing into a congregation of repressed Midwesterners, he might as well paint himself red and sing the *Internationale* for all the tolerance he could expect in this get-up.

He turned his t-shirt inside-out and found an oily rag in the trunk to tie over his head. It was truly the best he could do with what he had. As he trotted to the side entrance, he reflected he probably now looked like an Arab terrorist, the variety of human currently most despised by his fellow citizens. If Lutheran ushers carried side-arms...

But things had not come to that yet. Good? Bad? That was just how it was.

Still, however staid, however mediocre, however dull, this was still a congregation of Christian believers. Somewhere in each of them must lie the knowledge that the judgments of human beings are nothing.

Fat chance.

And what chance would he have against the judgments of God?

Like so many Christians before him, James finally surrendered his attempts at thought and simply hoped he could get through the next hour.

The side door opened into the rear of the nave, in view of only the last few rows of pews. The disadvantage of this was that those were the pews which filled up first. Ever since Christ had told the parable of the publican and the Pharisee, Christians had been breaking their necks to prove their piety by showing it wasn't showy. They did this by taking a back seat as ostentatiously as possible. Or maybe it was just easier to sleep in back.

But there were a lot of children there, hence a lot of distraction. Adults were rummaging for snacks and toys, mopping up drool, trying to hide hymnals whose pages their youngsters had just ripped out. As he slipped in and glided to the organ loft stairway, James noticed only one horrified face turned toward him. But it was a young woman who had too many children, a history of chemical abuse, and a bully for a spouse. She would probably dismiss him, as she had to dismiss most of her waking hours, as a hallucination.

Lucky, lucky. God was smiling on him now. There was no one in the organ loft except old Mrs. Losch, who had played the organ as a volunteer before his tenure at Mount Moriah. Widow of a minister, she had played the organ in churches since she was a girl, never apparently bothering to learn to read music or give much thought to the tonal system so pleasing to the Western ear. She had the curious distinction, in James' view, of never having hit an accurate pedal note in his hearing. He would have liked to forbid her to touch the organ but she was still asked, for sentimental reasons, to play at some funerals.

Playing or not, she never sat among the congregation, but always took her place in the loft, perched on the raised seats that the choir used, like a skull of cacophony at the feast of music. This was thought to be an extreme instance of humility, appropriate to a minister's spouse. James suspected that, given what ministers and their families see of human nature, she probably loathed the sight of human beings. Sometimes he wondered if she was trying to get up the courage to assassinate him.

Fortunately, she never spoke to him, nor even seemed to notice his presence. Indeed, she rarely stirred. Once, forgetting she was there, he had even changed clothes in front of her without provoking comment.

So he felt the worst was over. He was about to begin the prelude when Stephanie's husband entered the chancel and tapped the microphone on the lectern.

And then guilt pierced his heart. Stephanie. The woman he had loved and wanted. He had left her in her hour of humiliation. And he had not spared her one thought in his rush to get to this miserable organ bench and cover his own butt. What a swine he was. Guilty, terrified of being found out, he had overlooked the guilt lurking on the opposite side. He had left her. He had made it to the organ on time. But he had not realized that, after last night, there was no longer only one routine to serve.

His head jerked up at her name. Paul was talking about her. Stout, bearded, arrogant Paul had spoken his lover's name. He was telling his flock that Pastor Stephanie was ill this morning and that he would be conducting the service by himself.

James wondered: does he know? *How much* does he know? He must have seen them together. But he couldn't know all that had happened. Even if some ecclesiastical spy had phoned him with all the details, he surely wouldn't believe it yet. Humanity had not lost that many illusions. James himself had been there and he scarcely believed it.

And then James heard him say that there would be no music at the service, that the organist had called in sick and no replacement could be found. Yet Paul could surely see him sitting at the organ, ready as always. James stole a glance at Mrs. Losch, hoping for some conspiratorial outrage. He thought he glimpsed a stiffening of her jaw.

But this meant Paul knew or had guessed. For all James could recover from his drunken memories, Paul might have been watching them as they did it.

As large hearted and consumed with charity as Christians might become, there was still something atavistically enraging about being smugly dismissed by the spouse of someone you loved and had recently slept with. The famous human urge to protect one's self and one's own, one of the glorious drives we share with the animal kingdom, swiftly and efficiently shuts down all mental circuits and seals the mind off from the body until the crisis is past, so that the maximum amount of folly can be committed in blissful ignorance.

James hated this corpulent creep. He had hated him since the minute he had fallen for Stephanie and decided she deserved better. And maybe she did. Maybe she even deserved better than James. But that wasn't the issue now. It was man against man, with whatever weapons were near, dueling for the sake of a woman who at this moment probably despised both of them.

Perhaps it was even a little more than that: it was music against speech, with all the buried animosity that rivalry was capable of, despite their occasional harmonious blending.

Later, James would ponder whether it was the night with Stephanie or the morning with Paul that had sealed his fate. But now he wasn't pondering. He was pulling out the organ stops he would use to celebrate the Second Coming.

No music, eh? Listen up, Fat Man.

He was tempted to bury Paul in sound, show the congregation its money had not been ill-spent on the magnificent ranks of pipes that lay behind him. But all cunning had not left him. He bided his time, allowing Paul to finish his announcements, allowing Paul to think he would follow his hint as a good Christian sheep should and sit there silently in punishment for his sin.

Fat chance yet again. The human heart, including, and at this moment perhaps especially, that of James, had not come this far with that attitude. Or perhaps a good Lutheran should say: it had not come far enough for that attitude. But as dearly as he loved Lutheran theology, he wasn't about to let it run his life for him. And if it had a dim view of the trustworthiness of human nature, that was reason enough to doubt its own trustworthiness and more than enough to doubt that it entailed he should put up with this shit.

In any case, he was going to do what he was going to do, and that was that. Life can become very simple. Later he would reflect that it was a pity it could not become equally sensible.

The announcements were over. Paul moved to the center of the chancel to begin the service. James switched on the organ and heard his mighty creature take its deep breath and hold it, waiting for his touch. He opened his spiral hymnal.

So Paul would do the service without music? James would do it without words. He planned to move through the hymns and canticles in order. He knew, once he began, that the congregation would not hear Paul. If they sang with the organ, that would only make victory sweeter.

He flexed his fingers. Glancing at Mrs. Losch, he thought he saw her nodding. Paul raised his head from his hymnal, motioned his flock to rise, and opened his mouth.

And then Mount Moriah Lutheran Church heard Ralph Vaughan Williams' magnificent setting of the text 'For All the Saints', *Sine Nomine*, as it had never been heard anywhere. The first naked and powerful low pedal note, out of which rose the driving, relentless bass accompaniment, reverberated along the building's structure into the very nerves of the worshippers. They seemed to rise visibly from the shock wave. Before they could recover, the descending chords of the melody struck them like blows from the sword of God. A few impressionable people dropped into their pews under the assault.

But these were Lutherans, who could boast of having some of the most disciplined congregations still existing in Christendom. By the time James moved into the second verse, the bulk of the congregation had checked their bulletins, figured out what was happening, rallied, regrouped, and begun bellowing the words loudly enough to make James weep with pride.

Paul was still standing with his mouth open, as though that first note had turned him to stone. Like someone witnessing an accident, something obscenely out of place, he had been transformed into a pure observer, through sheer inability to categorize what was going on around him.

But the congregation had not only spent its money on an organ: it had also invested in an excellent public address system, one element of which Paul had looped around his neck. And Paul was no green recruit with a squeaky voice but a seasoned parish veteran, used to speaking above unruly students, crying babies, whispering adults. James' surprise attack had stunned him, but not destroyed him.

In the third verse, James began to notice an odd counterpoint to his music, a weird vocal chant intruding upon his measured notes. Paul had begun to read the unaccompanied parts of the service.

Worse, there were people in the congregation flipping pages to follow Paul. A few less stalwart individuals seemed to be completely demoralized. The singing was diminishing audibly.

James played on. The singing had been heartening but had not really been part of his plan. This had nothing to do with the congregation, even less with worshipping God. The congregation could fend for itself. So could God, for that matter. This was between Paul and him.

Through the final verse of the hymn, the battle was about even, the singing held up by several choir members who enjoyed nothing more than the sound of their own voices, the speaking held up by some council members who had always objected to spending money on the organ. Most of the worshippers were hesitant, either mumbling or humming, on the verge of complete liturgical collapse. Some of the former Roman Catholics in the congregation found themselves thinking nostalgically of the incomprehensible services of their youth, and felt more at home here than they ever had.

The end of the hymn became something of a watershed. By this time, even the slowest minds had grasped they were present at some sort of ritual contest. Just what shape the rest of the contest would take depended on what would follow the hymn.

Paul did not pause, nor did his volume diminish when the last 'Alleluia' died away. Without the organ's background, he sounded more like a madman announcing the coming of war than a minister praying for wholeness and new life.

James did not hesitate either, but turned to the first sung dialogue of the service, tapping out the minister's line, then blaring the response.

The congregation, once again showing its training, got the drift of things. Those whose faith was more aesthetic in nature followed James. Those who thought Christianity had little to do with art and imagination, much less fine art, followed Paul. Most of them simply closed their books and sat down, ready to enjoy whatever spectacle they were provided. It was what they had always wanted to do anyway, and they were grateful to be relieved of the necessity to participate.

As the contest wore on, with no end in sight, and as on either calculation the time for the sermon was approaching, the remaining participants finally gave up and sat down with the rest. Even the most eccentric of Lutherans are disposed to sit still for sermons. But, again, perhaps it's the only time they are not expected to participate and, what is more, it's easier to sleep then.

Paul was heading for the pulpit. James was in the middle of the psalm setting which would have been the last music played before the sermon.

One nearly deaf old man, in the front pew just under the pulpit, was still singing along to James' accompaniment. The organ was almost the only thing he ever heard when he came to church. Paul screamed at him to shut up. Then he strode down and shook the man's arm. The old man tapped his book and gestured to the organ, not surprised apparently at having to instruct the minister about what was going on in the service.

Paul then shouted that he was hearing things. As he began to threaten to have him committed to a nursing home, James' psalm came to an end. The old man closed his hymnal, sat down, narrowed his eyes at Paul, whom he had never liked, and switched off his hearing aid. It was little more than a symbolic gesture but he felt that, if modern preachers weren't going to use the pulpit for their sermons, they ought to learn that people didn't have to listen either.

The church had never seemed so silent. Paul again headed for the pulpit. James again bided his time. He allowed Paul the self-important shuffling of papers and the self-satisfied pose he always struck when he began to speak.

Theorists of preaching are fond of referring to the pregnancy of the pause before the sermon begins. This had never had a more graphic instance.

Once again James waited for the ministerial lips to part and draw breath. Congregation and organ held theirs. Did Paul imagine he had now won, through no effort of his own? Did he think James, who had just trashed the service, would at last fall silent for the sermon?

He began as though he did. But as the first consonant took shape on his lips, Bach's *Toccata and Fugue in D minor* invaded his ears.

It was not the most subtle performance of this masterpiece, coarsened as it was by James' extra-musical need to sustain maximum volume. But it was certainly James' finest rendition of it, since it was unspoiled by his usual anxiety over accuracy. He simply attacked it, gave no thought to his skill, and Bach did the rest.

After an almost imperceptible hesitation, caused by his disbelief that even such a low-down worm as James would put Bach to such a use, Paul had regained his composure. But by the time the fugue began, it was clear this was no contest. Unable to resist following Bach, the congregation was incapable of following Paul. But, then, they had never followed anyone's sermons that closely.

Paul was through before Bach. His dogged completion of his sermon could actually be taken as a kind of moral victory. However, since it was not a race, finishing first hardly signaled triumph, and, though it derived from nothing but a neutral fact about the relative length of two compositions, it was perceived by most people as a defeat. Bach aside, James was actually a better organist than Paul was a preacher. No one in the congregation was capable of recognizing that, but Paul's descent from the pulpit while the organ was still weaving its intricate patterns allowed them to think they did.

Paul made an attempt to continue with the service, which was possible insofar as the next parts were solo performances by him. But when he extended the offering plates, the ushers refused to come up until James had finished, as though it were an event too sacred to interrupt with the collection of money. He stood there, stubborn and alone in the chancel, holding out the plates, pretending that he was the only person in the building aware of what was going on.

In fact, with the singular exception of James, this was quite true. But, like every instance of lonely wisdom, it did Paul little good and only made him look like an idiot.

James, on the other hand, was having his finest hour and the sweetest moment of revenge in his life. But though at the moment he was the happier man, moments of happiness count for little in the grim sum of human life. And, like all human triumph, James' moment bore the seed of its own destruction. As any twentieth century rebel general could have told him, either he would have to kill Paul when he finished the fugue or his victory would be remembered only as a minor skirmish in a crushed insurrection.

The moment ended. Bach's voice faded. The ushers came up for the plates. To close out the service, James flipped to the Christmas section of the hymnal and played one carol after another. The congregation, with some gratitude for finally hearing music they knew, began to sing along. James kept at it until Paul recessed to the door and most of the church had emptied. A few carolers remained to the end and even gave him a little applause.

He sat on the bench, letting the glow of his daring and the memory of the music shimmer around him, like a man in a warm bed on a winter morning, unwilling to shift his position and feel the cold. It had been an hour when he had thought of nothing but music and the strategies of assault. He had forgotten himself and had lived only in the structures of sound created by his brain, his fingers and feet, his books and his instrument. And now the warmth was ebbing.

James felt again his body's depletion, he saw again his ludicrous attire, he thought again of Stephanie. He was here, she was—where? He thought of what had happened between them—what would happen now?

Again, time issued its laughing curse. He couldn't vanish, he couldn't sit here, he couldn't spend an ordinary Sunday afternoon at his apartment, watching baseball and wondering what Stephanie looked like without her clothes. He had to do something and, after destroying the Sunday ritual, in more ways than one, there was nothing normal to do. And there were people who actually hated routine.

Somehow rallying his strength, perhaps one of those ambiguous gifts of God, he decided he had to get to Stephanie. Somehow the mere physical proximity would have to do for a course of action. He shut up the organ and slid off his bench.

Mrs. Losch was standing before him, a wicked gleam in her eye. James gulped. Fine, he thought, I deserve it. let me have it, you old hag. So I'm a little unstable. But I can still play rings around you any day.

"Young man," she said, "I guess we showed that pompous toad who's boss."

It was probably something she'd dreamed of doing all her life. James kissed her on the cheek and dashed down the steps.

There was one person left in the nave, the janitor, who was straightening up the carnage in the rear pews. James had often had occasion to wonder why this man's relatives had never had him institutionalized. He waved at James. "Hey—that was...really different."

"Thanks." Moron.

Trotting out to his car as quickly as his spent body would allow, he noticed that Paul, ordinarily the last to leave, was already gone. At least he wouldn't have to face him in person.

But had he gone after Stephanie? Or had he simply gone home, not really caring where she was? Had James only been projecting his own turmoil upon him? After all, Paul had made excuses for both of them. Perhaps what James saw as arrogance was actually compassionate understanding.

Or perhaps Paul, who seemed so formidable, was actually quite wounded. Perhaps he had gone off to drown his sorrows in alcohol, as so many of his fellow citizens would. Perhaps he would be found in some gutter tomorrow morning, drunken and pathetic, one more casualty of James' night of lust.

Or maybe he'd gone home to watch the ball game, too appalled at his wife to care. Paul had undoubtedly glimpsed more than once the harsh side of Stephanie. Maybe he was glad to be rid of her. Or, rid of her or not, to have at last a trump card of accusation he could play against her in any hand, ever.

If he knew anything about electricity and explosives, maybe he had fixed a booby-trap in James' car, and was not gone at all but lurking at a safe distance, eagerly awaiting the instant when James would turn his ignition key and the next instant when his bodily parts, public and private, would bid a hasty and confused farewell to each other.

And maybe he had no more idea what to do than James did and no more of a routine to return to.

This last thought not only gave James no clue as to Paul's whereabouts, it also made him feel worse. He had been carrying his own desperation and confusion as a moral shield, as all victims do. But there was also the desperation and confusion of others, for which he was partly responsible. Or wholly responsible.

Earlier this morning, his mind had worked too slowly to please him. Now, if anything, it was working too quickly. A little fearfully, he started his car. No bomb. So: no quick death. More slow, complicated life instead.

But he couldn't let it be too slow, if it was going to make any sense at all. He raced back to the Interstate. He had to get to her. Then his fabulous mind could work on the next step.

This slow paced city with its low and comforting skyline, which had once delighted him, now seemed to him one more instance of mindless social growth and seemed to make as little sense as the last twenty-four hours of his life. If the modern world was so fast paced, why couldn't you ever get anywhere? Not only did he have to retrace his way through the maze he had come through an hour ago, he also had to fight Sunday afternoon traffic. James wondered if they'd all been to churches as inaccessible as his, and why they put up with it and did not stay home, in bed with someone they had to make no apologies to or about.

As if that were so simple.

Halfway across one of the deteriorating bridges that span the Mississippi, James had one of the few flat tires of his life. Never having had one in this car, and never having seriously considered the possibility, he spent half an hour searching for the jack. He finally found it mounted on a bracket next to the engine, of all places.

There had to be a Japanese engineer somewhere, whose father had perished on Okinawa, who was probably still smirking about this. James' father had served in the European theatre, which only made this seem more unfair.

By the time he had made it back to the house of revelry and shame, it was almost deserted. There were one or two people still in the process of waking up and one or two who James feared might never wake up. But that at least was something he bore no responsibility for, unless his memory still carried a few surprises.

With a more conscious and sober eye, the house looked even less worthy of human habitation than it had when he rose. For all the scarcity of bodies, there still seemed to be an immense amount of clothing lying about. Either the battle for it had reached a mortal level or people had left in some strange and scanty get-ups.

Stephanie was gone. He found the pillow she had slept under, its casing slashed and most of its filling emptied out.

One of his medical student friends was sitting against the wall in the bedroom, smoking, looking very pleased with himself. James wondered what the key to all this self-satisfaction was.

He squatted beside him. The young doctor, evidently well-trained in the medical profession's style of omniscience, gestured with his cigarette toward James' head. "Green," he said, "I'd definitely dye it green."

"I'll give it some thought. Listen: there was a woman here..."

"Of course, there was. Many women, many. As numerous, various, and fetching as the stars. What did you expect?"

"Please. I'm having a bad day. She was sleeping here. I'm trying to find her."

"Don't tell me. She had a matching haircut, right? Or is that a wig?"

"Right, right. Did you see her? Where is she?"

"Left. Some big ugly dude came to get her. Bad-tempered son of a bitch. Know him?"

"Yeah. Listen: how did they look? I mean, how bad tempered was he? Do you think—I mean, how did they get along?"

He took a long, thoughtful drag on his cigarette. "Let's see. A word here, a look there, a snarl, a nasty gesture. Pissed off, crabby, and like they could be that way because they had nothing to win or lose. You know, they got along like they were married."

"They are."

His friend laughed. "I know. You introduced me last night. You don't do this often, do you? You haven't built up much tolerance for real partying."

"Thanks for all the advice."

"No problem. It's Sunday. It's on the house."

James left. He supposed he would return to his apartment and clean up. The world often looked better after a shower. Of course, there were obvious limits to how far appearances could be altered, and he was probably beyond them.

Sitting in his car, he winced at how he had shamelessly abandoned her. And he winced at how easily the claim of marriage had re-established itself, in however tattered a form. With some amazement, he felt himself fill again with yearning for Stephanie. But now that yearning bore a history as heavy as urban blight.

What tormented him most was that all he had thought about was saving his own position. And considering what he had done during the service, he hadn't even managed to do that.

God couldn't be smiling now. She was probably laughing her head off. One more male had gone down in flames, flames he ignited himself. As he had no reason to go anywhere, he arrived at his apartment in no time at all.

Chapter Three

Although he never went to the church on Monday morning, unless there were a funeral or some other special event, James might have reaped some profit by breaking yet another of his life's routines. Had he done so, he probably would have run into the locksmith who was installing the new locks that none of his keys would fit when he finally did arrive, toward noon.

He stood before the locked front door in utter disbelief.

James was not entirely free of the human illusion that everything that happens near a conscious person is caused by, done in honor of, directed against, or is in some way relevant to that person. Nihilism is perhaps the only antidote to this, and James wasn't ready to swallow that yet, though it was beginning to look attractive. And, whatever the truth of skepticism, it remained true that some things were indeed caused by, done in honor of, directed against, or were in some way relevant to him. For example, this really had been done for him.

They were keeping him out. He was sure of it the moment he figured out that he wasn't holding the wrong key or turning it the wrong way. He was sure of it, even before he saw the neatly typed notice taped up to the right of the door, announcing the changing of the locks and the names of people who were authorized to apply to the secretary for new keys. His name was not on the list.

An oversight?

Unlikely. No, this was the first blow of Paul's counter-attack. What other blows might fall upon him, might indeed have already fallen upon him as he mooned in self-absorbed agony over a woman who was probably still cursing him, James was not yet ready to consider. The absence of his name from the list spoke with a clarity and eloquence he refused to hear at this moment.

He did consider breaking in. But there would be another lock to face in the organ loft. Still another on the organ itself. Would they have gone that far? As far as he knew, they might even have put locks on the restrooms.

And even if he had broken all of them, unhinged every door, laid open every physical barrier throughout the whole of Mount Moriah, there would still be the barrier of administrative decision, the door muscle could not splinter nor key of metal unlock, the tacit agreement of those licensed to decide, allowing some in, shutting others out, the silent mustering of the community around its own rules and regulations. They could change the locks everyday, and everyday he could break in and sit at this organ, and he would have accomplished nothing. Rules and decisions had put him there to begin with. Physically, he could sweep them aside, he could get inside the building. But he would be even further outside the community the decisions defined. He was powerless, by human decree.

And powerless in more ways than one, by more than human decree. He knew where she lived, he knew her telephone number, he had just slept with her. But he had a better chance of getting an audience with the Pope than of getting in contact with Stephanie. He would imagine himself calling her, driving to her home, waiting to get her alone. But he couldn't make himself do any of it. He couldn't face her. He couldn't face Paul. Two people he had talked with two days ago, a woman he had made love to, they lived in the same city as he, and they might as well have lived in a different galaxy. Physical proximity, which shines with hope for the confident lover, turned out to be as meaningless as all defeated lovers know it to be.

With the mindless persistence of those who are truly hopeless but have yet to realize it, he drove to the church again the next day. This time, Paul and Stephanie's car was in the lot. It was in the reserved space marked 'Pastor', right next to the space marked 'Organist'. It had once been his by right. Seeing their car, imagining only vaguely what seeing them would be like, he turned his car around and went home.

Home to what? His apartment, too, was the same. But he no longer had a life to fill it with. He thanked God for round-the-clock television programming, the only real friend of the friendless. For all the self-congratulating Christians do, it's only imaginary people who accept you for what you are. And that was only because they have no idea what you are, and no desire to have one. They don't even know you exist. And yet they would inhabit your living room at the touch of a button. Of course, they were silly, shallow, fit companions only for weak minds. But of how many real people could you say more? What a miracle television was, and what a blessing.

He did nothing for the next few days but eat and watch the tube. It was almost sweet to be reduced to a complete idiot. In this state, he would probably make some man a good wife: docile, undemanding, ready to get fat happily and neglect the housework. What more could a man want?

What more indeed? He was a man and had as little idea of what men wanted as he had of what women wanted.

One night, at last, he got a phone call. His heart pounded at the thought that it might be Stephanie. But it was a man's voice. It was a member of the church council.

"Yes?" said James. "What's up?"

"Oh, I just thought you'd like to know that we've had the locks changed at the church. Pastor Paul said he was a little concerned about vandalism. He said you were, too. Something about the organ."

I'll bet it was, thought James. "Right."

"Funny world, isn't it?"

No argument there. "Yeah."

"Guess we'll all sleep a little better now. Oh, say—"

James waited. He guessed he was probably about to hear the real reason for the call.

"I wanted to ask. I mean, I was notifying some people about the locks and I thought I should tell you, too, because you might have some things there. But, well—I heard you were leaving. Is that right?"

Well, thought James, at least it was comforting to know what I'm doing. He paused, then said, "That's right. I guess I am."

Emboldened, the man said, "I thought so. I heard Pastor Paul say something like that. I thought he said you resigned or something."

James paused again. It was another moment when life seemed simple. You sat at home and you did all sorts of things without knowing it. He shrugged. Why not? "Yeah. I did."

"Oh?" Transparent. He wanted details.

Sorry. James said, "Personal reasons."

"Oh. Can I help out? I mean, do you need anything, or—"

"I don't think so." Did he *need* anything?

"Oh. Well, good luck. Maybe I'll see you around."

I don't think so. "Yeah. Thanks."

"And if you need anything—"

"Right. Thanks."

They hung up.

Now he knew what he was doing. He was doing nothing. A disembodied voice had come to him, through the wonder of modern technology, and had given his life a new shape, as easily as a tongue licking a scoop of ice cream. More than one primitive culture, faced with an event like this, would have considered it a divine visitation. For James, a product of twentieth century Western civilization, probably too secularized for his own good, it was only so much more garbage to swallow.

Oddly, knowing that he was cut off from Mount Moriah gave him back some of the freedom and courage he would need to call Stephanie. He certainly would no longer need to worry about what it might mean for his job. Somehow it seemed more reasonable to think about her than about *why* it would no longer mean anything for his job.

He would begin with a new haircut. He had been trying several styles of combing it, with no success in making it look less outlandish. He had thought of trimming it by himself but could not get beyond the thought of raising a pair of scissors to his head. He would have to face the barber at the mall. They couldn't ridicule him too harshly. After all, he was paying them. For all the bad things said about capitalism, what could provide a more stable basis for a relationship?

His faith in the power of money was rewarded. He received neither a chuckle nor a question from his barber. How could the government have imagined it was adding anything to its currency by printing the slogan 'In God We Trust' on it? God? Trust *God*, who thought up *sex*? Please. Let's be more thoughtful with our economic life.

On the other hand, perhaps more than money had purchased his barber's decorum. Like police officers and doctors, the man had probably seen everything. There were, in fact, plenty of people drifting through the mall who had died their hair green (or purple or orange), mere children, clothed in leather and metal. Next to them, James might have passed for someone running for public office.

Nothing, of course, could be done to regain the elegant styling he had once had, but James was at least left with a presentable, slightly parted cut. Too short to be either modish or conservative, he looked like someone either newly released from the armed forces or well on his way to recovering from brain surgery, someone making a new beginning, who knew where the trail to success could be found.

Another illusion, but James did not object to the look. Lacking the substance, it was only that much more important.

With nowhere else he could think of to go, he went home. And with nothing else he wanted to do, he called the one person he thought he needed. He dialed Stephanie's home number.

Paul answered.

James hung up.

He tried again and again, at fifteen minute intervals, for two hours. Paul answered every time. Paul was probably enjoying it. Paul at least could speak. James only offered silence. He should have disguised his voice and asked for her the first time. After two hours of this, nonchalance was no longer a possibility. Finally, all he got was a busy signal. After a dismal evening, James went to bed.

Shortly after midnight, his own phone rang.

At least he heard her voice: "I just wanted to tell you to stop calling. Don't try to see me, don't write to me, that's it. Just stay away."

"Steph. You can't—"

"Look. I'm ashamed of myself. I can't even go out in public. I can't do this. It shouldn't have happened."

"What am I supposed to do?"

She paused. Then he heard it: "You left me. Do you know how humiliated I was?"

She waited. She wanted an answer no one could give. James said, "I'm sorry. I had to get to the service."

"I heard."

"I thought you'd be covered. I came back for you but you were gone. Steph, please—"

"It's over. It's over. Goodbye."

"But I can't even go back to the church. I found out I resigned without knowing it."

"What did you expect?"

"I don't know! Please. I want to see you. I have to see you."

"No. That's it. Just go away. You seem to be good at that."

She hung up. James couldn't even keep a phone conversation going. All these worthless machines at his beck and call, and he was powerless. He needed a different life. Something simple, something solid. Something that wouldn't scatter like ashes at the merest breath of wind. Something that didn't depend upon a thousand conditions, each easily withdrawn. Something basic, something indispensable, something that made you necessary to your neighbor and your neighbor to you.

He didn't need a new life. He needed a new world. He needed someone to take care of him, someone to tell him what to do. He needed a better life in a better place. It was the urge of the lost child and the religious dreamer: take me home, where things make sense, or made sense, or will make sense.

In the morning, he discovered that things were not quite as bad as he imagined or, from another point of view, that they were actually worse. To put it neutrally, he found out that he was still needed and wanted and useful to someone: several of his monthly bills arrived in the mail. They wanted the money he sent them so faithfully.

Love is less blind that it is said to be, at least where the beloved is concerned. But it often shows itself not only blind but deaf, wholly insensible, to the economic consequences of the fires it ignites. There may be some deep antipathy between biology and commerce that is only revealed in the ruinous effect passion has on worldly success. The jealous gods of sex and money easily and happily enlist each other's warriors, but only the rare individual can serve both without one or the other taking revenge. Without a regular income, James was going to be in trouble. He did a quick calculation. This month would be no problem. Next month he would have less loose change. But the month after that, while not penniless, he would have to choose between eating and paying his bills.

If he paid his bills, he would earn the admiration and gratitude of his creditors. He would please somebody. One of his credit card companies even printed a message of thanks on it for his record of prompt payment. But, as he had found out once when he had misplaced an envelope, this admiration and gratitude only lasted until the next bill was due.

Say he chose eating over paying his bills. One month of non-payment would create no serious problems. He would no longer be thanked for prompt payment. He could live with that. Even the second month of non-payment would probably not bring trouble. But that would be the limit. The utility companies would be cutting him off, to beat their winter cut-off deadline if nothing else. But that would be a minor worry, since he'd undoubtedly be evicted by then. And he supposed his credit cards would be cancelling him.

That gave him about two months or so of good citizen status, two more of uneasy grace, and then whatever dumb luck would provide. Say four, with not much anxiety, then total collapse. That would take him into the early fall and leave him facing winter with nothing. Grasshopper, farewell. Maybe he had a terminal disease he didn't know about, something so rare that specialists would pay him for the privilege of treating him. Well, he couldn't depend on miracles. None had shown up so far, and he'd been waiting.

Still, with four months and not a few skills, he had more time than most people were granted. He could look for a new position. Of course, he couldn't depend on a recommendation from Mount Moriah. Or would Paul not stoop so low as to destroy his chances for new employment?

Paul would.

As an alternative, James considered watching television for four months, then throwing himself on the mercy of the state. He had heard rumors of the great wealth to be had in the welfare system. But he suspected the rumors were exaggerated.

As he sat at his table, musing, savoring his coffee and smoking his cigar, the phone rang again. It was a fellow organist, who had heard he left Mount Moriah.

"News travels fast," said James.

"Small world, the Church. Are you looking for something new? If you are, I've got something."

It was too good to be true. "Try me."

"It's only a summer replacement, but it could be more. I'm going to be gone and, if things work out, I might not be back. There's a big church in Dallas I'm looking at. They don't know what to do with their money, so I'm going to see if I can't help them with that problem. But if you replace me starting next month, you'll be first in line for the job. Interested?"

"Yeah."

"Good. Hang on and I'll put you through to the pastor. She'll explain the terms. Hang on."

She? "Wait."

James couldn't have explained the machinery of judgment that went to work at that moment. At the mere thought of a woman cleric, the perverse demon of eros presented the image of him sleeping with her. Then he was overcome with fear. And the image sickened him as a betrayal of Stephanie. Who would not speak to him.

For no sensible reason, he couldn't take this position. He realized he couldn't even dream of approaching another church. He listened to the pastor politely, then made his excuses. She had a very fetching voice. And as he hung up he also realized that, theological truth and positive thinking aside, he really wasn't very much if he was no longer an organist and choir director.

The mess he was in was worse than he imagined, and it had little to do with paying bills. It was all too complicated. And he saw that it was only by virtue of life's complications that he was allowed to exist. But they made his existence vulnerable and, finally, insupportable. He needed recovery and change. He needed a simpler life. Simplicity, sense, solidity.

James thought about that for a couple of days while a desperate decision that he knew was forming inside him got itself into shape and presented itself to him with all the clarity of one more bill that had finally come due.

He had played at life. Play was at an end. He felt sillier than he had ever felt. Or perhaps he had always felt silly, frivolous, and simply had had enough money to avoid thinking about it. With nothing to do and nowhere to turn, he could still do one thing and turn one place. He could go home and regroup, at least spend some time thinking.

His father lived in a small Minnesota town near the Canadian border. His father lived simply, sensibly, solidly. His father had always thought he had wasted his life. As inclined as he was to agree with that judgment now, James was still not ready to let his father know that. But his father was still his father. That was one basic, solid, simple reality: if James went home, he would be taken in.

He called him the night he decided. A voice said: "Hello. McGrath."

It startled James momentarily, as though the voice had identified him without needing a clue, as though he had been connected to some pitiless, omniscient mind, to God. But that was how his father always answered the phone. James was more rattled than he thought.

"Dad? It's James. Listen: I'm pretty loose this summer and I thought I'd come up and stay awhile. Would that be alright?"

"Fine. Any time."

James heard a click. He couldn't believe that his father thought the conversation was over. But apparently he had. After a few minutes of pondering this, James wondered if he had imagined the entire call, if he would have to add hallucinations to his list of troubles. But he wasn't that rattled.

Irritating old coot. He never changed., Any time? Fine.

It took James a week to settle his affairs, store his belongings, cut the last threads that bound him to his life, and pack his car with what he thought he needed. Then he headed northwest on I-94 early one morning for an all day drive into an all new life.

He didn't bother to inform his father he was on his way. If any time was alright for the old fart, then any time it would be. A little anger and superiority didn't hurt. James was going home, like a frightened, baffled bride.

PART TWO

*in the darkness
drear*

Chapter Four

Madison McGrath was not distracted, busy, ill, or much more irritable than usual the night his son called him to announce his visit. He made the response that seemed necessary, saw no point in enriching the phone company by speaking to his son long distance when he would speak to him face to face in a matter of days, hung up the phone, and promptly forgot about the conversation.

His memory was in no way defective. On the contrary, it was excellent because it attended only to those things that required action. What would happen without his conscious intervention the elder McGrath left to fate. He wasted neither his time nor his mental energy.

Madison McGrath lived his life on a schedule whose rigidity would have drawn the applause of Immanuel Kant. If the community as a whole had not retained a few anachronistic shifts of activity in what had once been honor of the Sabbath (and was now, in his view, in honor of nothing, save perhaps sloth), each of his days would have borne an exact formal resemblance to every other. As it was, they were close enough.

McGrath rose early, near dawn, not unusual in a farming community. He recognized, as others did not, that since the advent of electricity, the need for early rising was more metaphysical than physical and implied moral elitism (an elitism, moreover, which required very little effort). He rose early, even though anything he had to do could be done later and much that he had to do could only be done later. This too was not unusual in the modern American farming community, dairy farmers excepted. Unless they wanted to watch the sun rise over the single crop which the government paid them to raise (or over the field in which the government paid them not to raise it), many of the farmers he knew could have slept to noon, if they weren't touring Europe.

McGrath breakfasted on toast and coffee, then walked his dog, an aging Black Labrador Retriever named Blackstone, who wore a blue collar. Then he read the paper and settled what correspondence he had. McGrath was a semi-retired lawyer.

Midmorning, he walked uptown to the post office, going out of his way to make a neat circuit of the town for chance conversation and exercise. (On Sundays, he omitted the post office but took the walk.) He returned to his office, above his garage, to work on the cases he was still handling. Some days, he had to drive to Carlsburg, the county seat, to be in court.

Around noon, he returned to the house for a light lunch, a nap, and serious reading in his living room. Before supper, he walked Blackstone in the country, out the cemetery road. He devoted his evening to light reading or the occasional visit.

For someone who rose so early, he retired fairly late, never having shaken his early student's habit of reading past midnight. He did not own a television set.

The bending of each day, against the forces of nature, community waywardness, and the heart's fatigue, into the same pitiless shape, like a row of Roman crosses holding a defeated army, or a row of rivets heroically set atop the world's highest suspension bridge, was the closest thing his life possessed to an aesthetic impulse. It was a life of order, a life of simple satisfactions, a life of austere discipline, and, through his profession, a life of enlightened service to the community. He saw it as the best any man or woman could achieve, relative to personal fulfillment and social utility.

And he often reflected that if all lived as he, or even aspired to, the world would be a much better place. If nothing else, with such rigid schedules and serious pursuits, there would be fewer traffic accidents and popular culture would generate fewer frivolous millionaires.

Yet the reality of Madison McGrath's day, indeed of Madison McGrath himself, was somewhat richer and more ambiguous than he liked to think.

He rose not so much at dawn, for the coming of dawn in Northern Minnesota varied too much for his taste, as at six o'clock, by the clock. And his alarm clock was a real clock (as all his clocks were), not simply a set of numbers projected into a mental void. It had the round face, the numerals, and the two steady hands of the clocks that kept time for Western Civilization in its days of glory. Digital clocks, he felt, were spawned by the annihilating skepticism of the modern temper. The circle spoke of sense, order, completion, regularity, and the sanity of recurrence, as did the evenly spaced numerals.

The numerals of his clocks were Roman numerals. This was not simply a distaste for the lawless tribes of Arabia, whatever their ancient achievements. It was another, even stronger, bond of continuity with the ordering spirit that kept the barbarians at bay.

And all the clocks were independent of the unpredictable comings and goings of electric power, being either battery driven or wound by key. Consequently, he was often the only person who knew what time it was during the longer power failures. Older residents of the town would sometimes call him up to find out. Sometimes he would tell them.

He was thus spared, to some degree, the dreamy timelessness and the breathless waiting that descended on lesser mortals when the electricity went off. As he loathed every form of electronic communication and positively relished reading by candlelight, with wine glowing in a crystal goblet, there was little the Minnesota power companies could do to inconvenience him.

Such independence had a price. As he remained perfectly in step with the relentless sweep of his autonomous second hands, he drifted further from the temporal moods of his fellow citizens. Objectively synchronized, he lost the bond of experiential sense which nourished subjective sympathy. He liked it that way. That was why he did it.

However, short of calling the Greenwich observatory in England, assuming the unreliable and incompetent English could still afford observatories (and telephones), he had no real way to insure that his time pieces accurately marked the passage of some greater design. That they roughly matched morning, noon, and night was not enough for him. That they were not designed to cope with the few seconds of inaccuracy relative to the earth's orbit which would accrue over a span of centuries he could live with. He needed something like a Supreme Court decision: neither the word of God nor the guess of a dolt, but a considered, informed decision, which would then become the standard.

When this problem first engaged him, some years ago, he somewhat arbitrarily designated his office clock as the master clock and, each day, reset all the others by it. Whether this amounted to anything more than roughly matching morning, noon, and night, McGrath did not consider. Besides, he had no schedule to meet but his own and thus no real need to know the time, except when he was due in court. But as the noon whistle in Carlsburg, by which even the county courthouse set its time, was notoriously erratic, no power on earth could help him there. He was always an hour or so early anyway, and the judges were usually late. Still, as far as his own life was concerned, he had preserved a rough equivalence with common experience, achieved uniformity in his own domain, and imagined he had achieved more. Art, science, religion, and law itself could make no higher claim.

As a matter of fact, the clock in his office lost a minute or so every year. At one time, it was as magnificent a machine as a Minnesota farmer could have shipped to him from Massachusetts. But that was ninety years ago. It was six feet high, in a walnut case with brass fittings, and even now its minor maladjustment was nothing but a testimony to its durability and precision. Still, drug stores now sold novelty watches the size of gumballs that kept stricter time. Thus does technology mock tradition. One might wonder why someone with McGrath's concerns would not move with the times. But to ask the question 'Why does Madison McGrath not throw out the walnut and brass clock bestowed upon him by his father and replace it with a plastic gadget made in Taiwan, Korea, or Japan?' is to answer it.

And yet the slight flaw in his master timepiece gave a certain limp to his punctuality. When he first got it going, setting it—after some hesitation—by his own town's noon whistle (said to be more reliable than Carlsburg's, but this might be local prejudice), his only bow to convention, he appeared the most exact of men. Then, over the course of several years, he could be counted on to be three, six, then ten minutes late. People assumed he was getting senile. When he noticed the fact, he assumed they were rushing things. By the year 2050 or so, he would be having serious problems, not that he would be around to enjoy them.

It stopped once, the day of his wife's funeral. He failed to wind it, not out of grief, but because the funeral director was delayed. He had no choice but to reset it by the other clocks in his home, making a nice circle of interdependence. Since most of these had even more imprecision than the sixteen-hundredths of a second the master clock lost daily, he ended up, after taking a precise average of their discrepant readings and factoring in a wild guess, regaining eight minutes and nineteen seconds of the time he had been losing. One might have said, perhaps too harshly, that the disruption of his clocks bothered him more than the loss of his spouse. What people actually did say was that he handled his grief very well. Some said coldly.

He mourned his wife very little, or so he would have said. The older he got, the more his youthful marriage and all that had come with it seemed to him as incomprehensible as swallowing tadpoles in a college initiation, something he had never even considered, even when young. She died quickly, from cancer, soon after it was diagnosed. He had tried to sue her physician for not diagnosing it sooner. Every year, on the day of her death, he sent the physician a copy of her wedding picture. Eventually, more out of irritation than anything else, the physician sued him for non-payment of his bill. McGrath argued that paying the man would be like paying a hit and run driver for the time he took to run you down and the mental anxiety his fear of capture caused him. McGrath lost.

In his professional career, this case was not an anomaly. McGrath had a penchant for what might be called personal animosity suits. McGrath lost often. But he had no great need for his percentage of the vast sums of money he often crusaded for, and he always enjoyed badgering the people who refused to pay *him*.

His dog had come to him in this way, as a settlement with an unemployed couple who had retained him to sue the same physician for botching a vasectomy. The wife had become pregnant for the eighth time but everyone, including McGrath, knew that the sperm in question this time had issued from another set of testicles which had never been in the admittedly questionable hands of the Carlsburg hospital. Taking the long view, everyone, including McGrath, thought this gave the child-to-be at least an outside chance of receiving a decent genetic heritage and a normal I.Q., if one discounted environmental influences. So the suit was perceived as not only groundless but ungracious.

On the other hand, it was not impossible that the operation had been botched as well and, besides, rural justice, as much as urban, has been known to err, sometimes in favor of the undeserving. McGrath had pointed out, at the hearing, the religious differences that the case involved. The couple were Baptists and the hospital was run and staffed by Seventh Day Adventists. When asked what that had to do with it, McGrath said, "My clients and myself believe medicine should heal people. This doctor and hospital appear to subscribe to a different creed." McGrath lost again.

The couple were not so much unwilling as unable to pay the, to them, astronomical fee McGrath demanded for handling their case and having to immerse himself in the sordid details of their efforts to thwart reproduction. After receiving a few threats, they offered to pay him by doing work on his property. The thought of having such morons in close proximity to his possessions repelled him, so he agreed to accept as payment one of the animals their home seemed to breed as profusely as it bred humans. Thus he received a surprisingly magnificent Labrador Retriever, whom he named Blackstone.

A little homesick at first, the dog quickly perceived it would be regularly fed, comfortably housed, and not have its life eaten away from within by parasites. The dog was now the only creature on earth that would kill for Madison McGrath. McGrath quickly perceived this, too, and an undying bond was formed.

Blackstone filled, indeed more than filled, the emotional space that McGrath would never admit his wife had left. Since Blackstone did very little except eat, sleep, greet him, walk at his side, and tend in silence to his own ineffable affairs, the emotional space could not have been very large, so it was easy to see how McGrath could overlook it. Blackstone had the additional merits of not being able to talk, spend vast sums of money, or colonize the bathroom at crucial hours.

Of course, no dog at all would have given McGrath even more of such advantages, so its mere presence must have offered him something. But that was the kind of thing McGrath's whole life was devoted to leaving undefined and unnoticed, unlike his wife's. Or his son's.

One social consequence of owning a dog was that it was another irritant for his neighbors. Urban Americans, addicted to nostalgia, loved to picture small towns as Norman Rockwell had, usually with a dog lying in the foreground. While they might realize the Bronx was no place for a dog, unless it was prepared to fight for its life, they thought of rural America as a haven for pets and small children. What they failed to realize was that rural Americans thought of any town with a population over 200 as just slightly smaller than New York or Los Angeles and regularly said of *them* that they were no place to raise kids or have a dog. Unfortunately, the FBI did not keep statistics on small town dog shootings or poisonings. McGrath's informal data showed they were high. He was one of the few dog owners left, most dogs now dwelling on the few remaining farms where they could be ground into insect chow by farm machinery or run over by delivery trucks.

The town itself had an ordinance prohibiting dogs from running loose, playing, or loitering. As much as McGrath loved the law and invested it with hopes beyond reason, here was a case where even he was prepared to admit it had gone over the edge. He was planning on challenging it some day. Until then, he enjoyed the thought of the town council lying in wait to nab Blackstone loitering.

To be on the safe side, McGrath kept Blackstone chained up during the day. At night, he would let him roam, for mobility in case of prowlers, and for the joy of having him tear up, befoul, and terrorize his neighbors' lawns, gardens, flower beds, and small children (if they happened to be out when they should have been in bed, usually because the parents were alcoholics).

But when he was asked why he wanted a dog, he would always say, "I felt the need for contact with an intelligent life form." The handful of intelligent people that heard him say that thought it was funnier than perhaps it really was. Madison McGrath was not that pleased to be spending his last years in the community he had tried to leave long ago.

He was the fifth child of a Minnesota farming couple of Scottish descent, the only one of the children to survive the flu epidemic of 1919, by virtue of being born two years later. His destiny thus bore upon it that illusory stamp of new beginning that immigrants found so alluring in America. Both his paternal and maternal grandparents had been in the long line of settlers from Scotland who had, by and large, responded to the harsh life of the Great Plains in the 18th and 19th centuries by perishing during one of their first winters. But they had settled this area first, well before the Scandinavian blight began, though the Swedes and Norwegians had worked hard to obliterate this fact from popular memory, just as the Vikings had tried to obliterate the Celts themselves a millennium or so ago. McGrath, however, had never forgotten who was here first.

Not that he had ever been particularly happy about it. He loathed farming and, when young, found every excuse possible to avoid it. World War II had served as an excellent one. In what could have been a prelude to a life of obscure strife, McGrath had served with the unsung First Army in the European theatre, upstaged constantly by Patton's Third Army on its right and the ponderous British on its left under Montgomery of the histrionic mouth and hesitant foot. Unsung, but not un-bloodied. McGrath had been through the terrible grappling in the Hurtgen Forest and the siege of Aachen. The utter shredding of strategy in the Hurtgen fighting down to encounters of platoon level and less gave him an insight into the mindless-ness of Vietnam that the American public at large, nourished on the tourist-like myth of advance from London to Paris to Berlin, simply had no concept of. More than once, McGrath had dreamed of shooting one of his young officers, whose grasp of military thinking amounted to little more than a collective death wish. For one thing, he could see them. For another, they seemed more immediately responsible for his misery than the German troops who were undoubtedly being led by the same species of lunatic. Fortunately, the Germans usually got them a day or two before McGrath's patience had been exhausted. But when less tolerant American troops turned on their officers in Vietnam, it came as no surprise to him. As a form of homage to the emotions of his youth, he represented a few draft resisters for the American Friends Service Committee during the Vietnam era. He even got a few off. It made him feel like one of the few liberty loving Americans left in a nation of slaves.

Looking back on his war, he could see that Western Civilization had as little no-tion of what to do with victory as he had when he was demobilized. College was the next most reasonable excuse to avoid returning to a life of dirt and animal excre-ment, so he took it. There he discovered the law and his spouse, the one a lasting project that became his only pleasure, the other an immediate pleasure that degen-erated into a lasting project. He took his degree from the University of North Da-kota, which had offered him easy access from his home but left him vulnerable to family claims.

They were not long in coming. His father had outlived his mother by several years, which looked to be a common McGrath fate, but his increasing frailty re-quired more and more of McGrath's time. Finally, he decided to move back to the family farm, once well outside, now just inside the little town where McGrath had gone to school. His wife, whose name was Marie, hated the town, whose name was New Culloden, in memory of the last time the Scots had made the English dirty their knickers, though they had paid for it dearly.

His son James was born the year his father died. Since his wife so loathed the place, in a last effort at domestic compromise, McGrath had moved his family to Fargo, North Dakota. He retained the farm which, since there were no debts at-tached to it, proved to be a rich source of income during the wonder years of Amer-ican agriculture. Prosperous farming became a matter of not growing things and being paid handsomely for it, and/or renting land to young farmers who would never be able to finance an operation of their own. Gone was the self-sustaining farm which helped the McGraths survive the depression, with its vegetables, chickens, hogs, and cows. The successful farmer need never sweat, let alone touch anything remotely organic. McGrath could enjoy this. Most of the toil was bureaucratic. He offered a more perfect example than anyone liked to think of what would come to be called 'the family farm'. That an entire nation would warp its economy to preserve this fiction would continue to amuse and enrich him until the day he died.

Not that he didn't value it. The rural lawyer, with a farm in his possession, was a role he more than welcomed, even with his strong demythologizing tendencies. It gave him the sense of an earlier, more integral republic, when animal husbandry and human rights animated the same cultivated minds and seemed amenable to the same enlightened efforts, the age of Adams, Jefferson, Madison, and Monroe. However make-believe, he preferred having a farm behind him to a used-car lot or a toxic waste dump.

And yet that wasn't the reason he had returned, after his son was in college and to his wife's undying grief. He was simply too abrasive and ornery to get along with anybody. His law partnerships grew bitter, the offices he hoped to win election to always went to his opponents. It became something of a sure thing to run against Madison McGrath. Embittered, and not that far from retirement, McGrath had returned to New Culloden ten years ago to establish a private practice. His wife promised to die in spite and she eventually did, though more of cancer than spite, asking that her ashes be carried to some civilized place. He buried them behind the garage, beneath his office window, which he considered highly civilized, much more so than any urban area in the continental United States. He hadn't seen their son since her funeral, five years ago. He could not say he experienced this as gnawing pain.

As the economies of Uruguay and New Zealand, indeed of most third world countries, could testify, farming was not the most solid thing to build a community on. As the town had boomed out to the boundaries of the old McGrath place, it had, by the time of his return, faded back. The human population of the county had fallen by half since he had come back from the war, though the ecological gap had been filled by deer, moose, wolves, hawks, and bears. McGrath would not have denied this raised the general tone of life, since most of the humans were stranded Scandinavians, inbred to the point of being on their last genetic legs. This was probably the reason behind the famous Scandinavian social conscience and its lavish welfare stipends: inside all Swedes and Norwegians was the knowledge that they would need help someday, when their brains curdled.

The McGrath house had always been surrounded by a thick grove of oak trees. When the town grew out to their property line, these preserved the house's privacy. Retaining an acre or so of the land he rented out, he allowed it to revert to wilderness, giving him an even larger buffer of uninhabited land around him. When the Minnesota farmers, obeying another metaphysical urge, uprooted most of the other trees in the county and did their fall plowing, only to watch in baffled wonder as their topsoil blew away year by year, McGrath's isolated home remained relatively dirt free. It was another thing that set him apart from his fellow citizens, another thing he liked.

He had had the barn torn down on his final return, having no livestock and no equipment of his own. His life-style was, thus, more suburban than rural, another far from unusual thing in the modern American farming community. McGrath, however, would never have uttered the word 'suburban' in connection with himself. He thought of his life as republican, Jeffersonian.

And he dressed the part. Each morning, before breakfast, he donned a three-piece suit, light for summer, dark for winter, complete with pocket watch. His goal was a kind of shabby elegance, or elegant shabbiness, so his shoes were usually scuffed, not a hard condition to maintain in a town with gravel roads and no sidewalks. Before leaving the house, he donned a broad-brimmed hat, also varied seasonally, and picked up one of the gnarled walking sticks he had gone to some trouble to collect. In winter he wore a thick woolen overcoat of a conservative plaid with a shoulder cape reminiscent of Sherlock Holmes. He would have been a perfectly dressed professional man of late nineteenth century America, but around him now even ministers and doctors wore blue jeans and sweatshirts. If clothes make a statement, McGrath's said "I am not part of this time and place" and came close to saying "I am not real." Yet he was far from the strangest sight to be seen in rural Minnesota and, though he would not have admitted it, far from the least accepted. He liked to think he was too ornery to be driven out. The truth was, he had been born there, and that counted for more than any amount of either conformity or eccentricity. The inhabitants of New Culloden accepted him, as they accepted thirty-below zero temperatures, fifty mile per hour winds, and mosquitoes. Madison McGrath was just one more aspect of their fate.

When he walked uptown to get the mail, McGrath could go part of the way on a paved road, U.S. Highway 59, which ran from the Canadian border to Laredo, Texas. His wife had often walked out to the edge of their driveway and put her foot on the blacktop, so that she might feel some tenuous link with more civilized parts of the world. McGrath hated the highway, since it was used by trucks which invariably blew his hat off as he paced uptown. At times he longed for civilization as much as she did, but he had no patience with the illusions of others. She also claimed to find civilization in church. He found this almost too hilarious to comment upon, though he managed to comment on it often. She had given both music and religion to their son, like some genetic deformity. As he often told her, swallowing his own sense of exile, "In New Culloden, I *am* Civilization." And that, as far as he was concerned, was that.

U.S. 59 bounded the west side of his property, which lay on the south side of New Culloden. The railroad tracks bounded it on the east side. Most of the town's business places and homes were clustered around the tracks, having made the wrong bet on the transportation of the future.

To the south of McGrath's property lay the Sometime River. It lay as though dead, since the dam had been built in the thirties, and would come to life only after heavy rains when the dam had to be opened. McGrath said of it: "Sometimes a river, always a sewer." He calculated it carried enough untreated chemicals running off from the fields to destroy human flesh in the space of one foolhardy crossing. It also carried enough plastic containers to be mistaken for a supermarket shelf. It was doubtful that most of the town, which lived upriver, meant this as a personal attack on McGrath's peace of mind and dreams of pastoral cleanliness. He, however, had always taken it personally. He sometimes fished garbage out and deposited it by night on lawns whose owners he suspected of being responsible for it. The owners, who in most cases were not, were still blaming the town's unruly teenagers for this. McGrath was aware of their mistaken conclusion and felt it preserved a natural balance, since the teenagers undoubtedly got away with things they should have been blamed for.

Even though he walked uptown to the post office six days a week, there was hardly ever a letter in his box. He couldn't remember the last time he had received one. On the other hand, circulars, advertisements, contests, and requests for contributions were there in great abundance. Despite all that had been done to make this a literate nation, McGrath received less correspondence than his father had at the turn of the century. More useless mail, but less correspondence. And most of his father's acquaintances had lived within a twenty mile radius, while his were scattered across the country.

When he had first returned to New Culloden, he had made a great effort to establish a regular correspondence with certain of his ex-partners, political friends, old teachers. He sent them brilliant essays: they sent him, when they bothered to reply, meaningless drivel. And even before he decided it was pointless, most of them had ceased replying. He assumed they were all idiots, a bad hand dealt him by fate. Actually, he had assumed that long ago and made little effort to hide it. That may have been why they had little interest in writing back, something that had occurred to him but that he refused to dwell on.

When he did receive a letter, it usually bore on his law practice which, by now, was not large. Though careful and methodical, McGrath had never been brilliant in anything but the offhand, abusive remark. He liked to think he was part of liberty's thin line of defense against barbarism on the one hand and tyranny on the other. Judging by the cases he handled, however, most people thought of him as little more than a thorn in their flesh. But he was ornery, a furious battler for his clients. And since rural America had not quite gone all the way back to settling scores with bullets, clubs, and knives, he managed to keep busy enough. Moreover, since he had little to be lost in social position or career possibilities, he was the lawyer of choice for anyone who wanted to take on the hospital, the school, the county, or anyone related to any of the other lawyers.

His serious reading had dwindled as his age increased and his immediate intellectual challenges decreased. His afternoon nap had lengthened, and his journals often lay unread in his lap while he stared out his living room window at the cemetery across the highway, the trucks breaking the speed limit, or the topsoil blowing away. He now caught himself watching the clock, eager for the hour to come when he would walk Blackstone.

His evening socializing had dwindled as well, though less from age than from lack of affability, or, as he would have said, lack of worthy partners. He still had a few acquaintances intimate enough to trade the occasional visit, but most evenings found him sitting with a book, his dog, his pipe, and some wine. It was a destiny he found not altogether unpleasant. Indeed, McGrath had always brightened in the evening and his mind remained nimble enough to enjoy works that most people would have found daunting as assignments for night school, if anyone around had had enough motivation to attend it. His taste in recreational reading ran to history and biography, with the odd volume of cultural doom-saying thrown in for spice. Henry Adams was one favorite, Francis Parkman another.

He read well into the night, setting Blackstone out to guard and to plunder around midnight. It was the only time he missed his wife, not that she had ever been of any use in a crisis. But another human presence had often eased his mind, when the night brought fears of marauders and intruders. His own combativeness then turned against him and made him edgy at every creak of the old house. The wine helped, as did the increasing lateness of the hour, but he had never gotten used to sleeping alone, a fact that only made him more irritable as he lay awake, and soon his longest and most restorative sleep would be happening in the afternoon.

He would have liked to keep Blackstone in with him through the night, but he thought he owed the dog his freedom. Besides, he thought Blackstone would be able to mount a more effective counter-attack from outside, should a prowler ever approach. None ever had, which only made McGrath more irritated with the fears he could not exorcise.

The night after he promptly forgot that his son had called him, he had an unusually difficult time sleeping. He heard Blackstone race by his window a time or two, heard him barking later some distance away. The wind made his protecting forest sound like a fleet of avenging trucks. A late spring storm was brewing. He must have slept then, because he didn't remember hearing the storm and there were puddles of water in his driveway when he walked Blackstone. The electricity was off, too, though he only took note of this because his refrigerator light hadn't come on. He smiled as he thought of the rest of the town, once again frozen in its technological tracks.

When he stepped out, then, to walk uptown, twirling his walking stick, he came out of an almost perfectly functioning world of the past, into a present that was severely malfunctioning, not only, as he well knew, from power failure.

He had heard a plane swoop over the house just before he came out. When he was halfway down the driveway, a dead bird fell at his feet.

It couldn't have been stunned by the storm, though the yard was littered with broken branches. Birds were tougher than that. Besides, the storm was over. He poked it with his stick. No apparent injuries.

The plane came over again, snarling and coughing. McGrath saw smoke trailing from it as it came into view, then the smoke stopped as it banked. It was the local crop duster, who had an airstrip on the north side of town. The man was such a hopeless alcoholic McGrath often wondered why he hadn't driven his plane into the water tower yet or tried to land on the highway in the path of a school bus.

He gave the bird another thoughtful poke, then crossed through the yard toward the river, instead of going uptown. He picked his way through the trees and came out on a crest above the river from which he could observe the fields south of him. He pulled his hat lower, planted his cane and waited. The plane made another pass over the land south of the river which McGrath was renting to two bothers, old Norwegian bachelors who looked like they were still packed in the grease they had been shipped in. The smoke trail appeared behind the plane, settled on the field, then in the distance the plane turned and came back toward him. Again appeared the smoke trail, which should have stopped at the end of the field. But as the plane finished its run, crossed the river and disappeared over McGrath's trees, the chemical death was still puffing out of it. It was just as he suspected. The careless pilot, his reaction time slowed by a few decades of alcohol consumption, was turning his property, perhaps the whole county, into a free-fire zone. For all McGrath knew, he could be using Army surplus Agent Orange. But then there would be no crops, either. Still, would those retarded Norwegians notice?

He shaded his eyes and peered down the river at the trees. He had probably seen this before but unconsciously dismissed it, attributing it to natural causes. But right along the river, like an artist's shading of its banks, there were dead or dying trees. Further in, they were still green which, to the casual eye, gave the appearance of universal health. But a careful look revealed those fronting the river were gone. It was too clear a line to be coincidental. The man was destroying his property.

He pounded his cane once like a gavel signaling a final decision. When he returned to his office, he would make some phone calls up and down the river, up and down the county. He would put that menace out of business. And he would have a great time doing it. With the plane still droning behind him, he resumed his schedule, rejuvenated by the thought of the coming crusade.

As he turned on the highway, a speeding truck nearly ran him down. He had to retrieve his hat. He complained on a monthly basis to the sheriff's department about the utter disregard of traffic regulations on the stretch of highway that ran through New Culloden, but he had yet to see a sheriff's car come down it for anything but a coffee break. New Culloden had no police of its own, the last man to act as combination police officer/maintenance man having quit when the city council refused to buy a new power lawn mower. With what they saved from his salary, they bought two (used) riding mowers but could find no one to take his position for the reduced (by a third) salary they were offering. The council decided to mow the lawns and maintain the town by themselves, and leave law enforcement to the county sheriff. The sheriff worked out of Carlsburg with two deputies who were usually busy driving alcoholics to the detoxification unit in Crookston, stopping men from beating their wives to death, and collecting bodies of car crash victims from back roads. In their list of priorities, they ranked speeding on the one mile of U.S. 59 that ran through New Culloden somewhere near mosquito infestation.

Law enforcement was a great source of debate in New Culloden, one of the few concerns McGrath shared with his fellow citizens. The city council debated it, if one could believe their published minutes, at almost every meeting. They loved debating it. It was paying for it that they disliked. Indeed, McGrath once remarked, they debated it with such energy that they had little left over to use the riding mowers they had traded it for. The only one ever seen mowing the considerable amount of town property was the mayor, when he wasn't responding to calls about marauding dogs.

Almost worse than the truckers were the town's senior citizens. As McGrath had outlived his wife, most of the Scandinavians seemed to have far outlived not only their minds but a good part of their bodies. Most of them had acquired driver's licenses before a sadder but wiser government began requiring minimal testing. It wasn't their speed so much as their accuracy that was the hazard.

Soon after the truck almost ended his day, McGrath had to step off the rather wide highway to allow a blind driver to avoid a manslaughter charge. The trembling, white haired driver was being talked uptown by his wife, who had never learned to drive, sitting beside him. Since the town's senior citizens were almost the town's only citizens, and most of the younger drivers had had their licenses revoked, with no effect on either their drinking or their driving, New Culloden nurtured a substantial indigenous traffic threat, which McGrath was sure the sheriff chuckled about when he complained about truckers.

Shaking his head as he did every morning somewhere along the highway, McGrath resumed his walk. He passed two churches before he made the turn to the post office, one Lutheran, to which his wife had belonged, one Assembly of God. McGrath always referred to ministers as vermin.

Both churches drew their architectural inspiration from the life around them. They had both been built during the last fifteen years, earlier buildings of equally clumsy design having burned down from the wiring installed by local all-purpose handymen who had grown up without ever seeing a light bulb, let alone a fuse. McGrath thought it was only a matter of time before these self-destructed as well. As the barns of an earlier era had resembled cathedrals, these buildings resembled potato warehouses, with slightly better cared-for lawns. McGrath saw nothing wrong with this. Neither did most of their members, for different reasons.

The failure of religion to strangle itself through inherent implausibility and egregious factionalism was a continuing puzzle to him. He was moved at times to attribute it to some as yet undiscovered flaw in the U.S. Constitution. But the founding fathers had probably never conceived the possibility of these unenlightened bigots banding together for mutual survival and trumpeting the ignorant claim that they had made America. If it hadn't been for the Constitution, they'd still be at each other's throats. Especially galling to him were holiday addresses by U.S. presidents, who broadcast the same illusion of a free country nurtured by religious faith. One could perhaps forgive the ignorance of the Inquisition, the Star Chamber, the torture and the punitive laws of centuries, but not of the Massachusetts Bay Colony, which had its own legacy of burning and banishing. Those people were not exactly the genial cooks they were portrayed as at Thanksgiving. But then, that a nation with a population of a quarter-billion people could do nothing every four years but run two morons for its highest office was another continuing puzzle to him.

McGrath was sure his blood pressure soared as he passed these two buildings every day. That was another reason he valued his walk. It made him feel young.

He was pleased to note that the younger generation had been making its contribution to religious life by tearing up the spacious church lawns with three-wheeler tracks. There were city ordinances against this activity, more stringent ones passed each year as a cheaper substitute for hiring someone to enforce the old ones. McGrath could see the point of these ordinances. But since the night one rider had tried to frighten Blackstone and been frightened into the river himself, his property had been relatively free of this nuisance and he could pretend to look on this youthful folly with the sympathetic eye of compassionate old age, which fooled no one. Besides, the frequency of fatalities from these vehicles helped to weed out the intellectually unfit of the young. Then again, perhaps these vehicles only took to the lawns to avoid being run over by senile Scandinavians. In the long run, the three-wheelers probably performed a more useful social function than the churches themselves, since they brought out the worst in the Christians and helped to reveal them as the hate filled, narrow minded, sanctimonious pipsqueaks that they were.

His shoes crunched on the gravel as he made the turn to the post office. There had once been an advertisement in the Carlsburg paper for a house in New Culloden, said to be "within walking distance of the business district." Since everything in New Culloden was within this distance, McGrath was highly amused, though he was one of the few people who still walked. This too was a puzzle to him, since the roads were usually graded in ribs which allowed a maximum speed of ten miles per hour before the steering column began to vibrate alarmingly.

If the post office had provided a mailman to deliver door-to-door, there would be little reason to walk to the business district anyway, unless one wanted to point out to visiting relatives the sites of defunct businesses. He walked past the boarded up creamery, the boarded up hardware store, and the site of the burned down body shop, still home to several gutted vehicles. The only buildings showing signs of life were the grain elevator, the post office, the bar (to which it seemed to be a point of honor to drive, not that its customers were any more capable of walking away), the grocery store, and the gas station. But, unlike the post office, the grocery store delivered.

It might be said, as a positive result of the population dwindling, that everyone in New Culloden knew everyone else, which could not be said for New York or even Sioux Falls, South Dakota. But would New Yorkers be happier knowing every other New Yorker? He doubted it. And virtually everyone in New Culloden, while knowing everyone else, also hated everyone else. While this was a difference, it hardly seemed to him to constitute an advantage.

This line of thought reminded him of the dead bird and the crop duster. There were so many chemicals used in modern agriculture that, in purely environmental terms, he might as well have lived in the middle of an oil refinery. And he had always felt that the law showed its uncreative side when it came to punishment for such abuses. Fines and jail terms meant very little and revealed a plodding, boorish tendency to befog distinctions at the precise point distinctions should be clarified, a problem which the legal mind should have been admirably suited to transcend. McGrath's own view was that, if toxic substances were carelessly used or disposed of, the persons responsible should be required to drink a few gallons. This would undoubtedly be a splendid deterrent, as capital punishment almost never was in, say, crimes of passion. Indeed, capital punishment would be a far more effective deterrent for anything but murder. Littering, for example, for which McGrath also had little sympathy.

As McGrath crossed the railroad tracks and the post office came into view, he saw a flurry of activity around it and also saw that its front wall, with both picture windows, had been demolished. Perhaps the government had decided to pull up stakes, ceding most of Minnesota to Canada. Or perhaps random terrorism had come at last to the American heartland.

This disturbance of his routine depressed him, but the near presence of serious misconduct, with the possibility of personal injury litigation, excited him, so he approached the carnage in relative equanimity.

Two workers, father and son of the family that owned the building and rented it at an exorbitant price to the American taxpayer, were sorting through the battered masonry, looking for bricks to salvage. McGrath saw in this the same impulse that would pry gold teeth out after a massacre, but he kept this observation to himself.

Instead, he remarked, "Faulty construction, eh? I always knew it wouldn't last."

Since these two, as McGrath was aware, had built the place, they made no response, less from anger than lack of ready wit.

The son finally said, "Car took it out last night. Lost control when he came around the curve."

"Anyone hurt?"

"Nope. Car even drove away. Can't see how it could."

"Well," said McGrath, "it shouldn't be too hard to trace. Something with bricks sticking out of its grille, I would think, and a drunken idiot at the wheel. Sure no one was hurt?"

"Nobody."

Pity, thought McGrath.

Around the bricks, a circle of onlookers had gathered, emotionally overwhelmed at having something beside the weather to talk about. He eased his way through them and picked his way through the bricks. Either the car had been going at an incredible rate of speed or the construction really had been faulty, or both. It had gone through the wall, collapsing it entirely, and rammed the interior wall which held the post office boxes. He approached his.

"Forget it, Madison," said the Postmistress, from behind her desk. "I've got all the mail back here."

"Gave the place a rigorous cleaning, I see, Ardell."

"It needed it, didn't you think? I shouldn't have taken down the cobwebs, though."

"We all make mistakes. No one hurt, was there?"

She pushed his immense stack of meaningless mail across the counter. "Nobody here. I had to come down around three in the morning."

"Oh? That probably caused you a lot of anxiety."

"I think I can handle it."

"Well, if you'd like to talk about your options, you know how to contact me."

"Yup. Right here, every morning."

He nodded curtly, gathered his mail, and went on his way. A quick glance told him his mail, as always, was hardly worth carrying home. The U.S. Postal Service was now fighting not only rain, sleet, snow, and dead of night, but suicidal drivers as well, and for what?

On the return leg of his walk, he stopped in at the gas station. Besides the bar, it was the only thriving business left, since most people did their grocery shopping out of town, choosing lower prices and variety over home delivery. And the station no longer thrived as it once had. At one time, its owners had three mechanics on duty and sold used cars out of the back lot. Now you were lucky to be able to buy a windshield wiper that fit, and the current owner was honest enough to profess complete ignorance of the internal combustion engine.

His name was Danny Danielson, roughly the age of McGrath's son, a far cousin of the family that had made the business great. He had inherited the station and a good share of the mercantile spirit, but not the boom years and large surrounding population of his fortunate ancestors. Great entrepreneurs, like great artists, need an audience equal to them. Danny, following his nose and pushing his own interests, had dumped the used cars and the auto-parts and turned the full-service automobile center into a convenience store and VCR home rental center at which you could also get a tank of gas. He was enjoying himself more, but he was still going broke. He had to supplement his income by delivering fuel oil and raising beef cattle. His wife Patty sat on an old rear seat of a Cadillac which served as a couch in the station, read old fashion magazines, and dreamed of exploring, travelling to, living, or dying in any continent in the world except North America. They were the only two Scandinavians McGrath would admit to knowing well, if he could not quite admit to liking them, which he did. But their brains would probably curdle soon, and he didn't want to waste any emotional investments, which he would never admit to having either.

He raised his cane in greeting. "Daniel. Patricia."

Patty raised her round, bespectacled face from her magazine, smiled brightly, and said, "Hi." Then she resumed reading. She reminded McGrath of Blackstone.

Danny, more dead pan, said "Madison," pronouncing it "Mahd-ee-sohn," with the accent on the last syllable. He did it, first of all, because he couldn't call anyone "Madison" with a straight face, and, second, because he thought it made him sound like a happy calypso singer with a joyous heart. McGrath thought the curdling process had probably begun.

McGrath set his mail on the counter and leaned against it. "Keeping the rabble in line, Daniel?"

"Doing my best. The gas flows, the junk food moves, and I got three new mad slasher movies in today."

"Destroying their will to live, eh?"

Danny laughed. "Exactly. Then, amigo, we make revolution."

Patty looked up. "I think this place is revolting enough as it is."

What she found most particularly revolting, and made no secret of, was the daily card game that went on in the station. Not so much the card game, as the card players. Danny had knocked out a wall and cleared an area for three tables, a magazine stand and a coffee urn. He had envisaged it as a kind of European café, where passers-by could read the morning paper, sip coffee, and play chess. Patty's comment on the idea had been: "Of course. Chess." She went so far in her mockery as to buy him three exquisite chess sets for his birthday.

The game area did prove to be an attraction. But it only attracted a handful of retired farmers, unemployed or underemployed farm workers, and aimless high school dropouts, all of whom could almost count high enough to stumble through a pinochle game. When she was being polite, Patty referred to them collectively as 'the frogs—croak, croak, croak'. She was sure one of the more cantankerous and mentally unstable older men had poisoned their dog, who used to enjoy smelling the odoriferous crotches of the players. Usually she simply called them 'the mutants'. McGrath was fond of the term and paid her the homage of adopting it for his own use.

One of the mutants rose from the current game, stretched, and came over to the counter. McGrath and Danny nodded to him. He remarked on the mildness of the weather. Danny agreed with him at great length. Patty snorted derisively. McGrath felt that the nod in recognition of his existence was more than his due and refused to join a discussion dedicated to proving that the sun was still shining but that, still, it could rain, though it might not, you never knew.

Since Danny himself had only joined in out of politeness, being much more inclined to discuss jazz pianists, oriental gardening, or the virtues of Marxism, the conversation quickly ran its course. Danny had once considered offering informal lessons in the art of conversation but Patty had pointed out both that no one would attend and that it would ruin his business, the mere suggestion implying that he thought the natives could use improvement.

The mutant stared at McGrath, as though waiting for another opinion on whether the sky was blue or not. McGrath stared back. They actually had something in common: like McGrath, this man had returned to New Culloden to take over the family farm. He had been working, unhappily, as a mechanic in the twin cities. Unlike McGrath, however, he had tried to work the farm himself, with as much or less knowledge of soil and crops as McGrath had, and much less knowledge of tax forms and bureaucratic loopholes. He now owed three times as much money as he had returned with, and spent most of his time working for more prosperous farmers on the few days each year they needed another hand on their machinery. He was the only human being McGrath knew who had a statue of a black jockey in his yard.

Now it happened sometimes that the mere presence of Madison McGrath, whose intelligence was legendary in New Culloden, though this was a source more of scorn than admiration, would goad the odd person into daring a sophisticated remark. This happened now. Seeing he would get nowhere with the weather, the mutant said, "Say—know what I heard on the radio this morning? They said that if all the Chinese jumped at once, they'd cause a tidal wave that would swamp North America. How about that?"

McGrath looked at the ceiling. "Who says Midwesterners don't deal with the deeper issues of our time?"

Convinced he had struck a rich vein, the mutant continued, "That would take a lot of organization, wouldn't it?"

"Undoubtedly."

"Course, they could probably handle it. Say—I wonder if we could do that to them. All jump at once and send a tidal wave their way."

Danny said, "We'd never agree on if or when or how to do it. In this town alone,

I could name a dozen people who probably wouldn't jump, just out of pure cussed-ness. Then there's the people who can't keep time."

"And," offered McGrath, "you'd have to worry about power failures. Clocks stopping."

"Shit. You're right. This country isn't what it used to be."

"Besides," said Danny, "we'd swamp all those cheap factories in Taiwan. And how about our bases in the Pacific? I think we're touching on areas of national secu-rity here."

"I never thought about that."

McGrath said, "Did you ever think of having a brain scan?"

"No, but I had my nose x-rayed once," said the mutant, as though this were a natural turn in the conversation. "Damnedest thing. I was twirling a padlock on the end of my key chain. Broke my nose."

"And they didn't do a brain scan? You've got to watch those head injuries."

"Never had any trouble."

"Well, as long as you don't overdo it."

"Oh, hell no. Well, be seeing you."

"Right."

Danny watched him leave. "He'll probably worry about the Chinese for a month."

McGrath said, "What radio station do you suppose he listens to?"

"Probably one of the CBC comedy hours."

"Humor is a dangerous thing in the wrong hands."

Patty came over to the counter. "To think that clown actually lived in the cities and came back to this. Not that other people aren't just as stupid." Her place in life was a sore point with her. Danny ignored the remark.

McGrath said, "If he ever writes his autobiography, which I admit seems highly unlikely, he could call it: *I Chose Hell.*"

"Come to think of it, Mahdeesohn, that wouldn't be a bad title for yours."

"A little too defeatist for my taste. No, mine would be something like—"

"*Life among the Mutants,*" suggested Patty.

"Yes. Very good, Patricia. Something along that line."

One of the few residents that neither McGrath nor Patty considered a mutant peeked in the door. It was Ben Beckett, whom McGrath sometimes introduced as 'Benjamin Beckett, Master of Arts', when, as happened rarely, he was with someone who did not know Beckett and whom he considered worthy of an introduction.

Beckett had never been able to decide whether he was a victim of a terminal mid-life crisis, hitting with unusual force because coming unusually late in life, a victim of teacher burn-out, or simply an idle vagrant showing his true colors belat-edly. After giving up on his doctorate, he taught literature and composition in a small community college for thirty years. He had spent the summers in New Cul-loden, renting a cabin on the lake that had been formed by the dam. One year, he had decided life in New Culloden made no less sense than anything else he was in-volved in, so he retired, bought a house, and stayed there year round.

Beckett said, "Guess what I just heard about the Chinese."

"If they all farted at once," said Patty, "they'd blow Western Europe into orbit."

"That too? This is more serious than I thought."

"We just heard about the tidal wave," said McGrath. "We're going to start filling sandbags tomorrow."

"And I used to think my students were the stupidest animals I'd ever met."

"Obvious you're not a native, Ben."

One thing McGrath loved about the station under the Danielson management was that it had an air of inspired time-wasting about it, something he associated with an earlier America of fire halls, general stores, and isolated army posts, where people of intelligence and some cultivation were condemned to spending many pointless hours doing nothing. They would much rather be somewhere else, but their jobs wouldn't allow it. Yet their jobs filled neither their time nor their minds. They thus offered entertainment on demand to anyone who would pass by. Most modern equivalents of such jobs were held either by the culturally handicapped, who found them challenging, or by people who enjoyed watching television. The Danielsons were neither, and their servitude gave McGrath an opportunity to enjoy them, while their freedom would have meant they never had time to see anybody. Beckett, a frequent visitor to the station, carried the same quality about him like a special atmosphere, with less excuse.

Yet McGrath was too methodical and driven to remain idle for very long. He now made a great show of taking out his pocket watch to signal he was preparing to leave.

It was no more than a show, first because the time had nothing to do with his departure and, second, because his watch had stopped years ago. That he never had it repaired was not a matter of carelessness or forgetfulness but of standards that were rigid to the point of absolute paralysis. There was no jeweler within three hundred miles that he would trust to look at it. He had every intention of having it repaired someday and, until then, he saw no reason to give up the habit of consulting it.

Not that repairing it would accomplish much. All his life, McGrath had stopped every watch he owned. Timepieces that would run for weeks on his desk would freeze in a matter of days if carried on his person. This was a great source of irritation to him, who was so punctual.

"Well," he declared, "enough frivolity for one morning. I have to march along."

"I'll march with you," said Beckett.

"Drop in again," said Danny. "Maybe we'll run a special on life preservers for the coming flood."

Patty stretched out on her car seat. "Maybe we'll make a t.v. commercial. You could be in it, Madison. You know, say something about the Yellow Peril, being prepared, forewarned is forearmed, no more Vietnams, a sound mind in a sound body."

"Amen," said Danny. "Eternal vigilance is the price of freedom. Or is it eternal ignorance?"

"You two worry me," said Beckett. "If you don't watch out, you'll wind up like me."

"One of us already has," said Patty, and at once regretted it. Like many of the things she said, it struck a bit too close to the truth and was a bit too sharp an underlining of a self-deprecatory remark. Danny raised his eyebrows. McGrath waved his cane to end the banter.

"We're off."

"Walk with God, Yankees," called Danny.

Definitely curdling, thought McGrath, though still above average. He set out on the return loop to his farm, and Beckett loped along beside him.

Since Beckett's retirement, he and McGrath had become relatively frequent companions. They did not so much complement each other as present two extreme instances of human types, with no clue to the continuum that connected them. Where McGrath was fastidious, Beckett was slovenly, dressing in jeans, torn and frayed white shirts, and loose fitting sweatshirts, with an army parka for winter. McGrath was not short, but appeared so among the Scandinavians, and was rather dark. Beckett was tall, and his hair had turned gray when he was young, from, he said, too much contact with college athletes. But they could follow each other's conversations and recognize the names of the authors each was reading. McGrath liked Beckett because he suffered fools no more gladly than did McGrath. Beckett, who thought of himself as whimsical and tolerant, liked McGrath's arrogance and sarcasm. And they were comfortable enough to walk together in silence, McGrath according to his daily schedule, Beckett with nothing better to do.

They turned at the boarded theatre. It had once been packed every Friday and Saturday night, but the decent citizens of the town had been more and more outraged at the movies that the manager had to show to remain solvent. He finally sold the theatre to a local farmer who vowed to show nothing but general family entertainment. The people who complained never went to movies anyway, and the new fare did not slake the regular customers' thirst for flesh and blood, so the theatre soon closed. The city council showed old horror movies in it on Halloween night, a concession decency made to the lower passions in the hope of forestalling real horrors, a curious reversal of its usual view of the consequences of art. McGrath, who never went to movies either but hated censorship of any sort, had mounted an ironic campaign against the horror shows on the grounds of consistency. He wrote a letter to the local paper, arguing that if sexy movies encouraged sex, *Abbot and Costello Meet Frankenstein* would encourage either idiotic behavior or the creation of man-made monsters. McGrath was horrified to receive a letter of congratulations from the Assembly of God church council. Beckett thought it was hilarious and hoped they would make McGrath an honorary member.

Between the theatre and the highway lay the old elementary school grounds. The school had been a victim of consolidation and the town's children were now bused to school in Carlsburg. The first floor of the building was currently leased by the Assembly of God for its Christian American Heritage School, which offered a facsimile of modern non-education, but only up to grade eleven, since its staff were opposed to its students going on to college.

As they neared the highway, they came upon Einar Ekdahl, the town's mayor, mowing the school lawn. Ekdahl had negotiated intensively to get the Heritage

School into the facilities. It was one of the things he boasted about as injecting new life into the town. McGrath thought it not much different than boasting about having a venereal disease.

Ekdahl, a rotund, nervous little man, waved at them. Beckett waved back.

They reached the highway.

"Well," said Beckett, "I think I'll go up and challenge Patty to a game of chess." He started to turn away.

"Oh, Ben. My son telephoned me. He's coming up for the summer. Why don't you come over for dinner when he gets here? I'm not sure what day he's arriving." It was the first time he had thought of James since their talk.

"Sure. Just give me a call. Afraid to face him alone?"

"What nonsense."

Instead of thinking further about this, McGrath waved and let James fall from his mind again. As he headed for his office, he thought of the calls he had to make up and down the river. He felt good. That careless pilot had his blood pumping.

Chapter Five

As James followed the Interstate toward the Dakotas, his public radio station started to fade. He hoped it was only the first of many things about the twin cities that would simply vanish from his life, conjured away by distance. He knew he could pick up the station on some other frequency, but he put on one of his tapes instead: *Don Giovanni*. That would take the edge off the next three hours of driving and, moreover, would make him feel more self-contained, more self-directed, than allowing himself to be subjected to some undergraduate's afternoon programming.

Then he remembered the sexual entanglements of the opera: love, death, and damnation. An unfortunate choice. But he left it on. It was in Italian anyway. And he was leaving all that behind. He whistled along with the orchestra.

The mere fact of his decision, being on the road, thrilled him. There was something intoxicating about having all he needed in his car with him, a life stripped down and compacted, no vulnerable links to institutions or people. He sensed the attraction of banditry: living out of motels and convenience stores, more at home on the highway than anywhere else, never having to call a plumber, robbing liquor stores.

Undoubtedly, that had its down side, too: being gunned down by armed clerks or, worse, captured and imprisoned. The price of failure went up with the rewards of success. A life of complete freedom risked the complete loss of freedom. James had had a life of moderate freedom and relative bondage; having botched that, he was now relatively unbound but still not all that free. He supposed that was the price of a cautious, mediocre life: the utter reversal of its terms, through failure, still didn't get you anywhere.

And yet the feeling of travel, the knowledge that he was not returning, cleared his turmoil a little. If his life was not quite sensible yet, it was at least a little more simple.

The country around him was clearing as well. There were fewer buildings, then fewer towns, fewer cars around him. At times, he could imagine this magnificent four-lane divided highway had been hewn out of hill, forest, and prairie solely for his pleasure. It was a comforting illusion, and he welcomed it.

After Don Giovanni had been carried off to hell, accompanied by the heavenly music of Mozart, James pulled off the road to study his map. It had been years since he had been to New Culloden; with some surprise, he realized he hadn't been there since his mother's funeral. For that, he had flown to Grand Forks and his father had met him at the airport. So it had been even longer since he had driven there. Rather than risk getting lost on lesser highways, which would have cost him another phone call to his father, with no guarantee of getting help, he decided to swing all the way into North Dakota and catch Interstate 29 going north. That would leave him only a small stretch of country road and only one turn to make. Moreover, he could go through Fargo for one last lungful of city air before hurling himself into the country.

Even though James had grown up in Fargo, he was out of it and on the way to Grand Forks before he knew what was happening. He supposed North Dakota had to list something under the category of "city," but what he had driven through, searching for some sort of central urban landmark before he stopped, struck him as nothing more than a housing complex with a department store or two. So much for stopping in Fargo. He would have to be careful not to miss Grand Forks.

But perhaps this was the glory of life out here: even the urban areas were rural. Their scale was small, they fit a human being's hand, foot, and eye, they offered a home, roots, smiles of recognition, civil servants that knew you by sight and by first name and probably your mother's maiden name as well.

His very perceptions had been distorted by city life. No wonder his life had become a snowballing catastrophe. It's a wonder he wasn't wanted for murder.

Afraid of making the same miscalculation he had made in Fargo, and in urgent need of a restroom, he took the first Grand Forks exit and stopped at a mall on what he would have called the outskirts of the city but for all he knew might have been its center. He hit the restroom, grabbed some food, and headed back to the road, leaving the last place on the map to qualify as a city before the Canadian border.

When, north of Grand Forks, he finally left the Interstate, he could almost believe he was an early settler coming to an untamed land. Obvious signs of civilization were all around him: paved roads, power lines, houses, farms; but there were so few of them. What struck him most was the sheer amount of non-human and non-manufactured things: trees, rocks, dirt, grass, all of it wild and filled with confident power.

He saw a man standing in the back of a pickup at the edge of a field. There was a herd of cows facing him. He could have been Adam, risen erect for the first time over the new creation, calling the animals to him to give them their names. James marveled. He was made uneasy by house pets. And here was a man sharing his life with dozens of large brutes, watching over them. And drawing strength from them.

James knew that his grandfather had raised pigs, chickens, cows. But he had never discussed farming with his father and his father had certainly never reminisced about it. He would have to bring up the subject. It might become a bond between them. James had to admit there were few others.

The turn he had to make was in Carlsburg. Judging by the map, he would have about twelve miles to go after that. As he made the turn, he saw a sign that said: Canada, 30 miles. As did most Americans, James thought of Canada as being somewhere inside the Arctic circle, though he in fact knew better. But its proximity still sent a shiver through him. And there was no mention of New Culloden.

He was sure he was on the right road. And he knew the town was still there, because he had talked to his father. He felt for a moment like one of those travellers in the first chapter of a horror story, journeying into a world beyond reality. He dismissed it as a consequence of frayed nerves, eight hours on the road, and the need to urinate again.

If he was struck by the presence of nature when he left the Interstate, he was overwhelmed by it now. The thin U.S. highway seemed ready to vanish at any moment, frightened away by the ancient forest which had never relinquished its claim to the land. He began to fear he really had taken the wrong road. But he saw a road sign: U.S. 59. Then the trees cleared, and he could see they were thicker in appearance than in reality. There were many cultivated fields, stretching to each horizon.

Just a mile or two from New Culloden, there was a farmer tending a grass fire. Now here was a life with depth, a life in partnership with the earth. The man was burning the prairie to renew his land. It was a rite of spring, and the gnarled old farmer probably looked no different than the men who had stood in his place several millennia ago, performing the same act with more primitive tools but with the same care, concentration, and purpose. It was a fitting image for his homecoming and for all he hoped from it. The highway curved slightly, and then New Culloden was before him. He slowed down to make the turn into his father's driveway.

It was early evening, and the sun filled the air with soft, golden light. The shadows were long and dark, and the green foliage shone like wet jewels just raised from the deepest ocean. Across the road, there was a fat little man driving a lawn mower in the cemetery. His shadow made him seem a lean knight on a powerful horse, beating back the primitive, keeping one of the haunts of his people safe from the hungry disorder of chaos. The man waved to him. Everything gave off the air of the warmest, most welcoming home.

Except home. There were no lights in his father's house and the door was locked. Any time is fine, but don't expect any welcome. James walked around the yard.

It was large, and the grass was lush. Where he lived, it would have ranked as an almost extravagant park, and the taxes alone, not to mention the cost of security, would have prohibited private ownership. The trees that surrounded it on every side gave the grounds the aspect of a small castle or monastic retreat. Nature was close, but controlled. It was a perfect balance. He took a deep breath of satisfaction. Father or no father, he was going to enjoy this. He strolled back down the driveway.

The knight of the cemetery was still making his devoted rounds. The noise of the motor spoiled the image, but it was much less than James was used to. Then, coming toward him out of the far distance, on the road which ran along the cemetery toward the setting sun, preceded by two long shadows that moved like nervous but well-trained servants, James saw his father and his dog.

His father must have seen him, too, but he didn't quicken his pace. James remained where he was, a gesture somewhat more filial than returning to brood in his car, but far from effusive. Neither was of the sort who would lessen the distance between them by elated sprint and open arms.

As McGrath came closer, his dog trotting easily at his side, he seemed thinner to James, his clothes hanging a bit loosely. But, then, he also seemed to be emerging from a time warp. With the sun behind him like a halo, the dust of the road around him, he could have been Abe Lincoln, pondering a case or turning over the phrases of an address. He was carrying his coat, and his sleeves were rolled up. His vest was open and his tie slightly undone. He looked serene, a man who knew his worth and could be at ease with himself at day's end. When he was almost at the highway, James raised his hand in greeting, McGrath, as though he hadn't noticed him, looked off to the south.

What an act, thought James. His father seemed to be enjoying the picture he made. James supposed he was meant to admire the noble profile.

The dog was not as histrionic. Sitting at McGrath's feet, at the highway's edge, Blackstone had locked on to James for the last hundred yards like a missile guidance system. His head was slightly cocked and his mouth slightly open, watching James while his brain considered the issues of identification and appropriate response.

McGrath turned, appearing to have just noticed James, which he had, being preoccupied with his crop dusting crusade and imagining he heard the buzz of the maniac's plane, raised his hand in greeting, and, with a word to the dog, started toward him. He didn't hurry.

But the dog did. Blackstone sprang from his stance as though the race had begun for the last meal in the world's life. James wondered if his father's word to the dog had been 'kill'.

He had read that it was pointless to run from attacking animals because they could overtake any human, no matter how driven by mortal fear, up to and including Olympic sprinters. In fact, if animals had a sense of humor, it was probably aroused most often by hearing of the "world record" times in track and field events. But James couldn't remember what it was you were supposed to do, if not run. Stand and die, he supposed, as a lesson in courage and the achievement of a moral victory. So he stood there, most of all so that he wouldn't look foolish in front of his father. Besides, if the dog hurt him, he would have something legitimate to be angry about. If the dog killed him, he could curse him from the grave.

With exquisite co-ordination, as though he were chasing a squirrel up a tree, Blackstone crossed the highway at full speed, stopped instantly with his rear paws on the toes of James' shoes, uncoiled, punched two dusty paws into James' chest, nearly drove James' nose up into his brain with his snout, and covered his face with licks.

"Don't be so scared," said McGrath. "He just wants to greet you."

That makes one of you, thought James. "I know," he said, lying.

Blackstone pranced around him, wagging not so much his tail as his entire body. He had reached the limit of his powers of communication.

His father shook his hand firmly but curtly, as he would that of a new client who looked like he might not be able to handle the fee. That seemed to bring all three of them to the limit of their powers of communication.

McGrath said at last, "How was the trip?"

"Oh, fine." James tried to laugh pleasantly. "It's a long drive up here."

"Depends where you start from." His father could always make facts sound like insults.

McGrath started up the driveway. James sighed and followed him. Rural paradise or no rural paradise, he was going to find this difficult. Walking in the older man's wake, he felt reduced to a child again. He was even tripping over this stupid dog, as though he hadn't learned to walk yet.

They reached the car and McGrath wondered how anyone of sound mind could condemn himself to squeezing into a car this small.

James thought his father was frowning at the Japanese name. "So shall I pull into the garage?"

"That's where I park mine."

James controlled himself and only nodded.

"And," continued McGrath, "you'll want to move it so I won't hit it when I back out. Park it behind the garage." He had been looking at James' luggage, trying to estimate how long he was staying. The contents of the car seemed more appropriate for a year at school than a summer visit. "Sure you brought enough?"

"What I didn't bring I can always steal."

McGrath straightened up and turned to his son, as though the rituals of greeting were over and the moment of real business at hand. "So what's up?"

It took James by surprise. The old lawyer with his hands in his pockets and his coat draped over his arm was treating him like a defendant, cornering him for the truth, off the record, just to satisfy his own curiosity. James was maddened to find that his voice shook when he answered. "Oh, this job was only supposed to last so long. I was an interim director. I thought I'd give myself a break." If he believes I'd come here to do that, thought James, he'll believe anything.

"How long did you have this job?"

"Three years or so. About three and a half."

"Funny length for an interim: 'three years or so, about three and a half'. Doesn't it strike you as funny?"

"Hilarious. That's how they do things, okay? That's just—how they do things." One more remark, thought James, and I get back in the car and drive away.

And go where?

McGrath had been a lawyer and a parent long enough to know James was lying. He also knew that right now he would get nothing out of him. And he was long past feeling the need to fight his child's battles. Still, he persisted: "You're sure nothing's wrong?"

"What could be wrong?" How about: everything.

"Well, too bad you didn't call. Dinner won't be much. It's usually just Blackstone here and me." McGrath made it sound like an argument that he should go.

James was tempted to say: I can always run out for another can of dog food. Again he felt he had entered some horrible fairy tale, where he would have to say the right word or everything would be denied him. What he said was: "Can I stay or what?"

McGrath seemed surprised at the question. "Of course. Why not? Come on, come on. Let me give you a hand."

The house was much gloomier than he remembered it from the visits of his college days. Dark wood, heavy furniture, with very little color anywhere. A book with red binding that was lying on the table seemed like a vulgar foreign guest, uneasily tolerated.

McGrath led the way upstairs to the room James used when he came home from college. There were two rooms upstairs, the other having been the master bedroom. Since his wife's death, McGrath had slept downstairs, in the room that was formerly his den. Lacking a woman to keep happy in the living room, McGrath no longer needed a den.

The dust was so thick and undisturbed in the room that it could have been grey paint.

"I never come up here."

James attempted a teasing remark. "I guess it could stand a little cleaning."

"So clean it." McGrath set down the bags he was carrying and went down for another load.

James looked around at the tiny room. He remembered freezing up here one Christmas vacation. Surely he would leave before then.

And go where?

Now that he was here, it was as though God had granted him an instant of omniscience and he saw how utterly senseless his decision had been. But if he was not ready yet to think beyond being here, he was certainly not ready to think *about* being here.

James spent the next two hours carrying up his things and doing some basic cleaning, his father helping with the carrying, then disappearing into the kitchen. Blackstone ran up and down the steps with them, then curled up on the bed to watch James work.

"Don't plan on sleeping with me."

Blackstone received this comment with an affronted air, as though he had more important things to do than keep humans warm.

When James had done what he could to the room, the dog leaped from the bed suddenly and ran down the stairs. James assumed it was time for dinner. And, like some half brother of the dog, he stopped unpacking and followed him down.

He was surprised to see another man present. He was leaning against the sink, sipping wine, while his father stirred things on the stove.

"Ah, you're here," said McGrath, now playing the host. "This is my friend, Benjamin Beckett, Master of Arts, Citizen of New Culloden and the world, and one of the finest minds this side of the Mississippi."

"The Mississippi doesn't come up this far," said Beckett. "We can't really be said to be on one side or the other of it."

"Alright. One of the most irritating people north of Arkansas, then. How's that? Ben, this is my son."

James extended his hand. No name, just: my son. A label. My son, my dog. "James," said James.

"I know," said Beckett, and made him feel like an arrogant child. This would not be the easiest meal of his life.

To his surprise, however, it went very smoothly. His father served spaghetti with a sauce he had concocted himself. Beckett kept their wine glasses filled. Most importantly, the two older men spent most of the meal talking to each other. Beckett seemed to bring out a humorous side of his father that James had never seen, or at least had never recognized as such.

And they ate by candlelight, two slender candles in pewter candlesticks. This was something that James had heretofore associated only with women. Women, that is, in whom he was taking a romantic interest. He could not remember his mother ever using them.

The atmosphere began to win him over. There was something at once substantial and playful about these two old friends conversing in the evening, the flames of the candles reflected in the glass of the dining room cupboards, in this dark room with its oaken table and straight-back chairs. This was the ease that accompanied a life of depth.

The meal over, Beckett pushed his chair back and took out his pipe. McGrath lit a cigar and offered one to James, to his amazement. For reasons, he could not fathom, James refused it.

"Don't smoke?" said Beckett. "Not for religious reasons, I hope."

James cursed himself, first for not accepting his father's offer, second for not being able to say he was dying to smoke and that he had his favorite cigars upstairs, and most of all because he had failed to slip easily into their mood and broken the spell of the evening. He began to stutter an answer that he could not complete.

"Well," said McGrath, "this isn't our mandatory smoking area. That's my office, eh, Ben?"

He felt again like a child in an adult world, whose status had just been underlined. So, forcing himself, he said, "I have my own upstairs. I'll just run up and get them."

"Oh, by all means," said McGrath, graciously enough, and James wondered why he found it sarcastic.

But his stumbling seemed not to bother them, and when he returned, Beckett was pouring more wine. James estimated that Beckett was out-drinking them by at least two glasses to one. It seemed to have little effect on him.

As James sat down and attempted to look relaxed, Beckett pulled a thin manuscript from his coat and pushed it over to him. It was stapled together and gave off the unforgettable smell of mimeograph fluid. James had not imagined, in this age of copy machines, that he would ever smell it again.

"What's this?"

Beckett lowered his eyes in mock humility. "A small creation of mine. It's actually from a much longer work-in-progress. As you can see, I print them myself. It's for you, a small present."

James looked at the title: *Nomina et Numera: selected phone numbers from North American phone directories, 1979-1983.* James fingered the pages politely, without attention. "So it's—"

"A kind of modernistic epic."

"Ben's a poet," said his father. McGrath had a mischievous look in his eye. James wondered if both of them, only his father, or only he himself had consumed more wine than he thought.

"Really? How—"

"*Don't* say 'how interesting'," said Beckett. "Anything but that. Or were you about to say how strange or bizarre or unlikely? I think that's it: unlikely. That's what I am in your eyes. Correct?"

"I guess. A little."

"No doubt you expected to find out here nothing but frontier life, served by a few of the less dispensable professions."

"Such as the law," said McGrath, raising his glass.

"Medicine," continued Beckett, "a skeleton crew of police officers, mounted, as the later Roman legions were, to make up by mobility what they lacked in numbers,—"

"Also, verminous fanatics," said McGrath.

"He means the church. That, too, and let's not forget the ever present tentacles of the federal and state governments."

"Here, here."

"But never, I'm sure, a lonely man of literature."

"Not lonely, Ben, never lonely."

"Correct. A lone man of literature."

James reasoned vaguely that if Beckett were so alone, he would have to count as an unlikely instance, which seemed to be the point he was arguing against. All he said was, "I hadn't really thought about it one way or another."

Beckett smiled. "Don't take me so seriously. I'm teasing you. I think I'm pretty bizarre, myself."

"Bizarre," mused McGrath, "I wonder if there's some Semitic root to that word, something connecting it to 'bazaar.' What do you think, Ben?"

James thought they had all had too much to drink. There was something a little unnerving about getting steadily drunk with his father. It made James feel even more of a stranger.

"Seriously," said Beckett, "I do write. This is from my magnum opus, currently growing slowly, but growing. I'd like you to have it. Read it later."

"Alright. I will. Thank you."

Outside, a loud siren began to wail. Blackstone, who had been lying peacefully beneath the table, trotted to the window and howled with the siren as it rose and fell.

"Fire," said McGrath, and rose from the table. "I'll find out where it is." He hurried to the phone.

"Lawyers," said Beckett. "Alas, they're addicted to the misfortunes of others."

James smiled politely.

"And what do you do?"

Nothing, thought James, but said, "I'm a church music director."

"And you are presently employed where?"

"I am presently unemployed, to tell the truth."

"Ah. Well—" Beckett raised his glass. "To better days."

"Amen." They drank. Beckett refilled his own glass, but James put his hand over his, still half full.

"Unemployment is a condition with which I am not unfamiliar. The thing to watch out for is the panic. It comes from primitive fears: I am not useful so I must be punished. My advice is: relax. Enjoy it while it lasts. There's much more to life than work."

Was that all I did? thought James. *Work?* "Right. I'll relax."

"So we'll be having you around a while, then?"

"Afraid so."

"Drop in and see me. After you've looked at my book. We'll talk. Oh, and—you strike me as a reader—I'll let you borrow some of my books. Best library in miles."

"Well. Thank you."

"You know, in some ways, I've fashioned a second career out of unemployment. I only wish I'd begun at an earlier age. Of course—" He grinned wickedly. "It *does* help to have a pension."

"Yeah. It would."

McGrath returned, chuckling. "Ben, you know that idiot Knutson that lives south of my land? He was burning his field—"

"Oh, I saw him," said James. "He was out there when I drove up. Thin old guy, a little stooped over."

"Yes, and not from the weight of his brain, either. He's burning his field, he thinks the fire's out, and he goes home for supper. But it isn't out. While he's enjoying his sardines, it is, on the contrary, creeping ever nearer. Knutson rises for one last check, but too late—" He paused.

"And?" said Beckett.

"The damn fool's barn burned down."

James thought it sounded like the sort of disaster rural people rushed to remedy, but the two older men dissolved in laughter.

"Burned down his own barn!" said McGrath, slapping the table for emphasis. "This is a new high for the Knutsons."

Beckett was wiping tears from his eyes. "That calls for a toast. To Oscar Knutson. Long may he entertain us!" He drained his glass. "Gentlemen, we'll never top this. I can think of no more fitting close to an evening. James, come by sometime. Lawyer McGrath, I bid you good even."

"Thanks for your book," said James. He folded the papers and put them in his back pocket.

It was almost midnight. After Beckett's departure, McGrath insisted on doing the dishes. James' habits would have left them there, perhaps for a day or so, in homage to a pleasant evening. McGrath cleaned so thoroughly James would not have been surprised if he had begun to shampoo the carpet.

His father worked silently. James assumed he was tired or, more likely, had no idea how to communicate with his son, now that Beckett was gone. McGrath never considered the issue. He was simply following routine. He never formulated the thought: James can like it or not, it makes no difference. Though that is what he would have said, had he been asked.

But when he was done, he bid James come outside with him. It was time to set Blackstone free.

The dog was out the door and away into the night before either man was out of the house. Hands in his pockets, McGrath walked into his yard. James, again a son, following a parent whose purpose he could not guess, walked behind him.

The night air was cool and fresh, with just a trace of smoke from hapless Knutson's barn. To the north, New Culloden's lights glowed behind the trees. But above him, James saw more stars than he had ever remembered seeing. Layer upon layer, they were like fine lace draped on the black satin gown of a queen. Here was the distant, unearthly beauty of the heavens that the modern city would always deny him. Inebriated, he was loose enough to gasp, "What a beautiful night!"

"Hmm? Oh, the stars. Yes, you can't see them very well from here. You have to go out to the lake, get up on the high ground. Best view, and no lights at all there. If you like that sort of thing."

"This is nice country."

"The United States? Well, we still have a few kinks to work out. We'll make it, though, if we can keep the fanatics and ideologues in their place."

"No. I meant the area. This is a nice area."

"Oh. It's alright. Good as anywhere, I suppose." He thought a moment. James couldn't see his face. "Your mother never liked it."

"I know."

"You won't either." McGrath shook his head slightly, to dismiss the topic as he would a pesky fly. He continued, "I let Blackstone out every night at midnight. He comes back on his own. He gets walked in the morning—you might need a leash, he might not follow you. He can stay in the house or, if he's outside during the day, he has to be on the chain behind the garage. He gets an evening walk. You saw where we walked. I'll write down what he gets to eat. He likes to spend the evening inside, then out again at midnight. I'm telling you this in case you ever have to manage things. Got it?"

My son, my dog, my dog's manager, my son. James wanted to say: oh, planning a trip now that I'm here? But he said, "Okay."

"Because if I have to be gone, or if I'm tied up in court, and you're here, there's no reason his schedule has to suffer. Dogs are very orderly creatures, one of their many points of superiority to humans. I don't want to have to contact you on a daily basis to make special arrangements. These things should just be done. If you're here, you can do them. Of course, if I'm here, I have the primary responsibility. Do you want me to go over it again?"

"I think I can cope." What was eating the old fart?

"Good. We can talk about general rules tomorrow. And I'll work on a list of shared duties."

James sighed in bewilderment. "Whatever you say."

McGrath walked on, oblivious to the sarcasm. He was now following his earlier line of thought. "Yes, to be more precise, a *nicely conceived* country. We are the fortunate heirs of brilliant and canny men." He stopped and looked not so much at his tree line but through it, to some image only his mind could see. "I love America." He turned to James and raised a finger in qualification. "The *idea* of America."

He continued: "What's our glory? Are we smarter, handier? Take a good look at the mutants around you. American know-how? You should have seen what the

German tanks could do to ours. The only decent car built in America right now has a German engine. Natural resources? Go to Africa. Southeast Asia—why, a man could spit on the ground there and raise a bushel of rice. No, it's the law. The law. The idea of America. The *thought* of a life together, given shape in law. That's our glory. That's all we are."

He paused, turned to James, then turned away and said quietly, "You should have studied law."

James knew it was coming. He had heard it before and he expected to hear it again. Part of him, defeated and confused, wanted to shout agreement. But he would never utter such words to this man. To someone else, perhaps, but never to this man, who wanted so much to hear them. For another part of him knew better. That part urged him to bellow an argument. But he didn't do that either. He shrugged, and said "Life's strange."

McGrath's head snapped around. "It isn't life that's strange." He started back to the house and called over his shoulder, "You didn't move your car."

So James moved it, feeling as though he were losing another argument every inch he travelled.

His father was reading in the living room when he returned. He didn't look up. James went upstairs. He was thankful there was a bathroom upstairs, so he wouldn't have to come down again. If there were a kitchen, he would have considered laying in supplies and never coming down.

As he undressed, he found Beckett's manuscript in his pocket. He sat down at his desk to look at it.

He liked Beckett. He did think him an unlikely character to be living in New Culloden, but thought too that he might enjoy knowing him. And he intended to take him up on his invitation to drop in. If nothing else, it would be something to take him away from his father.

Strange title: *Nomina et Numera: selected phone numbers from North American phone directories, 1979-1983.* He wondered what the poem would be like.

He opened it, turned one page, then another. In amusement, then dismay, he paged through it from cover to cover. That was all it was: names and phone numbers. From, he supposed, North American phone directories. Undoubtedly, 1979-1983.

James closed the manuscript. He decided Beckett had been wrong. They had been able to top Oscar Knutson's barn burning after all.

Chapter Six

In the morning, when James finally wandered downstairs after a night of nervous nightmare, his father was already gone, engaged on his daily round. The first thing James saw when he looked out the kitchen window was a set of seven large letters, burned or cut or dug into the front lawn. They spelled out: FUCK YOU.

He thought his father was probably not capable of conceiving such a message as a suitable lawn decoration. Though this did more accurately represent McGrath's sentiments than a sign of welcome would, the phrasing was certainly not his style, nor would any short, printed message be. Besides, in that event, the letters would surely have faced the road. These faced the house, to facilitate reading by its inhabitants. James didn't think it could be meant for him.

Someone had left a message for Madison McGrath.

James looked for his father, but couldn't find him, either in the house or in his office in the garage. Blackstone, tied on a long chain behind the garage, patiently observed the habits of this new creature.

More than the message, it was the calculated intrusion its mere presence implied that frightened James. He approached the desecration for a better look, moving cautiously, as though he were inspecting an alien life form. The grass was neither dug up nor burned. The letters, at least six feet long, and admirably neat, consisted of brown, dead grass. Some sort of chemical had been used.

Someone had left a very serious message for Madison McGrath.

Going back to the house, he looked at Blackstone, who looked at him. "So where were you when all this was going on?" The dog cocked his head, waiting for a more intelligible remark. Probably out chasing some female, thought James, correctly. He supposed he understood. Oh, yes, he understood.

He had intended to drop in on Beckett this morning, to see if he could gain some insight into his fascination with phone numbers. Now he would also ask him who might have a serious quarrel with his father.

Before he went uptown, he regarded his hair in the mirror. It was mending and could even pass for the sort of haircut a man might habitually choose if he spent a lot of time wearing a helmet or had had an unusually severe upbringing. He had expected his father to comment on it but, knowing his father, shouldn't have. The thought crossed his mind that anyone might have showed up claiming to be James McGrath and his father would never have looked closely enough to detect an imposter.

He left the house, looking again at the front lawn to make sure he wasn't imagining things. FUCK YOU. Its very permanence suggested a determination which chilled James.

It was not the only horror he was to encounter. As he came up the highway, he saw New Culloden for the first time in years. He saw it in daylight, with the eyes of someone who had just chosen it as a place of exile.

It was so run down, so dirty, so dull and spiritless, of a drabness that must have been beneath the utilitarian, that James' mind was denied the usually pleasant, beckoning mystery of a new neighborhood. When the houses were anything but square, they were square with a smaller square as a clumsy addition, whose roof leaked. When windows were not cracked, they had boards over them. It seemed suitable for not much more than driving through at great speed, by night. He wanted to hang himself.

New Culloden's inhabitants looked to be of two kinds: doddering old people, mumbling to themselves, who had recently been released, after many years of drugged incarceration, from a cruel nursing home that had been condemned, and the kind of people he had always hated in high school, who tended not to appear in the circles he had recently moved in and whose fate he had occasionally pondered: the athletes, cheer leaders, good dancers, and early blooming bodies of both sexes, now pot bellied, drunken and decrepit in their thirties. If he didn't hang himself, he would be driven mad by boredom in a month.

Then he thought he saw Stephanie's car turn down the road from him.

His heart leaped with hope, and he quickened his pace. It parked by the post office and he thought he saw Stephanie get out. He knew it was impossible, but it was equally impossible for him to dismiss the chance. She might have followed him. She might have found out where he was. She might have come to throw herself into his arms, his life, yes, my love, yes, whatever the price, I want you, yes. Oh, God, let it be her.

James reflected that he seemed to pray only in moments of acute sexual distress. But if God were a woman, and she knew anything about men, she would surely understand. And surely have mercy!

Even the post office seemed to be a shambles, but James did not allow this sign of a government outpost collapsing to deflect his exuberance. He hurried inside, forcing himself not to calculate the odds of Stephanie actually being there. If he could have had a vote on the moment of his death, he would have chosen the moment he had first imagined he saw her. As he reached the door, even his own easily duped and desperate brain was telling him not to make too much of a fool of himself; it couldn't possibly be her.

His brain, of course, was right, though as far as his heart was concerned that was just one more strike against it and one more reason for ignoring it whenever possible.

Out of breath, feeling as thought his throbbing blood was broadcasting his idiocy to everyone, he tried to examine the woman without being too obvious. She was a little older than Stephanie, a little broader, a little more wrinkled, and far more unkempt. Her clothes were bright, loose, and careless. She glanced at James, an inevitable gesture because he was wheezing and in his haste had almost bumped into her, and she smiled, a gratuitous gesture which surprised him. Her eyes were large and merry. Her hair was light brown and so wind blown as to look knotted in places.

And she had the softness and promise that any woman not quite hideous might have offered to James in the shape he was in. He was smitten, if not by love, at least by definite interest and the possibility of attraction.

This made him feel both a traitor and a fool. On reflection, he realized Stephanie herself made him feel that way. Perhaps that was to be his fate with women. Holding on to whatever sanity remained to him, he looked away without returning her smile. He tried to think of something he could ask the woman behind the desk.

A young man walked in and gently socked the woman who was not Stephanie on the arm. "Morning there, slick."

"Hi, Tim." She had a fetching, deep voice, breathy. James would like to hear her breathing in passion. "How are you?" She asked it coyly, as if his health were a private joke between them.

The young man shrugged. "Oh, you know, not really much more suicidal than usual."

She hooted and grabbed his neck with both hands, strangling him. "Here. I'll help."

The Postmistress was undisturbed. James wondered if this were a common occurrence in New Culloden.

"Thanks. Much better," said the young man.

"Got time for coffee?"

"Time? Are you kidding? I've got nothing *but* time."

They collected their mail and left.

James watched them climb into the woman's car. They seemed a pleasant pair. And the woman…

Perhaps New Culloden would be tolerable after all.

He turned and found the Postmistress staring at him, as though he were the oddity. But he had thought of some business to pretend he was interested in. "Hi," he said, "I'm going to be staying with my dad for a while and—"

"I know," she said.

"My name's—"

"I know," she said.

"So…if you could put any mail I might get in my dad's—"

"Where else would I put it?"

James nodded. "Well, Thanks."

"You're welcome."

No secrets here, thought James. Perhaps if he lived here long enough people would begin telling him what he was going to do in the future, saving him the agony of decision. Perhaps that was the source of the legendary stability of rural life. Since everyone knew everything you did, you simply continued to do what they said you would, assuming they would undoubtedly be correct and not wanting to embarrass yourself by proving them wrong. It probably was as sensible a way to live as any other.

He headed for the gas station, to ask directions for Beckett's house. He could have asked the Postmistress but didn't want to display his ignorance of what must be, to her, one of the basic facts of existence. And perhaps this was the source of the legendary stupidity of rural people. Since everyone knew everything about you, you hated to risk admitting you didn't know everything about them, so no one ever learned anything.

So obviously, thought James, excited by this line of thought, anyone new, anyone unknown, would have to be destroyed, because of the threat posed to the area's fragile system of knowledge. And so—

One night here, he thought, and I'm turning into a lunatic.

He entered. Several men playing cards looked at him suspiciously. It was a look that said: we have every right to be here, but who are you? For a moment, he was tempted to say: good morning, I'm Madison McGrath's boy, don't lynch me. Then he felt foolish for the fear, and slightly amused that only a short time ago he was thinking of lynching himself. He must not have been serious. But most of all, he hated the impulse to hide behind his father.

Yet perhaps that would have made it worse. Perhaps one of them had left the message on the lawn. Perhaps fear was not so out of place. Perhaps he should get his directions and get to Beckett's house. He probably needed somebody to talk to. His mind wasn't doing so well left to itself. He turned to the counter. The attendant was looking at him with a playful smile on his face.

Then James noticed the music. It wasn't rock music, it wasn't country and western music, and, what would have been worst of all, it wasn't a canned orchestra playing characterless renditions of the world's most recognizable melodies made almost unrecognizable. "Why, isn't that—" He was about to say: the morning concert on Minnesota Public Radio.

The attendant put up his hand to silence him, thought a moment, then said: "I think that's the great fugue from the last act of *Schwanda the Bagpiper*. By—uh, let's see—Weinberger. Patty, what was Weinberger's first name?"

A plump young woman lying on a car seat looked up from her magazine. "Casper."

"Not that warmonger. Weinberger the composer."

"I don't know. Duke, maybe, or Wolfgang. Those sound right. Wolfgang Duke Weinberger. But maybe Duke was only his nickname."

"I'm sorry I asked."

"So am I." She returned to her magazine.

Through the gloom of his morning, James felt a mild elation rise. Of the many surprises he had encountered in New Culloden thus far, as well as the even more dismal non-surprises, none was more welcome than stumbling across a man who listened to such music habitually and could use the word "fugue" in conversation without feeling the need to either apologize for or define it. James smiled broadly—one of the most sincere smiles in his recent memory—and said, "It's Jaroslav or Jaromir, something like that, but I don't think I would have recognized the piece."

Without looking up, Patty muttered, "You won't have to feel like the Lone Ranger around here."

"Jaromir—that's it," said Danny. "Jaromir. Looks like we share a common interest." Grinning, as delighted as James at the discovery, he extended his hand. "Danny Danielson—owner and proprietor of this august emporium."

"Hi." James was about to introduce himself when Danny put up his hand again. James thought: of course, why bother? He probably knows more about me than I do. Maybe I'll ask him to read my palm.

Danny was squinting. "Um, let's see. You walked up, so you're probably not a tourist."

"What's a tourist?" said Patty.

"Silence, please. You'll have to excuse my assistant."

"Wife—for the moment." She corrected. "Had and held for worse, for poorer, in sickness, till death."

It was too good a routine to be improvised. And at last here was someone who didn't know him. James was enjoying himself more and more.

"Yes, this is Patty, my beloved wife. Now—not a tourist or a traveller because if your car broke down you'd look more desperate. Hence, a visitor."

"He's been reading Sherlock Holmes," sighed Patty, "if you couldn't tell.,"

"But I don't see any monograms or obvious resemblances to old family portraits or genetic deformities or discolorations due to the various diseases I've studied extensively or—"

"Oh, give us a break."

Danny closed his eyes. "May I?" He waited a moment while she hummed a tune quietly. "Thank you. So: you're a visitor, undoubtedly a close relation of someone well known to us—as, I feel I must admit, everyone around here is. But other than the fact that you're a person of some cultivation, I knew absolutely nothing about you. Still, I'm very glad to make your acquaintance."

"Holmes, you astound me," said Patty.

"James McGrath. You're right about the visiting relative—I'm Madison McGrath's son." James thought he heard an interested silence fall on the card players but he felt relatively safe in the presence of an actual stranger. The pleasure of being able to tell someone who he was before they told him was delicious.

Patty looked up and her face brightened with cheerful mischief. James found himself surprised again. He hadn't imagined the mention of his father's name could delight anyone. She said, "Oh, my God. Madison has offspring? This is news."

Well, thought James, that means he doesn't exactly talk about me all the time.

"She's not from around here," said Danny. "Born in Carlsburg, all of fifteen miles away. A complete alien."

James shrugged. "Well, I was born here but that's about all. We moved away, then I was at school when my dad moved back." My dad: the words had an odd taste. As did: born here.

"I guess there are worse fates," said Patty. "One of them being coming back. But why didn't Madison tell us about you? I know! It's all part of his act. He wants us to think he was born a wise old man. Well. How about that? Madison actually—" She giggled. "You know what I mean. It's a little hard to imagine."

Amen, thought James, but he said, with an impulse of filial loyalty that surprised him further, "Oh, we've drifted apart. One thing and another. Let's say we live in different worlds."

Yes, the woman was definitely made for mischief. She smiled wickedly. "Well, I've heard it put less politely. But think of it: Madison's flesh and blood."

Danny said, "I think we've had enough biology for today. And, for your information, I happened to know Madison had a son."

"Sorry, Holmes. You know what a bumbler I am."

"So," said Danny, ignoring her, which seemed to be another well practiced routine, "up for a visit?"

"More or less. I'm between jobs." James nodded as though he were saying something utterly commonplace, hoped he wasn't nodding too self-consciously, then felt it was a good time to change the subject. "But you seem to know your music."

"I studied it in college."

"Among other useless things," added Patty.

"Among other delightful, enriching, but unfortunately non-lucrative things."

"And you play—?"

"I *pound* an occasional tune on the piano. But I'm really nothing but a good audience."

"Well," said James, "God bless good audiences."

"But how about you? Teacher?"

"No, I was an organist. Am an organist. Choir director."

"An actual musician. Keyboard and voice. I'm impressed. We'll have to have you to dinner. Staying long?"

"Let's call that question," said Patty, "our basic intelligence test."

"Not too long, I hope."

"Bingo," she said. "And I'm very glad to meet you, too."

"You've even managed to please my wife. More impressive still. We have to get together. I'm sure we'll be seeing you around, so we'll have you over some night."

"After we check our social calendar."

"Okay. It'll be fun. But—why I came in—I was looking for directions. Do you know Ben Beckett?" A stupid question, he supposed.

"If you hang around awhile, he'll probably come by. He and Patty are chess opponents."

"Believe it or not, you're in the social hub of New Culloden."

"I told him I'd drop in on him."

"Okay." Danny walked to the door. "Take that street left, past the school, then instead of going toward the highway, go left again and it's just beyond the tracks. First house."

"Thanks. Nice to meet you guys."

"Stop in again."

New Culloden, like a lucky harbor, seemed to have gathered in some interesting cargo from the shifting cultural tides. Life here might not be as bad as James had begun to fear. If it offered both simplicity and the odd learned eccentric, it might be more than tolerable.

He followed Danny's directions and soon saw Beckett's house. It was strange to be walking on gravel roads and stranger still to feel the bulk of the town so low around him. Even in Jewel Lake, which he never walked in anyway, there was pavement and a tighter, higher, more enclosed sense of space. But here the sky's weight was almost palpable. It was as though it had caused everything to squat and spread.

Perhaps this was the ancient source of the Midwestern figure. People sunk into themselves under the heavy sky and grew mostly sideways. But maybe there was just nothing to do but eat.

He put that grim thought away, reflected that neither Beckett nor his father was very stout, nor yet was Danny, resolved to keep a better grip on his mind, and entered Beckett's yard.

It was fairly ragged, which seemed fitting to James. The lawn was well past its first need for spring mowing. There was a space that had been used for a garden, complete with last summer's sagging bean poles. Next to the house there was a substantial stack of cut wood. The house itself was small and neat, but needed painting. It seemed a good place for a poet to dwell. Though he had to admit: if Ben was a poet, his poetry was the strangest he'd ever seen.

Beckett heard him coming up and swung open the door, extending his arm with a flourish. "Young McGrath. How pleasant." As much as Beckett claimed to loathe teaching, he found himself missing the chance to perform before a younger audience and never let such an opportunity go by.

"Mr. Beckett. I thought I'd drop in if you weren't busy."

"Dear God, no one's called me Mr. Beckett since my last IRS audit. Make it Ben."

"Alright."

"And busy is for business people, the carrion crew of capitalism's latter days. Nothing's ever hurt by being postponed. Come up, young friend."

Beckett stood aside to let James precede him. He had put a lot of effort into the effect his rooms would have on visitors, and he took great pleasure in watching their reactions. Since most of his visitors could have recited their contents with their eyes closed, from long familiarity, a new guest was a rare treat for him.

But James disappointed him. The room looked like a cross-section of some library's basement level of stacks, expanded slightly to make room for some useless donated furniture, with a mimeo machine in an ink-splashed alcove and a kitchen area to the right, whose table was piled with manuscripts, folders, and stray sheets of paper. This was no more than normal for James' acquaintances, perhaps the only oddity being that the kitchen gave some signs of being used for producing food. But James credited that to Beckett's age and necessity, so did not remark on it.

Beckett, like a holy man waiting for a final sign to validate his discipline, had waited for someone to arrive some day and exclaim: why, here it is, the very womb of literature! Since James acted as though he had only entered his own apartment, Beckett supposed he'd have to keep waiting.

James did point to the mimeo machine. "I have to tell you: I always loved that smell and I never thought I'd smell it again."

"Brings back the old school days, doesn't it? Bury your nose in that fresh syllabus on day one. What will they remember from today? Computer screens? It's a sad world that's come upon us. Well, that's someone else's problem. But I picked this up for a song at a church bazaar. I couldn't believe they were selling it."

Looking at the condition of the walls that surrounded the machine and noticing fugitive splashes of purple ink further into the room, James couldn't believe anyone had ever willingly used it.

"Have a chair," said Beckett. "Would you like some coffee?"

"Don't bother to make any just for me."

"Are you serious? I'm never without it."

"Then sure, I'll have some."

Beckett searched for an extra cup in the kitchen. "Coffee, tobacco, books—you've touched ground, young friend. We are not rich but the essentials we possess in abundance. And delight in sharing."

Since Beckett insisted on being called by his first name, James wondered why he had to be addressed as Young McGrath, young friend. But any friend of his father's was probably half out of his mind.

James could see coffee spilling from each overfull cup as Beckett whirled from his counter. It drizzled over his manuscripts without apparently getting Beckett's attention. Remembering his consumption of wine, James thought it probable he had already been drinking heavily.

Beckett, however, thought manuscripts all the better for a few human stains. It was his own kind of ornamentation and illumination. He often spilled things on them on purpose.

He shoved a cup at James. The hand was steady enough. Perhaps, thought James, I'm being hasty. He is an entertaining old coot. And the coffee was real coffee, thick and strong.

"So," said Beckett, sitting opposite him, "how do you find our little town?"

"Nice enough."

Beckett laughed. "Oh, bullshit." He seemed to unwind instantly, as though needing the first polite absurdity to be at ease. James was won over.

"You're right," he said. "It's not much."

"Glad to hear you say that. For a moment, I was worried about your sanity, not to mention your honesty. Of course, politeness can be a useful thing. Only in this house it's limited to human relationships, not judgments of value."

"Fair enough," said James and cleared his throat, pulling Beckett's manuscript from his back pocket. "Speaking of which: I read your—poem, you said?"

The old man had a wonderful, fetching laugh. It was musical and enlivened his features as the deepest of joys would. "Yes, that's what I said. A poem. Of sorts."

"All it is is a list of phone numbers."

"*All?* That's *all* it is?" Beckett was on again, enjoying his own performance. "Do you know how much life that puts you in touch with? How much drama? What ecstasies, what sorrows? It's all there: work, play, intrigue, desperation, love, hate. And as shifting as the moon: use it in the afternoon and hear one song; use it at three in the morning when the wind is howling and the ghosts walk and you'll hear quite another."

James took the bait. "But I can do that with an ordinary phone book."

"Yes, but would you? No, because a phone book has one use: it gives you the numbers *you* want. This gives you the book's own realities. Besides, you'd never pick just these numbers."

"So the numbers mean something."

"I hope not. Nothing is more itself than a number."

"But there is a principle of selection."

"Not at all. If there were, you could duplicate it. These are random choices. That's their chief beauty and their chief claim to utter, unfettered inimitable reality."

Ruling out harmless insanity and the possibility of an elaborate, compulsive practical joke, James assumed he was in the presence of a definite aesthetic theory. The man might not be off his rocker, but the theory was.

And yet what a blessed find: a debating partner. James narrowed his eyes quizzically as he sipped his coffee, then set down his cup. "Okay. Two points, then. What does this do to the reading of it? I mean, you don't just sit down and read this."

"You can. But that's not the point."

"Right. So you lose the reader. And, point two, what's behind it? What's trying to get out? In other words, don't you lose the writer, too?"

"Very good! Of course, you do."

"So what's left?"

"Phone numbers—and all that and anything that and nothing but what that implies."

"Right." James picked up his mug and settled back in his chair. "Right."

"And that's not enough for you?"

"Well—no."

"But you see what a prejudice you have. You think this makes no sense because you first think it should make sense." Beckett seemed to be intensely serious. "At one time, so did I. And, of course, lots of things do, God bless them. But I decided you could perish as easily through too much sense as too little. Hold it—let me light my pipe."

While he waited, James glanced at the shelves of books that surrounded him. The titles spoke of broad taste and vast curiosity, the grouping of the books spoke of a drive for order. In a sense, Beckett must be their heir, the embodiment in this time and place of what they had striven for and stood for. They made James even more curious about what Beckett thought he was up to.

Puffing furiously, Beckett gestured at his books. "Mine own people and inheritance. Relics, sad to say, of earlier days. I don't mean I don't enjoy them anymore. On the contrary. They're the people I'm spending my last years with. But there was a time when I considered it my absolute duty and greatest pleasure to devour every last idea and story and poem and drama ever conceived—and write my own to boot." He grinned. "That was obviously a young man's dream."

"Not such a bad dream."

"Still, dreams and realities, you know. Comes a time to wake up. And it struck me one day like a bolt of lightning: I can't do it. There are too many of them. I'm outnumbered."

"Don't you think that's always been true? Shakespeare couldn't have read all he had to read, Bach couldn't have heard all there was to hear."

Beckett was enjoying this as much as James was. He had closed his eyes to take in James' point. Without opening them, he said, "So?"

"So," James continued, "why should that bother you?"

"It didn't bother me, it influenced me. Sent me in a different direction. It was my way of regaining creativity. Getting back to the old foul rag and bone shop."

"Listing phone numbers?"

"You see only the last stage of a journey. Call it a series of experiments in literary collage. I probably should have given you one of my earlier pieces. Oh, let's see—I put together a thousand random sentences from the letters of Cotton Mather. They made almost too much sense."

"The Puritan minister?"

"A brilliant man, believe it or not. And there he was with his European mind on the shore of what to him was an immense wilderness. I suppose, nowadays, we're more aware of the cultures that did surround him. But I imagine the existence of Native American cultures only isolated him further."

"Mather was another random choice?"

"Oh, not at all. My methods were still impure. I liked him for that lonely post of his: seventeenth century Europe shrunk to one man's brain and hardly a soul to share it with."

"Lonely post in the wilderness—like you here?"

"Like all of us. Everywhere." Beckett paused, a great seriousness having come upon him. But he waved it away with his pipe. "Well, to make a long story short, I decided to purify my methods. You might say the phone book provided a genre of its own, suitable for my emerging purpose. Fist I collected the most exotic names I could find. Then, with a kind of triumph of discipline, I turned to the most ordinary. Somewhere in this room there are a few copies of *The Book of Smith*. But, for obvious reasons, putting that together was no challenge at all, and not much fun. So now I pick them at random. Sometimes I'll get a real charge out of one—or even fish out someone I happen to know."

"Well, then," said James, "in other words, you hit something that means something, something with an interest beyond itself."

Beckett arched his eyebrows. "An irritatingly correct point, young friend, which has not escaped my notice. But I accept it as a human flaw."

"But you *are* pleasing yourself?"

"Yes, I suppose."

"And nothing else?"

"What else is there? Or are you still worried about the *reader*? Look around you: who really cares?"

James suspected he had bumped up against a deeper issue and felt vaguely impolite. "I guess I see. Still—"

"Yes? There are readers? Re-read Dante lately, have you? Just to pick an author at random."

"No. And, to be honest, never have."

Beckett rose and scanned his shelf. "Here. The Ciardi translation." He tossed it in James' lap. "You be a reader. Go ahead, it's not just a challenge. No one should go to their grave without reading Dante. If nothing else, he may be right about what you'll have to face."

"Okay."

For a while, Beckett talked of Dante and was so captivating that James asked him if he had ever done any teaching. This amused him greatly and Beckett launched into a discussion of his experiences with education which paralleled his experiences with literature, only with the former he had to assail not only his own ignorance and finitude but the ignorance and finitude of others as well. He concluded: "So, you see, even if I did comprehend all things, I would still have the task of passing on my wisdom to absolutely uninterested and impermeably dense nineteen year olds, who comprise a chilling mystery in themselves. A daunting task, for the stoutest heart. Thus, surrounded by mysteries on all sides, and just having survived my first heart attack, I retired to this place and these tasks that we have been discussing."

Again, James felt they had descended to something fundamental, something that probably wasn't any of his business. After all, who was he to argue with Beckett's use of his own time? And yet there was something about where Beckett had landed and something in Beckett's defiant defense of it that made James want to challenge him to mortal combat.

Luckily, as with most occasions that seem to call for mortal combat, at least in the still civilized parts of the Western world, this one ended with empty coffee cups, the need to be on one's way to find a bathroom, and a turn to lighter topics.

As he rose to leave, James said, "Oh, Ben, there was a woman I bumped into today and I wondered if you knew her." Now what's making me ask this? thought James, as if his beleaguered brain couldn't guess.

"Without a doubt. Do you have a description?"

"Oh, thirtyish, thirty-five. Light hair, blue eyes. Wind blown look. A deep voice, big smile."

He got one of Beckett's in return. "Well chosen, young McGrath. Of course, I can't speak with certainty but you probably met Kathy Frei. Don't worry. You'll meet her again. You won't be able to help it. Small town, as you've noticed. You'll like her. I would say she's probably just your type."

James' mind, usually dormant because hopelessly at a loss in anything to do with women, told him there was something a trifle puckish in Beckett's tone. "She looked interesting."

"That she is, my boy. That she definitely is."

As so often lately, James found he needed another change of subject. "And, say: I don't know how to ask this. But—is there anyone who'd bear a grudge against my dad?" He told Beckett about his discovery of the lawn message.

Beckett didn't seem surprised but, on the other hand, he didn't seem dismissive of the event. "Lawyers make a few enemies," he reflected. "And—let's say, in an area like this, there are a lot that can be made."

"And my dad's good at making them?"

"A reasonable assertion."

"Any ideas?"

"Why not ask him?"

James nodded. Why not try to figure it out from tea leaves? "Well, I should go."

"Drop in again. Don't be shy about doing it regularly."

"Alright. I will."

"And enjoy Dante."

Above the doorway there was a beautiful hand-lettered sign which James hadn't noticed. He stopped to take it in:

> What people call health…
> is a mistake.
> Fragility
> is the only endurable
> condition.

"Like it?" said Beckett. "Lettering was a former hobby of mine. The quotation's from Shaw. And I haven't a clue to what he was getting at."

James reflected that Beckett didn't look very fragile. He didn't bother to grope for a clue to what Beckett was getting at by hanging it up.

Beckett continued: "Still, it has a nice ring to it."

"Well—I'll see you again. Thanks for the book. And the coffee and the talk."

"Ah, thank *you.*"

It had been an hour in another world for James. Waking to misery, exile, and mysterious assault, he had found himself sitting with a scholar debating aesthetics. However demented the theory, the discussion had taken James away from his own problems, and for that he could have kissed Beckett. As he walked home along the unpaved road, a book under his arm, in the bright noon of a mild spring day, he felt despite himself a freshening of life and purpose.

The old man was an imposing character. To have come here with his books and his discipline, at the end of some twisted journey of the mind, and to remain still functioning, with however narrow a purpose, demanded a certain respect. James would enjoy sparring with him. He recalled meetings with musicians in the Twin Cities where the only subject discussed was money. Now here he was in the wilderness discussing the purpose of art.

Of course, thought James, let's not forget that what he's up to is the anthologizing of randomly picked phone numbers. Somewhere in that old brain there were a few circuits gone haywire.

But he was feeling good from the morning's contacts. And the woman he had seen in the post office was not wholly absent from his mind. Kathy—what was it?—Frei.

As James walked sprightly away, Beckett had stood in his doorway, feeling as pleasantly renewed as James did. What James could have no sense of was how starved Beckett was for conversation, argument, the provocation of intellectual resistance. He too would be glad to have the other man around.

But the story of the vandalism disturbed him. As often as the phrase "fuck you" appeared in human discourse, from the belligerent to the playful, it was no joke to have it emblazoned on your lawn deliberately through chemical agents by a midnight messenger. Could anyone bear the lawyer a grudge? It would be easier, Beckett supposed, to number those who couldn't.

He was worried about the elder McGrath and not for the first time. But he wasn't about to reveal that to the younger.

Beckett sighed and went inside. That was, after all the trouble with making sense. You always managed to piss someone else off. He picked up a phone book from Atlanta and started flipping pages.

Chapter Seven

After his return from Beckett's, James went searching for his father. If someone had scarred the lawn as a mere prelude to napalming the house and its inhabitants, James thought he might like to know about it. Suspecting that his father would be the last person to tell him anything only made him feel more of an idiot.

Perhaps that was the secret to life: it was nothing but a long and subtle demonstration that you were an idiot. Perhaps if you accepted that more sooner than later you would find peace. Still, James had often been willing to accept it, no more so than lately. Perhaps there were further secrets to be discovered. Such as: accepted or not, idiocy hurts. And: there is no peace.

After failing to find his father in the house, he carried his book up to his room. Maybe Dante would help make sense of things. Beckett's phone numbers were obviously not a strong contender. He tossed the book on his bed. He thought he'd save it for the evening, as though he had everything in the world to do and the mid-day hours were precious.

Outside and on his way to the garage, he got a few barks from Blackstone, in greeting, irritation, pleading, or affronted outrage at the intrusion he could not tell. The dog was on his chain so at least James didn't have to worry about being attacked. James waved at him with what he hoped would be taken for friendliness, making the old human bet on animals having more insight into his gestures than he had into theirs. Who knows? He might need a friend in the animal kingdom someday.

Blackstone settled down and wagged his tail. He was as willing as any dog to accept another member into the family pack, especially one of so inferior a quality and unlikely to challenge his position as top dog.

James went into the garage. The car was still there but, for all James knew, his father only kept it there so that his would have to sit outside. Against the back wall of the garage was a wooden stairway up to the loft his father had converted into an office. Feeling a little like an intruder, which he supposed he was after all these years, James ascended it. On the way up, he marveled at the order and cleanliness of this area that most American males felt obliged to reduce to chaos.

He knocked at the door at the top of the stairs. Hearing nothing, he tried the knob. Of course, it would be locked. As he was descending, a great roar came upon the building, lowly whining and guttural, as though the garage had become part of some greater engine which had begun to turn over in wrath. He stumbled down the stairs and ran outside.

Blackstone was leaping into the air at the end of his chain, barking madly. James saw a plane beginning to climb at the edge of the tree line. He stood motionless, half expecting an explosion to obliterate him. None came, one more solution to his problems denied.

The dog had stopped jumping. James looked at him and said, "Looks like the raid's over." Blackstone glared, then barked as though he knew better. Perhaps he did. Perhaps it was the first wave of a surprise attack by the Canadians, sick of playing second North American fiddle to the vulgar Yankees, and who could blame them?

But the plane did not return and none followed it. One more isolated maniac, thought James, and isn't that comforting? "Told you," he told Blackstone, wondering why he kept addressing the brute. The dog barked again and seemed determined to remain on alert. James returned to the house.

His father was eating lunch at the kitchen table. James wondered where he had come from, if he hadn't been hiding, which he didn't dismiss as impossible. Madison looked up and said, "Where have you been?"

Out molesting children? seemed to be the implied accusation. James decided to state the obvious. "Out. Did you hear that plane?"

Madison's eyes narrowed. James thought: now, even he can't blame that on me. But it was clear he wasn't pleased to discuss it. Madison said, "I'm not completely deaf."

"It probably wouldn't matter if you were. Are we near a landing strip or something? Wasn't he a little low?"

Madison leaned back as though he were trying to decide if his son deserved to know what was going on. If so, he decided he didn't. "It happens once in a while."

James nodded in irritation. "Well, since we're on the subject of lunatics, did you notice the little message on the lawn?"

Madison regarded his half-eaten sandwich with sadness. This conversation was spoiling his lunch. He got up and walked toward the kitchen window, as though he had no idea what James meant, but said before he got there, "I saw it." He stared out the window with his back to James.

"So?"

Madison turned his head slightly. "Yes? Continue: so…?"

"Well—is somebody trying to start a correspondence? C'mon. What's it about? Do you know who did it?"

"I'd say—" Madison paused, with a faraway look that seemed to be scanning the chronicles of crumbling civilizations. "—it was some member of the human species."

"I gathered that from the spelling."

"Nothing for you to worry about," said Madison brusquely, as though they were discussing a minor accounting error.

"So you know who did it."

"I have no idea."

"So how do you know it's nothing to worry about?"

"Nothing for *you* to worry about," corrected the lawyer.

"I *am* worrying."

"Then you're wasting your energy foolishly and there's very little I can do about that."

Case closed, James supposed, and tried to recall how many serious conversations with his father had ended this way. Probably quite a few.

Madison got out some foil to put around the remains of his sandwich, indicating just how thoroughly James had destroyed his lunch. "While you're around," he said, "we might as well discuss our schedule." He gestured to a chair and finished clearing up.

James sat, too obediently to please himself but unwilling to make a debating point out of an invitation to comfort. Thus, he thought, are inferiors put in their place. He wondered if their schedule would include a turn at night sentry duty.

But their schedule, as Madison presented it, turned out to be McGrath's own schedule with the variables smoothed down by delegation to James. The early meals could be taken in common, if, and only if, James did not speak much, especially at breakfast. James made a mental note to avoid them. Supper should be taken in common to ease preparation but Madison would do the cooking. "Unless," he concluded, "you have a habit of overeating, which doesn't seem likely, but I mention it for the record."

Madison would continue to clean the common areas. James would clean his own and wash his own dishes. "And, of course, if you work in the garage, you'll tidy up after yourself."

Work in the garage? Either his father was being deliberately aggravating or he had no idea what James' life was like.

The main responsibilities he was given were mowing the lawn and doing the grocery shopping (though Madison would provide the list). Though not impossible to work into a rigid schedule, both activities were bound to the vagaries of seasonal spurt and organic drift which McGrath perceived as constant threats, unstable buffer states along a volatile border, and was happy to be rid of.

"How about the garbage?" asked James, thinking it was right up his alley.

"I handle the garbage. Understand? I deal with the garbage."

James put up his hands. "Fine. Maybe I can work my way up to it—I mean, if I really apply myself."

"What?"

"Nothing. A joke."

Madison looked at him and seemed on the point of unbending. "This isn't a business, it's a shared household. It just helps to be clear on these things. You're not a hireling."

"I know, I know."

"And I'm not either. So we share tasks. If you're going to be touchy about little things, it's going to be difficult."

"Sorry."

Madison waited for more and James waited for him to continue. James could have provided the speech himself: this is my house, you dropped in on me, you're the needy one. He didn't know if he was being unfair to the old man or not. But right now, he'd settle for discussing daily tasks forever, rather than confess his confusion.

Madison obliged him by rapping the table and summing up. "I think that covers things. Now I'm used to a quiet life so I don't relish interruptions during the day. I thought I'd just make that plain. People—" He paused, looking over James' shoulder, either to soften the point or to take the measure of some ghost. "People can wear on one another. In my profession, I see a good deal of that. You might say it's the very cornerstone of my profession. It helps to be clear on things. I assume you've acquired some studious habits so I'm not anticipating many problems. We can talk, of course, in the evenings. I don't mean to sound like an ogre."

His father was actually offering him a refuge with no demands. James should have been grateful, knowing he was spared prying and chatting, enforced socializing and planned activities. But he allowed himself to feel mildly offended and he supposed he would have felt that way unless Madison had embraced him and pulled him on his lap for an hour's crying sleep. But this was the wrong father for that. And, he supposed, the wrong son.

Anyway, he probably would have been pissed off at that too. So he said, "No, this will be fine. Thanks for letting me stay." It was only polite but, irritation aside, who else could he have asked to let him in?

Madison rapped the table again and stood up. "I have to do my reading now. By the way, how long were you planning to stay?"

It was a question even God could not have answered for him. "I—wasn't sure." He took some measure of the void he was facing, guessed at his father's tolerance, his own ingenuity, and fortune's possible smiles, and said without conviction or hope: "Maybe for the summer." He added, "Didn't I say that?"

"No. You said you were loose for the summer and you wanted to stay a while. I assumed it was more than a few days or I wouldn't have discussed this. But I have no way of knowing if "a while" is part or all of a loose summer or if it lacks definition altogether."

I couldn't have put it better myself, thought James. "I guess I don't have anything else planned for the summer. You know, I might—later." Like?

"That's fine. Our arrangement should work that long. And then?"

He wouldn't quit, would he? "Back to the grind, I guess," said James. Right.

Madison nodded. "Let's assume the summer, then."

That was easy. Much easier than: and then?

"So," continued Madison, "I'll make a calculation about room and board and send it to you. Just so it's on a regular basis. I assume you've arranged things with the post office."

His father was going to bill him. Through the mail, no less. Somewhat stunned, James nodded and Madison retired to his journals.

Well, James thought, everything has a price. And given the nature of things, the worst ones probably aren't financial.

When James had finished his own lunch, careful to remove all traces of his presence from the kitchen, he peeked into the living room. His father was sitting in a chair facing the window. His journal was closed on his lap, and he was asleep. His head lay turned against the back of the chair. He was drooling slightly and his breath rasped a little. Somehow the mere fact of his being awake made James feel both superior and intrusive. He turned away, a little ashamed, a little smug, as irritated as always with his father.

He thought about taking another walk, then went upstairs to his room and lay on his bed with Dante. In a few moments he had nodded off.

So they began their life together.

Before long, James had acquired enough of a routine to get over the disorientation of his first days. Because the tasks he had to do could be done almost anytime, he could rise late and keep his own hours.

The mail was always stacked and sorted on the table by the time he came down. Though he had sent out change-of-address notices to his magazines and written to a few of his friends, there was never anything for him. He allowed himself the luxury at times of thinking he had ceased to exist. Reading Dante, he thought New Culloden might serve as the home of the virtuous pagans, not exactly hell because they hadn't been that bad, but far enough from heaven to be pretty bleak.

Grocery shopping would have been a familiar pleasure if there were anything to buy. Though the check-out women were jovial, and contemptuous enough of government to smoke in the store—something he could not remember ever seeing anywhere else, there was so little choice on the shelves that the liberated atmosphere of the place failed to excite him. He soon became well known and could kill an hour buying a roll of toilet paper but he would happily trade this easy familiarity for a more sophisticated brand of mustard.

Eventually, he decided, he would expand his shopping trips to take in other towns. But he was hoarding that hopeful pleasure for a later date when he might need it more desperately. Besides, he had no idea of how far he might have to go for things to be different. And in New Culloden he charged everything to his father. If he went elsewhere, he would have to ask for cash and he wasn't ready to face that.

It was surprising, with so few things to buy around him, how fast he was spending his own money. He supposed the act of spending was one of freedom's last expressions. But what he thought was a substantial cushion was disappearing more quickly than he had anticipated.

At least there were no bills from his father lying on the table with the rest of the mail yet. His father, if no one else, should have no doubt that he existed. Perhaps he had only been kidding, or had decided to ease up. Or perhaps he decided James was doing enough lawn mowing to deserve a free ride. There had been frequent rains and James was learning about the down side of spacious lawns: someone had to mow them.

He had been a bit apprehensive about using a power mower, never having done so. But how absurd it was to assume his father would own one. He was lucky he didn't have to use a scythe. Madison provided a fine specimen of an old-fashioned mower, but the job took forever. And if James waited too long between cuts, he might have been better off with a scythe. He wondered how his father had managed it without him. But perhaps he had always hired it out, though anyone who took the job, unless they had their own mower, would have to be insane. Just as he was, he supposed, for doing it without griping.

Mowing days were never among James' best. That his best were often nothing but his shopping days, when he would discuss weather, inflation, and the quality of produce with Inez, Myrtle, or Rhonda at the grocery store while sharing a smoke at the cash register, was not exactly something to lift his heart.

He had a routine, something he had always valued without being obsessive about it, but he would admit that he hated it. His life had become something of a variation on, or parody of, his father's, lacking nothing but a purpose. But compared to his own prelapsarian existence, it lacked much more than that.

He felt childish when he realized one thing he lacked was a television set. Hardly an addict, James still took some pleasure in watching the evening news and the occasional movie. He couldn't believe his father didn't have a television. But in New Culloden you might end up watching it around the clock, just on the chance of hearing a literate sentence uttered on some substantial topic, if only in an old movie.

The Danielsons turned out to be a godsend in this environment. James put in many hours at the station, singing a kind of duet of misery with Patty and solving the problems of the world with Danny. He dined with them as often as he could without feeling a crushing obligation to return the invitation. That would mean negotiating with his father and he wasn't up to that yet.

But as delightful as the Danielsons were, there were only two of them and what James had hoped was the tip of an iceberg, only the most evident specimens of a substantial community of interesting individuals, turned out to be all there was of it. Or all that he could see so far, and he'd had his eyes peeled.

Not that he'd met everyone. For example, the one other person of obvious interest to him, the woman who was not Stephanie, named Kathy according to Beckett, had never crossed his path again. Every so often, he had seen her from a distance, but that was all. He still mistook her for Stephanie but that did not make her unique. He kept imagining Stephanie's head on women getting out of cars or turning a corner ahead of him, kept imagining her car disappearing down another road.

He kept hoping she'd write to him. But he didn't have the courage to write to her. And he knew her address.

It was something of an emotional landmark for him, then, when these imaginings started to fade. Not having met Kathy Frei, and having imagined meeting Stephanie so many times only to be disappointed, he realized one day that he had begun to look for Kathy Frei as herself. Thus are loves traded in, he supposed. It was like your body replacing cells. Years pass, they're all different, but you're still you. Was this passion so indifferent to object? Was one as good as another?

He thought the optimistic position on that issue was probably that one was not as good as another, though he wouldn't have staked his life on it. As with so many other things, how could you ever know? You could be either a fool for looking or a fool for not looking. And perhaps that was just it: look or not, there you were, the same fool.

At least, adding up what he had and had not run into, there had been no more lawn messages or plane attacks that he knew of. "FUCK YOU" was still there to be read whenever the desire was upon him, but there were times when the thought was not so foreign to his mood. As lawn decorations go, it wasn't the most pointless.

The fear those early assaults had struck in him had passed and he dismissed them now as random nonsense. Those who inhabited the earth had had to dismiss a lot of things that way and there were more than a few modern philosophers who dismissed everything that way. James would not have known how to decide what the optimistic position on that issue was.

More palpable mysteries surrounded him in the ordinary run of things: there were the noises, for example, of the trucks and trains that sped through New Culloden without cease, carrying the commerce of others. They must once have stopped here or the town would never have existed, but they did so no longer. The town was thus perhaps the greater mystery and must obtrude on the wider world as nothing but an inconvenience, so many minutes lost per year for shipping in negotiating its slight curve.

The noise of traffic, however, was something he was accustomed to and he noticed this only because there was so little of it. The grind of local tractors was something new. As they came in and out of town or moved back and forth in the fields, their purposes were as mysterious to James as those of anything else, as severed from his own awareness as traffic on the Interstate.

And yet, he knew, they didn't have to be. They were driven by men he saw daily, even occasionally spoke with at the gas station. Why, Danny was one of them, as were the husbands of Inez, Myrtle, and Rhonda. He had no idea what they were up to but, if he made the effort, he could find out. This, after all, was the glimmer of light that had brought him here: to be where things were small enough to make sense. Simple tasks, simple connections.

Perhaps that was what had drawn someone like Ben Beckett to this place. What Beckett was up to with his collection of random data seemed to bear some relation to what rural dwellers were up to. Here we are, this is what we have, let's put it all together. And if sometimes it spells "FUCK YOU," well, where was perfection on this earth?

James began to sense a kinship between himself and Beckett which the older man seemed to sense as well. He ended up at Beckett's place after many of his solitary walks, enjoying the learned but light talk, the strong coffee and the sense of a kindred soul. He was impressed by watching Beckett plant his garden, and more impressed to learn that Beckett cut his own wood and heated his home with a wood furnace. This was the artistic life with no apologies and with immunity from threats.

As uneasy as he still was in New Culloden, James admired Beckett's easiness and thought he might learn to imitate it. His father too seemed easily of the place. And their days together had gone more easily than James expected. It helped that they rarely saw one another.

The one thing that nagged James, living as he did, was that compared to men like Beckett and McGrath he was something of a parasite. And he could never forget: he had voyaged out haughtily into the great world and been beaten back by the storm. And that was something that his routine underlined for him every day.

He found himself staying up late each night, reading in his room, unable to deny that it gave him the illusion of independence. Also, the coming of night brought with it a kind of freedom from the responsibility of significant achievement that daylight seemed to demand. But if the pleasure was tainted, he hadn't become foolish enough to avoid it, so he ended his days reading Dante and felt, if not ecstatic, at least not suicidal.

One mild Saturday night, with a slight breeze coming through his window, he was holding himself at his desk to finish Dante's *Purgatorio*. He had never managed to free himself from flipping back and forth to Ciardi's notes and was still unable to remember if Dante had been a Guelph or a Ghibelline, not to mention what that would mean anyway. At what seemed like the hundredth reference to another Italian he would have been just as happy not knowing about, it struck him that right at the heart of this timeless epic was a ridiculous and haphazard collection of the most ephemeral enmities and spites.

These men and women had been nailed into the world's libraries and most of them were, like Beckett's phone numbers, utterly random choices. They just happened to strike Dante's fancy or stir his ire. Any hundred other Italians or Russians or Zulus would have done just as well.

Yet Dante was the least random of artists. There was a difference there that would bear exploring. James closed the book and looked out the window. He wasn't going to explore it tonight. The mild breeze, nature's kiss upon strolling lovers, made him lonely.

He wondered where Dante might deposit him: among the misguided lovers, he supposed. It was rather nice of Dante to place such souls as high as he could among both the damned and the saved who still needed purging. Anyone who shed a little pity on illicit love affairs was alright with James. He hadn't thought of Stephanie very much and now, when he tried to summon up her image, called up Kathy Frei's instead. Well, so be it.

The stars were thick and bright outside. James thought it would be nice to sit under them, then realized there was nothing to stop him from doing so. He had, he further realized, been treating himself like a prisoner. And all the time he had the sweet freedom that came from literally no one caring what he did. He went outside, smelled the air and felt like a giddy fool. Looking at his watch, he saw it wasn't all that late and thought he might enjoy a drink at the bar. He had yet to visit it but, by now, was well known enough to enter as something more than a stranger.

So he simply walked down the driveway and headed uptown, astounded that it was so easy.

He was startled when a dark form lunged out of the trees at him. But it was only Blackstone, who fell into step beside him. The dog was probably happy to have a companion, and James wasn't so sorry himself. I must belong here, he thought. You can tell by the dog.

Just down the street from the post office was a bar he had heard spoken of as something of a community center. It had the unpromising name of *Mudhole Bar and Grille*. Country and Western music floated out of it as James drew near and set his teeth on edge. But then, he wasn't here for a concert. As he was almost to the door, it burst open violently. A body floated out of it and fell at his feet. There seemed to be a good deal of blood on the man, at least more than James was used to seeing on the bodies he encountered.

An immense man, a head taller than James, with arms the size of municipal sewer pipes, followed the body out the door and began beating on it with a pool cue. The size of his hands made the cue look like a toothpick.

The music had grown louder. James thought: I'm not here for a concert but I'm not here to fight for my life either. He was used to a somewhat higher form of inebriation. He turned away. For a moment, Blackstone lingered, wondering perhaps if there would be some raw flesh to devour. Then he followed James.

James was going where, he supposed, he had wanted to go all along. He was heading down the street that ran along the river. He had managed, by hint and observation, to find out where Kathy Frei lived and it seemed not a bad idea to pass by there occasionally.

She had a tiny house, smaller than Beckett's and in worse repair. Her front lawn had several evergreens and not much grass, giving the house a rough and sheltered look. There was a car outside, a car James knew wasn't hers. He could see lights in her windows and imagined he heard low music. He listened, hoping not to hear a country twang.

It was soft piano music and he heard soft laughter as well.

Now, thought James, this is the moment to sigh and walk on and hope for a new and brighter day. So, feeling like a swine, he crouched behind one of her trees and peered into the window. Her face was shining by candlelight. She was standing above someone who sat on her couch.

James' heart started to pound. The someone's hands rose from the couch and began to unbutton her blouse. She swayed to some inner melody and arched her back as he freed her breasts. She bent down to kiss him.

James wondered if he dared move closer. He knew he was beyond the bounds of civility here, not to mention nobility, but watching this was better than watching someone being bludgeoned with a pool cue.

His foot snapped a twig. He waited, breathless. Safe. Then all at once Blackstone began to howl and bark wildly. Oh, Christ! thought James and turned to run, only to have his legs cut down by the charging dog, racing after some invisible prey. For a dizzy moment, he lost contact with the ground, then regained it with great velocity, severe shock, and, to him, deafening collision. He lay on his side and hoped for the best. He could still see them through the window. The man was peering over the couch, but Kathy was laughing with her head thrown back and her hands on her hips.

However, this was no time to linger in admiration. He rolled across her yard and on into the next, then waited, crouched, waited, and dashed for home. But dashing quite that far was beyond him so he soon settled into a morose plodding. After a time, he caught up with Blackstone who was now in the process of mounting a female dog.

"Oh, yeah?" said James and felt on the ground for a rock. He winged it at his erstwhile companion and hit him in the side. Blackstone yelped and disappeared into the night. "How do you like it?" called James, feeling good about such a direct hit and so poetic a revenge, not unworthy of Dante.

And then he came to himself on that gravel road: throwing rocks at a dog after almost being caught peeping in a woman's window. Stooping out of spite to spoil an animal's pleasure. What a picture of humanity he offered. How low he had sunk. One more lesson in what freedom was all about. And so much, once more, for the urgings of lust.

He went home and put himself to bed, thinking it highly probable that he would never venture out again. Maybe that would be simple enough for him.

Chapter Eight

Whether it was out of abysmal self-disgust, the rising insistence of a long neglected need, or the merest itch of habit, James was moved the next morning to attend church. He had avoided it thus far with the professional's irresponsibility, no task to be done there hence no reason to be there. It was as though his regular attendance these last few years had been nothing but a matter of employment.

But Sunday had come again after several Sundays had gone by and the urge to be there was upon him when he awoke. He didn't know if he needed to seek some higher freedom or if, like some convict long imprisoned and newly released to a bewildering world, he only wanted his old cell back.

The thought of going made his hands go oddly cold and, more oddly, he found himself weighing yes or no as though he were making the most serious decision of his life. Time, still his enemy it seemed, would not solve the problem for him. It was still early enough to walk to any church in New Culloden, if not crawl there. In other words, it was up to him.

So he dressed and started out.

There were two churches in New Culloden. The Assembly of God was obviously out, for aesthetic reasons if nothing else. He would place himself back among the Lutherans.

It was a bright, windy morning and the day was starting to thicken with the early summer heat. Only a few of the people entering the church were known to him, though he supposed he was known to all of them. Knowing whose son he was, they would probably not think he was coming. And they would probably be stunned if he walked in, for the same reason. James was ready to give a fortune, had he had one, for a little anonymity. On the other hand, if he were in possession of a fortune, he wouldn't be standing on this highway.

He lingered a bit, still wavering. The church's sign board gave him no sign, only the name: First Lutheran. But as he came closer, the organ prelude drifting from within sent him a double message. Its quavering tones, wheezing out a tune of unpalatable sweetness, told him there was no question of his spending an hour in the same room with that instrument. But its very existence reminded him of the paradise he had once inhabited and gave a different shape to the aching of his heart. Music. He had not had music in his life these last weeks. And he missed it.

So he passed by, took one of his routine walks, avoiding the streets of last night's shame, and returned home, humming hymn tunes, his own devotion.

But it came to him that afternoon: his mother had owned a piano. It was an old, high-backed spinet which he had practiced on for hours. He was certain she had brought it with her to New Culloden, but it was nowhere around.

His father being gone, James checked in all the rooms to make sure he hadn't overlooked it. But he came upon nothing remotely musical. The house had seemed gloomier than he remembered it from his visits, but now he saw more deeply. It didn't seem gloomier, it *was* gloomier. Pictures he vividly remembered had disappeared. The drapes were all dark and thick. Not only was there no piano in the house. There was no trace of his mother's existence. Not a picture of her, not a knick knack she had owned, not a floral pattern she had chosen.

Amazed, James went from room to room again, half hoping to find a small sign of her memory, half hoping for the absence to be complete, thus making his amazement complete. But his wild conclusion was right. There was not a trace of his mother's existence in the house.

Except himself. A chill came upon James, as though he were the last sign of an unwanted truth that some omnipotent avenger meant to erase entirely. Though he could credit his father with the sentiment, he doubted he would go that far. But it was an eerie discovery. Incredulous, he searched the house gain. Nothing. Not one thing.

Even the master bedroom upstairs, which could easily have been used as a storage place for what must have been an immense amount of possessions, held nothing that might indicate that more than one person had ever lived there, except for the double bed. And that wasn't exactly conclusive.

He's kept more of me than he has of her, James thought. There were things from his youth still left in his room, undisturbed. The thought did not flatter him so much as make his mother's removal all the more deliberate. It must have taken a great deal of time, but that would have been the least of it. It had needed clear and narrow purpose, determination, a ruthless will to search every corner and yield to no exceptions. James could not believe it had been hatred, but he had as hard a time thinking it was mortally wounded love that had caused it. McGrath had been cleaning up, and that's all he had been doing. And that was chilling enough.

But perhaps it was not the woman so much as death that the old man was clearing out. Perhaps it was a kind of exorcism, the only one possible for a hard headed man, defiantly materialistic. He wondered if it had worked. He had no reason to think it hadn't.

For himself, however, the very completeness of her absence brought her back to him. Her laughter, her frivolous moods, her cultural passions, her hopes for him, her delight in his talent, and her pride in his career.

Yes, his career. Why is it, he thought, that everything eventually makes me feel like a worthless failure?

One of these days he was going to have to find his way back. And, for now, he had one pleasant and promising thought: he would find a piano or an organ somewhere. He might not have a job, but that was no reason to play dead. And no reason not to play music, if only for the joy and peace of it. If Beckett could be satisfied copying out phone numbers, music, even unpaid and performed for his own ears, was sure to give him something. With this aim, the smallest spark of a purpose, his life brightened a little. He felt as though he had reclaimed part of himself from his father's dominion.

That night, he asked his father what happened to the piano.

"Why?" answered McGrath. Not this and that or such and such but: why?

"Well," said James, "I play, you know." While his father could make facts sound like accusations, in his father's presence James could only make them sound like confessions of weakness. He realized that any statements he might add—I need one, I'd like one, I want to keep in practice, we could play chopsticks together, flowers look good on them—could be parried by his father *ad infinitum*: why?

McGrath said, "I don't."

James nodded, hating the feeling that he had lost an argument through a simple tally of skills—and he was the one with the skill!, but he persisted. "I was thinking—I mean, if you gave it or even sold it to somebody, I might be able to get it back."

"Why?"

"To play."

"Here?"

"Well—yeah."

"I suppose…we could have worked something out," said McGrath and smiled. "But it's gone."

"I *know* that. What did you do with it?"

"Why do you want that one?" answered McGrath.

"Well, that was just the one I was thinking of, and—it was mom's, and—well, I thought maybe if you'd only loaned it to someone—"

"I disposed of it."

Did he eat it, wondered James, and he just doesn't know how to tell me? "Well—where? How?"

"It's gone."

"I've grasped that. *Where* has it gone? Who has it?"

"I really couldn't say. I disposed of it. I'm afraid it's gone."

"You disposed of a lot."

James wished he hadn't said that, not from remorse but for fear of what he might unlock. But McGrath took it with what James had to assume was the same attitude that had motivated the disposal. "Yes, I did. The sheer bulk of what one life can collect is staggering."

"You kept a lot of my stuff."

"I wouldn't do it forever, I assure you. I've assumed you would come for it some day."

"My baseball mitt? My toy trucks?"

"If not for yourself then for your child, were you to have one. If you don't think you'll ever need those things, then you should do some disposing of your own."

"Okay, okay. But—about the piano. I'd like to get hold of one anyway."

"Where would you put it?"

"How big is Blackstone's doghouse?"

McGrath's eyes narrowed. Humor was not a good tactic with this man, James saw. He almost admired his father's ability to look affronted while being the one doing all the goading. But he said, "Joke. Just a joke. I don't know. Where was the old one?"

"In the living room."

"Well—"

"But then I had a study. Now I use the living room as my study."

"I wouldn't play it when you were there."

"You don't understand. I am not going to renovate my house just because you're visiting it."

"What would it hurt for it to sit there? We're not talking about knocking out walls here."

"Where else would you put it?" answered McGrath.

"I guess—I really don't know."

James expected him to gloat but he continued in the same neutral tone, as though they'd been discussing barbers. "It might suit you better to see if you could arrange for the use of one. The school in Carlsburg must have some. Why, I believe the school here has one still in it somewhere. They might let you use a room. There are other people who use the building. You might find that very satisfactory."

Not as satisfactory as you would, thought James. He said, "Who would I see about that?"

"Our illustrious mayor. Mayor Ekdahl. You'll usually find him mowing lawns or picking up garbage."

"That's the mayor?"

"This isn't Minneapolis."

"Well—I'll ask."

Mayor Ekdahl wasn't hard to find. He was the knight-like figure James had watched in the cemetery the night of his arrival. And he'd seen him almost every day, a stout, short man, with a fervent expression, patrolling the boundaries and empty lots of New Culloden atop his riding mower, leveling the unruly sprouting of the earth into uniform carpets with relentless devotion, as though if he let up the whole town would be smothered by wilderness and vanish. His constant presence and determination made the threat seem palpable. If he missed a few days, the shaggy weeds that stretched themselves to the sun and scattered in demented patterns looked sinister, a slave class slipping its shackles and forming a laughing, lawless army mustered around the brooding trees.

When James came upon him, a few days later, the noon heat was making the air shimmer and, combined with the lush growth spurred by the spring rains, must have been making the mayor's job seem like an endless nightmare. James, with one relatively small plot to manage, had been dreaming of being lost in the Amazon with a dull machete. The mayor's nocturnal terrors were probably beyond imagining.

He waved at Mayor Ekdahl and tried to indicate he wanted to speak to him. He wasn't sure he had succeeded since the mayor continued on his path, spraying rocks against James' legs as he passed. One sizable rock made a not negligible impression on his shin.

Dangerous beast, thought James. He tried yelling but the roar of the mower defeated him. Approaching the thing struck James as foolhardy.

Then, at the end of the lot, the mayor suddenly rounded, veered, charged James, and braked at his feet. It was either a demonstration of skill or the carelessness of stupidity. James leaned toward the latter judgment.

"I've been wanting to meet you," bellowed Ekdahl. "I like to greet our new citizens. I'm the mayor. Einar Ekdahl."

"I'm Madison McGrath's son, James."

"I know. Always happy to see people move in."

Qualifications seemed unnecessary luxuries at such a high decibel level, so James let "moving in" stand as a description of what he was up to. He wasn't sure, under the circumstances, of how to go about negotiating for the use of a piano.

For Ekdahl, however, the roaring and spitting of his machine must have been an ordinary atmosphere. After explaining that he hated to shut it off because it was nearly impossible to restart, he began to sing the glories of his town.

James smiled and tried to seem interested in the fifty percent or so of the words he managed to hear, wondering how many hours a human being could tolerate such racket without permanent hearing loss and at least partial brain damage. Piecing together Ekdahl's portrait of the town and comparing it with his own impressions, James thought Ekdahl had probably passed the limit long ago.

As nearly as he could tell, New Culloden was, in the mayor's eyes, a mere step away from becoming a major tourist attraction. He was hoping to lay out a golf course. He was trying to get funding to build a mall. Next year, he was going to sponsor a rodeo.

"But it's hard to get people involved, you know, they don't like to get involved. We could use a young fellow like yourself."

"Doing what?" shouted James, trying to imagine himself attending a rodeo, let alone organizing one.

The mayor's face brightened. It might have been the most positive response anyone had ever given him. "Helping me, for starters! Helping me. You could be my assistant, you know. I need an assistant."

"To do what?"

"Well—I'd like somebody to take over the mowing, you know, free me up for organizing things."

James pictured himself on the mower, muscles tautening through the summer days, skin growing bronzed, sweat glistening as his body dehydrated, bones and joints turning to dust as he was shaken mercilessly hour after hour. He could acquire a macho swagger while his health lasted, down a few beers at day's end with the rest of the labor force, maybe crack a few skulls up at the bar. He could think of nothing more unpleasant.

"Sorry."

"Clerical work, then, you know, writing applications for grants, making contacts. There's a lot to be done here, a lot to be done."

"I don't know how long I'll be staying."

"Think about it."

"Okay. Listen—is there a piano I could use in the old school?"

"What?"

James supposed he was stretching Ekdahl's ordinary conversational parameters. He yelled louder. "A piano. In the school. Is there one I could use?"

The mayor beamed. It was one more activity he could imagine going on in his beloved town. "Sure, sure! By all means! The doors are open all day. There's a good one in the gym, a good one. Up on the stage."

Promising to think about his offer, James bid him goodbye. He didn't think he could stand much more noise. But before he had gone very far, he heard the mayor run up behind him. He had left the mowing beast parked in the field, rumbling and sputtering.

"I wanted to tell you," said Ekdahl, "that I'm really excited about your civic spirit."

What spirit? thought James. "Thanks."

"Involvement, you know, that's what we need, involvement. Think about this: I've been wanting to change the town's name—*Lake* Culloden. How's that? Lake Culloden. Highlight the lake, you know, as a tourist attraction, for tourists, so they know we've got one."

"Has a nice ring," said James, wondering what possible difference it could make.

"I'm bringing it up again at the council meeting next month. Give me your feedback, I'd like to have your feedback on this."

The roaring of the lawn mower changed its pitch and James saw it lurch into movement. The mayor looked back and started after it. "And think about that job!"

James watched him waddle after his runaway creature. He caught up with it, tried to mount, then slipped off and fell. It would have been the first time James had ever seen anyone killed by a lawn mower. But the mayor rolled clear. The beast continued on across the lot Ekdahl had been cutting, dropped into a ditch, and stalled.

Silence rose around James like a divine blessing. The mayor stood up, waved at James, and trotted after his mower. For a moment, James considered helping him but finally concluded he didn't need much more of a reputation for civic spirit. By the time he reached the school, two blocks away, he could hear it roaring again.

The building was open and there was indeed a piano in the gym. It was up on the stage behind a few hundred folding chairs, pieces of old homecoming floats, several lengths of pipe, and a few rolls of linoleum. The gym had retained the aroma of sweat and defeat from the basketball seasons of the past. But perhaps it was still used. There wasn't much dust around.

James managed to clear a path to the instrument.

It had at least once been a piano. When he first ran his hand along the keys, he thought he had gone deaf—but one or two finally sounded, out of tune. Yet it had once played notes, as he had. And there he was, touching it. This one wouldn't do, but he would find one somewhere. The very attempt had been bracing.

On his way home, he thought about the mayor's offer. He was again glimpsing a life that could be his: he could be part of a community's functioning, at a level he could not even dream about in Minneapolis. It was almost tempting.

He mentioned it to his father at supper.

His father said, "Work for that moron? Don't be absurd."

So later that week James told Mayor Ekdahl he would be happy to assist him in some clerical capacity. The mayor was ecstatic.

James didn't know if he was on his way up or only sinking lower. He didn't know if he was embracing simplicity or descending further into chaos. And he didn't bother to ask himself if he was going to spend his entire life doing things only because his father objected to them.

PART THREE

we feebly struggle

Chapter Nine

The secret of Scandinavian culture, Madison McGrath had always held, was constipation. These people could never let anything go. Every few months, from sheer human necessity, they might produce a potato pancake or a painted plate, but they would feel compelled to apologize for it. When they celebrated something, which was rare, they were capable of devoting hours of labor to forge one paper-thin object of decorated dough which would be joylessly consumed in seconds.

It was no wonder that when they let go they went berserk. The breed had no balance in it. Their artists and thinkers who had attained international repute—Ibsen, Strindberg, Kierkegaard, Munch, Bergman—were all idol smashers, haunted fiends, people who screamed for free air with no idea of either how easy or how pleasant breathing was meant to be. They had sold their visions of torment and alienation to a foolish era as a picture of the human condition, when they were only a repressed protest against painted plates piled with lefse in airless drawing rooms where no voice was ever raised.

Not that McGrath ever read or watched any of their productions. But he knew what they meant, and he resented it. Whatever they did, the normal or the abnormal, the Scandinavians clogged the works.

And that his own son would stoop to working for one of them stretched his tolerance of them, that son, and freedom of choice itself to the limit.

Einar Ekdahl. What could possess James to become that man's assistant?

One might have expected McGrath to admire the man's energy, but he had learned to be wary of Scandinavian activity. It was only disguised constipation, radical disorder. In the projects and ideas that Ekdahl rained upon the community, McGrath saw only chaos, the anarchy of a Scandinavian run amuck, promising only more clogging and strangulation somewhere down the road.

It was sometimes said, in New Culloden, that if Einar Ekdahl or Madison McGrath were to give a speech in praise of the goodness of life, the other would have rushed home to hang himself. They had taken opposite sides on every issue that had ever arisen in the town. Thus far, their score was about even, Ekdahl having recently won on leasing the school building to the Assembly of God, McGrath on abolishing curfews for minors.

But that James was working for the man, consorting with him openly in public, daring to repeat his inanities at the dinner table—this was too much. It presented McGrath with another of those mysteries of life human beings seemed to generate effortlessly, mysteries he had spent his life avoiding when he couldn't destroy them, and here was one eating and sleeping in his own home.

"*Lake* Culloden!" he had roared, choking on a carrot and slapping the table in wrath. "*Lake* Culloden. Can the man be serious? A *tourist* attraction? That—that—that lake is nothing but a plugged drainage ditch. It's man made! Hasn't he heard that Minnesota has thousands of lakes? Real lakes! How can a man made lake be a tourist attraction in Minnesota? Maybe in Death Valley—just as a monument to bullheadedness—but in Minnesota? *And* it's going to become one by changing the name of the *town*? Analyze that for me, James. Convince me I'm missing something. Changing the name of the town is going to alert people to the fact that there's a lake here which only an idiot would bother to visit—have I got it? That's the new blueprint for the boom?"

"That and the mall," said James. "And, of course, the rodeo." James had never seen his father sputter before. He quite agreed with his father's analysis. But the conversation wasn't about agreement and James knew it, even if Madison did not. James knew it and was enjoying every minute of it. So he said, "What's the big deal? A rose by any other name, you know."

"Yes, and the same goes for a weed. There's my point. Thank you."

"It isn't your point at all. My point was that an uproar was pointless. Your point is just the opposite."

"Indeed!"

And yet there was some use to James' treachery. His closeness to Ekdahl and his willingness to divulge the nonsense concocted by the fool served to alert McGrath to any new schemes in time to thwart them. As soon as he learned that changing the town's name was to come up at the next council meeting, he prepared a petition against it and began collecting signatures.

"Hand it over, Mahdeesohn," said Danny, when McGrath appeared at the station with it. "I'll be happy to add my John Henry to that."

"Hancock, John Hancock. What are you going to do—hit it with a hammer? You're confusing the steel-driving man with the ostentatious signatory. Does no one study American history anymore?"

"A facetious remark, my friend, offered in full awareness but one which I will happily withdraw. C'mon. Give me your petition."

"Don't you want to know what it's about?"

"Certainly not. I'm a merchant. I agree with everything. That's American capitalism. Besides, I've carried around a few in my day and I know what a bitch it is."

"Well, sign it, sign it. Another one of our mayor's schemes. He wants to rechristen us 'Lake Culloden.'"

"An excellent idea."

"Damn you, Daniel. This petition is in opposition to that."

"Did I say 'excellent'? I meant 'exasperatingly silly'."

"Sign it, you amoral scamp, and let me move on."

Patty wasn't around, so McGrath looked over the station for other possible signatures.

Most of the card players were enjoying—or perhaps not enjoying—one of their seasonal employment spurts, as the farmers were seeding and fertilizing and could actually make use of the unskilled, unintelligent, and unambitious labor force that the industrial revolution and the welfare state have reduced the peasantry of the world to. The farmers always seemed bewildered at the lack of ingenious, motivated workers lying about waiting to be hired for sub-standard wages on the two or three occasions a year they needed them. They looked upon the available laborers as one more device invented by a soft nation to cheat them of their due, while the laborers looked upon the opportunity as an intrusion into their leisure, albeit necessary to maintain their unemployment benefits. This gave all of them what McGrath looked upon as the supreme Scandinavian satisfaction of both sides of a bargain sinking into acrimonious misery.

But right now it checked his purpose. There were only two unemployable old Norwegians, named Odin and Tor, sipping coffee in the station, kept company by Beckett, who was perhaps engaged in some undercover anthropological research. These two were of poor quality, even by Norwegian standards, and, lacking a card game to watch, lacked anything to do and everything to do it with. The absence of the card game had no doubt struck them as one more mystery of the world's turning, as impenetrable as the coming of snow or the phases of the moon.

Beckett, who had overheard McGrath's presentation of his petition, smiled as he approached. McGrath raised his eyebrows. But a name was a name. He filled a coffee cup and joined the group.

As he placed his too official looking document on the table, he could feel the men become tense. They pursed their lips and began moving their heads slightly from side to side, hoping to forestall any overt request by these evident negations.

McGrath had expected this. He began by trading a few pleasantries about the weather and a few deprecatory remarks about the usual summer tourists. This was firm ground. But if he had hoped to build an edifice of agreement on it, he was disappointed. As soon as he fingered his petition, both of them rose silently and left.

"Thank you, citizens," he said, after they had gone.

"Stirring up trouble again, Lawyer McGrath?"

"I'm not the one doing the stirring. That idiot Ekdahl wants to change the town's name. And why? To attract tourists, if you can believe that."

"An outrage. You should have told those two they'd be forced to bathe and wear neckties. And register their firearms. You might have gotten further with them."

"Could they own bathtubs and neckties? It seems unlikely. Or even firearms? Surely they would have blown their own heads off by now. God knows I would have if I were in their shape."

"It's all a question of perspective."

"True. And how's your perspective, Ben? Will you sign?"

"But of course. It's almost an extension of my work, maybe even a purer form of it. Nothing but names. You know, I believe petitions are undervalued as an art form. I might take around a few."

"You have to care about something first."

"Ah. A pity."

"Will no one debate with me? Don't you want to know what's at stake?"

"I heard you talking to Danny. Besides, if I debated with you, you'd only badger me until I gave in. And you expect me to sign anyway."

"Because I'm right!"

"Of course you are. Give it here. A rose, after all, by any other name would smell as sweet."

"That's not my point at all."

"Well, then, a rose by any other name would not smell as sweet and I'm even happier to oblige you."

"Fiend."

And yet, as McGrath well knew, a name on a petition, whatever the motivation, was still a name. And the first ones were always the hardest to get. Few people enjoy the nakedness of a blank petition, any more than they enjoy appearing naked themselves.

But before the day was out, he had a substantial collection and he hadn't even twisted many arms yet. That afternoon, in his office, he looked over the names lovingly and savored the thought of sliding his document, heavy with ink, identity, and anger, across the table at the hapless mayor.

His eyes fell on Beckett's florid signature. It had begun to irritate him that Beckett got on so well with his son. This was only one aspect of the disruption James was causing throughout the entire system of his life. But, unlike whistling, clattering silverware, or mowing in uneven rows, this was not only a point against James, easily filed in the mental brief McGrath added to daily. It also bore on Beckett and himself.

McGrath would never dream of applying notions like resentment or jealousy to his own heart, so he refused to probe his irritation very deeply. He could not even decide who was the object of his ire—James or Beckett—and this only irritated him the more.

His office had now become his sanctuary, through no real decision and no real need. But as Natty Bumppo had been driven further west as civilization spread, so McGrath had been driven out of his own home by the mere presence of another human being shrinking his private space. But he would not have said he was fleeing civilization. Indeed, he might have said he was organizing its last stand.

Most of his books were in his office, all of his files. There stood his father's clock. He had a roll top desk and a swiveling wooden office chair, curved to his back with wooden arm supports perfectly matched to his elbows. The office was heated in the winter by a black wood stove. At the school's closing, he had managed to salvage portraits of Washington, Jefferson, and Lincoln and a free-standing globe, two feet in diameter, showing the world as it was in 1900. Imperialism was something McGrath loathed, so the globe was more an aesthetic than a political statement, or rather: it was a political statement of a non-nationalistic sort, having nothing to do with colonialism and everything to do with craftsmanship, decent materials, integrity of design, and durability.

And yet it sometimes bothered him that he could not find at a glance the precise boundaries of Kuwait or Lesotho.

The only modern things in his office were the telephone and his own brain. Thanks to the inefficiency of the telephone company and the splendidness of his brain, neither was precisely in step with the last quarter of the twentieth century.

He loved his office. What he hated was feeling forced to be there through the return of his child, who had yet to offer a cogent reason for that return. But this again was only one aspect of a greater disruption.

McGrath could not quite grasp what had come upon him. It was nothing but the return of a son he didn't know very well to a life that had no place for him. But the very simplicity of that, the unquestionable claim of biology and history, was defeating every attempt of his at order. There was always someone else there to be considered: in cooking, in bathing, in sitting and reading, some other eye, ear, mouth, and body was always there to be considered.

That it was summer made things worse. To maintain the solitude of his afternoons, he had taken to his office. But his office, in the garage attic, became an inferno in the late afternoon. The time for Blackstone's walk arrived each day like a governor's reprieve on death row. To make some other arrangement was beyond him, since admitting the inconvenience was distasteful.

He filed his papers, locked his door, and went outside. Blackstone was lying in the shade, panting a little from the heat. Summer was hard on him, but he still perked up in expectation of his walk. The dog's devotion to routine warmed McGrath's heart. Before he went, however, he walked across his property to examine his trees for further deterioration.

Thus far, he had been unable to drum up much concern about the sloppy pilot. It occurred to him that his anti-mayoral petition was having more success only because the issue seemed trivial to most people. The only one responding to his agitation against promiscuous crop spraying seemed to be the pilot himself, who had increased his attacks on McGrath's property.

The message James had found, which McGrath was sure had been left by the pilot, was only the most overt attack. His office was buzzed at least twice a week, the drunken sot being apparently gifted with an instinctive knowledge of when McGrath would be there. Once or twice, in the morning, he had found crude skull-and-crossbones drawings taped to his door.

McGrath was not pleased to find himself turning from an accidental victim to a consciously chosen victim. He was, of course, chronicling these violations and abuses. But he knew the limitations as well as the power of the law. When he took this person to court, it would have to be to destroy him completely. Anything else would be far less than enough to secure his peace. Sharing his dilemma with James was out of the question.

His trees seemed not much worse than they had when he had first noticed the damage. If McGrath had been fond of trees, this would have given him some consolation. But for him the struggle was one of principle, right, and sane conduct, which doomed him to perpetual dissatisfaction. Having found no fresh atrocity to enrage him, he was about to return to his yard for Blackstone when he turned his ankle on a fallen branch and fell to the ground.

McGrath dreaded physical incapacity, and a sickening fear, which he was powerless against, came upon him. He frantically checked his limbs for breaks and sprains. Finding none, he felt ashamed of his own terror and quickly stood up.

Then he noticed the tear in his right trouser leg.

Cursing nature, society, and himself, he went to the house, hoping like a truant child to escape the notice of its other occupant. James was in the shower, loudly singing one of the maddeningly complex melodies which unnerved McGrath. But at least he would escape notice. He hurriedly changed and rushed out to his dog and his routine, putting his clumsiness, his terror, and his shame behind him as well as he could.

That his own land and his own body could rebel against him and topple him so easily was hard for McGrath to swallow. To know it was one thing, to feel it another. How strange and bitterly comic, that mind and will were powerless against soil and bone. For McGrath, there could be no more damning judgment on the universe.

He unchained Blackstone and headed out the cemetery road with the dog at his side. The sun was still high, and what had recently been a mild sunset walk was now a little grueling. How the deists could ever have compared the lunacy of nature to the majesty of clockwork remained utterly bewildering to him.

Just beyond the cemetery, there was a slight rise in the road and over it now McGrath could see a jogger coming toward him. Jogging was an urban fad which had not made many inroads into the cultural network of New Culloden, and he wondered who it could be.

Soon he saw it was Patty, coming slowly toward him in a pink sweatsuit. He should have known that she would be the only one in town likely even to have heard of jogging. On the other hand, he had never seen her move very quickly or very far. She waved at him. Somewhat in spite of himself, he cheered up.

Blackstone ran forward, tongue out and tail wagging, to meet her. She continued to McGrath, then stopped to pant and smile. She took off her glasses, wiped the sweat from her face and wheezed. McGrath found himself thinking she looked young and pretty, then wondered if his mind was going soft for taking pleasure in that. He put it down to the shock of his recent fall.

"Patricia," he said, "you look both fetching and formidable. But I had no idea you were an athlete."

"Oh, Madison, you're such an old flirt."

The inaccuracy of this remark was so overwhelming he ignored it. "Is this a new endeavor or have I simply not noticed you out here before?"

She put her arm through his coyly. "I'll tell you a secret. Not to be told to anyone, now. Violations will be punished by excruciating torture administered by a sadistic woman."

"Surely you can't mean yourself. But you insult me. I am the guardian of untold confidences."

"Okay." She had her blonde hair in a ponytail and she gave it a proud little flip. "I'm in training for a big event."

"Yes?"

"Big event. You *know*. I'm going to have a baby."

"Oh, is that all? And does the American Medical Association require this of you? Now there is an organization of sadists."

"Just staying healthy, Madison. And what do you mean: 'is that all?' Can't you work up a little enthusiasm?"

"Ah, but you know I've warned you about having children."

"The expert speaks. I'll have to tell James how wicked you really are, though he probably already knows it."

"Why the secrecy?"

"Oh, we want to tell our parents first. It's the first grandchild, on both sides. So we promised each other not to tell anyone else. You know a small town: Tell one, tell all."

"I'm happy to see you make an exception in my case."

"Well, you're special. Even if you like to pretend you're so tough."

"There isn't a trace of pretense in my character."

Patty giggled. "Oh, no, of course not. Speaking of James, how are you two bachelors getting along?"

"Fine," he said. "But does your use of the term 'bachelor' suggest a strain of matchmaking in your nature? In my own case, I must warn you that I never forgive meddlers."

"I know you're a lost cause. Don't get excited. I was only wondering. Danny and I have enjoyed having him around. How long's he staying?"

"The summer, I believe."

"Too bad."

Madison shrugged. Everyone he knew seemed to enjoy his son.

"Well, I'd better push on. A healthy baby in a healthy body, you know. See you around."

"Don't overdo."

She started back toward town and Blackstone trotted along beside her. McGrath would have liked her to walk along with him. And he felt a little jealous of Blackstone leaving. But he shook these thoughts away.

Yet he could not help reflecting that he could be easier and more jovial with Patty and Danny than he could ever be with James. More of the lunacy of nature, he supposed. If he didn't know better, he could believe the world had been designed by a Scandinavian. He turned to continue his walk and, in a few moments, Blackstone was back at his side.

His ankle ached a little. He looked over his shoulder and watched Patty turn up the highway. She was waving at someone in a car. He felt old, and it was the feeling, far more than the fact, that infuriated him.

Chapter Ten

The New Culloden city council met the second Tuesday of every month in the community center, a square building of concrete blocks James had at first mistaken for an abandoned warehouse. Beckett said they met on Tuesday in sometimes real, sometimes mock homage to Tiu, the Norse god of war.

The community center was almost always locked, being used only for council meetings, senior citizen lunches, and an occasional rummage sale. James, who was used to the city, thought this unremarkably normal. Madison considered it a perfect ironic commentary on rural community life.

James had found, to his dismay, that his job would entail attending city council meetings and acting as their secretary. Most of the time, he was kept busy applying for state and federal grants available for community development. So far he had only succeeded in acquiring a flagpole, which Ekdahl installed behind the life guard station at the lake. By the night of his first meeting, he had yet to be paid and he intended to bring this up to the council. But when he arrived, Ekdahl handed him an envelope.

"Here's your salary. I thought I'd give it to you here to save on postage, you know, every penny counts." The envelope was taped closed. It was a colorful envelope from some lottery, advertising thousands of dollars worth of prizes. It was addressed to Einar Ekdahl.

James was about to pocket it when the mayor said, "Go ahead. Open it." The man beamed at the very thought of an official transaction.

James shrugged and slit the flap with his finger. Instead of a check, the envelope contained some bills and some coins. James counted them.

Then he counted them again.

Pointlessly, he counted them a third time and looked inside the envelope for stragglers. He had received exactly $8.33. It could only be a joke. Indeed, he was sure it was a joke, but he knew it wasn't one of those jokes meant for humor. It was one of those jokes Life was fond of and that his own life had been receiving in abundance. He said, "High tax rate?"

Ekdahl whispered, "No taxes at all, don't say a word."

Now James had agreed to work for $100. He realized that he had never asked if this were weekly or monthly. He had assumed, for such a job in such a place, that it would be monthly. He had never thought of asking: monthly or yearly? He said: "This would make, then, one hundred dollars a year?"

Ekdahl took a seat next to him. The room was filling up with council members. He whispered more quietly, "You're worried about the four cents. That will come as a Christmas bonus, you know, end of the year. And forget the taxes. This is between us."

James repeated tonelessly, "This would make, then, one hundred dollars a year."

"With the four cents, yes, exactly. To the penny."

And for this he was going to be forced to attend meetings? For this he had exposed himself to his father's sarcasm? For eight dollars—in single bills—and thirty-three cents, eighteen of them pennies?

At that moment, two things happened that stopped the words "I'm sorry, I quit" from coming out of his mouth. His father walked in the door, and Ekdahl said, "Remember: don't mention this to anyone. I'm paying you myself, out of my salary, you know, you're my personal assistant. They all think you volunteered."

They might have thought so, but his father didn't. He had told his father he was *being hired*. McGrath would never overlook a detail like that. The presence of his father at that council meeting did more than convince James to leave his salary unmentioned. It moved him to pray that no one else would bring it up.

The childish desperation of Ekdahl, his eagerness to stir up community activity, touched him, too. And he was sick of his father's tirades against the Scandinavians. The very paltriness of Ekdahl's payment effectively purchased his loyalty.

James slipped the envelope into his pocket and opened the secretary's notebook. He nodded to the mayor and the mayor winked back, patting him on the head as he stood. James was sure McGrath noticed the gesture. He would probably equate it with the handshake of a Nazi. And feeling his father's eyes upon him, James felt it as such, and hated himself for it.

It occurred to him that he was agreeing to do something he had no desire to do, for a salary that was an insult, only to side with someone it embarrassed him to be seen with and to avoid the embarrassment of revealing how little he received for it. It was one of those insights that seemed to show the hand of God in the world at its most malicious. Or the human mind at its most helpless. Of such self-defeating urges, anyway, did his life seem to be made.

James was not going to enjoy this meeting.

Mayor Ekdahl extended his hand to McGrath, who had taken a seat against the wall of the room. "Welcome, Madison, you rascal, and what are you up to?"

Always polite with officials, as he thought this the best way to show his contempt for them, McGrath shook his hand and said, "I'm observing the working of our democracy. The last time I passed the post office it was still flying the stars and stripes. Are you implying that I need a special reason to be here?"

What bullshit, thought James.

McGrath continued, "Or would you like me to leave?"

Ekdahl laughed heartily. James reflected it was probably not a bad method for dealing with his father. The mayor said, "You devil! Stay, stay, you know, we're always happy to have you."

McGrath sat primly in his seat. After his exchange with the mayor, he gave no indication of being acquainted with anyone in the room, let alone the father of one of them. James felt his presence all the more.

The meeting was mercifully non-controversial. James was as thankful for this as it was possible for him to be. He thought nothing transpired that could make any fair-minded observer dismiss the council as a pack of fools. But his father hardly qualified as a fair-minded observer.

And they all knew whose son he was. More absurdly, they all imagined he had volunteered to be Mayor Ekdahl's assistant. Depending on their estimation of Ekdahl, they must think him either retarded or rebellious. In any case, as he sat there in a cold sweat taking the minutes, he felt like the third, accidentally formed angle of some triangle of aggravation that everyone was taking the measure of. Even with the stiff competition the rest of his life could provide, sitting in this meeting might rank as the most stupid thing he had ever done.

As they approached the end of the agenda, James began to ponder the reason for his father's presence. The fact that it unnerved him had been the salient fact about it, but he doubted even his father would stoop to such a petty thing. He had no idea why McGrath was sitting there.

And then, the last item, Mayor Ekdahl broached the issue of a possible change in the name of the town. A few council members shifted in their chairs, some glanced at McGrath.

Ekdahl presented his reasoning at great length but James sensed that he was losing his audience. He was sure the rest of them knew something neither he nor the mayor knew. And James knew his father had something to do with it. Beyond these perceptions, which the mayor seemed blissfully ignorant of, James was as much in the dark as Ekdahl.

Fascinated, James watched his father rise as the mayor concluded. Churchill must have risen like this to stun Germany with his determination after Dunkirk. And his father was, if anything, more certain of victory than Churchill could have been. McGrath cleared his throat. "If it please the chair, may I speak?"

Ekdahl smiled like an innocent mouse seeing its first snake. "Of course, of course, we're always happy for input here." He looked around. Nobody looked that happy to James.

"I assume the will of the people of this town counts for something in these deliberations."

"The people? That's what we're here for, you know, to serve the people. Why? Do you have some opinion on this? It's just an idea, of course, open to debate."

"Well, my own opinion is that it's the most idiotic suggestion I've ever heard, absurd in itself and supported by laughably inconsequential arguments, a suggestion more likely to defeat than advance any of the purposes linked to it. But I would not presume to interrupt this assembly on the strength of one citizen's opinion, however enlightened. I have with me a petition, bearing the signatures—by my tally—of just short of two thirds of the registered voters of New Culloden. Through this petition, they declare themselves to be in unqualified opposition to any alteration of the town's name." McGrath placed his petition, now several pages long, on the table between two council members and pushed it slightly forward with his fingertips. They looked at it as at a rat dead of plague. McGrath concluded, "I respectfully submit this on their behalf. Thank you." He sat down, expressionless.

Even James knew by now that in New Culloden, on an issue that did not require action for the sake of public safety, one dissenting voice was enough to settle that things would remain the same. Once McGrath spoke, New Culloden was destined to remain New Culloden. The petition sitting on the table was so far beyond necessity to be sheerly gratuitous, a pursuance of delight and assault for their own sakes. Had most of the council not already been disposed to agree with him, such an ostentatious display of pointless effort might well have backfired.

Ekdahl was frowning. McGrath had placed the papers so that the mayor could read the names. He reached for them and spread them out.

James was astounded, both at the amount of activity this represented and the names themselves. There were Danny's and Beckett's, and later on Patty's and even Kathy Frei's. He couldn't make himself believe that anyone he knew cared about the name of the town one way or another. So he read the petition as a testimony to his father's personality. It was nothing but Madison McGrath staring up at him through the signatures of other people, and James had had no idea he was so immense.

The names of half the city council were also on the petition. James wondered if the rest had refused or if McGrath had just not had the time to get to them. A quiet man sitting across from the mayor said, "I move we table this issue until the next meeting."

McGrath snorted.

Ekdahl said mechanically, "Is there a second to the motion?"

There was not. Another man, who had signed it, said, "I move we forget about it."

Someone else seconded without being asked.

"All in favor, say: aye."

`Everyone did.

"All opposed, same sign."

There was silence.

"Carried, then," said Ekdahl. "Any other business?"

James wrote "There being no other business, the meeting was adjourned," closed the notebook, stacked it on the mayor's folder and left. Where he fit in all this was unclear to him, but clearly enough he fit awkwardly, and he was hoping if he got outside quickly he could be hit by a falling satellite or at least avoid his father.

But as he hurried out the door, he tripped over a soft, thick, dark object and pitched to the sidewalk. His palms were scraped, but mildly. He turned his head in irritation. Blackstone sniffed at him impassively.

"Great. Thanks, you big lug."

He brushed himself off but he was too late to get away without being seen by his father, as McGrath had as little desire to linger as he did, though for different reasons, and he was the next person out the door.

Since they were headed for the same house, they walked along together, Blackstone prancing before them. James readied himself for the gloating oration he was sure would come. But he did not know his father so well as he thought. What he heard instead were some wandering reflections on the nature of petitions, their limited use, the necessity of clarity and brevity in their drafting, even some of McGrath's memories of the social unrest of the sixties, which had for James, a pre-adolescent at the time, something of a mythic stature.

His father was treating him more like a colleague than a foolish son. It was a transformation both unexpected and difficult to assimilate. Perhaps it came from the mere sitting together in some political arena. Whatever the reason, James received it as a token of mercy, even if it still savored somewhat of a put-down.

There was a definite spring in McGrath's step, a youthful swagger. It was the step of victory. James walked with his hands in his pockets. He felt the envelope he had received from Ekdahl. If he were going to mimic his own state of mind with his posture and movement, he supposed he would have to crawl, with hung head and protruding tongue.

McGrath was taking his victory lap. James was only going home. And it wasn't even his home.

Chapter Eleven

The summer heat was becoming unbearable in the afternoons. But Minnesota summers can be very pleasant, each day ending in a mild evening of soft light, cooled by a light breeze. James enjoyed retiring to his room to spend the night reading. If he let his mind wander a little and primed himself with a few glasses of wine, he could almost imagine he was on a long vacation.

But he was getting tired of Beckett's book selection. Beckett never let him browse along his shelves, which he would have loved to do, but insisted on pressing his own choices on him. In addition to Dante, he now had *The Name of the Rose*, Balzac's *Lost Illusions*, Barthelme's *Snow White*, and Stanley Cavell's *Must We Mean What We Say?*, marked at the essay on modern music.

He did not dislike Beckett's choices so much as his own lack of them. The structure of his reading felt too much like the structure of the rest of his life. He wanted to walk between the stacks of some immense library, casting the net of his fancy. Lacking that possibility, he decided to make his first trip to Carlsburg. There was a library there. One room, he had been told, in a building that housed both the fire department and the sheriff's office. He would also enquire at the school about getting the use of a piano.

His first enthusiasm to secure an instrument had passed, and he wasn't sure why. He had the vague sense that he no longer had a right to touch one. The thought of playing brought him a kind of fear now. He hoped it was nothing but broken habit.

One afternoon, on a wave of unusual desperation, he had called the Minneapolis church his friend had referred him to. But they had already hired someone else. The pastor's voice was still fetching, but it now stirred neither desire nor terror in him. He had, no doubt, run away too quickly. It was the revenge of passion. The passion had ebbed, but he was still away.

When he announced his plans to go to Carlsburg, his father gave him a grocery list.

He hadn't driven in weeks, except to move his car when he mowed the lawn. Driving reminded him of having places to which he must go. He had the freedom of doing whatever he wanted, in the very middle of the productive day. He would use roads, machines, buildings, and merchandise that others built, grew, stocked, and maintained. Utterly free, he was utterly useless. He felt as though he had betrayed something, though he couldn't have said what. Maybe if you became useless, it meant you had betrayed everything.

It didn't take long to get to Carlsburg or to gather his father's groceries. He decided to save either the pleasure or the disappointment of the library for last, so he went up to the school.

They were happy to oblige him. The superintendent reminded him of Mayor Ekdahl. James was told he could use any one of the practice rooms, especially since it was summer. If he came during the day, he wouldn't need a key. As he was leaving the office, the superintendent asked him, "Will you be here in the fall?"

"I—don't think so."

"Well, we sometimes have openings. Could you direct a band?"

Not willingly, thought James. "I haven't done much of that."

"Chorus, then?"

"Chorus. Yes."

"Maybe we can work something out."

James didn't know what to think about that. Except that, if the man really were like Ekdahl, nothing would come of it.

But he sought out the practice rooms, nervous excitement rising in him. He entered the first one and closed the door behind him. It wasn't beautiful, but there it was. It played notes and it was in tune. He sat down at the bench. He should have brought some music with him.

From memory, he ran over the first three Hanon exercises. He did as much as he could recall of Mozart's *Rondo alla Turca*. He started Bach's arrangement of Walther's *Christ Lag in Todesbanden*. Then his fear defined itself.

It wasn't about the instrument or the music. It wasn't about his skill. It was about what it all was for. And that didn't have to do with the position, or the money, or the regularity. It had to do with what he didn't have: a purpose. He hadn't learned and performed these things in a vacuum. He had done it for somebody, some tribe whose unspoken thoughts needed the touch of his skill to be born. That was what he didn't have. Worse: that was what he couldn't see anywhere around him.

But he played the Bach anyway. Despite himself, he felt a delight at what sprang out from the union of himself, the instrument, and the long dead Germans.

But again: not just Germans. Walther and Bach weren't composing scales when they came up with this magnificent creation, so stately and intense, its maze of notes winding through and binding up sorrow and joy. They were conjuring up the spirit of the resurrection, shaping hope out of dread, shaping it for a community of voices, a gathering of souls.

He wondered how often this piano had been touched by such a piece. Perhaps he had brought the instrument a gift of grace. James had been touched by it. Often. And he had touched others with it. That was what he didn't have. And he was going to need more than an instrument to get it back.

For the present, however, an instrument was what he was going to have to be satisfied with. After a few more hymns, he looked at his watch and found he had spent over an hour in the room. His father's broccoli was probably rotting. He had to hurry to the library.

He had asked directions to all these places in Carlsburg and had been given one all-purpose answer: you can't miss it. This turned out to be true. It was easy enough to find a building with a fire truck and a patrol car parked next to it. But the library inside the building was another matter.

He found that he had to go through the sheriff's office itself, down a corridor to a door marked REST ROOMS which opened into a square hallway with three more doors: BUCKS, DOES, and LIBRARY, as though three sexes came here, reduced to brute errands. He couldn't tell if it was meant as a compliment or an insult to the life of the mind. But he couldn't imagine many teen-aged intellectuals making the trip down this hall to take their first crack at *The New Yorker* or their first peek at Freud.

When he entered the library, he knew he had made a mistake. Beckett's collection made this one look like a doctor's waiting room. A woman sat at the desk. She had frizzy hair and eyes that had dulled beyond the possibility of eagerness. She had her feet on the desk.

Since they were the only two people in the room, James felt he had to say something. "Thought I'd look around."

"Oh, really? Well, that shouldn't take long."

She was right. He had to force himself to pretend an interest in the shelves: lots of generic romances, mysteries, westerns. This had clearly been a bad idea.

He thought there was no point in making the broccoli suffer any longer, but he didn't want to rush out too quickly, as though he had taken a wrong turn to the BUCKS room and was only staying out of politeness. Nor did he want to seem to be leaving in disgust, which would have been closer to the truth. On the other hand, to stay at length was to collaborate with the mind that had assembled these volumes.

This was another one of those situations that lacked noble choices.

James didn't think the woman at the desk could have chosen the books. The air of defeat she had about her suggested she knew too much for that. She was smoking a cigarette. She blew smoke rings, one inside another. Maybe, like the piano he had just come from, she needed to be touched by something splendid in her profession. He wished he could carry her a collection of Elizabethan tragedies, or Hildesheimer's *Mozart*, or Virginia Woolf's diaries. Unfortunately, he wasn't going to find anything like that here, and he would have settled for Kipling or Dickens.

He could ask her for some obscure information, something about the difference between Benedictine and Trappist chant or suicide rates in the fourteenth century. On the other hand, it might only depress her. She might be out of tune. Being in tune was harder for humans than for pianos.

He decided to leave her on her own. He would take the cowardly, practical way out and pretend he had come to read the newspaper. He saw they carried both the *Minneapolis Star* and the *St. Paul Pioneer*.

The woman was a chain-smoker. James was rather impressed by this in a librarian. He wondered if she had brought it with her into her career or been driven to it. He sat in the only chair available, an imitation leather chair with several slits in the imitation leather and a wobbly leg. He flipped through the papers.

But this, too, had been a bad idea. There were his cities. There were the places he had gone and the things he had enjoyed. There they were, in paper and ink before him, in his lap. It was temptation, accusation, and mockery at once. They were there and not there, because they were primarily elsewhere, the cities and all they offered. He looked upon the stories and the ads in the paper with the insatiable yearning the dead must have if they are conscious.

"You from the cities?" asked the librarian. She was now sitting on her desk, bringing her closer to him.

"Yeah."

"I lived there once." Prisoners in Siberia must sound as she did then.

He may have been imagining things. But he thought he saw a hunger in her, an offer of something, anything, in trade for a little life. Sorry, he thought, no sale.

"Attractive cities," he said and quickly folded his papers.

"You bet."

"Well, I'd better be going. Errands."

"Come again."

"Right."

Music, women, books. They didn't seem all that useless now. What was it about life that always convinced you that you were standing in the wrong room? Or was it just *his* life? This room, at any rate, was the wrong one. Leaving the woman there, he felt like a rescue team abandoning the last survivor of a coal mine collapse.

On the way back to New Culloden, his engine started to whine, then the speedometer dropped to zero. He coasted to the shoulder. He decided to spare himself the comedy of opening the hood.

He collected the most perishable groceries in one bag and hitchhiked up to Danny's station. Danny directed him down the street to a man who ran a repair shop and owned a tow-truck. James rode back down the highway with him. When the repairman got the car back to his shop, he told James it might take a while to get parts. A long while.

"But can you fix it?"

"Anything can be fixed. It's all a matter of time. And money."

He carried the rest of the groceries to Danny's station and went to get his father's car to ferry them home. Car trouble usually enraged him but he found he was taking this calmly. After all, he already was where he had to be, or could walk there in minutes. Wanting his car back was a small thing.

He wanted his life back.

Chapter Twelve

Kathy Frei watched James walk past her house. It was the third time he had gone past in an hour. Each time, he pretended not to be searching her windows and her back yard for a sight of her. Men were so helpless.

The poor things were full of desires that choked them. If they couldn't make themselves use their fists to get what they wanted, most of the time they just went without it. They didn't have the sense nature gave chickens. She felt sorry for them.

She should run out to him and yell "Hey! You want to fuck?" She giggled at the thought of what he might do. Or not do. He'd probably never come by again.

She was watching him from within her living room. She was back in the shadows, standing with her hands on her hips. It was the stance she met the world with: she found it gave her an edge in almost any situation, friendly or hostile. It could express easy companionship, condescension, determination, rebelliousness, amusement, or disdain. Kathy usually didn't need the edge. She just liked to have it.

This wasn't the first time she had watched him watching her. She had noted his arrival early, as everyone in town had. And she had noticed his interest. Given the population of New Culloden, and the paucity of choices within the prime mating years, she thought it would be only a matter of time before he offered to buy her a beer or take her to a dance.

But he had put off what she saw as an inevitable approach for so long that she had begun to think he was deliberately avoiding her. Not to have met by this time in a town the size of New Culloden was an achievement in itself, requiring conscious effort and considerable social skill. If anything was going to happen, she was going to have to take charge.

He looked lost and abandoned, and she had an affinity for lost things. Cats and dogs came to her door as a last resort when scavenging grew too lean or winter too cruel. Teenagers who had lost the code to their parents' affections were drawn to her forgiving smile and patient ear. Men who couldn't dance wanted her as a partner.

She had done enough wandering and scavenging herself, misplaced enough of her own codes, found herself without grace or partners. She didn't think there was anything worth not forgiving. Men, of course, were the hardest. They hated to admit they had anything to forgive.

If James came by again, she decided she'd go out and face him. Such an elaborate ceremony of circling and yearning was beginning to irritate her. If he was a jerk, at least she would settle that. Besides, the road by her house was hot and dusty. This anonymous devotion of his deserved at least a glass of iced tea. And she was between lovers. She wouldn't mind having a new one. Before winter came on again, it would be nice to secure some man to keep her feet warm.

It didn't take James long to show up for the fourth time. She wondered, if she let him pass, how many times he would keep it up. He must be desperate for something. And if he was anything like other men, he would have no idea what it was.

She walked out her front door confidently, her hands in her pockets, not even pretending she was doing anything else. She was barefoot and had her hair tied in a red kerchief. He looked like he was going to faint.

"Hi," she said and stuck her hand out like a used car salesman. "About time we met, don't you think?"

"Um, yeah, I guess—what do you mean?"

"Well, you've been up and down here so many times you've started to distract me."

"Oh, I'm sorry. I was just wandering around. I didn't mean—"

"Uh huh. Are you thirsty? C'mon, let's have some iced tea."

He threw out his arms and said "Okay", as though he had nothing better to do, but she could tell he felt like the luckiest man on earth.

"It's cooler inside," she said, when James dawdled at the step. "And I don't bite. Or are you worried about your reputation?"

He was so surprised by her bluntness and outmaneuvered by her verbal dance that he could only shake his head stupidly as if his reputation were really an issue. If he hadn't wanted to meet her for so long, James might have been put off by her. Her way of talking left him nothing to say. He wondered if she turned everyone around her into a straight man or if she was simply used to compensating for taciturn men.

"Not worried, huh?" she continued and playfully slapped his stomach with the back of her hand. "Maybe you should be."

James thought: and maybe she does bite.

Kathy waved him to the sofa and went into the kitchen for the tea. She kept her house spotless and neat, and was far more fastidious about it than she was about her own person. It was part of her respect for things, her natural grace. Because her own feet loved the feel of mud was no reason, in her eyes, to assume her chairs would also enjoy it. This gave her an odd detachment in her own home, as though she were a slightly underprivileged visitor. She felt that way about the entire planet, and thought it was best for everything. She wasn't high on possession. She never locked her door.

James sat on the sofa, remembering the night he had watched her swaying above it, being undressed by some other man. It made him feel a little tainted, marked by original sin before the relationship had even begun. But he couldn't deny it made him that much more delighted at her invitation.

He noted a piano against the back wall with music stacked on it. If anything, it was in worse shape than the piano he had used in the Carlsburg school. He wondered how well she played.

When she brought in the glasses, she said, "My name's Kathy, if you didn't already know."

"I did. Frei or something, right?" he said, as if he didn't know.

Kathy thought of the husband she had not seen for years and of his name. She had sloughed it off with her youth, her daughter, and the grip of other places. She said, "Or something. Right."

"I'm James McGrath. But, if you're like everyone else, you already knew that."

"Don't be too sure I'm like everyone else, but I did know that. Madison and I are old friends."

"Really?" It was still odd to hear his father addressed as Madison, as though he were a person and not his father, and odder still to hear this woman address him so. It brought a vague sexual uneasiness with it.

"Let's say we shared a courtroom once."

"Ah."

"Does everyone call you 'James'? Why? It seems so formal."

"I guess everyone always has. Do I strike you as formal?"

"Yes." She laughed loudly. "You need a better name: like Hawk, or Savage Elk. It would probably do great things for your life."

"I'll consider it."

"So, James, what brings you up here?"

The constant, aggravating question. He sighed.

Kathy caught the vibration. "Sick of being asked, right?"

"You guessed it," he said and loved her for catching it. And because she was a woman, and just this woman, he felt the tale of his folly rising within him, eager to be told. "To tell you the truth," he began, "I didn't know where else to go." Then he told her about Stephanie and all his misadventures. She found them funnier than he thought they were, but he found he didn't mind that.

Perhaps each face has an expression natural to it, imparting an atmosphere, inviting a situation to evolve one way rather than another. Hers was amused, understanding, sexy. It was an expression that loosened tongues and quickened hearts.

Kathy took his measure as his story unwound. He was younger than she was, slightly younger, but much less travelled, less ill-used, more pampered and uptight. He was someone who could imagine that both foolishness and responsibility meant something.

Before experience had enlightened her, she had gone to school with eager, devoted boys like this, those who thought the world—or their place in it—mattered so much. But they had played for higher stakes then, almost twenty years ago now, in a sour nation they had set themselves to sweeten and save. Many of them had been jailed, some—not the worst—were still. A few had died. This worry and fear and fret and effort, how self-important it was, how useless.

After his story had tumbled out of him, they sat quietly, as if waiting for the future to begin the next episode by itself. Then he said, "You remind me a little of Stephanie." He smiled shyly.

James wasn't sure why he had said that. At one time she had, but she did no longer.

Kathy wondered how much slyness his shy smile hid. She thought probably not much. She said, "From what you've said, we don't sound at all alike. Your friend seems pretty humorless."

His eyes brightened. "I think you're right."

But she understood why he had said it. He was handing her a precious memory and telling her she might take its place. It was the kind of invitation Kathy was quick to sense and just as quick to avoid. She said, "You're pretty humorless yourself, James. It isn't as though you've been sent to a concentration camp. Maybe getting out of there was a real break."

"How's that?"

"You're out. You're loose. You're not showing up on time. You're not kissing ass. You're not worrying about your next paycheck."

"Yeah, but see—I am. What's next is a big question."

"Oh, c'mon," she shouted, as though he had said the most outrageous thing in the world. "What's next is whatever's next. Right now, sitting here talking to me is what's just come next. Not enough for you? Watch out: it doesn't do to make a woman feel unwanted. And you sitting there feasting on my iced tea. James, wise up: what's next is never a question."

James realized she hadn't asked him that question everyone seemed to force on him: what are you going to do next? But perhaps he had always forced it on himself. Kathy obviously didn't care what he did next and thought he was a fool for caring. She couldn't have done more to enthrall him.

"Well," he said, "maybe you're right. I'll consider that, too. You're filling me with such good advice."

"We pioneer women aim to please."

"So—well, what do you do?"

"Usually whatever I please."

"Okay. But for *your* next paycheck."

She stood up. "C'mon. I'll show you."

She led him through her kitchen. She had a rough, confident sway to her hips, but their fullness prevented them from looking anything but feminine, anything but desirable.

Behind the kitchen, a large, shed-like room had once been lamely attached to the house. It was now Kathy's work room. She stood aside and waved her hand at the contents, more in teasing than in pride. "Here it is. I arrange junk."

"My God," said James, surprised and impressed. "You sculpt. I had no idea. Good heavens. Of course: junk sculpture."

"I prefer to think of it as arranging junk. Less tempting to the ego. And much, much more accurate."

It was hard for James to tell, with some of the pieces, where one stopped and another began, or indeed where the pieces stopped and the raw materials began. But there were some stunning arrangements set on tables. Wires, glass, engine parts, stones, and an occasional domestic object, a hairbrush, a hand mirror, a butter knife, or a thermos bottle, composed together into forms at once dynamic and peaceful. For this woman, there was an odd completeness to them where he would have expected a shagginess. And they were confident. Confident and strong.

"Why, these are wonderful."

"As I said, they're my next paycheck. It's junk, James. I prefer making pots. These are somebody else's passing fancy. But right now they pay a little. If I could grow my own clothes and gasoline, I'd chuck it and do nothing. Or just go naked. Maybe I'll still do that one day. Rejoin the animals and get back some sanity."

"Not so easy to go naked in Minnesota."

"Haven't you ever rolled naked in the snow, James?"

"Not sober."

"I can see I have a lot to teach you."

James wondered how much of an invitation this was. He cleared his throat. "Be my guest."

She made no reply, so he said, "You actually support yourself with this. I'm impressed."

"Don't be. I don't need that much support. And I haven't sold that many. Right now I have a grant from something called the Northwest Council of the Arts. A fool and his money, as the saying goes."

"Don't knock it. And don't knock yourself either. There's some great stuff here."

"This stuff is *not* myself."

James ignored her. "This one is great." He was looking at a pair of columns made of barbed wire and toothpaste tubes. Each had a photograph caught in it. Between them were pieces of sharp tools: half of a pair of scissors, an axe head, a screwdriver blade. Each tool skewered part of another, torn photograph. The wires and tools were welded to the bottom of an upside-down frying pan. Ceramic fingers reached out from under the pan. On the pan's handle there was a plastic cradle for batteries from a portable radio, with wires stretching to each barbed wire column.

"If you put batteries in, does it do anything?"

"No. That's the point. It's called 'Portrait of a Marriage: batteries neither included nor helpful.'"

"Pretty ferocious thing."

"It's harmless, James. You've been standing there and there isn't a mark on you. Completely harmless. All things are, really, looked at in the right way. It's all in the eyes."

"Hey! This is you." He was pointing at the picture in the right column. He looked at Kathy. Earlier he would have described her face as contented, happy. But now he saw what he could not have seen without a comparison. The girl in the picture was happy. The woman in the room with him had won her way back to happiness after a long time of something else.

"It *was* me. I had it lying around. More junk."

"I suppose it would be indelicate to ask about the other two pictures." There was a man in the left column. The torn photograph was of a small girl.

"A husband. And a daughter." She said it as though the identities were generic, nothing to which a personal pronoun could be applied, not a matter of bond or possession. For her, now, that was the truth. She continued, "You can't imagine how irrelevant the concept of delicacy is to this situation."

"Oh. Sorry I raised the issue."

"Please, don't be silly. It's life, James. Sometimes it's time to go. For everyone. Sorrow is beside the point."

He thought the composition he was looking at held another point of view, but he kept this reflection to himself.

So she had been married. And had a daughter. It was not something he would have guessed. It didn't seem to fit with the way she presented herself. Or perhaps, since they were no longer around, it did. Perhaps shedding entanglements was what she was about. He looked at the barbed wire and thought again: maybe she does bite.

When they returned to their drinks, he pointed at the piano and said, "I see you play."

"A little."

"So: play a little."

"I don't audition, James. Or entertain. Once upon a time, I gave lessons. But now I just use it to relax."

"Why'd you stop giving lessons?"

"Too much effort for too little return. Too much constraint for too little pleasure. Not for me. Maybe that's something you could do while you're here."

"That's something I've thought about. But I've had a hard time finding an instrument. Right now I'm using one at the Carlsburg school."

"That's silly. There must be one around town. You could probably even find somebody who wants to sell one."

"Well," said James, a little flushed, seeing the possibility of an ordinary bond with her, "how about this one?"

Kathy smiled. It never helped to cave in to their every whim. It gave them the illusion of having rights. "This one's taken. Not for sale or rent. Even occasional use is frowned on by the owner. But why not try one of the churches? I think the Lutherans have let people give lessons on theirs. You could use their organ, too."

"I bet. I heard their organ."

"Arrogance becomes you, James. I'd cultivate it if I were you."

"Okay, I'll ask. Maybe it's a good idea."

"I know the minister. Come to think of it, you really do remind me of him."

"Oh?"

"Uptight, frustrated, slave of duty. You know: good scout."

James wondered if the unlucky minister in question had made a similar trip to this house. And been similarly entranced. If so, was he still? He said, "We should get along then. We can work on merit badges together. Whittling, knot tying."

"Very appropriate: knot tying. It's the untying that's the real trick. But that's beyond the scout repertoire."

She threw herself into her chair and reached for her glass. James thought it was probably time to leave and ponder this creature in private. But she gestured to the couch. "Finish your tea."

"Oh, I should go."

If he thought she would urge him to stay, he was wrong. She said, "I'm glad we finally met. Don't be a stranger."

James felt as though he had passed a test. But, like all real tests, it was probably only the beginning of something even more difficult, less amenable to judgment and calculation. Well, he would see. He needed an interest in life. And she certainly promised to provide that, one way or another.

Still standing, he gulped what was left of his iced tea. She sat there, in her own careless peace, having accomplished all she had set out to do with him. Utterly fascinated, he watched her drift into self-absorption, reach for a pouch of tobacco and roll her own cigarette.

But Kathy was never as self-absorbed as men tended to think. His fascination was foreseen and intended as part of this momentary arrangement and, pleased with him and with herself, she duly noted it.

Chapter Thirteen

"Suppose," said Danny, "one day you come up with something so off the wall it's perfect. You're at your piano, right? You're composing—uh—you're composing 'The Stars and Stripes Forever.' You're almost done. But you need one little thing. It comes to you in a flash: the piccolo part in the trio. It's amazing. You've outdone yourself. Suppose that happens. Now, my question is: do you say 'son of a bitch, I can die now, I've touched greatness, I'm at peace'? What do you think?"

It was a normal day at the station: few customers and much aimless conversation. Patty and Beckett had been playing chess. Kathy had dropped in to see Patty. James, who had been on one of the aimless walks which more and more often led him to Kathy's house, had seen her inside and joined them. Danny had been musing on human fulfillment.

"I think,' said Patty, "you've finally flipped your lid." Looking at Beckett, she moved her bishop and added, "Check."

"And mate, I fear," said Beckett.

Danny persisted. "What do you think, James? Would the piccolo solo be enough for you? Give you satisfaction, make it all worthwhile, be the finishing touch?"

"Wouldn't you rather hold out for—I don't know—something like that vocal part in the fourth movement of Mahler's second?"

"The particular example isn't the point. Make it anything you like. You realize you've done something special. So whatever else happens, whatever else, you're satisfied. Yes or no?"

"I think I would be," said Beckett. "The work is done, in other words. Now come age, hell, death, and fury—so what? Artist dies, work lives on."

"But," objected James, "you'd have to know that, wouldn't you? I mean, that this was it, this was the crown of your work. That you couldn't do any better or any different. I guess I don't think you could know that about either the one thing or your work as a whole. You always want another shot."

"Only if you're not satisfied," said Beckett. "So the particular example, or some particular example, is part of the point."

"No, he was talking about a different kind of satisfaction, something final and lasting. I guess I don't think anything like that would last. You'd be beyond it, one way or another. The proof is: who stops?"

"Lots of people."

"But because they've decided they've already done their best?"

Danny said, "Of course, we're thinking about artists. But athletes, say, sometimes do that. Still, are they satisfied in just that way?"

Patty said, "Are they worth talking about?"

Danny ignored her and looked at Kathy. "You look silent and thoughtful. What's your vote?"

"Speaking for myself, I'm satisfied right now. And I can't even play the piccolo."

"Lucky woman."

"Luck has nothing to do with it. Put it this way: if you can be satisfied without it, you can be satisfied with it; if you can't be satisfied without it, you probably won't be satisfied with it."

"I think you're on to something," said Danny.

James said, "I think you're missing something."

"Oh? What?"

"Well, I'm not sure."

"Then I'll tell you, James. It's mindless ambition. But whether that's a defect or not is debatable. I'd say having that is *really* missing something."

"That's very good, Kathy," said Beckett. "I think she has you, James."

"It was Danny's problem."

"Oh, I just raised it as an abstract issue. I'm perfectly satisfied. With everything."

Patty said, "That makes one of us." She turned to Beckett. "Another game, champ?"

"Thank you, but I must return to my own work. Still looking for that magical moment."

"You see," said James, "there's my point."

"Let me rephrase that. Still looking, since I have the time for another magical moment. I too am perfectly satisfied. Are any of you young people going my way? I'll allow you to bask in my serene radiance."

"I am," said Kathy. "I'll see you guys around."

James had been hoping, as he always did when he was near Kathy, for some moments alone with her. He was sorry to see her go and too inhibited to reveal his desires by brazenly joining them. So, he reflected, here I sit unsatisfied.

"I wonder," said Danny, when they were gone, "if those two are as content as they say they are."

"Well—are you?" said James.

"Of course. I never lie about happiness and contentment."

"Oh, spare us," said Patty.

"But it seems to me,' continued Danny, "that they're the two people I know who are least likely to accomplish anything at all."

"I don't know," said James. "Maybe that was her point. They're satisfied already."

"Knotty issues, my friend. Far beyond our ken."

"And completely meaningless," added Patty.

"The only ones worth discussing, my love. Now, if we were to analyze *dis*-satisfaction…"

"I would probably excuse myself so I wouldn't nave to witness your murder," said James. "Time for me to be off anyway."

"Coward," said Patty.

James looked wistfully after Beckett and Kathy. He had managed to spend a good deal of time with her the last couple of weeks. They had talked, gone to a street dance, gone swimming at the lake. But she was as far from him as she had been when he was only dreaming about her. Kathy had the knack of binding people to her while keeping herself detached. At the *Mudhole*, where they went for drinks, she was always the center of attention but seemed to have an invisible shield around her.

Proximity had at least given him a clearer view of her physical qualities. She was older than he had imagined and, on close inspection, looked it. But wrinkles became her. And the slight heaviness of her body was carried with grace. She was a fluid dancer and she could swim faster and farther than James.

But if he had been expecting to slide into an easy attachment, he had picked the wrong woman.

He walked down to the garage that was mending his car. They had yet to acquire the necessary parts. James wondered if they were negotiating directly with the Japanese instead of simply phoning the Minneapolis dealer. Or if they had ordered special parts that could only be hand forged by Sumo wrestlers atop Mt. Fujiyama during a solar eclipse.

Having nothing better to do, and wanting to do something that tied him to Kathy, he went at last to the Lutheran church to inquire about their piano. He had been putting off this appointment and would never have approached them but for her.

The heat was intense and the gravel roads were dusty. James thought he must never have walked so much in his life as he had this summer. The dust seeped through his shoes and each evening he found himself with blackened feet.

The doors were open at First Lutheran. Someone was mowing the lawn. James went inside.

The oddness of entering a church again. With no right to be there. Churches theoretically are homes for the homeless, havens for lost souls. But property and ownership grow together. Your habitual haven becomes yours, not someone else's, and is unwillingly shared. And James himself had enjoyed being one of the insiders. Perhaps the returning exile is not that different from the intruder: both are strangers, both demand the making of room, both have the lack of shared time against them.

This was nothing like his beloved Mount Moriah. The lack of imagination that had named this church "First" had extended to every inch of its physical presence. The lawn outside was nothing but lawn: no trees, no use of space. Save for the irreducible presence of altar, pulpit, and pew, which had been domesticated as far as possible by streamlining, padding, and lack of adornment, the rooms could pass for large living rooms in a bedroom community, suitable for use as soap opera sets. The organ was an electronic abomination.

There were two pianos: one in the nave, one in the fellowship hall. They were, though ungainly in appearance, passable in sound. Kathy had been right. Not only was it silly to drive to Carlsburg, especially as he was now dependent on his father's car, it was also silly to settle for the school's beat-up instruments when he could use these.

He heard someone else in the church as he was examining the piano in the nave. The young man he had seen mowing the lawn was coming up the main aisle. He had on a grey sweatshirt, whose arms had been cut off, which bore a mock university emblem and the words: Catatonic State.

"Can I help you?" he said, so hesitantly as to imply that he probably couldn't, hoped he wouldn't have to try, and was very sorry about both.

"I was just looking at your pianos."

"I'm the pastor," said the young man, as though he needed to point out he wasn't an instrument, and as though he thought it would never occur to anyone to take him for a minister.

"Hi. I'm James McGrath. I'm spending the summer with my dad. He lives just down the highway. And I was wondering if I could drop in and use one of your instruments from time to time."

"Oh, Sure. We only lock up at night. As long as there's nothing else going on. Feel free."

At Mount Moriah, a request like this from a stranger would have necessitated a discussion by the entire church council, a referral to the music committee, and a recommendation sent back to the council. It would have been tabled at each stage for months. James was charmed, though he himself would have resisted the request more than anyone.

"Well, thank you," he said. "How about if I wanted to give a few lessons?"

"Great! I love to have things going on. Scout troops, singles clubs, senior citizen crafts—the more the better. Keeps the community humming. Great. Hey—maybe you'd like to play for us sometime. Work up a solo piece. We like to have special music. Always happy for new faces."

"Well, maybe."

"Say—you don't play the organ, do you?"

James cleared his throat. "Oh, I've been known to."

"Really? Wow! Well, would you like to? Hey—wait a minute. What did you say your name was? I forgot already."

"James McGrath."

"Oh, sure. Somebody told me about you. Kathy! You know Kathy Frei? You're the one, right? Up from the twin cities? 'Been known to'—c'mon! She says you're the best."

"She's never heard me."

"But you're a church organist, right? That's you, right?"

"I suppose. But I'm not really looking for anything regular. I'm—well, this is a kind of vacation for me."

"Hey—we won't work you to death. Just think about it, okay?"

"Okay."

"Have you looked at the organ? We just got it about a year ago. C'mon, I'll show you."

On hearing it, James had assumed it was someone's cast-off home organ and was stunned to learn that anyone of sound mind had recently purchased it expressly for use in a church.

"Look," continued the pastor, "it's great. You don't even have to know how to play the pedals. It does it all for you."

"Quite an advance." The very thought made James ill.

"Yeah, we're really happy with it. We got a big contribution for an organ fund a few years ago—well, before I came. They were still getting contributions and letting it pile up, but I convinced them to cut it off and get this one. We don't need anything fancier. And this one sounds just as good."

This was too much for James. "Really? What did you pay for it, if I may ask?"

"About twenty-five thousand. Pretty stiff, anyway. But I couldn't see throwing any more money away on it. I'd rather send it to the Hunger Appeal."

James sighed. In ten years, this instrument would be obsolete; in twenty, it would be beyond repair. A small pipe organ would have been here when the most recently baptized children were in their graves. He said, "So how many thousands did you send to the Hunger Appeal?"

"What do you mean?"

"Did you keep getting contributions of that size which you shifted to the Hunger Appeal?"

"Not really. I assume there were some, though."

"So how many fewer hungry people are there?"

"I don't know. A few, maybe. What do you mean?"

"How many? You decided to settle for this instrument so you could use your money elsewhere. So how much did you get and how much good did it do?"

"Well, that's not the point. Giving's a kind of self-discipline."

"So giving for a better organ would be self-discipline, too."

The pastor laughed. "You professional organists are all alike. C'mon—first things first."

Why not settle for an accordion, then? thought James. The man was a moron, and James knew the type. The great causes were always elsewhere, and meanwhile they let the life around them remain impoverished. Keep the community humming. Right. James would rather whistle an accompaniment rather than touch this computerized atrocity.

"Well, anyway," continued the pastor, "this shouldn't give you any trouble, should it? If you ever played for us?"

You couldn't imagine, thought James. But he said, "No."

"So maybe we can call you up?"

"I'll think about it."

"Great! And feel free to drop in anytime. Play, give lessons. Whatever. Listen, I've got to finish cutting the grass. The older people really appreciate a neat lawn. We could hire it out, but," he chuckled, "why waste the money?"

"Why, indeed?"

"Well, stay as long as you like. Oh, by the way, my name's Tim. Tim Franklin."

James had thought he looked familiar and now he made the connection. He was the young man he saw Kathy strangling the first day he went to the Post Office. He wondered again about their relationship. And he wondered why he hadn't seen Tim around much. But he supposed the pastor didn't frequent the beach or the *Mudhole*. And if he were avoiding Kathy for some reason, he would be unlikely to encounter James, who was pursuing her.

James nodded and said, "Thanks for letting me use your piano."

"Hey—no problem."

James considered returning home for some music but he had an appointment with Mayor Ekdahl in a few hours. He decided to check about his mail at the Post Office.

Every day, his father returned with the mail. Every day, James went through it hopefully. He had yet to receive anything. Not a bill, not one of the magazines he had notified of a change of address, not the cigars he had ordered. He couldn't believe his father would throw them away. Some connection must be missing.

When he entered the Post Office, now rebuilt from its spring disaster, the Postmistress disappeared immediately, then returned with stacks of letters, packages, journals, and circulars. She looked disgusted. She said, "I knew you weren't dead, so I saved these. Your mail may not be important to you, but the space it takes up is important to me. I wish you'd come and get it a little more often."

"But my dad picks up the mail. Isn't it in his box?"

"It was until it started to fall out of it."

"So...I don't understand."

"Your dad picks up *his* mail. This is *your* mail. Haven't been crippled up, have you? I expect he thinks you should get your own."

"I guess so."

James was livid. The old fart hadn't said a word. Worse, there were even bills from his father for room and board. Second notices, no less!

The Postmistress was kind enough to give him a couple of bags to carry his mail in. But he was too infuriated to go home. He had a key to the community center from Ekdahl, which he had never used, so he went there instead, to brood over his mail and his misfortune in solitude.

Once there, he separated the mail into bills, personal letters, meaningless ads, catalogues, and magazines. There was a substantial amount of each, save for personal letters. There was only one of those and it was from Stephanie. A slight quiver went through him. That one could wait a little.

He opened the package of cigars he had ordered from his tobacconist. He looked at the sign on the center's wall that read: THANK YOU FOR NOT SMOKING. It was one of Mayor Ekdahl's modernization schemes, and the mayor was very proud of the sign as it was the first in the county. James thought about it for a moment, saluted the sign, then lit up. Bliss.

He paged through the two issues he received of *The New York Review of Books*. It was like getting a message from God, one of the more pleasant ones. He lit another cigar. Complete with incense. He started to feel a little better.

The bills, however, were formidable. They were going to take a big chunk out of his remaining funds. If he had nowhere to go by the end of the summer, he would have to start looking for work in earnest, be reduced to menial labor, perhaps even stoop to playing First Lutheran's organ. Or throw himself on his father's mercy.

He started to feel worse. Accepting that as a kind of equilibrium, he opened Stephanie's letter.

He didn't know what he expected. Love letter, hate letter, he didn't know. Something other than a friendly inquiry, he supposed.

It was short. It was, of all things, a kind of apology. She wrote:

"I think what happened between us unhinged me a little (a little?). I don't know what I want to say. It's sort of hard—I mean, given one has a past, people have different lives, these things happen, not everything can work, you can't have everything, etc.—anyway, it's sort of hard—I mean, it's been hard for me to bury feelings and go on and keep working and smiling, etc. I'm not being very clear, but I think people like me are always kind of yes and no, they want this and that, and they end up doing things sort of half way and then everything gets to be a mess and other people get hurt. And they can't do one or the other really, I mean, part of me has probably always wanted to be someone else but part of me didn't or couldn't really.

"Sorry. See: I feel as though I should apologize to you. People that are married and in careers, that should be it. You see these movies where married people get involved with somebody else—and it's always a mess, the people are jerks, they shouldn't have done that. Because there was no way they were going to make any kind of break. Part wanted to, part didn't."

She wished him well. She asked about his hair. Hers was presentable. She was somewhat reconciled to Paul. She hoped maybe she'd run into James sometimes. They could smile about their escapades.

James wasn't ready to smile yet. He wasn't sure what to think about Stephanie's letter. He wondered if she was still being yes and no, apologizing and terminating on the surface but underneath hinting a need for contact. He wasn't ready for that either. Or: he was beyond the need himself.

The letter had not set him yearning. Once he would have felt Stephanie's dilemma in his bones, pitying her for the tension and straining to tilt her toward yes. He now felt indifference.

He was here because of her, but whatever would happen to him had become detached from her. And he was honest enough to conclude it was a little (a little?) unfair to blame everything on her. He was here because of his own choice and his own blind gropings. He didn't think he'd reply to her.

That night, he asked his father why he hadn't told him about the mail.

McGrath said, "You assured me you'd take care of it."

"But I thought you were bringing it home."

"Did I ever bring your mail home?"

"No, but I thought you would if I had any."

"You did have some, and I didn't."

"But I didn't *know* that."

"I'm neither your keeper nor your slave, James."

James was ready to explode. "We're talking about communication here."

McGrath said, without looking up, "Speaking of communication, I assume I won't need to send a third notice to you for your room and board."

"I guess you won't!"

"There. You see how easy life can be when you pay attention to details."

James spent the evening hot with fury paying bills. But when it was over he had more money left than he had feared he would. He indulged in the great pleasure of reading some thoughtful book reviews. He took a shower. He reread Stephanie's letter with no feeling whatsoever and decided definitely not to reply.

It was still early so he walked to Kathy's to invite her out for a drink. He wanted to tell her about visiting First Lutheran and hoped to share a few jokes about its pastor. Perhaps he had needed Stephanie's letter to show him his life was shifting.

On the way to Kathy's he dropped his payments into the mailbox outside the Post Office. If the old coot was going to bill him by mail, he could walk up here to get his money. Even if it cost James the postage.

Chapter Fourteen

It had not rained in so long that the grass was turning brown. Habitual mowers, like Mayor Ekdahl and Tim Franklin at First Lutheran, were now out watering instead of mowing. Happily for James, his father thought the practice idiotic and wasteful. James found himself with a little more time on his hands.

But this only underscored how little there was to do with it in New Culloden. He would have tried to spend it with Kathy but she was out of town. She had simply driven off one morning and had yet to return. James wondered if she wanted to make a statement of independence, even though there was still little need to declare independence of him. Danny assured him that for Kathy it was normal behavior. But he also pointed out that her whole life was a statement of independence.

James liked Danny, his contentment and his ease with life. He could think of nothing better to do than while away the time at the station.

On his way there one morning, a car roared up behind him, screeched to a halt and blared its horn, almost causing James to have the heart attack he sometimes wished would end his misery or at least cause people to pity him more. It was Patty, exercising her peculiar sense of humor. She beckoned him inside.

Patty was headed out to the lake. She was going to camp overnight with two of her girl friends from the twin cities. Her backseat was piled high with camping gear: tent, stove, sleeping bag, provisions, axe, entrenching tool, first-aid kit, pots, plates, fuel for the stove, inflatable rubber raft, paddles, inflatable mattress, backpack, hiking boots, folding chairs, water jugs, toilet paper, books, lanterns, insect repellent, three sun hats, and two walking sticks. Patty loved gear, equipment, stuff of all sorts. It allowed her to combine her twin passions for adventure and for catalogue shopping.

"All this is for one night?" said James. "There are people who could live off this stuff for a year and feel like they'd gone to heaven."

"What people? You?"

"Well, maybe it would do me for a week."

"No, it wouldn't. I sense in you a real non-camper, James. I'll bet you've never spent a night in the woods."

"You win."

"*Never*? Oh, my. How about winter sports? Do you like to cross-country ski? There are some great trails around the lake."

"Never done it."

"James, you're hopeless. You're as bad as my husband. You've never tried cross-country skiing?"

"Nope,"

"Well, you have something to look forward to this winter. I'll take you."

"Actually," said James, "you don't strike me as that much of a wilderness guide. The only thing missing from this back seat is an inflatable white-picket fence."

"Don't laugh. I've ordered one. Made in West Germany."

"Wouldn't it be simpler to stay home and watch a movie about Africa?"

"I'm not a minimalist, if that's what you mean. All the stuff is part of the point."

"You can get movie stuff, too. Lots of it."

"I have, James, I have. But, seriously, we'll have to go cross-country skiing. Are you going to be here this winter? Or did you say you were leaving? Anyway, you could always come up for it."

He looked out the window. "Oh—who knows?" He didn't.

Patty turned her eye of mischief on him. "Why are you *here*, James? You don't fish, you don't hunt, you don't camp, so that covers the cultural life of the area. And I'll bet you didn't come for the climate. Myself, I find one afternoon with my parents will satisfy me for months—so you must have seen enough of Madison by now. What's keeping you here?"

"If you have any more questions," he said, "feel free to trot them out. I can keep saying 'who knows?' all morning."

"You know, I'd love the cities. These friends of mine I'm camping with—they make me green with envy. They have the best of both worlds. Live and work down there, then, when they hear the call of the wild, they drive up here. God! I'm jealous. You know, I think I'd even love traffic. Traffic! At least you'd know you were surrounded by people with places to go."

Patty had been dazzled by the tales James had sometimes told of his life in Minneapolis, though James could not imagine how much or why. The very thought of an urban area, where the lights did not go out in the early evening, where men and women aspired to sartorial brilliance, where speed and light and the buzz of activity were as common as air, loosened in her an erotic yearning. She was a Carlsburg girl and she had watched her high school classmates, no brighter than she was, make their moves downstate while first her own frivolous dawdling and then marriage had kept her bound here. She wasn't that interested in what James was doing. She was simply brooding on what she wasn't doing and where she wasn't living and what she yearned for her life to be.

"Let's not spend all morning sitting here in my car," she said. "It tends to overheat when it idles. Reflects its owner. Let's drive around this big town and see what's cooking."

She squealed ahead and raced past the station, horn blaring.

"Drop me anywhere back there," said James. "I was going to visit your spouse."

"Our station's always there. It's like God. Always there, always the same. So why hurry?"

She went up and down New Culloden's gravel roads, raising a dust trail behind her. Few inhabitants were visible. Patty and James shared what they felt was the only enlightened approach to morning: to rise at such an hour that as little as possible was left of it. Thus, when they made their sweep of the town, most of the population had already returned to their hovels and were watching television or looking forward to their afternoon naps.

"Is this a ghost town or what?" said Patty. "And speaking of ghosts, guess what I've been doing lately? Driving relatives to the doctor. It's endless. I think they must plan to all get sick at once. We're just about the only ones our age left around here, so we've become the official caretakers. I mean, they're nice folks, I don't mind it. But God! It gets to be a chore."

"Maybe that's what I'll end up doing."

"Well, you're lucky you've only got one. And he's probably immortal."

They were passing Beckett's house. James said, "There's Ben. Drop me here. I'll make my way back to the station on foot."

"Think you can handle the excitement?"

"I'll manage."

She slowed down barely enough for him to step out, then was off again, covering him with dust, waving out the window without looking back. Beckett was weeding his garden. He rose and stretched his back as James entered his yard. He said, "Risking your life driving with Patty, I see."

"Just a little taste of life in the fast lane."

Beckett arched his back and massaged it with both hands. "I'm just old enough to consider giving up my garden and just foolish enough to keep at it. Let's go inside and have some coffee."

Coffee and literature were Beckett's two unbreakable habits. He drank his thick brew regardless of the heat or time of day. Once James became familiar with his habits, he realized Beckett was far more often to be seen with a coffee cup than a wine glass, though his capacity for alcohol seemed on occasion boundless. James accepted a cup out of politeness but let it cool. Beckett reclined in his easy chair, simultaneously fanning himself and pouring the steaming liquid down his throat.

"It's probably about time I gave up gardening. If your time's worth anything to you, it really doesn't pay. Then in the fall you have to either can the stuff or let it rot. The last few years, I've been giving most of it away. I think this year I won't even bother to pick it. Just invite people in to take what they want, then plow the rest under and forget about it. *Requiescat in pace.*"

"Amen."

"Correct response. Thank you. Oh, well, it's only the last of many hobbies. It's probably time for me to start thinking of getting rid of everything. In a few years, maybe I'll just open the doors and give it all away: clothes, furniture, books, appliances."

"Be sure to call me when the books go."

"I'll do that. But it has a kind of appeal, don't you think? Stripping things down to the last essentials: a chair, a table, a pencil, a man writing on his last piece of paper."

"You'd need a coffee cup, too."

"Oh, amen to that."

"Well, hence, coffee, water, kettle, stove, fuel—"

"Yes, yes, and a pot to piss in. But I'm talking about a master image here, not necessarily pure fact. A way to see what's most yourself."

Beckett looked rather worn and tired. His face was still red from working in the heat. James wondered if he thought himself as near to his end as he was hinting, and if the end was really purpose and goal or simply an ordinary human final end.

Beckett reached for his pipe and continued musing. "Believe it or not, when I first came here, I meant to devote myself entirely to domestic crafts: grow my own food, weave clothing, build furniture. I even bought a goat to milk. O, pioneers!, you know."

"Sounds ambitious."

"You wouldn't believe the time and effort involved! Well, I couldn't do it. Oh, I *had* the time and I *could* take the trouble, but when you walk by the grocery store every day you start to wonder what the point is."

"Then there's the difficulty of raising coffee beans in Minnesota, growing grapes."

"There is that. Always be a flaw in the pattern, you see. But, mostly, I just wasn't cut out for it. I decided if this society was good for anything it was for taking the necessities off your back. So I gave that business up. Gardening's all that's left. I was then going to devote my life to photography."

"Back to technology, in other words."

"Bizarre, no? Well, to make a long story short, I eventually found myself driven home to literature. I couldn't stay away. Paper, pen, forming those little black signs, getting your mind to dance in step. Couldn't live without it. Had the habit. Harmless enough, anyway."

"That was your idea? To be harmless?"

"There are worse things. But, no, the goal was just to do it. And in such a way that reflected where I had come—well, where we'd all come. I once wanted to be a novelist, did I tell you? I have a ridiculously large stack of manuscripts somewhere."

"I'd like to read one."

"You can't; no one can: they're unreadable. I wouldn't press them on the most bored person on earth. Absurd plots. I blush to say it, but I seriously looked forward to making money with them."

"I'm shocked."

"Scandalously naïve, I know, for a man of my background and experience. But illusions die hard. I remember the last one I wrote. I thought it was my ticket to fame and fortune."

Despite himself, Beckett grew animated at the wakening memory of one of his fictive children. He put down his coffee and gestured broadly with his pipe, tracing abstract patterns of smoke which hung about him in the still air. "It dealt with two fundamentalist Christian students at a Texas Bible college. They couldn't forgive the evangelists for not making the gospels exhaustively detailed, factual accounts of the life of Christ. They wished they had been there, you see, with video cameras—from the quickening womb to the empty tomb, as it were. Would have had it all, settled all the arguments, asked all the right questions, nothing left to chance. Anyway, they're determined this will never happen again. But how to know what's significant? They tape as much as they can of everything around them. But that's a little spotty to satisfy a really deranged intellect. So they make a pact to tape only each other. Even then, though, *action*, the *point* of activity around them, is a little elusive. So then they have to scale down their lives—to fit the camera. Clever, no? Well, they end up sitting in a room, face to face, taping each other. Their own contribution to the foundations of later Christian witness. Starve to death. The ending's a little sensationalistic, but the book had its moments. Revenge of life on facts."

"Sounds intriguing. But not exactly tailored to the best-seller lists."

"An understatement, young McGrath."

James thought of Beckett's phone numbers and wondered if this were a case of an author turning into his characters. But Beckett continued his reverie and he didn't interrupt him.

"At any rate, all that's behind me—along with teaching, woodwork, goat milking, cameras, weaving. It makes me feel rather fit and trim—simply to have left behind so much. I recommend it. Unclogs the mind." Beckett relit his pipe. "What a chatter about nothing. I really must be getting old and foolish. More coffee?"

"No, thanks. I'm going to be on my way."

"Greet your aged parent for me. I think I'll treat myself to another cup before I face that damn garden again."

"Take it easy, Ben."

On the way to the station, James thought of Patty and Beckett. He had become attached to both of them, and their charm for him seemed to come directly from their struggles with the life around them. Beckett did seem to have reached a kind of equilibrium with his epic retreat from human puttering and his focus on a narrow self-dictated task. It was an equilibrium that James envied and mistrusted at once.

Danny was struggling with his inventory when James entered the station. "Greetings, gringo," he said. "And God make you prosper for giving me an excuse to take a break. Shit. No matter what I do, this stuff comes out wrong every month. You don't think Patty could be drinking the oil, do you? At the rate of, say, a quart a day? Some sort of aberrant urge connected with the menstrual cycle?"

"Sounds unlikely, but I'll ask her if you want."

"Where the hell could it go? Well, screw it. Who cares? It's not like a case or two is going to make any difference. I'd just like everything to check out. Just once, to restore my faith in mathematics."

They slumped together on Patty's Cadillac seat. James said, "I didn't think anything worried you."

"Hmm? You mean my inventory? Oh, 'worry' is putting it a little strongly."

"I have this idealized picture of you: always calm, always smiling. The world's going up in flames around you and you're wondering what all the fuss is about."

"Sounds like me. If I could convince myself my wife wasn't consuming all manner of petroleum products, I wouldn't have a worry in the world. Tell me, James: how long's it been since you've been psychoanalyzed? I'm really worried about you."

"Another worry. You're destroying my faith in things."

"Ah," said Danny, "here we sit: two of the bankrupt heirs of bourgeois capitalism in its post-imperialist phase, spinning the wheels of our minds in a vacuum."

"For want of anything better to do."

"Such as what? That's the point, I guess. Take heart, Yankee dog, better days are in store. Oh, by the way, speaking of better days, has that woman you're chasing come back yet?"

"I haven't the faintest idea what you mean. And, no, she hasn't."

"She comes and she goes." From the seat, Danny could just reach his desk with his long legs. He stretched them out, crossed his arms on his chest, and sighed. "Kathy, Kathy. I went with her once, have I told you?"

This was news to James. "No."

"Many moons ago, amigo. When we were young and merry and life was sweet. Well, not so young. About ten years ago, before I took up with the mercurial maiden I eventually wed."

"Kathy never gives out much information about her past."

"No, she doesn't. But she was just getting out of her marriage at the time. She came back here with her daughter to take care of her mother. That's her mother's house she lives in."

"What happened to her mother? And her daughter?"

"The one died, the other split. It surprised me—well, it surprised everybody that she came back. Not a person you associate with ancestral bonds. Anyway, we went out a few times. I never really cracked the shell."

"I know the feeling."

"She always seemed to go for older men. Like our friend Ben, for example."

"You're kidding me."

"No. They were really hot for a while."

"Danny, you amaze me. How do you come by all this great information?"

Danny cleared his throat. "The gas station is the rural equivalent of the confessional or the psychiatrist's couch. Of course, the confessions usually come disguised as boasts and tall tales when they aren't disguised even further. But, come to think of it, I'll bet that's true of confessionals and couches, too. I think we may be on to something here. We haven't been wasting our time after all."

"So Kathy and Ben—this was how long ago?"

"Oh, a few years now. As I said, she comes and she goes. Even so nimble a mind as my own starts to lose track of things after a while. I can't really recall the sequence of all her escapades."

"Sounds like she's been around."

"And then some. The first time I met her husband—this was before we went together—I was delivering some fuel oil to her mother. I walked in with the bill and there he sat at the kitchen table, completely naked, cleaning his machine gun. A complete lunatic."

"Whatever happened to him?"

"I think he died, but I'm not sure how. I don't think it was violent. Come to think of it, I'm not even that sure he's dead. She doesn't say much about it."

They were silent for a time, James trying to imagine Kathy's life, Danny at peace, regaining his composure from his botched inventory.

"Hey, Danny," James finally said, "Patty asked me this morning why I was staying here—"

"The woman *will* pry. I'm sorry, but there's nothing I can do about it."

"Well, okay, but I was going to ask you the same question."

Danny smiled. "Patty's always after me to move out."

"So I've noticed."

Danny raised his right hand. "But wherever you go, you always take yourself with you."

"Yeah. I've heard."

Danny raised his left hand, then extended both in a gesture of happy, comfortable futility. "So why waste a trip?"

Chapter Fifteen

If familiarity begets ignorance, and if the taking of even the unusual for granted is part of having a home, then James and New Culloden were becoming familiar to one another and he was beginning to feel about this place as he had once felt about his apartment, or at least the elevator up to it. He was noticing less and less.

The most outstanding thing that he was failing to notice was the increase in litter to be found each morning in the yard. Madison assumed that James was either unobservant by nature or overly accustomed to filth. Whatever the reason, James usually didn't notice it. And when he did, he dismissed it with the thought that his father had reserved the disposal of garbage for himself. And Madison did dispose of it, often before James was up.

In contrast to his son, at least in his own eyes, Madison McGrath was the most observant of human beings: no detail escaped him, and no hidden pattern could resist his deductive powers.

In his legal practice, he managed to see through the stories of his clients and had to defend them in spite of his knowledge of their guilt. Indeed, a lifetime devoted to the law had convinced him that most people were, if not guilty as charged, at least guilty enough or more than enough. But he feared, more than the release of a few petty criminals, the arrogance and the often equal guilt of a police state, which his beloved republic—cheered on by various strains of vermin—was always tempted to become. Shorn of their power and judged simply as students of human nature, the police were without equal. If McGrath wanted an analysis of a human situation, he would much rather consult a police officer than a psychoanalyst. Through the vicissitudes of post-war American wandering and moral confusion, the police had shown a remarkable ability to stay in touch with reality.

This did not keep McGrath from despising their authority and thwarting them whenever he could. But he was, in his way, a fair and generous man and gave credit where it was due.

He also recognized the limits of power, most immediately in the case of his increasing litter. His perspicacity led him to conclude that his enemy, the crop duster, was behind it, goaded into further malice by rumors of McGrath's campaign and the two or three not very abusive letters McGrath had sent him.

The ultimate and final settling of this pilot problem still lay beyond some distant horizon. But McGrath was being drawn to some less than ultimate solution, one which would raise his status from hapless victim to combatant. Guerrilla warfare seemed the most promising thing. He was saving the litter, carefully bagged and stored, for a massive counterstroke. In the meantime, other irritations bloomed to maturity, thriving on the heat of summer as did the crops and wild vegetation, though without the promise of certain death later in the year.

First among them was James, his wayward and probably irredeemable son. A much lesser mind than McGrath's could have grasped by now that James had lost his last job through some act of egregious stupidity and that he was floundering with nowhere to turn. The precise details no longer interested McGrath, consumed with the nuisance of another human presence and the eagerness to be rid of it. All McGrath wanted from James now was the date of his departure.

All he got was maddening provocation. Einar Ekdahl was actually parading his alliance with James as the greatest boon to New Culloden since the damming of the river. (Put in less laudatory terms, McGrath would agree with the comparison.) The work James had done researching and applying for grants had begun to bear fruit.

Every public building, every city lot, and many not so public buildings and lots could now thank Ekdahl for a new flagpole. Ekdahl's own yard could boast a half-dozen, two of them flying the Canadian flag, to make tourists from Manitoba feel even less like they had left home than they usually felt in Northwestern Minnesota.

James had also landed, through a deft juggling of population figures and a vague statement of boundary lines, a pair of urban renewal grants from a downstate commission that had little idea of what life was like on the Canadian border. Houses that should have been fire-bombed, or at least condemned, were now being repainted with money from a neighborhood redemption project. Since the actual painting still required human effort, and since such effort would require the loss of time spent wandering aimlessly to the gas station or watching daytime television, Ekdahl was forced to do most of the work by himself.

James' other grant allowed the mayor the time to do this: it provided for the hiring of a dozen underprivileged teenagers to do the menial jobs that usually claimed Ekdahl's time. For the first time in history, both of New Culloden's riding mowers were in operation at once. This lasted for a week or so, until the unsupervised children began sneaking away to drink and dally with one another. Soon Ekdahl was mowing lawns well into the long Northern Minnesota evenings after a day of house painting.

But the mayor was in his glory. Buoyed by all the activity and energy he saw around him, most of it his own, he had begun to buy up property near the lake, planning for the day when he could establish a shopping mall there.

He stopped McGrath on the road one day, paint brush in hand, to interest him in the project. "Madison," he said, "speaking as a fellow citizen, you know, someone involved in public life, don't you think a shopping mall would do a lot for this town?"

"No."

"Well, it would get people interested, you know, pull in business."

"Don't be absurd."

"You could even have an office there, endless possibilities."

"Do I strike you as a merchant or have you completely lost your mind?"

"You rascal! No, an office, you could have your office there."

"I have an office."

"Oh, you have an office, sure, but you could have a place where people could drop in, you know, you'd have more visibility."

"Drop in? You mean without an appointment? How repellent. And I'm quite visible enough, thank you." He glared at the mayor. "More so than I wish."

"Just think about it, you know, it doesn't hurt to consider things. Always open to new ideas."

"Let me ask you something, Einar. Where's the money coming from for this mall?"

"I've put up my own so far but there's lots of interest, lots of interest. You know, if you believe in something, you get behind it."

"Thanks for the lesson in progress," said McGrath and went on his way.

It was among people such as this that Madison McGrath was forced to spend his life. He had begun to blame it all on James and he would never forgive him for it.

That evening, he was offered a chance to strike back at Ekdahl. He received a phone call from the outraged mother of one of the teenagers who had been hired for the summer. The family was hardly underprivileged but they were equal to James in juggling financial data. James, who kept hoping someone would call to offer him a miraculous new life, rushed downstairs when the phone rang and stayed to listen in.

"I must say," said McGrath, "this sounds incredible even for our illustrious mayor. Why would he cut off your son's toes? Was there some provocation?... Well, for example, was he walking in his food?... Ah, the lawn mower. But what was he doing underneath it?... Then why didn't he hear it coming?... Could you elaborate on 'busy'?... I see, I see. Was there an injury to the young lady as well?... Shorter legs, I imagine. A pity—I mean, for your son... Sue? Of course, we can sue. Come and see me tomorrow at eleven.... Yes, and my sympathy to your son. Goodnight."

McGrath clapped his hands in glee. "Now he's done it. That cretin you work for was out there in the dark mowing weeds while two of his alleged employees were involved in, let us say, more personally rewarding pursuits. Their ears filled with sweet nothings, undoubtedly dazed as well by drink, they were deaf to his approach. Turned the boy's foot to ground beef."

"My God."

"Spare yourself. I know the family. Nothing they've ever done requires feet. But he's mine, Ekdahl's mine! I'll show that imbecile, that buffoon, that self-important Norwegian menace—"

James could only take so much of this. "Show him what? What are you going to show him?"

"Ah, forgive me. I forgot I was speaking to his right hand man, his prince, his heir, the jewel of his work force, his boon companion and partner—wait: partner? partner? Do I smell a co-defendant? Someone whose moronic endeavors are equally liable for the injuries inflicted on this innocent lad? Someone as culpable as the careless driver, someone who placed the instrument of destruction in his hands, who set the scene, who put the actors in place for the tragic finale?"

"You're going to sue *me*?"

"Why are you working for that lunatic?" screamed McGrath.

"What is your problem?" screamed James.

And, in truth, neither knew the answer. But from that moment, James began to think his father was not simply eccentric, not simply irascible, but completely off his rocker.

The foot case was settled quickly, out of court, despite McGrath's efforts and to his great disappointment. Because the accident had occurred outside the boy's normal working hours, and because Ekdahl was operating his equipment in almost complete darkness, an ungrateful city and an indifferent state left him to fend for himself. Eager for cash, the family settled for what Ekdahl could get from a second mortgage on his house.

James, who did believe his father was capable of suing him, was relieved to find he had not. But he was not entirely untouched by the consequences of this episode.

The cool conversations of the townspeople, burying equal amounts of affection and anger, had become even more frigid around him. Less and less was he asked if it was hot enough for him or if he thought it might rain. Curiously, he found he missed this austere badinage. He had done nothing, but everyone—both Ekdahl's partisans and his father's few supporters—seemed to blame him for the animosity that was being stirred up. He sensed that he had been claimed by struggles that transcended the simple, normal choices he was trying to make.

Chapter Sixteen

His life brightened a little near the end of August when Kathy finally returned. Her first night back, they had a few drinks at the *Mudhole*. As she walked him home, he complained about the tensions he felt, the rage of his father, the haplessness of Ekdahl, his own pitiful lot. "I mean," he said, "I feel like I'm not getting to settle anything for myself, like my life is stuck on somebody else's desk, waiting for God knows how many decisions to be made by God knows how many people. And anything I do, any dumb little thing, gets sucked into somebody else's big issue."

"James, is this a prison sentence you've got here or what? Leave. Take off. You're free. Go."

"It's not that simple."

"It's just that simple. That's your problem. Your life's on somebody else's desk? If it is, you put it there."

"Oh, c'mon. I don't control these people."

"Right," said Kathy. "But they control you. So whose fault is that?"

"Theirs. There's more of them."

"But there's just you to worry about you, and just you for you to worry about."

"Maybe my head's a little fuzzy. Say that again."

They were at the driveway to his house. The moon had just cleared the trees ahead of them. It was full, golden, large, unreal in its serenity and unique solitude. Kathy said, "Look. There it is. There's peace and rest. That's what you need. Why don't you go there?"

"The moon? I grant the attraction, but I'm a little old for the space program."

"You're hopeless, James. I'm not sure I can save you."

It was time to leave her again, and he didn't want to. He never knew when he would wake to find she'd left town, on some journey she would never discuss. He put his arm around her shoulder and started up the driveway. She moved easily against him. He saw something fitting in Kathy walking him home. With her, he felt very much the privileged partner, waiting on her whim and pleasure. He thought: well, if she tries to kiss me or have her way with me, who am I to resist?

But there was something in the driveway. Some things. A lot of them. James and Kathy stopped. "What on earth?" she said.

They were white, bag-like objects, dozens of them. The blatant abnormality of the apparition could make any explanation plausible. Perhaps some lunar James, some interplanetary melancholic, burdened by who knows what extraterrestrial longings and puzzles, had looked at planet Earth one lonely night and decided to come *here*, and this was his luggage.

Kathy moved closer, James following. The white, immobile objects in the moonlight looked eerie, foreboding. James wouldn't be surprised if they started to glow, leap, spit fire, metamorphose into something worse.

Kathy kicked one. "Well, shit. They're garbage bags."

James walked among them, bewildered. "What do you suppose is in them?"

"*Garbage*," hissed a voice beyond them. James was certain his heart stopped.

His father stepped out of the shadows. Blackstone was at his side. McGrath wore a black turtleneck and had a black knit cap pulled low on his forehead. This is it, thought James. He's flipped. They'll say I drove him to it. Damn this miserable world.

"Madison! How rakish," said Kathy. She sounded delighted, as though she met lunatics every day and always looked forward to it. "What are you up to?"

"Call it a redistribution of unnatural resources. Call it a small payment on an account past due. Call it justice. I'm putting this stuff back where it belongs. I can do it myself, but if you're game I'd be happy for assistance."

"Why not?" she said. "Lead the way."

"Whoa," said James. "What's going on?"

McGrath sighed. "If you can recall ever being up before noon, you might remember a fair amount of litter on this property. Well? Ring a bell?"

"I guess. So what?"

"So did you think it was accidental? A shift in continental wind patterns? It was deliberate and malicious mischief. Tonight, I'm going to—let's say I'm going to restore someone else's property. An act of benevolence."

"Then why by night? Why the get up?"

"I'm a busy man. And it might get cool."

"Dad—"

"Here, I made some slings. They go like this. One over each shoulder and you've got four bags. Then one in each hand and we each carry six. They're light, I kept the loads small. We'll have to go by foot. But with three of us, that's only—four trips."

"*Four trips*? To where, for God's sake?" cried James.

"Keep your voice down." McGrath was hoisting his bags.

Kathy punched him in the ribs and whispered, "Live a little, James."

"Live a little? Live a little? This makes sense to you?"

"Follow me," hissed McGrath. "We'll avoid the main roads. If you get separated, keep the moon on your right, bear northeast."

"But *where* are we going?"

But McGrath was moving out, Blackstone at his heels. Kathy was chuckling. "What a great old coot your father is."

"Oh, right. He's only flipped his lid, that's all."

Kathy was loaded. "He's right. They're light. Coming, James?"

"Fuck. Why me? Why me?"

"Because you're *here* and not *there*, James. It's still just as simple as that."

"Okay. Wait up."

"You hurry up. I don't want to lose him." She ran off.

"Fuck." But he loaded up and caught up with her and soon they had overtaken his father.

McGrath was crouched at the end of his property, still in the trees, peering into the quiet darkness of unsuspecting New Culloden. He turned as they crowded behind him and in a high-pitched whisper that raised goose bumps on James' flesh he recited the only lines of poetry James had ever heard come out of his mouth:

"Scots, wha hae wi' Wallace bled,

Scots, wham Bruce has aften led,

Welcome to your gory bed,

Or to victorie."

Blackstone, his ignorant blood catching the thrill of the hunt, shot into the darkness ahead of them. McGrath gestured forward with his arm and trotted after him. Kathy followed, and James, reluctant, furious, and terrified, trailed along.

Of course, he thought, let's all follow the dog.

They moved across lawns, over fences, through hedges, and around the hulks of useless vehicles in overgrown lots. They glided silently past dark houses, lit within by flickering television screens, like humorless and extravagantly pathetic jack o' lanterns. Then they were in a drainage ditch alongside the crop duster's landing strip, and this was where they were going. The plane stood outside its hangar. The hanger's doors were open.

Everyone is vulnerable, thought James. Isn't it stupid how much we depend on one another? "Drop your loads," said McGrath. "We'll leave them here until we transport all the bags. Same route. It'll be safe since this is our first strike."

First strike? *Strike?*

"Too bad about the moon," continued McGrath. "But we have surprise on our side. And justice. *Let's go.*"

By the third trip, James' pace was slowing. Kathy lagged behind to keep him company. McGrath passed them on his way back. "*Hurry.* I'll wait for you at the house with the last load. I don't want to be lying in that ditch wondering where you are. It's midnight. Come *on.*"

So they hurried, James understanding the hurry even less than he understood his participation. Almost within sight of the ditch, Kathy and James were scampering across a street when someone hailed them.

"Well, hi!"

James screamed, jumped a foot, dropped his bags, and tripped. He reflected that he fell a lot in New Culloden. His father was probably affecting his inner ear.

"Calm down," whispered Kathy. "Act nonchalant."

"Nonchalant?"

"Hi, Tim," she said aloud. "Beautiful night, isn't it? Don't you love the moon?"

It was Tim Franklin, the Lutheran pastor. He sauntered up with his hands in his pockets. He smiled broadly at Kathy, then glanced at James lying on the ground, then frowned at the garbage bags. "Uh—yeah. What's—uh, what's up?"

Kathy looked at James, James at Kathy. She hefted her garbage bags. James rose. Kathy took a deep breath, then was overcome with laughter. She kept trying to speak, Tim waiting with a puzzled smile, but it was all too funny for her. Finally, she gasped, "Tim—you don't want to know."

James was still a long distance from a humorous perspective and likely to remain so. He said, "We could tell you, and you might even believe us. But it still wouldn't make any sense. And she's absolutely right: you do not want to know."

Tim nodded, thinking he was being teased. But he looked at the bags again. Kathy shrugged. And the desolation in James' face finally convinced him that he wouldn't want to know and that he probably didn't want to be around to find out either. "Well—" he said slowly, "I guess I'll see you guys around."

"I guess you will," said Kathy.

"If only in the newspapers," added James when he'd left, "or on the wall of the Post Office. Wanted: dead or alive. Preferably dead. This is the suspect's own preference. Not very dangerous but incorrigibly stupid."

"Too bad they don't execute people for excessive melodrama. Your troubles would be over."

McGrath was fuming when they returned to pick up the last load. "Where have you two been? We've still got to unload. Get the last of it and follow me."

There were only four each for Kathy and James this time. McGrath held two larger bags, bulging and evil smelling.

"What's in there?" asked James.

"A little contribution of my own. Oh, and Blackstone's as well. Call it a dividend. It should go nicely in the cockpit."

"Dad—"

"Forward!"

Blackstone had vanished after the first trip. Some sixth sense of imminent frolic had guided him back now and he rejoined the party when they arrived at the ditch. He lay alertly at McGrath's feet.

James looked at the bags surrounding him. He could scarcely imagine the amount of refuse they contained. A lifetime of fastidious behavior had not prepared him for this moment.

"Alright," said McGrath, "This is it. I'll go first. I'll do the actual dumping. Take the same loads. Drop the first loads in the hangar, then the next loads at thirty paces short of that and so on. I'll start on the plane, then proceed to the hangar and work my way back. When you drop the last load, take off. We'll meet at the house. Clear?"

"Dad—"

"Roger that," said Kathy.

McGrath scrambled out of the ditch with his two bags of organic death. James looked at Kathy. "We really aren't going to do this, are we?"

"And miss the fun? Where's your spirit of adventure?"

"Maybe I didn't get the right genes."

But Kathy was on her way, too. Blackstone peered down at James from the edge of the runway. Oh, well, thought James, it's only garbage. It's not as though we're murdering somebody. He hoisted his bags.

Kathy passed him on the way to the hangar. She was breathless, alight with excitement. She slapped him on the back. When he passed the plane, McGrath was leaping from the wing and heading on. The odor drifting from the cockpit was like the breath of Satan. At least he's a lawyer, thought James. He can defend us if we're caught. But his fees are probably outrageous.

McGrath was emptying Kathy's bags across the hangar floor. Milk cartons, newspapers, meat wrappers, vegetable bags, cereal boxes, plastic bottles, tin cans, candy wrappers, and chicken bones tumbled away from him like some inept, monstrous creation. James dropped his bags at his feet and ran for the ditch. Less to go this time. Faster I do it, faster I'm done. Home to shower, read, stare blankly at the police—who? *me?*

Blackstone was dashing from one side of the runway to the other, weaving in and out of the bags Kathy and James were dropping. Suddenly, obeying some inscrutable impulse, he began to bark.

"Quiet," hissed McGrath.

Three quick barks, followed by two more. Three, two. Three, two. Again and again. A sense of rhythm? wondered James. A code? Some message that needed to be delivered just here, just now?

McGrath was falling back on the ditch. They could see the white bags rising in his hands and fluttering as they emptied. Blackstone continued to bark.

"I suppose," said James to Kathy, "he's been trained to foil lawbreakers."

They could hear McGrath shouting something about loyalty.

Some lights went on in a house behind the hangar. Kathy elbowed James and pointed. "That's where he lives."

"Who?"

"The guy whose property we're trashing, dummy."

"Great."

McGrath was almost finished. He was at the last pile of bags. James and Kathy waited in the ditch, too entranced to leave. Blackstone, for reasons of his own, had stopped barking. They could hear him running again in the darkness.

It was at this moment that Kathy saw the door of the pilot's house open, that McGrath lifted the last bag, that Blackstone vaulted the ditch and headed for home, that James saw what might be a shotgun barrel protruding from the open door, and that Einar Ekdahl's pick-up truck appeared on the road that paralleled the runway, freezing Blackstone in its headlights.

He was headed home late, last lawn of the day mown with undoubtedly less precision than he wished, and he was probably weary, no doubt bleary-eyed, his mind dwelling either on the day's work or the new day's coming glory, in any case not watching where he was going, blinded by memory and by hope, severed from night, road, truck, dog, awestruck audience, and shotgun.

They heard it fire.

"Who'd he hit?" asked James, his eyes closed.

"He fired in the air," said Kathy, then she cried, "Look out!"

Blackstone, picking an unfortunate moment to make a stand or simply transfixed by the lights, stood his ground. She closed her eyes.

Ekdahl braked, awakened by the blast. McGrath slid into the ditch. They saw the shotgun lower at the most evident troublesome object, Ekdahl's pick-up. Blackstone crouched, baring his teeth.

Ekdahl swerved, he lost control on the gravel, he bounced across the ditch. Blackstone stared after him, contemptuous, victorious. Ekdahl missed McGrath by inches. Another blast, sparks flew off the hood.

The truck was headed for the plane, on a collision course. Ekdahl's mind was not keeping pace with events. Or perhaps he was distracted by all the litter dancing before his headlights. With more than enough time to turn, to brake, even to coast to a stop, he was speeding toward the plane as if drawn by a magnet of destiny. Maybe they were going to murder somebody after all, thought James. Or at least help.

Another blast, followed by a tire blowing. McGrath said, "Pretty good shot for an alcoholic."

Out of control again, Ekdahl barely nicked one wing and sailed on into the hangar. McGrath shook James and Kathy. "Time for bed, children. Follow me."

They crossed the road crouching low, to the sound of shattering wood, crunching metal, and human curses. Blackstone wagged his tail when he saw them.

James stopped, fearing for the mayor. But he could see him climbing from the cab and waving his arms. The other man was screaming, shaking his fist.

Kathy yanked his arm. "C'mon, James. Only a real loser would let himself get caught now."

Despite himself, running after her in the wake of all this made him feel giddy.

He wondered, out of all the things he might wonder, if sharing this night would make it any easier to get her into bed.

He doubted it. The moon was higher, paler now, but still serene. It looked more inviting than ever.

Chapter Seventeen

McGrath got out his most precious bottle of scotch for a small victory celebration once they had made it back. He held up his glass for a toast: "Here's to order, sanity, proportion, and right."

A curious toast, thought James, for a curious evening. But he drank and, after a few more drinks, began to lose a little of his anxiety. It was good, and rare, to see his father in a jovial mood. Though not that rare, it was still very good to have Kathy sitting next to him with her hand on his thigh.

There was a sense in which this evening was no more than a logical consequence of Madison McGrath's involvements and his ire, and James let it go at that. McGrath himself would have argued the same position, more eagerly and forthrightly. What he had done was a simple extension of his values and his routine.

That it was an extension along an axis that led to chaos, that it was a logical consequence so extreme as to be absurd, as only extremely logical consequences can be, was dimly apprehended by James but quickly dismissed in the euphoria of personal survival and general conviviality.

After an hour of retelling the night's events from their own perspectives, they sank into their own silences over their glasses. Eventually, Kathy shook herself and rose. "It's a shame to end a night like this because nothing I could possibly do tomorrow can match it, but I really have to go." She stretched and yawned. "Whoo! I hope I make it home alive."

"I'll walk you," offered James.

"No—I walked *you* home, remember? If we keep that up, we'll be wandering forever."

"There are worse things."

"Like?"

"Uh—how about: walking home alone?"

She nuzzled his hair and kissed him on the forehead. "The serene heart is never alone, James."

He felt bright and happy at her kiss, but then she gave his father an identical kiss. McGrath beamed. James was deflated.

"Let out the dog, would you, my dear?" asked McGrath.

"Sure. And call me if you plan anything else. I wouldn't have missed this for the world."

James reflected on that. For the world? Well, for the *world*, he would have missed it, certainly. Perhaps even for—say, North America. Perhaps not for Texas or Nebraska or Arkansas, but for Minnesota or even Virginia, he would have missed it. Certainly.

Maybe that was his problem with Kathy. Maybe he was too dull. Maybe she needed adventure. Maybe she'd marry his father. He could accept her as a step-mother. James wondered how she felt about incest. Christ. It was time for bed. He left his father washing the glasses and climbed to his room.

McGrath tidied up. Beyond the hatred of leaving a mess, it was a way of prolonging a satisfying evening. He touched his forehead, surprisingly pleased at the memory of Kathy's lips. Then he checked the locks, turned off the lights, and retired to his room.

Out of habit, he reached to his stomach to undo the buttons of his vest. For a moment, he was disoriented, tugging at the wool of his sweater. Of course, he recalled, I'm wearing a sweater. I changed earlier. Then he reached up to undo his tie.

This second mistake made him snort with irritation. He felt a pressure on his head. At first he thought he might still be imagining her kiss and he felt childish. Then he realized it must be from his cap. He thought he had removed it earlier. He reached up to pull it off. Then he forgot what he was doing and reached again for his tie.

Chilled with terror, he turned to his mirror. He wasn't wearing a cap. But the pressure was increasing, like a thick belt tightening round his skull. He put his hands up to massage his temples. In the mirror he saw his left arm still hanging at this side.

Then he thought he raised his arm but he found himself sitting on the floor. He took a few deep breaths, waiting for the next treacherous report from his nervous system. But everything seemed stable now. He knew what he was wearing. He moved his arms, made fists. Everything seemed normal. He stretched his legs and they seemed fine. The pressure in his head was gone. He stood up and looked in the mirror. He saw nothing unusual.

Until he noticed the clock. Four-thirty. But it had been wrong before. He went back through the house, turning on lights and peering at his timepieces. Despite the usual early morning discrepancies, they were all close enough to give him pause. He must have been sitting on the floor for two or three hours.

He went to the kitchen to pour himself another drink. This was what he got for thinking about young women. Kisses, indeed. This was what he got for having a son. Perhaps he had overextended himself.

Nonsense. He sipped his scotch and looked out the window. He could hear birds chirping. The sky over his garage was growing lighter. He swirled the whisky in the glass and sighed.

It wasn't nonsense. It was the inevitable defeat of the mind by the body, intellect's retreat from organic breakdown. It was age and sickness and stupidity and death and he hated all of it and he hated himself for being a slave to it. He hated it and he feared it. Incapacity. The drooling lip and the drifting eye. The return to diapers and the hands, unloving now, not maternal, of women, most of them only a step away from being institutionalized themselves, less intelligent than Blackstone.

He shivered, then downed his drink. He needed sleep. He was never this morose unless he was tired. If he started worrying about the relative excellence of his prose style, he would know he'd been up far too long. What he had been worrying about he dismissed from his mind as he rinsed out his glass. Things like this happened to everyone. It was nothing to be concerned about.

After using the bathroom, he again turned off the lights and entered his room. This time he undressed without confusion and snorted derisively at his own fears. He was fine. He had probably only fallen asleep. He would think no more about it. He got into bed and fell asleep in the proper place.

James awoke about an hour later. He was dreaming his father was chewing him out for some unexplained but inexcusable offence. But he wasn't dreaming. He was alone in his room, but he could hear his father's voice. It was faraway, but—there it was again—he could hear his own name.

Frightened, he jumped up and stumbled down the stairs. Maybe what he thought was anger was a cry for help. When he got to the ground floor, he slowed down. He hadn't been wrong: it was anger. The voice was surly, guttural. McGrath must be talking in his sleep, chewing out his son in his sleep.

This is the limit, thought James. But he crept to his father's room to make sure. The door was open a crack. James pushed it open slightly more. The room stank of sweat and the sourness of age.

Early dawn illuminated it. McGrath's face was white, contorted in rage. His eyes bulged under their lids. The sheets were in knots. His pajamas looked like a straight-jacket. His hands gripped the pillow, then tore at the sheets. A stream of indecipherable muttering poured from his mouth, pierced by obscenities and by James' name. Holy shit, thought James. If this is what it looks like from the outside, what's it like on the inside?

The natty, erudite, and arrogant man, who strutted like a peacock among pigs, who assumed the voice and tone of God in the absence of any other serious contenders, who sipped wine, read books, analyzed and constructed arguments, who defied nature with the acquired stance of a rigid culture, had been reduced to this smelly, quivering body of loose, clammy flesh. James would not have been more sickened and shocked if his father had turned into a cockroach. But more unnerving than the physical contortion was the thought of what must be loose within. Here was the inescapable descent into the body, its chemical reactions, its collection of horrors which cannot be bargained with or shouted down, its ugly revelations, its dominion of disorder beyond law and sense, where you meet at last the things that are hidden, in all their force and power. And one of them was named James.

James didn't know how long he watched, but McGrath finally calmed down. His breathing was slower. His face regained a human composure. James felt ashamed for watching. He felt, less clearly, ashamed for the way things had turned out between them.

His father had probably looked at him this way once. Well, knowing his father, maybe he didn't—or maybe just once, if only by accident or special request.

But he would have liked to touch somehow the man his father had been then: younger, less angry, bright, more hopeful, his own age. He would have liked to meet his father as an equal. And then—

James shrugged and turned away. Then they probably wouldn't have gotten along at all. What little bond they had now was probably the closest bond they could ever have. Things had turned out between them just the way they had turned out. Kathy would probably say it was just as simple as that, and it probably was.

Chapter Eighteen

James held his breath for a few days, waiting for the house to be bombed or for his father to begin cackling and howling as he descended completely into madness. But nothing out of the ordinary happened. God, who James felt had a special fondness for rewarding frivolity with tragedy, must have been doing her eyelashes at the time of their adventure.

He did have a slight scare one day when he came upon his father in a daze. McGrath was sitting at the table when James came down for breakfast. Used to not being answered, James eventually realized he was not being heard. McGrath's hands were flat on the table. His eyes were wide, vacant as James had never seen them.

He slowly sat down opposite his father. "Dad?"

McGrath blinked.

"Dad?"

"Read the first amendment lately?" said McGrath.

"What?"

Then McGrath came to. He looked at James, looked down at his breakfast, then glanced at the clock.

"Are you alright?"

"Why wouldn't I be?"

"Well, you seemed a little out of it. You were just staring at the wall and I couldn't get you to answer me."

"It's called thinking. Not usually visible to the untrained eye. What did you want?"

"Well, nothing—"

"So what's the problem?"

"Dad—do you ever, you know, have a check-up or anything? Yearly physical?"

"I assume you're referring to medical care. You've undoubtedly been as brainwashed as the rest of the country, but let me attempt to begin your enlightenment. There is absolutely no evidence that the human race is better off with the medical profession than it would be without it. In some cases—childbirth, for example—their successes are only relative to the early disasters they themselves brought about. They probably kill as many people as they help. And for this they expect to be paid. Paid? Enriched, endowed, honored, worshipped."

"Sure, they make mistakes. They're human, too. But—"

"Human, eh? If you're going to start flattering them, this conversation is over."

Like most of their conversations, it had been over before it began.

James considered discussing his father with Beckett or Danny but to present his worries fully would have involved mentioning their raid on the airfield. He decided the fewer people that knew about that the better.

The presence of Einar Ekdahl at the scene of the crime had evidently provided enough of a smokescreen to blunt the pilot's revenge. Or perhaps he feared too pointed a response would only call forth greater havoc. In any case, litter had reappeared on McGrath's property, but in quantities just small enough to conceal malice. Ekdahl's lawn was now getting the same treatment. Moreover, all of Ekdahl's flagpoles had been cut down one night with a pipe cutter. The stumps stood in his yard, in their concrete bases, looking like the rough beginning of a permanent barricade around some beleaguered embassy. The last falling pole had gone through his picture window, which was now covered with plywood.

Ekdahl bemoaned the rise of vandalism in New Culloden. James sympathized. But he had other things to worry about. Himself, for example. It was September now. And he was still in New Culloden.

Ekdahl's summer workers had quit to prepare themselves for the return to school, leaving him with not much of a net loss in man- and woman-power but with a feeling of loneliness. The air was cooler, if not actually cold yet. Soon what stunted trees the area possessed would be turning to their fall colors and dropping their leaves. McGrath would be selecting darker suits and carrying one of his sturdier canes. But, for James, only two incongruous facts stood out in all this autumnal realignment: that it was September and that he was still here. Apparently, he could no more change one than he could the other.

One drop of mercy finally fell upon his arid exile. His car was at last fixed. Perhaps the approach of Labor Day, bringing a reminder of the dignity of manual work, the pride of honest craftsmanship, and the tradition of American know-how, had spurred the local mechanic to triumph over the inscrutable labyrinth of the Asian engine. The bill was astronomical. But he was mobile again. He asked Kathy to dinner and a movie in Grand Forks, the nearest facsimile of an urban area.

He drove over roads of her choosing, which she assured him cut miles off the distance. The country was even more uninhabited than what he was used to around New Culloden.

Kathy was resplendent. Multiple bracelets on each arm, long ear rings, and an elaborate jeweled necklace gave a sparkle to her natural vivacity and warmth. Her dazzling costume, in place of her usual peasant garb, sang of her freedom. She dressed as she pleased, just as she did what she pleased. And if it pleased her, she could look like a queen, albeit of a small and eccentric country.

Grand Forks was about eighty miles away, so with turns, twists, gravel roads, dodging farm equipment and beet trucks, the drive took about two hours. But he had her to himself, buoyed up by the freedom and movement of the wonderful modern automobile, in a cocoon of intimacy. He rediscovered the shameless pride and power of an American male, negotiating curves with one hand on the wheel while gesturing nonchalantly to the fetching and captive female beside him.

When Grand Forks came into view, he was overwhelmed by the appearance, now to him almost magnificent, of what was only a moderate sized town. But here was at least semi-urban sleaze. Blocks and blocks of actual stores. Restaurants—plural. More than one place where people actually came to eat and drink away from their hovels. Domestic architecture that was, if still base, at least more imaginatively so. Traffic. Traffic lights, not just the odd 'yield' sign. Lanes where one could *only* turn right and not simply do as one pleased—oh, charming necessity born of commercial bounty. He had been away too long. He loved it, he loved it.

They were to eat after the movie. With Kathy's help, he found the theatre and was more impressed than he thought he could be. They were going to see *The Woman in Red*, not the greatest movie ever made, but good enough for a night out. More than good enough if it was your first night out in months.

It was a thrill to be again among people who were actively seeking out pleasure, to give himself to the music and the images of a film, to hear an attempt at clever dialogue, to gaze at the grace and the touching awkwardness of beautiful women and men. And to do all this with a beautiful woman beside him. If he didn't feel so elegant and cultured, he would have torn her clothes off in the middle of the theatre and forced himself into every opening of her body.

When it was over, Kathy directed him to a restaurant that a year ago he might have taken for granted but now struck him as a kind of inner sanctum of delight. He felt he had entered the temple of human ingenuity, where human need was transmuted into splendid luxury. And why not?

"Why not?" he said. "It's so simple. Why can't people do this all the time?"

"Here we are, James. We're doing it."

"But for the first time in how long? I've got to get back to this."

Kathy laughed. "Oh, James. You're *here*. You're already *at* this. You can be here anytime you like. What's the problem?"

"Well—don't you ever feel stunted in New Culloden?"

"We're living out your fantasies tonight, not mine."

"Oh." This spoiled his vision of happiness a little. "So what are yours?"

She spread her arms and grinned. "You see them every day. They're whatever I happen to be. When I get one, I do it. You really have to loosen up, James."

"Well, *I'm* enjoying myself tonight."

"So am I. And of course you are., You're here and of course you're enjoying it and you can do it again and there's nothing to it. You're not in Paris or London or Rome or New York, you're in tiny Grand Forks, North Dakota, and of course you're enjoying yourself, and why do you persist in feeling so miserable about it?"

He opened his mouth to reply but she held up her wineglass and stopped him. She said, "Let's drink to a lovely evening and then let's order dessert."

So, putting aside his complaints, he set out to enjoy the rest of the night. But there was always a slight abrasiveness to Kathy, a sense that one must either not raise topics around her or else be willing to combat her, that always raised a barrier before him.

But they were easy enough with one another now to be comfortable riding silently home in the car, with the night deep around them, the dashboard lights glowing and the radio playing softly. She hummed along with it occasionally. He would not have guessed that she would know old standards like "The Way You Look Tonight" or "Fly Me to the Moon," but she did. The wave of his enjoyment would find a fitting crest in a naked a"nd passionate embrace, but he couldn't help wondering if that too was only his fantasy, not hers. If his house was dark, he would invite her in for a drink and see what happened.

With about twenty miles to go to New Culloden, the night seemed to grow closer around them. He thought it might be a storm brewing but, looking out the side window, he still saw plenty of stars, no clouds at all. But his lights penetrated less and less of the road ahead.

"Am I going blind?" he asked, "Or does it look to you like things are getting dimmer outside?"

"Things?" She sat up and gazed intently ahead for a few moments. "It's definitely things. Like your two headlights. Whatever you do, don't stop."

Just then, a stop sign came into view. James stopped. The headlights dimmed to nothing and the motor died.

"Nice going," she said. "Why'd you stop?"

"Stop sign."

"James, you are so uptight. In all the dozens of miles you can see from here, do you anywhere glimpse the vaguest sign of the headlights of another vehicle, and so some *reason* to stop?"

He turned the key a few times. He couldn't even hear a friendly click, a bare flutter of an indication that he and this vehicle had been through a lot together and might reasonably be expected to summon up some sacrificial reserves of strength for one another.

"It's probably your alternator," said Kathy.

James didn't find this very comforting but wasn't sure he was meant to. It was just more useless information about the trials of life, the futile human charting of what had again gone wrong, as we awaited our own graves and the eventual death of the sun. God really knew how to kick you when you were down. He supposed sex was now out of the question.

They pushed the car, mercifully light, to the side of the road. James had never seen so black a night. It impressed him with the awful challenge most of his human ancestors had faced between dusk and dawn. At this moment, he would have dammed every river in the world for a little more widely-spread electrical power. The only yard lights he could see, those brave little beacons of isolated farms, were miles away, and there was no guarantee anyone was living there.

"Now what?" he said.

"We can wait or we can walk."

"Walk? It's probably—"

"About twenty miles. Relax. Somebody will come by. The walking's just to keep busy. Look: it's warm, we won't freeze, the stars are out, we've got each other to help fight off the wolves—"

"Not even as a joke. Please. Don't say that even as a joke."

"*Relax.* Anything we're likely to meet will be more scared of us than we are of it—well, unless we meet some homicidal maniac."

"Great."

Her laughter sounded loud, daring, vulnerable in all this lonely stillness. "So what'll it be?" she said. "Care for a stroll, or do you want to torch the car and hope somebody comes to investigate?"

"Okay. Let's walk. What really kills me is now I have to cope with this to-morrow. And send it back to that garage."

"Modern conveniences, James. They spoil us for real living. They're the masters, we're the slaves. We probably ought to torch it."

"Yeah, yeah. Let's go."

And she was right. Before they had walked very far, a truck pulled up next to them. James was getting tired of Kathy being right. The driver shouted out the window. "That your car back there? Little Japanese piece of dog shit? Well, climb aboard, kids. I'll take you home in a real vehicle. Where you headed?"

"New Culloden," said James.

"Shit. Are you ever in luck. Going right by there."

"Thanks for stopping."

"Shit, boy. I'd pick my worst damn enemy up out here. Can't leave no damn human beings on the road at night. Shit. Might need help someday myself."

James, sitting in the middle, was subjected to more of this tolerant populism, as well as an excursus on the folly of buying foreign cars, until they reached the curve into New Culloden. Kathy seemed to find it hilariously amusing.

"Next driveway's fine," said James.

"How about the little lady?"

Now that was an interesting question that had not occurred to James. He assumed she would get off with him. On the other hand, she might appreciate a ride to nearer her own home or even, given the nature of life, decide to accompany this profane gorilla on into Canada and beyond. From still another point of view, perhaps this chivalry of the road only extended to fellow males and women constituted a crude form of payment. James wasn't sure he would do very well in a fight against this person, but maybe Kathy could take care of herself.

"Here's fine for me, too," she said, giggling.

"Fine's fine, and it's all fine. Next stop's your stop."

He stopped at the driveway. They got out.

"Related to old McGrath?" asked the driver.

Since he was out of the truck, James risked saying, "Yes. He's my dad."

"Well, shit. Why didn't you say so? Tell him 'hi' from Stumpy."

"'Hi' from Stumpy."

"Yup. Best damn lawyer I ever met, your dad. Sued the mortal dog piss out of my brother-in-law for me once. Son of a bitch. Well, you tell him 'hi.'"

"Right. Thanks for the ride."

"Next time, sonny, buy American. Ask your dad. He'll set you straight on that."

Yes, thought James, on that and on so many other things. The world was so full of helpful people, eager to give such helpful advice, that he felt like throwing up. The house was dark but so were his hopes, and he turned to say good-bye to Kathy.

Then she said, "Why don't you invite me in for a drink?" and his heart leaped again for joy.

He said, "Great. C'mon," just as Blackstone leaped upon him, growling and clawing.

Dogs, much like doctors, he supposed, are as liable to make mistakes as anyone. Undoubtedly, the watchful brute, using what little intelligence he had, had expected that since James left by car he would return by car. Undoubtedly, too, Blackstone must have found it easier over the years simply to put himself into an attack mode, relative to all nocturnal pedestrians, saving the loss of precious seconds that might be wasted in useless discriminations, when a pause or an error could have mortal consequences.

All of this James was willing to concede as true. But if it was, then where the hell was Blackstone when the lawn was being trashed night after night? And how long would it take him to realize he'd goofed and let go of James' arm?

Blackstone actually calmed down much more quickly than James thought and stood regarding the newest member of the McGrath pack, puzzling over what he had done with his strange sounding, foreign smelling car. Instead of being happy about this, or being even happier that Blackstone had gone for his arm instead of his throat, or Kathy's throat, James turned his own rage and the night's repressed fury on the dog.

He grabbed his collar and yanked him up on his back feet, walking him toward the chain. Blackstone whimpered in surprise and hopped at James' side, twisting and flailing his front paws. James slammed the dog down next to his chain, fastened it roughly to the collar, and picked up one of the sticks Blackstone liked to chew on in quieter moments.

"Here, you miserable dog: see how you like being chained up all night. And don't you ever come at me like that again."

Blackstone's ears were down. His great eyeballs rolled in confusion, as though he had concluded James was losing his mind. Seeing the dog's fear, James reached the same conclusion. He dropped the stick.

Taking out his frustration on a helpless dog might be the very thing to make the woman he was with despise him completely. She had come up behind him. Now she walked past him slowly, over to Blackstone. She stooped to pet the dog. Blackstone licked her face as she stooped, and James prayed to be swallowed by the earth. One more unanswered prayer.

He was, again, utterly ashamed of himself. He took a breath and muttered, "Ready for that drink?"

She didn't look at him. She said, "You know…let's skip it." Then she walked away, back through the yard, not even going past him to the driveway. Over her shoulder, she called, "Be seeing you."

It sounded like an absolute and eternal dismissal. He hoped with all his heart that she meant it literally, that this too would pass, that she would be seeing him. Then again, maybe she had been talking to Blackstone.

Chapter Nineteen

What strange rivals were sex, shame, and sleep, one always driving the others from the arena of consciousness, yet never escaping their pressure. Shame was upon him now, making sleep impossible and leaving no room for a wakeful dalliance with erotic fantasies. Yet it grew deeper and more absolute from lack of sleep, it burned more painfully because he had earned it in front of her.

James would have no peace until he talked to her again. He sat numbly in his room until he couldn't stand it anymore. He wanted to walk to her house but decided that physical presence would call up too many other factors. He needed to apologize and he didn't need to confuse the issue with wanting to stay or wondering how to go or trying to decipher the look in her eyes. He decided to call her, even though it was now 3:00 a.m.

He crept downstairs, hoping not to rouse his father. He went to the phone but couldn't find the phone book. James had rarely called Kathy, so he couldn't remember her number and he didn't want to risk anyone else's wrath in the state he was in. He looked on, under, and through every conceivable place the book could be. He couldn't believe his last hope for this night would be thwarted by a misplaced book.

Then he got an inspiration. He went back upstairs and, after rummaging through his desk, found his copy of Beckett's *Nomina et Numera*. He flipped through it and found "Frei, Kathy." It was good for something after all.

He hurried back to the phone and dialed her number. He let it ring half a dozen times, unable to believe she had gone peacefully and deeply to sleep while he had suffered all night. He counted the tenth ring. Then he was convinced she knew who it was and was deliberately ignoring him.

Finally, it was picked up. A hoarse voice said, "Hello." It was a man.

The shock of what that must mean went through James. He was humiliated. His first urge was to avoid further shame and hang up, but he hesitated and the man said again, "Hello?"

If he hung up, he would never know and he would be alone for the rest of the night with his imagination, something he'd had a taste of more than once in his life and would rather avoid. So he blurted out, "Is Kathy there? I have to talk to her."

"Who?"

Oh, God. It couldn't be anything so simple as a wrong number. Could it? He took a deep breath. "Kathy."

"Kathy who? Oh, well, that's a stupid question. Kathy whoever isn't here. In fact, no one who could conceivably be named Kathy is here. I just woke up so I can't be absolutely certain someone hasn't moved in during the last few hours, but I've been living alone for, well, years. But I'll check if you like."

"Oh, my God. This is Ben, isn't it?

"Who is this?"

"Ben, I am so sorry. This is James. I was trying to call Kathy."

"And you decided to check here first at—great heavens, three in the morning. You know, I'm really flattered."

"I must have dialed the wrong number."

"Well, it's rather dark at this hour. And we do have one or two digits in common."

"I'm really sorry."

"Good luck. I think I'll turn in."

"Sorry."

James hung up, trying to smile at his error but unable to shake the thought now of her being with someone else. He dialed her number carefully again. It was answered on the second ring. Ben said, "This wouldn't be James again, would it?

"Shit. What am I doing wrong? Maybe the phones are screwed up."

"Let me ask you something, James. You wouldn't by any chance be using my humble poem as a guidebook for this nocturnal search. Would you?"

"Yeah. I am. Why? Are there misprints?"

"Not as such, no. But there's a certain creativity in the entries. Remember: I told you this was meant for adventure."

"In other words, you mixed them up."

"Mixed them up, made them up. I really didn't want to intrude on anyone's privacy."

James took a moment to absorb this. "Ben, what's the point? They're all in the phone book anyway."

"That's not my responsibility."

"Yeah, but—what's that do to your theory about collecting?"

"It's still a collection. What else would you call it? It's just done with some poetic license. Anyway, I think it's a little late for a philosophical discussion."

"Wait a minute, wait a minute. You just happened to give yourself Kathy's number?"

"A harmless indulgence."

"Ben, you fraud."

"Found me out, have you? That's what you get for waking me up."

"Okay, okay. Well, then, is Kathy's number under your name?"

"No—I think that's the sheriff's office."

"Now I'm shocked."

"My little joke. It's full of them really. But finding out for yourself is half the fun. James, I don't mean to be rude, but I do try for an hour or two of sleep each night."

"One more question, and I know this is going to sound pretty dumb, but do you *know* Kathy's number?"

"Ah. I once did." There was a pause. "But I can't recall it. I'd look it up but I have about two hundred phone books here and I'm not sure where—but, tell me, James, why don't *you* look it up?"

"Can't find the phone book."

"Your parent probably locks it up at night. I can certainly see the wisdom of that policy."

"Ben, I really am sorry I woke you up. I didn't do it on purpose."

"Don't be sorry. I haven't had this much fun since midnight."

"Kathy's real number wouldn't by any chance be somewhere in your book, would it?"

"Certainly not. Why would I want someone to call her at three in the morning?"

"Yeah. Okay. I can think about that when I'm more awake."

"Good night, James."

"Oh—I can't resist asking: who would you get if you called my dad?"

"If memory serves, I think you'd get the Assembly of God parsonage."

"You know, when I wake up, I'm going to think this was all a dream."

"It is. Good night."

James put down the phone. He supposed he could call the operator, but contact with a human voice had punctured a little the shell of his anxiety. And the absurdity of Ben's arrangements had moved him a little from his shame and his panic. It occurred to him that this was probably the key to modern art.

He could call her or see her tomorrow. There were other human beings out there with lives just as nutty as his. If you never got what you wanted, what was the big deal? Thoughts like this whirled in his head and brought him, if not peace, at least the blunting of desire.

He returned to bed and lay awake for another hour or so. He composed elaborate speeches to Kathy, explaining how it was that life had brought him to the point of attacking an innocent dog. They all began brilliantly but on reflection struck even their author as pathetic and mindless. Maybe that hinted at the real explanation.

At last he had a thought that was practical. Blackstone was still chained up. If his father discovered him that way, James would have to explain his conduct to him as well as to Kathy. Once again he rose and went downstairs. This night was becoming memorable in ways he never imagined.

The dog looked at him with more irritation than fear when he approached. James unchained him, hoping to be perceived as a liberator or at least a deserving penitent. Blackstone, when the chain was a safe distance from his neck, looked at James haughtily and began to bark.

"Quiet."

But the dog knew when he had won and scolded James until he retreated to the house.

Accepting it as the only measure of success likely to come to him until a new day brought new opportunities, James reached his room undetected and lay down finally, resolved to offer the world no more interference. Blackstone's barking and then his father's rising gave the drifting of his mind a strangely comforting background.

He slept until the noon siren woke him, unusually late even for James. His need to do something about his car and his need to face Kathy pounced upon him like angry creditors. He felt slightly cheated again that he hadn't died in his sleep or that the dawn hadn't remade the world in a more sensible way.

The noon siren seemed to be going on and on in steady bursts. He sat up, rubbing his eyes. It was the phone. It was probably Beckett taking his revenge. He let it ring. And it did, like a rebellious slave freed at last from its overseer. So he had to rise, force his stiff legs down the stairs, and answer it.

"Look, Ben—"

"Surprise, surprise." It was Kathy.

Kathy. Miracle of miracles, the dawn had actually given him a new day. "Oh, hi. Um, listen—"

"No, you listen. Summer's almost gone. If we're ever going to run naked through the park, we're going to have to do it soon. How many good reasons can you think of for not doing it today?"

Like the fool that he was, he let his head speak before his heart. "Well, I have to do something about my car. And I was supposed to meet with Einar to do some planning for the rodeo."

"I can't believe you actually thought of some! I can not believe you're this up-tight. Nothing's going to happen to that car. How long did it take to be fixed last time? Months? So what's one day going to matter? It's as safe out there as it is in your driveway. Safer, probably. And Einar! James. *Einar*? You can meet with Einar anytime. I'm offering you adventure, romance, excitement, sex, you moron. Tell me you're going to turn that down."

She was saying everything he wanted to hear. He said, "I guess there's nothing that can't be put off."

"You guessed right. I'll pick you up in an hour."

"What should I bring?"

"Just bring yourself. My fantasy, my treat."

"Sounds good."

It sounded very good.

Chapter Twenty

It was a disaster. James would look back on it often, during the lonely months to come, as a fitting close to his summer.

He had gone out in high spirits, not only because he was with Kathy but because she was who she was. Here was a woman—a woman, yet!—who lived the simple, self-reliant, and free life he had come to New Culloden to find. And while he found himself mired in the complexities of others, she just lived it. She didn't wait for the world to arrange itself for her pleasure, she didn't complain, she didn't yearn hopelessly for miraculous saviors. She did what she pleased. She was utterly happy and utterly free. She could probably survive on dandelions and raw fish that she caught with her bare hands. If she were the only survivor of a nuclear war, and who was a better candidate?, she could probably find a way to reproduce from scratch. The woman was immense, powerful, everything he wanted to be.

And she had invited him not only for the day, but for the night as well.

Lake Culloden, the man-made horror McGrath raged against was about two miles out of town. By September, it was usually so rank and uninviting that no one, no matter how drunk, would consider getting into it. Consequently, the lake and its environs remained relatively deserted until the hard frosts of late December and early January brought out the ice-fishing crowd.

Thanks to Ekdahl, the area surrounding the lake had been developed over the years to accommodate hikers and campers who didn't mind primitive conditions. The local residents, many of whom had grown up in homes even more primitive, were impressed enough by the rude efforts of Ekdahl to refer to the area around the lake as "the park." James, who associated parks with drinking fountains, sidewalks, vendors, orchestra pavilions, jugglers, and folk guitarists, thought it more wilderness than park, if not quite the Forest Primeval.

He was pleasantly surprised and aroused when, on the drive out, she told him she intended to spend the night under the stars. Arousal faded a little when he realized that she meant it literally. She never used a tent.

"What if it rains?"

"Does it look like rain to you?"

"Weather conditions change."

"If it does, we'll get wet."

James had been thinking of more than rain but he didn't dare say so to Kathy. Tents, if they were not fortresses, were at least minimal barriers between whoever was inside and whatever might be outside. For all James knew, a pack of Siberian tigers, marooned in Alaska at the last spring thaw, then driven down through Canada by the slim pickings among the caribou herds, might at that moment be crossing the border of Minnesota, ravenous and merciless, ready to settle for human flesh. They could be in James' vicinity in a matter of hours. They were sure to hear him whimpering and, if the smell of fear would attract them, James was a goner. The presence of a tent might confuse them or distract them for a few moments while he shot himself to avoid capture.

"Did you bring a gun?" He hoped he sounded nonchalant.

Kathy thought this extremely funny. "I never use anything but a knife. I don't think it's sporting. Besides, it's unlikely that we'll have to kill anything bigger than a mosquito."

"What about—" But Siberian tigers sounded a little farfetched. "Well, what about wolves?"

"Protected species. Shooting wolves is strictly a no-no. If we meet one, we'll have to negotiate."

What about *my* species? thought James. He hoped there were liberal and ecologically concerned pressure groups among the local wolf packs that were hard at work protecting the lives of humans.

"While we're on the subject of animal life..." He cleared his throat, but finally conceded to himself that nonchalance was beyond him. "Um, are there, you know, many snakes in Minnesota?"

"Pretty ignorant of our own environment, aren't we? Well, let's see. The biggest I've seen, and I haven't really gone looking for them, was, oh, no more than six feet long."

"Ah."

"I'm kidding, James. I'm kidding. Take it easy. I didn't know you were this much of a wimp. Did you bring your teddy bear?"

"Forgot it."

"That's okay. Maybe we'll meet a real one. But watch out for the claws."

Then, too, reflected James, the lower animals might be the least of their problems. There were also human threats to consider. He had read accounts, which seemed ever more frequent, of deranged men living alone in sparsely inhabited areas who one day, out of some twisted desire for human contact, would seize a hiker or jogger or camper and keep them captive for weeks, months, sometimes years.

He hadn't bothered to tell his father where he was going. He felt the urge to call home but thought if he mentioned it he would be finished with Kathy for good.

They hadn't even arrived at the lake yet and he was a nervous wreck.

Kathy drove to the most remote campsite. Her idea of camping was a far cry from Patty's. Out of her trunk, she took two old canvas knapsacks which James didn't think could hold an adequate first-aid kit between them. She tossed one to him. "Let's go."

"Where?"

"Somewhere a little more remote than this."

"Oh. Good. But we'll come back here to camp?"

"No, we will not come back here to camp. Why?"

"Well, where's our stuff?"

"We're carrying it. A couple of messkits, some beans, some bread, some wine, a little coffee for tomorrow. What else do you need?"

"Don't you need some kind of stove and sleeping bags and, I don't know, stuff. Camping stuff." He could do without an inflatable white picket fence. But she hadn't mentioned toilet paper.

"Trust me. We'll make do. C'mon."

He was at first too apprehensive, and then too hot, too bug ridden, too wheezing and chafed and miserable to enjoy walking beside her. He hadn't dressed for this. Come to think of it, he hadn't led a life that prepared him for much of anything. Maybe the Siberian tigers would do him a favor. He hoped they were fast eaters.

In a half hour, he was as miserable as he had been the night before, though for different reasons. A half hour later, he was not only miserable but completely disoriented. If he pissed her off now and she left him, he'd never find his way back.

Southeast, he told himself, if I just keep heading southeast, sooner or later I should bump into Minneapolis or Dubuque or maybe even Chicago. He'd like to hear the Chicago symphony.

He hadn't even let himself think about what he might encounter if they did run naked through what was looking less and less like any park he had ever seen, what parasites he might pick up, bearing what strange and untreatable viral infections. He assumed she had meant that literally too. It no longer sounded quite as exhilarating. Unluckily, he didn't keep completely silent about all this.

"Whine, whine, whine," Kathy said finally. "Give it a rest."

Right.

At last they reached a kind of clearing which she declared would serve as their camp. To his surprise, James found they were on a slight elevation. Also to his surprise he could see part of the lake. He had imagined they had walked much further. He could see for miles but in all those miles he could see nothing human: not a home, not a road, not a cultivated field, not a telegraph pole, not a tower, not a beer can. He supposed that was why she had chosen it.

It was the kind of view James had only seen in pictures. The landscape itself was unimpressive but, if one forgot the lake was man made, it was its inviolate quality that demanded attention. Too bad James didn't have any to give it.

Kathy stretched her arms. She said, "Just think. It was all like this once."

How depressing, thought James. He was glad he had missed it.

She tossed her knapsack to the ground and began to undress. "Oh! I've got to get out of these clothes. Just feel that sun!"

And what did she think he'd been feeling all this time? What did she think had been boiling his brain and raising rashes on his thighs? He watched her undress, watched her shake her hair loose and stretch and coil in the sun like a happy animal, and he couldn't muster up an erotic thought, not even for the sake of politeness. Next to heat, the most evident sensation he felt was nausea. Probably, if he concentrated hard enough, beyond that he'd find a little fear of being eaten alive or poisoned or maimed. Stimulation, desire—this was not their moment.

And it probably wasn't their moment for her either. Kathy wasn't one to move toward her desires obliquely, under false pretenses. If she said she wanted to run naked in the park with you, she didn't mean she wanted to go to bed with you. If she did, you would get the message without a smokescreen. Right now, James supposed, she wanted to run naked in the park. And to think at this moment he could be sitting in the station, looking at fashion magazines with Patty and discussing modern architecture with Danny.

"C'mon, c'mon," she said, coming towards him with a child's open smile, "This is your big chance. You don't get an offer like this every day."

At least she was still in a good humor. And she was so matter of fact about her nudity that he began to give way a little before her charm.

She helped him off with his knapsack. From it, she removed a small bottle. "This will help with the bugs. It's a herbal cream. Completely natural. No deadly chemicals. Drives them off without killing them."

Well, thank God for that, thought James: the last thing I need on my conscience is a handful of dead bugs. Then he thought: but that's it—she wants to warn them off so I won't have a chance to kill them.

"Stop staring, James, and undress. Open to the world."

It wasn't as easy as it sounded or as he thought it would be. The more clothing he removed, the more awkward he felt, until he could have believed his nervous system was shutting down from embarrassment. He decided the situation was lacking in that charged atmosphere of lust which helped burst the shell of civilization. The truth was he felt extremely stupid standing there without his clothes, preparing to run down some undoubtedly snake-infested path. He didn't even like to run. How could he be expected to enjoy it in the nude?

Kathy appeared to him now in the unfortunate light of one more person making him do something he didn't want to do, in some place he didn't want to be.

He wished he were in his room reading.

She smeared some of the cream on his back, then handed him the bottle. "Let's *go*, James. Loosen up." She closed her eyes and her nostrils flared as she breathed deeply. "What a day!"

When she thought he was sufficiently coated with her humane insect warning cream, she led the way out of the clearing in what was to her a moderate jog and to James just short of an Olympic level sprint. He quickly fell behind.

His genitals flopped about with no definite rhythm that he could possibly adjust to, and he began to appreciate the ingenuity that had come up with the jockstrap. Her cream seemed to be attracting mosquitoes and there was a grasshopper snarled in his public hair. It probably carried some bizarre form of plague that doctors would confuse with venereal disease, causing him further embarrassment. He slapped it away in panic.

Then he lost sight of her. He could hear her laughing as she outdistanced him. Then all he could hear was his own breathing. His tender soles broke on knobby sticks. He stopped and bent over, gasping. She was gone, on an errand of her own delight. He wanted to die or be able to breathe, God could take her pick.

His breath came back eventually. And he received one of the more comforting insights of his life. I don't have to do this, he thought. There is no reason I have to do this. I am a free person, I am dying of fucking discomfort, I am not getting paid for it, and no one on earth can make me do this. I may not be able to solve all my problems, but I can solve this one.

He turned around and walked back to the site of their camp, such as it was, at his own pace. He felt the delicious and rare, for him, strength of resolution. But, once he was dressed, he knew he couldn't find his way back to the lake, and they had come in her car anyway. So he still had to face Kathy and the night, not necessarily in that order, grim thought, and he wasn't sure which would be worse. Probably the night, Kathy or no Kathy.

She came first. All things considered, her arrival and the subsequent mutual preparation of supper were relatively free of tension. She was doing her best to ignore his ineptitude, and he was doing his best to collaborate with her.

But when the sun was setting and they broke out the wine and he, relaxed now, tried to sit closer to her, he could feel her tense up. James looked into the fire she had built. He thought a moment, then said, "Okay. I'm not cut out for this. I admit it. I'm sorry. There are a lot of things I can't do."

Kathy shook her head slowly and said, not unkindly, "I can't believe you're as uptight as you are." And much of the evening was spent by her telling him other things she couldn't believe he was. He took most of it passively, since he was not going to be in the woods for more than one night and he formed another resolution: to avoid this woman. Well, at least for a day or two.

He concluded, smarting under her harangue, that the freedom he admired in her was not without its missionary side, that one thing she was not free of was a reforming impulse that one might not have associated with her. He knew she didn't preach like this to everyone, saving her advice as a compliment for her intimates. But it was a compliment he would rather be spared.

How American she seemed to him, then: preaching to him on a hillside, like some sweating revivalist, loud, cocky, secure in her purity of heart, anxious to lead him to the light if only he'd give her the chance. These were perhaps slightly unfair thoughts but James welcomed them as a self-protective shield.

Still, he thought, when they split up into their separate blankets and the fire was dying out and he looked at her comely form while listening for dangerous noises, still, if she was a revivalist preacher, she was the only one he ever wanted to sleep with. Except perhaps, whispered his treacherous mind, except Stephanie.

Oh, lord.

Was there something in these visionary women that made them irresistible to him? He would have said that Stephanie and Kathy were as different as night and day. But now... Who knew? Who knew? Life was amusing. You had to give it that. He fell asleep.

James awoke, uneaten and unbitten, slightly after dawn but closer than he had come in a long time. Kathy was squatting at the edge of the clearing, naked again, urinating without a trace of self-consciousness. She smiled at him.

And all his desire for her and the ease he really did have with her at times came back to him. A little late now, but he took comfort in the thought that it couldn't be the preaching that drew him to women like this. The smiles, maybe, the legs, the laughter, the tenderness, almost anything but the preaching.

Her attraction for him grew the closer they got to New Culloden. Yet the sense that he had failed her nagged at him. When she dropped him off, he said, hopefully, "I'll see you."

She only waved, though she did smile.

Later, he went up to the station to turn his misery into a comic tale for Danny's amusement. Patty told him Kathy had left town and wouldn't be back for months. He tried not to sound shocked and hoped he didn't look as surprised and hurt as he felt. "Where does she go when she does these things?"

Patty said, "California. Florida. Mexico. Wherever she wants. She's a real human being."

Danny assured him it was perfectly normal behavior for Kathy.

He went home and thought about that, and about his feelings for her. All he could come up with was the usual human confusion. Had she planned all along to go away? There was no way to know and, with Kathy, no way to know if that would make any difference.

One of the last things she had told him before she fell asleep was a dream she had had. It involved a large, smooth head appearing between her legs, its teeth buried in her crotch. "That's your problem, James. Your mind has you by the balls. You can't let it do that to you."

Last night, he had swallowed that as one more morsel of her extended analysis of his character. He supposed it was both fascinating and flattering, and very distracting, to have a beautiful woman care enough about you to analyze you.

But in the wake of her departure, he saw what he had missed at the time: it wasn't his dream she had analyzed; it was hers.

PART FOUR

*within your
great design*

Chapter Twenty-One

It was late September now.

And James was still in New Culloden.

He was tired of repeating those two phrases to himself. They weren't making any more sense together but, as the days and weeks wore on, they were making less nonsense. If he couldn't explain them, he still had to act upon them. He had to make some money. Like a leaf that had to admit it was dead, James had to let go of hope, descend to the earth, and consent to be trod upon.

The season brought other changes. Along with the leaves, golf balls were now falling on the McGrath lawn. No one had been hit yet but Blackstone had a near escape. Watching the plane come low across the tree line, by now a regular sight, Blackstone had stared open-mouthed at the falling white balls, perhaps concluding it was an early and unusual snow fall, perhaps created by the wonder-working human species, as it fell not from clouds but from an airplane. They bounced all around him, startling him with their impact. He sniffed them inquisitively, wishing not for the first time that he could fathom the purposes of the master race.

Einar Ekdahl hadn't been as lucky, having been struck on the head while he was out inspecting the site of his mall-to-be. He was hospitalized for a few days with a minor concussion. He could no more than Blackstone figure out the motive behind the bombardment. In fact, when asked, he preferred to say that a bird had dropped a rock on his head. After saying it a few times, he appeared to believe it.

James worked out the chain of events something like this: the pilot, while still carrying on his limited war against McGrath, had decided to number Ekdahl permanently among the enemy because of the night his truck had crashed into the hangar; Ekdahl provided him with further motivation by setting up a driving range on the edge of his mall site, as another tourist attraction and as an advertisement for the mall; this happened to be near enough to the airstrip to make sure a continuous supply of unretrieved golf balls would be left upon it, providing the pilot not only motivation but ammunition; by switching from litter to golf balls, the pilot would not only continue his harassment of McGrath but hopefully deflect his fury toward Ekdahl, the ultimate source of golf balls in New Culloden.

One chilly night, McGrath hurled a bucket of them through Ekdahl's bedroom window, one by one.

It was hard to blame this on anything but a fellow human being, but Ekdahl's civic spirit could not be dampened. He had high hopes for the driving range next summer. And despite a universal lack of interest in the mall, he had managed, with what little money he had left, to start construction, certain the interest would come when the presence of the building established itself. Since all Ekdahl could afford was a steel building that looked like a potato warehouse, James doubted it. Ekdahl kept James busy making arrangements for the rodeo, set now for the early spring, at the start of the rodeo season. In Ekdahl's mind, prosperity for his town was one year away, and a little ungrateful vandalism was not going to stop him.

There was much for James to observe and admire here, in this panorama of elegant schemes and steadfast determination, but none of it helped solve his personal dilemma. As he had thought, the school had no opening they could offer him in their music department. But, before he capitulated entirely and sold his body as unskilled labor, he decided to advertise aggressively as a piano teacher and voice coach, based at First Lutheran.

The response astounded him. By filling his afternoons and evenings, Monday through Thursday, he could earn a living that was, by New Culloden standards, more than adequate, even considering what his father charged him for room and board, which he had found to be, by New Culloden standards, exorbitant. Most of his teaching would be rudimentary, but there was a high school senior named Lori whom James wished he could have tutored when she was younger. He gave her lessons in both piano and voice. She had enough technique and receptivity for James to think that a year's work might carry her to a level that would be challenging for him.

He saw how much he had missed this part of his life, and he began to feel strengthened.

As a consequence of the time he was spending at First Lutheran, James got to know and to like Tim Franklin a little better. If still an idiot, he seemed a fairly affable one, harmless enough as young pastors go. In a town that could have passed for a geriatric ward, Tim was a prophet of youth and bemoaned the lack of energy and enthusiasm of his congregation. His efforts to sustain a youth group among the town's future felons and alcoholics were laudable, if not successful. He was constantly after James to lend his talents to the Sunday service, though he was too tolerant and polite to suggest that James attend.

One Thursday night, he was waiting for James after his last lesson. "You've got to help me. Our regular organist is visiting her grandchildren and our substitute's got the flu. You're my last chance. How about playing this Sunday?"

"Do it without music. It won't kill you."

"Oh, c'mon. Would it kill you to play?"

"It might."

"Okay, so it might kill me not to have music."

"That's your problem." The fact that he had begun to sound like his father was not lost on James, and it frightened him a little.

"One Sunday. Please. You know the service. It'll be a snap."

"How about Lori? I'll show her some stops to use and she can skip the pedal part."

"Believe me, I already asked her. We're talking bottom of the barrel here, James."

"Well, thanks."

"You know what I mean! C'mon. Will you do it?

So James agreed and, much as he hated to touch an instrument of such low quality, he found himself looking forward to the experience.

When he showed up early Sunday morning, Tim informed him he'd have to accompany a soloist during the offering.

"Thanks for all the notice," said James.

"We're pretty informal here. Hey, it'll be a snap. How hard can it be?"

But no soloist arrived and soon it was time to start his prelude. He went up to the organ, which was at the front of the nave, to one side of the altar.

He had found, the day before, the organ to be quite as terrible as he thought. Twice his feet had gone off the edge of the pedal board, searching for notes this particular instrument had decided to live without. Sounds that his scores demanded were simply not to be wrenched from it. Playing it was like singing with a rag in his mouth.

And yet: there he sat at the organ bench, endowed with the right to be there by a web of decisions and tacit hierarchies similar to the one that had once evicted him. And there was the congregation, accepting him and expecting something from him. There was even the little flutter in his stomach that in former days always told him it was Sunday morning.

Into this beloved knot of purposes, habits, and gifts, he began to send his notes. It wasn't great, it probably couldn't even be called music, but it seemed, just then and at last, something that was peculiarly him.

Tim tapped him on the shoulder and whispered, "The soloist is here. She wants to practice."

James frowned and hissed, "Tell her she's two days too late. She can come back next week."

"Give me a break, James."

"Give *me* a break. I'm already giving you a break. Tell this woman to get lost. I can't stop now."

"Who's going to notice? What's the big deal?" Questions like these seemed to be Tim's answer to everything.

Faced with Tim's persistence and knowing the blind determination of volunteer soloists and preferring practicing now to having her march up to the organ in mid-service, James nodded and brought his piece to an untimely end. He conceded Tim was probably right: nobody would notice. They had probably heard worse, and would again.

So, feeling like a fool, he walked back through the nave, avoiding the stares of the congregation, and went into the assembly hall to find the soloist. She was standing next to the piano. She was built like a Wagnerian heroine but James guessed she was probably short of breath.

He sat down at the piano and waited for her to hand him the music.

She said, wheezing a little, "Well, what do you want me to sing?"

He couldn't have said how many precious seconds he wasted in trying to grasp her question. Finally, he said, "You're joking, right?"

Now she looked puzzled. Humor was obviously a waste, too. Rather than strangle her, he said, "Look. Since we only have three minutes, why don't you pick this time? Let's do something you know."

"If that's alright with you—"

"That's absolutely wonderful with me. What have you got?"

"Well, I usually just sing something out of here." She showed him a little paperback titled *Your Favorite Country and Western Hymns.*

He repressed the urge to say "you're joking" again. He threw open his arms in a parody of graciousness. "Just name it."

She shuffled her feet coyly. "I thought, maybe, well, this one."

It seemed to be, insofar as any single hymn could be, a compendium of all the worst in nineteenth century church music. It carried to even lower depths the melodic and harmonic atrocities that Doane, Kirkpatrick, Lowry, and their ilk would suffer in hell for. James couldn't bear to look at the text.

"Okay," he said, swallowing hard, "Let's run through one verse and figure we can get by on that. Have you got another copy?"

"Just the one."

This was too much. "I see. In other words, no. Then how do you expect me to play and you to sing?"

"You don't know it?"

"Madam, do I strike you as the sort of person who would carry around drivel like this in his head day after day just in case he had to accompany someone?"

"I thought everyone knew this. How long have you been playing the organ?"

James took a deep breath. "Let's just say I'm not from around here."

"Well, you play it and I'll look over your shoulder. That way, if you get lost, I can nudge you easier."

Touch me and die, thought James.

But she turned out to be rather nearsighted. And since the print of her book demanded, if anything, superhuman eyesight, she and James looked like two Egyptologists on unusually intimate terms, peering at an indecipherable set of hieroglyphics. Fortunately, her voice barely rose above a whisper.

But he got through the service well enough, consoling himself with the thought that he was only a substitute, none of his friends were there, and in fifty years he would be dead, so why would anyone bother to remember what happened today?

And he didn't feel like killing Franklin when it was over, because part of him had taken a little satisfaction from it. He went so far as to smile, remark that it hadn't been bad, and, no, he wouldn't mind doing it once in a while.

This was all that the regular organist and her substitute, who, like James, had both been praying for a miracle to change their lives, needed to tender their resignations. In a week, Tim was badgering him to take over the organ full time.

"No. Absolutely not."

"It's your fault, you know, James, that I'm stuck without an organist."

"My fault? It's my fault? Explain, please."

"Well, if you hadn't shown off so much with your fancy playing, this would never have happened. Those women are afraid to come back. They think everyone will be laughing at them."

"Everyone was probably laughing already, if they're that bad, which I doubt. They're just using me as an excuse. Besides, it's your fault for begging me to play."

"You agreed."

"Oh, I agreed! Excuse me!"

"What's the big deal, anyway? You show up, you play, you go home. It's nothing. A musician like you could do it in his sleep. Hey, we pay ten dollars a week, too."

"Princely."

"C'mon. What's the problem?"

It was only, James decided, his not wanting to, his poor individual faculty of choice, mere preference. So he gave in. Perhaps it was simply Christianity itself, absorbed at some subconscious depth of the soul, that never allowed the seasoned church worker to tell people to get lost with a clear conscience. He gave in. He began playing every week. It wasn't that bad.

His father's fury was boundless. "First Ekdahl, now the Lutherans! What's next, James? Hare Krishna? Pushing drugs? The Flat Earth Society?"

"I really don't see why this is an issue."

"And second hand! That I should have to be told of it second hand! By one of those senile women that frequent that temple of nonsense. Asking me—daring to accost me on the street—asking me if I'm proud of my son. Proud, indeed!"

"Making you proud of me was not the point."

"Oh, that's a relief. I feared I was missing something. Regular organist at—*regular organist!*"

But James had expected this. And it was with a bravado born of the irritation he knew he had caused and the relative independence his earnings from his lessons would now give him that he picked this precise moment to say: "I suppose you want me to move out, then. I know I said I'd be gone in the fall but it doesn't look like I will be now. And my activities cause you so much discomfort that you'd probably be happier if I moved out—right?"

McGrath snorted, glaring at James. His eyes were bright and piercing. "You persist in thinking I'm an unreasonable monster. You've always thought that. Of course, you can stay. I would no more turn you out than I would shoot my own dog. If you're staying in the area, I would prefer it to be here. It's simply that—" He paused, then turned away. "Never mind. Enough has been said."

And this James had not expected. He thought the old buzzard would be happy for any excuse to be rid of him.

So, in some ways, had McGrath, until the moment came. And McGrath could not have explained his shift in feeling. Perhaps the spectacle of James moving elsewhere, perhaps boarding with Ekdahl, would have meant further public shame. Perhaps he had grown fond of having someone to berate. Perhaps he was sleeping better now, with someone else in the house. None of these things could be pleasantly and calmly entertained by McGrath as an explanation for his conduct. So he banished the question from his mind and never thought of it again. At the very least, James' continued presence would give him that much more to be furious about.

So James forged a new routine, a kind of thin reprise of his late career, out of his teaching and performing. He began to feel an affectionate tug as he passed First Lutheran, and he looked forward each day to the work with his students.

The nights turned colder and the days were crisp and clear. The smell of burning leaves drifted through the darkening evenings. The human beings who were still reasonably sentient felt that quickening of interest and activity that autumn brought, whether from the habit of returning to school or from some more ancient urge, the soul's mustering of forces before the coming of winter.

At Halloween, New Culloden, along with other rural communities, worked hard at reviving the more traditional aspects of the day, wherein the dark spirits stalked the world in fact, not just in costume. Traffic fatalities increased. The sheriff's department worked overtime. Danny's station was broken into and his small stock of tires was set ablaze in the middle of the street. Houses were covered with eggs, and trees with toilet paper. The letters on First Lutheran's sign board were changed to 'Luther in Farts'. All the street lights were shot out, and a bullet pierced the post office window.

James had planned his own celebration for the following Sunday, which First Lutheran was observing as All Saints' Day. Willing to tolerate mediocrity on a week by week basis, though less so as the weeks rolled by, James had pressured Tim into allowing him to introduce several hymns new to the congregation, hymns James was astounded to learn they didn't know. These he would gather into the All Saints service: his beloved Vaughan Williams' *Sine Nomine*, then the folk tune Vaughan Williams had arranged as *King's Lynn*, and finally one version of the sweeping *Lasst Uns Erfreuen* from the *Geistliche Kirchengesange*. Under threat of resignation, he blackmailed Tim into using a longer Eucharistic prayer. And he himself would sing an anthem based on the old Latin hymn *Kyrie fons bonitatis*. Lori would accompany him. It would be, for him, a return to form and, for the congregation, a vision of ritual's possibilities, courtesy of James and the Western musical tradition.

He should have known better. He did, he supposed, but he could not eradicate from himself all traces of what Kathy would probably dismiss as mindless ambition. Still, was it so mindless?

The snowballing debacle began early Sunday morning when Lori called him to say she couldn't make it.

"What do you mean: 'can't'?"

"My dad needs me."

"*I* need you. How can he need you more than I need you today?"

"We have a sick cow and he had to help the vet so I have to do the milking. And by the time I get my other chores done, I'll never make it."

"Can't you do them later?"

"My mom says I have to stay. I'm really sorry, Mr. McGrath."

Conscientious girl, she told James she had already called the woman who had preceded James as organist. She would accompany him. She was getting the music from Lori and would meet James an hour before the service. Later, James would reflect that that was the moment he should have chosen to hang himself.

He was at the church an hour and a half before the service but the woman didn't show up until fifteen minutes before it was to start. She looked peeved. "Where were you?" she said.

"Here! I've been waiting."

"Didn't that girl tell you to come to my house to practice?"

James, controlling his panic and the homicidal rage he seemed to feel all too often around older women, spoke very slowly and quietly. "I. Don't. Even. Know. Where. You. Live."

"I just live up the *road*."

"Right. Forget it. I misunderstood. Look: shall we skip the anthem? Or are you ready? What do you think?"

She sniffed. "Oh, I'm ready. Of course, it's a little different."

"Okay. But you're ready. Fine. We'll wing it. I've got to get up there."

When he began the prelude, he thought he had done all he could and, given the context, it should have been enough to be splendid. But things started to unravel during the opening hymn. No one joined Vaughan Williams' paean to the nameless saints of the Christian church. No one sang. Absolutely no one sang. Stealing a glance, James saw that most people didn't have their books open.

It was God, the Superwoman who never forgot, getting back at him for what he had once done with this hymn. Or it was simply the normal behavior of his fellow citizens: the newer a thing, the less responsibility they felt to notice its existence. This hymn was not one of the things they were born knowing. Tim was no help, since he usually spent the time during the hymns editing his sermon or doodling on his bulletin.

The ordinary parts of the service began well enough. James, however, had spent the week coaching Tim on the chant, which he had never attempted before. After two quavering lines, which James was prepared to accept as a good effort, Tim laughed out loud and said, "Hey. I think I'll just speak this stuff."

James was so aghast he missed his next cue.

When the time came, he walked with some trepidation to the piano to join his accompanist for the anthem, convinced now that it had been foolhardy to proceed without Lori and without practice.

It too began well enough but then, somewhere in the middle, he was never sure exactly what happened, the woman moved into some bizarre key, James lost his pitch, he tried to follow her, she strayed further, he reversed course and tried to force her back to the proper tonality, she apparently skipped or added a repeat, he was no longer sure, and the performance crossed a frontier of dissonance that vaguely recalled the more tortured works of Schoenberg, both technically and thematically.

As if to bestow mercy, Tim, as was his habit anyway, shortened everything he could, forgetting all the promises James had squeezed out of him.

But James was glad to see it end. Every defeated part of him ached to scrap the postlude and go home. Improvise some variations of 'Yankee Doodle' and swallow the cyanide pill he wished church musicians would all carry implanted in their thumbs. But he finished with Bach and pleased, at least and no doubt only, himself.

He went home in a daze. He napped, and then, late in the afternoon, sorted things out. His students made him happy enough, Lori especially. It wasn't altogether revolting to play there on ordinary Sundays. But what he had intended as a triumphant breakthrough had been his comeuppance. They all knew in their bones what he foolishly refused to accept. Mediocrity was easier, more pleasant, reliable, safer, more satisfying, capable of longer duration, less likely to disappoint. To try for more is to risk coming up with less. To try for more *is* less, guaranteed, sure to be awful. This was absolutely clear when you failed, as you inevitably would. He put on a record. It was the Deller consort, singing the music of Henry Purcell. He listened to the sweet, apparently effortless blend of voices, shaped by so much skill, so much, tutored to form such beauty. He couldn't shake the sound of his own croaking when that woman mangled the accompaniment.

He turned up the volume. Alfred Deller's counter-tenor voice, brilliant as crystal, pierced him like the eye of God. He turned it louder, distorting the sound, but it was still less distorted than his own performance. He lay on his bed, holding his knotted stomach.

Downstairs, McGrath jerked awake from his nap. He had been dreaming of riots and massacres. Then he realized it was only James' music. He gave it a few seconds of tolerance, since James had never blared it before, then pulled himself up and headed upstairs.

James was lying on his bed and didn't see him approach. Hearing him was out of the question. What Deller did not drown out, the sounds in James' memory did. McGrath stopped short of the door to his room, perplexed by the sight of James deafening himself.

Then James could stand it no longer. He leaped from the bed, ripped the needle across the record, tore the record from the turntable, and pounded it against the corner of his desk. McGrath backed away and crept down the stairs. He had seen enough to understand, because he had seen this before.

It was the hatred for quality born of failure and frustration. It was the rejection and the acceptance at once of the accusation leveled by achievement. He had seen this before, many times, in his dead wife, James' mother. They shared it between them, like the color of hair and the ironic lifting of an eyebrow. It had eaten at her in New Culloden longer than cancer had, and now it was eating at James. It was the curse they carried for the sake of their passions.

McGrath felt a pang of memory and of pity. He thought of going back upstairs to talk to his son. But more than pity and memory, witnessing the outburst had brought him the distaste he always felt for unanswerable demands and incalculable yearnings, snares and storms that always made him recoil in impatience or anger or horror. He listened for a time, but no more sounds came from upstairs. He took Blackstone on his walk. When they were returning, he saw James leave the house.

James walked for a few hours, alone, avoiding dinner with his father. They nodded to each other when he came in, and they retired to their separate rooms. McGrath soon forgot the incident. For his part, James figured he would eventually get over it. When, on Tuesday, he saw how stupid he had been to destroy his most treasured record, he concluded he was probably going to outlive this humiliation and be available for however many more there were to come.

And then, just before his students began arriving at the church for the afternoon sessions, he got an unexpected lift. He was arranging his music on the piano in the assembly hall. A tall, pretty woman with dark hair and large, soft eyes, dressed elegantly in black, pushed the door open a little and knocked on it. "Excuse me," she said, "Are you busy?"

"No. Come on in. Can I help you?"

"I'm Kris. Kristina. Carlson." She was very nervous and much younger than she seemed at first glance. "I go here. I mean, to this church. You don't know me." She pointed her finger at him. "But I know you. I mean, I've been here. When you played. At the service."

As awful as he had been last Sunday, he didn't think a parishioner could be so upset as to want to shoot him, so he said, "Yes?"

"Well—" She started to blush and began waving a hand in front of her face. "Whew! I feel so stupid. Um, you give lessons. I tried to get one of my kids to take them from you but I couldn't talk them into it. I'm really sorry."

James nodded without comprehension. "So—you've come here to apologize?"

"No! Oh, no." She giggled. "Geez. Um, no, what I mean is—do you do moms, too? I mean, older people. Give lessons to older people? Moms, you know."

"I'm sorry. Your kids don't want lessons, but you talked your mother into taking them?"

"No! No! God, why can't I just say what I want? They're for me. Me. I want to know if I could take lessons. If you gave lessons. To people. Like. Me." Her face was as bright red as any face he had ever seen.

And he saw in her eyes a naked and defenseless yearning for the world he sometimes took so lightly, a dream of music and skill and beauty, purified by years of burial and denial. He felt at once utterly unworthy and utterly privileged. If he had a thousand students and not one single moment to spare, he couldn't have denied her.

He smiled, in pleasure, in gratitude, and a little in self-defense before so much unveiled passion. "Sure. Sure, I do. But first you have to promise me one thing."

She looked stricken, as though she knew he were going to ask for the one thing she couldn't give, the promise of sexual favors or the sacrifice of a child. "What?"

"You're going to have to relax."

"Oh! Ha! I guess I'm a little. Yeah, well. I guess. You know. I'm nervous. A little. Nervous."

"I picked up on that that. You can go home and work on it."

She nodded seriously. "Fine. I will. And then—come right back?" Or—?"

"Look. Kris, is it? Kris, please relax. Okay? Okay. I have students coming in now—"

"Geez. Right. What a klutz. You must think I'm stupid. But I'm just. Nervous. I mean—"

"You can come Thursday night. How's that work for you? My last lesson's over at seven. So come then, we'll go about half an hour or so. Can you come every week?"

"Oh! No problem. Oh, God, this is great. Should I bring anything?"

"No. I've got some books you can use. We'll go at it a while to see where you are, which way we want to go. And it'll be a treat for me to have an adult student. This'll be fun."

"I bought some music." She rummaged in the large bag that was slung over her shoulder, then stopped and reddened again. "I guess I should have waited, huh? You want to see it?"

"Yeah. Sure."

She pulled on a book, then stopped again before she had it out of the bag. "I guess I was trying to work up my courage. I thought if I had, you know, some money invested, I'd be more likely to ask you."

"How long have you been wanting to?"

"Three weeks. I mean, that's how long I've been carrying the book around and walking by here without coming in."

"Three weeks?"

"Well. Or four. You want to see it?"

"If it's still there. Of course."

"Pretty dumb, huh? Well, I was—"

"Nervous."

"Here it is."

It was a volume of Bach. *The Well-Tempered Clavier, Volume One.* James himself wouldn't exactly have been able to breeze through all of them. He flipped the pages, marveling at this student who had fallen into his hands.

"I looked," she said. "Up on your bench. One day after the service. You had something by him. So I thought. It would be fine. And the man at the store said—well, I mean, I *know* Bach. I mean, the name. I don't—is it alright?"

"Uh—you have excellent taste, but just how proficient are you?"

"Well—"

"Have you had any lessons?"

"Not really. I mean, no. I always wanted to."

"Look. This is great. It really is. But we'll start at a little lower level, okay? Huh. You really checked out my music?"

She nodded shyly.

"Keep this. I'll get you a book. But keep this, and someday you'll play it and that'll be the day I don't have anything left to teach you."

"Oh! I'll never get that good. I just want to. You know—"

James looked at her steadily. "Oh, yes, you will."

She looked down. "Well, I'd better go. Thursday night. Great, this is great." She turned quickly away, then turned back. "Thanks. I mean it. Thank you. I've always wanted to do this."

"It'll be fun. For me, too."

"Oh! I should have asked. How much—I mean, should I pay week by week? What do you charge?"

James smiled. "Let's forget about that at first. If you like it, we'll work something out."

"Oh, I'll love it! I know I will. But okay. I'll see you Thursday. Thanks. Geez. This is going to be great."

If she hadn't left then, he was afraid he would have wept for joy.

Chapter Twenty-Two

As Thanksgiving approached and James was anticipating the enjoyment of a lingering autumn, the first snowstorm came. It covered everything with a wet, heavy slush that made the power lines and tree branches sag with its weight. The roads became hazardous, and the bland conversation of New Culloden was seasoned with tales of winter driving adventures, though James could not wholeheartedly share in these, his car still being in for repair.

With the coming of winter, the station became crowded with an influx of mutants, though it would be hard to say whether they were being driven in by the snow or driven out by something else, since one never saw them anywhere else and it was hard to imagine them working or indeed dwelling anywhere. Patty's theory was that they were professional actors, hired seasonally by wholesale stores and the sleazier malls to make the lower classes feel more at home and, at times, superior; in the winter they were dispensed with because of the holiday crowds, and they retreated to places like New Culloden to hone their skills.

"Think about it, James," she said. "Have you ever seen people like this anywhere else? And do you ever see them while you're doing your Christmas shopping? Never. Q.E.D."

Both James and Patty, who had the station and its pleasures to themselves for most of the summer, resented their return.

"On second thought," she said, "I give up my theory. That's giving them too much credit. I think what we see here is the deterioration of the gene pool, the end of the human line, the final gasp of this particular genetic code after who knows how many millennia."

"About fifteen hundred to two thousand," muttered Danny, turning a page in his book.

"Excuse me," said Patty. "Do I hear an uninvited comment?"

"You said, 'who knows how many millennia'. The fact is I know: about fifteen hundred to two thousand millennia. One and a half to two million years since the emergence of this particular genetic code."

"Danny, you are so irritating. Who *really* knows?"

"Well, if we're talking about things like tool-making—"

"I'd say that would be a little sophisticated for this bunch."

"Oh, well, then, you're right, my sweet, as always. Once we get beyond tool-making, we're dealing with guesswork and serious questions about classification. No one really does know. You could say four, five, six million years. Some would push it all the way to fourteen."

"Anyway, a *lot,*" said Patty. "Only to come to this. There's the future, James.

People are worried about the arms race? In a few years, we'll all be like that. Pouring coffee will be a challenge. Figuring out how to pee or, more likely, how to keep from it at socially inconvenient moments. Rather sad, when you think about it. Which is why I don't, until these assholes remind me."

"You don't think your picture is a little bleak?" asked James.

"No."

"I think," said Danny, closing his book, "that genetic problems are more local than universal. What we need to do, as far as our area is concerned, is organize a raid on some place like Massachusetts. Carry off a truckload or two or those passionate, high class women and use them as breeders."

"It's too late for me," said Patty. "Look, James. I already married one of them. And now I'm carrying his offspring."

Patty's pregnancy was, by this time, an open secret in New Culloden. They had shared the information with so many people that the only ones left now who were ignorant of it were their parents. The normal time to inform them having passed, they had not been able to find a way to bring up the subject. And then, as Patty always said, you never knew how parents were going to take some things. She fantasized about raising their children in secret until they graduated from college, then presenting them as distant cousins. Not even Danny could be made to see the point of this.

As they silently pondered, for a moment, the fate of the human heritage, Tim came in.

Due to James' influence, Tim had taken to dropping in the station on his way back from the post office. He had, for some time, avoided this mark of a native's behavior. Patty decided he was losing his grip and that it was time for him to leave for another assignment. But, since Kathy liked him, he had been accepted as something other than a mutant, even though he had neither the cynicism nor the intellect to otherwise qualify. But what, Patty had said, could you expect from Kathy? The woman had gone out with *truckers*. Thanks, James had said. Oh, James, she replied, I'm not talking about *you*—believe me, I'm rooting for you.

Tim was looking tired. They had been averaging a funeral a week for the last month, and the strain was showing on him. He had come to announce another one. "Hi, guys. James, I've been looking for you. We've got another funeral. This Friday."

"Oh, man. Hey—Thursday's Thanksgiving. Can't you ever say 'no' to these people?"

Right," said Patty. "No more dying. It's hell on business."

"I mean," said James, "why not Saturday? Or even next Monday? Who wants to have a funeral the day after Thanksgiving? Everybody should get that day off."

"Well, the kids want to get home—"

"Sure, and this way the funeral can just be a part of their visit. How convenient. Don't you find that a little gruesome."

"I didn't kill the man, James. He died. That's when they want it. What am I supposed to do? Do you think I enjoy doing these things? Or trying to deal with these relatives?"

Patty said, "How's this for a recruiting slogan? Join the ministry: live in hideous locales and argue with morons."

"Or this," said James. "The ministry. It's not just a job. It's penal servitude for life."

"C'mon, guys. You're talking about my life."

"Don't mind them, Tim," said Danny. "They've been breathing exhaust fumes for too long. Why don't you two go outside and roll naked in the snow?"

"I'm pregnant, if you haven't noticed."

"*Bounce* in the snow, then. James can hold your hand. Do something. Anything. You're driving me nuts."

Tim perked up a little at the thought of young, rather than aged, flesh. He glimpsed a new candidate for a future youth group taking shape before his eyes. "Wow. You guys are going to have a baby?"

"Don't tell me you didn't know," said James.

"No. And nobody's said anything to me."

"Well," said Patty, "it's a secret. Was. Well, still is."

James explained, "First it was a secret until they could tell their parents. Now that everyone knows, including you, it's a secret *from* their parents. It's very complicated. I wouldn't worry if I couldn't understand it."

"Well, it's really great. Congratulations, you two."

Patty said, "Everyone is entitled to their own opinion."

Tim shook his head. "How can you guys be so cynical all the time? This is great. Babies are great. New little people. Life."

"We were just discussing that."

"I'll bet. You have my congratulations anyway. James, stop over sometime this week and we'll plan the service. I've got to go. And cheer up, for pete's sake."

When Tim had gone, Patty said, "There but for the grace of God go I, James. A little blur in the gene transmission and, poof, you're smiling all the time, you're shaking hands with people, you're trying to spread happiness. It's a pitiful sight. Well, I certainly know what I have to be thankful for this Thanksgiving." Then she could stand her act no longer and burst out laughing. "Tim's really not so bad."

"No, he's not," said James.

"You wouldn't guess this, James, and it's an even bigger secret," said Danny, "but the woman you are philosophizing with is positively glowing about the prospect of giving birth."

"I'm stunned."

"Don't believe him, James."

James said, "No comment. And I'd better go after Tim and get this over with. But I thought I'd risk saying this before I left: I really like you guys and I think it's because you're the most normal people I know. Pregnancy is a very normal thing."

The mischief came back into Patty's eye. "Did you know Madison warned us against having children?"

"That makes me feel wanted."

She patted his arm. "*We* want you, James."

"Maybe you can adopt me."

"It's tempting. You're already weaned, toilet trained, you can walk, talk. Now if you were only rich!"

"That, too, is probably a very normal response."

"If you tell me I'm normal once more, I won't be responsible for what I'll do to you."

"She means it, James."

"Better go. Stay warm." He waved and walked out of the station into the damp, cold air.

The sky was filled with swirling, grey clouds and the wind made him gulp. The sidewalks were a mess of slush. Danny was hoping it would melt before he had to shovel. James zipped up his coat and slogged and slipped away.

Patty opened the door and called after him, "Remember! Today is the first day of the rest of your life!" Then she threw back her head, laughed like a loon, and retreated inside.

James paused and looked back at the run-down station fondly. The lights were on, Patty and Danny were continuing their banter, the thick heat was keeping out the cold, the wind, the snow. It was one of those indispensable human havens, and it had really served as one for him. If the core group of humanity that frequented it often mocked and derided the peripheral hangers-on, well, that was not so different from other havens the world offered. New Culloden would be the worse without it. At least it would be for him.

Living as a bachelor, James had become used to spending Thanksgiving as a guest. He had also spent some lonely ones. He had hoped to spend this one with the Danielsons, but they were dining with relatives. He wasn't sure what to expect form his father, not the most celebratory of creatures under any circumstances, let alone those officially decreed, especially when they closed the post office.

But he woke on Thursday morning to the smell of a turkey roasting, and he curled in his bed, shamelessly enjoying the child's pleasure of warmth and good smells, of watching a light snowfall through the window of a house someone else paid for. It wasn't why he had come back here, but it was a good feeling.

The churches in New Culloden took turns each year hosting a Thanksgiving service, and this year it was the Assembly of God's turn. Tim went as a duty but James couldn't bear the thought. He told Tim he was avoiding it as a subtle gift to his father.

McGrath loved Thanksgiving because he looked upon it as a parody of national aspirations and a good joke on religious fanatics. Though the Fourth of July still meant freedom, Thanksgiving for most people meant food and football. He thought it was fitting that the Puritans should be remembered primarily for eating. And he always found it amusing that American presidents used the occasion to discourse on liberty and human rights, things which would have made the original pilgrims vomit. These addresses proved two things to him: that the American people were immensely tolerant of the hilarious statements made by their leaders; and that, if there was a growing ignorance of American history, it hadn't begun with the most recent generation of students. All in all, Thanksgiving found McGrath in good humor, or what passed for such for him.

When James came down, his father was happily clattering around the kitchen. Blackstone was curled up attentively next to the stove. James had had to admit, over the last few months, that his father wasn't a bad cook. McGrath told him Beckett would join them for dinner and that he was bringing a guest.

"Who?" said James who had, to his own irritation, acquired the rural suspicion of the unknown.

"He didn't say."

But when they arrived, late that afternoon, to the sound of Blackstone's barking, the stomping of snow from boots, the shaking of snow from hair and coats, to the accompaniment of laughter, when he heard her laugh, James knew it was Kathy. She looked more beautiful than he had remembered and he was torn between the joy of seeing her and the senseless jealousy of seeing her arrive with Beckett.

"Hail, McGrath and son," said Beckett. "I'll see to the wine."

"I thought you might," said McGrath. "Welcome back, Kathy." McGrath felt the urge to hug her but successfully resisted it.

"Good to be back."

Beckett and McGrath went into the kitchen together and James was left alone with her. Kathy gave him her friendly, understanding smile that always seemed a little sad and hopeless, and also a little condescending. She had the gift of resuming relationships effortlessly, if not of maintaining them. She saw James' turmoil without really understanding it and she saw that she was near the heart of it. But she could be glad to see him and knew that, in a while, he would be glad to see her.

"When did you get back?" he said.

"Last night. I always come back this time of the year."

"Home for the holidays?"

"*Here* for the holidays. Just something about the place I like in the winter. And I guess I really don't do it always."

"Don't want to get in a rut."

"Nope."

"Well. It's good to see you."

The four of them sipped wine together and James couldn't take his eyes off her. He felt absurdly jealous of sharing her attention with the two clever old men, like an awkward younger brother with a crush on his elder's girl friend.

When the table was prepared, Kathy said, "Maybe we ought to say grace."

"Why?" said McGrath.

Beckett shrugged. "Tradition? Atmosphere?"

"Perhaps my religiously inclined son, as a representative of the organized wing of superstition, should offer one."

"I'll pass," said James.

Kathy continued teasing. "Oh, it has to be the head of the household."

Beckett said, "I quite agree."

So McGrath, looking pained and malicious, put down his carving knife. "Alright. Bow your heads, you jackals. O Lord, may this day's food be as thorns in the mouths of mine enemies; may your hordes of followers shatter on the rock of your contradictions; and may this great land, conceived in liberty, no thanks to the faithful, spew them forth like sour wine. Amen."

"Dad, give us a break."

"I don't know about anyone else," said Beckett, "But that certainly added something to my meal."

The conversation at dinner, as befit McGrath's conception of the day, eventually turned to civic ideals. "I'm not blaming the young," he said. "All we have to do is look around us to know that stupidity is not a possession of one age group. If anything, the young have been victimized by what's passed for education in this country in the twentieth century. But look at the sad state they're in. How *can* they be citizens? Why, I just read the other day that most teen-aged girls would rather have a baby by Mick—Mick somebody—"

"Jagger?" suggested James. "Mick Jagger. Rock singer. You know, the Rolling Stones."

"No, I don't know. But they'd rather have this Jagger person's baby than become an astronaut. I don't mean to imply that our space program makes any sense. But you see my point. What a shrinking of ideals."

"Well," said Kathy, "when you talk about Jagger, you're aiming pretty high."

James said, "I suppose they have as much chance for either. Actually, as far as women astronauts go, I think Jagger's ahead statistically."

"The sad truth," said Beckett, "is that sex is part of all our fantasy lives, whereas going to the moon isn't."

"Come, Ben. Wouldn't you like to be the first poet on the moon?"

"Of course. I thirst for the honor. But, then, as in so many things, I'm the rarity."

McGrath chuckled. "Ah, the only thing worth being. Rarest of the rare."

"Wait a minute," said James. "How does that square with what you were saying about democratic citizenship? It sounds a little elitist to me."

Beckett grinned. "He has you there, Lawyer McGrath. Admit it. You're a closet royalist. Always have been."

"I'll admit nothing of the sort. And you have this damnable habit, Ben, of appointing yourself conversational umpire."

"Now you're being evasive."

"And you're proving my point."

"It seems to me," said James, "that you could argue that excellence and democracy aren't very compatible."

"You could *argue* anything," growled McGrath.

"Didn't Tocqueville suggest something along that line?" said Beckett. "The paradox of democracy: honors individuals but dooms them to conformity."

"Tocqueville? You're quoting a Frenchman to me? A Frenchman? They can't cope with sewage, let alone civic affairs."

"That doesn't affect his argument."

"Who's your next authority? Mrs. Trollope? Let me tell you something. There isn't a society you can name that has specialized in excellence. None. But if I had to choose one, for all time, in season and out, that would allow it to flourish, I'd take a democratic society without a moment's hesitation. Royalist, indeed."

"I think" said Beckett, "the issue is social pressure, psychological pressure."

"Psychology be damned."

"Wouldn't you admit," said James, "that at least in point of fact democracy tends to level things? That in fact it hasn't encouraged excellence? Whether or not it could or might or should—" He had the feeling he was speaking through an alcoholic haze.

"No," barked McGrath.

Kathy laughed. "Well, I guess that's settled."

"Tocqueville!" shouted McGrath, and he was off on a diatribe against foreign visitors to the United States.

James eventually found himself wishing he could watch a football game. Then he thought of offering this impulse as evidence for his argument. But McGrath would probably take it not as a proof of James' general point but as evidence of personal failure. And he supposed his father could offer his own life as counter-evidence. Maybe everyone's life proved their own point.

He found this a grim thought. Worse, he suspected that somewhere along this line of argument lay a victory for his father. So he kept his mouth shut, drank more of the wine Beckett kept pouring, and stared at Kathy, dreaming of undressing her.

McGrath insisted on cleaning up when the dinner was over, and Beckett offered to help. James would have too, if only to make a comment about social pressure, but sat too long trying to phrase it, decided against it, and ended up feeling irresponsible. There was simply no way to win with his father.

Kathy announced she had to be off.

"I'll walk you," said James, to his surprise, effortlessly.

"Yes, yes," said Beckett. "Be off, children. We can manage."

She had a long black scarf that she wound around her neck and over her ears which made her look silly and splendid at once, irresistible. James fetched his coat and they left. The holiday had reduced the volume of traffic roaring along the highway, and the lightly falling snow made the air close and quiet. Kathy didn't want to walk down the road, so they made their way through McGrath's forest barrier.

"I love walking through the woods in winter," she said. "Especially in these early snowfalls. No tracks anywhere. You're alone, you're first. Everything's clean. Now *that* is excellent, wouldn't you say?"

"Yeah, I guess."

They walked slowly, James searching for ways to bridge this time and the last he had seen her, Kathy oblivious to the necessity. He finally said, just to hear himself speak, "It's funny how much my dad enjoys Ben. I don't usually think of him as very sociable."

"He likes him because he's given up."

"What?"

"Sure. Ben has that charming air of the talented failure who's not trying anymore. Very pleasant, especially for someone like Madison."

"Meaning?"

"He thrives on all his warfare and turmoil but he never gets anywhere with it. He needs someone like Ben to help him relax."

"Oh, c'mon. What a thing to say."

"I'm not putting them down. All relationships have their strange side."

James risked saying, "Is that why you like Ben?"

"You've been feeling jealous since the moment I walked in. You really are hopeless. He invited me to come along and I thought it would be nice to see you. I thought you'd enjoy seeing me."

"Oh, I do. I do." He paused a moment, then said, "I always wonder where you go, when you just take off."

Kathy smiled. "To see lots of old friends. We're all pretty scattered. When I grew up—things were pretty wild. Lots of people crept away to points unknown, licking their wounds. They still are."

"You, too?"

"It's been a long time, James. You heal, if you let yourself heal."

They left McGrath's woods and started down the road to Kathy's house.

She would never let him into her life, open the door of her past for him. He wondered if she treated everyone this way. When he talked with her, he felt like a drunk fumbling for his house key, wondering if he were standing at the wrong door.

It made him feel out of tune with her, stumbling. He searched for something to say to bring them together. "Speaking of my dad, did you know he warned Patty against having children?"

"A little late for that now."

"Talk about a crusty old buzzard. It made me feel a little unwanted." He intended it as a joke but, even to himself, he seemed nakedly pleading for her sympathy. Once he said it, he felt stupid and ashamed. So why had he said it?

"I can't believe you take these things seriously. Or let them bother you. You're here, James. Whether you're wanted or not is beside the point."

"I'm not sure I like the sound of that either."

"You're so self-obsessed."

"No, I'm not."

"Yes, you are. You've got to wake up to what's around you, go with it, live with it. You're not going to change your father or yesterday or the weather. And you're not the only one who has a say about the future. You've got to look around you. Work on you, you, you."

"Now *that* sounds self-obsessed to me."

"You have to take your pick, I guess."

He supposed there was no way of winning with Kathy either. She and his father would make the perfect couple. The could correct each other forever. God spare any children from falling into their hands.

Being, in some sense, in the hands of them both, James felt defeated. Throw in the fact that God had not spared him this fate, and why should she?, he felt cursed.

Realistically, he reflected, I have probably consumed too much wine too early in the day. To be on the safe side, he said nothing for the rest of the walk.

But she put her hand on his shoulder when they got to her door, as a friend or a lover might, and said not unkindly, "I'd like to have you in, but I really have to go. But don't be a stranger. Let's get together."

"It's a promise."

The next day's funeral was, for James, a matter of going through the motions. If the Sunday fare of the community showed a narrow taste, such occasions narrowed it further. He could foresee a day when the Christian heritage would shrink to one verse of 'Amazing Grace' and some dimly remembered version of the Lord's Prayer. He supposed people inevitably turned to the past at these times, looking for the comfort of the familiar. But then their choices amounted to an indictment of their past. He refused to believe that anyone's spirit was strengthened or uplifted by the handful of sickening hymns he was asked to play over and over again.

The church ladies always served a lunch following funerals and James, out of politeness, had been forcing himself to attend. Tim usually sat with the family so James always made for an empty table, ate quickly, and left.

He was concentrating on his plate, as though marveling at what the day's chefs had managed to do with their cheese and olive sandwiches, when his student Kris walked up.

"Can I sit with you?" she said.

"Please do. I hardly ever know anybody at these things."

She swooped into her chair with the same eagerness he had come to admire during her lessons. Interestingly enough, she had managed to find enough food to heap her plate with. Maybe it was a question of attitude. She said, "I really appreciate your playing. I'm so glad you're our organist now."

"Confidentially, I don't do that much. I'm sure a lot of people could handle it."

"Oh, don't say that! You're a lot better than the ones we used to have." She shuddered in mock horror. "Ugh. I'd never have asked them for lessons."

"I mean for what people want. They don't ask much of an organist."

She nodded quickly. "I can tell. The stuff you like is so different from what they like."

"You can tell, huh?"

"Oh, yeah! It's—I don't know, it's like they're singing the same song even when it's a different one."

"Soap Opera principle," said James. "Same thing over and over again. Same awful thing."

"Right! Right! Oh, I like your stuff. That's the kind I want to play."

"Still going to get to that Bach?"

"God! You must have thought I was so dumb."

"No. No, I didn't." He wanted to say: I thought God had sent you in a rare moment of mercy.

"Well, then, maybe I just will. Who knows?"

"You're doing fine."

"Really? I seem so terrible. To myself. But—when I'm down, I think about how much the music, well, or the books or anything like that, of other people mean to me. Then I can see the point of going on with my own."

"You'll make it. Maybe someday you can take over from me."

"Ha! I'll never get that good. And—I suppose you won't stay here that long. I mean, why *would* you? So I'd have to get pretty good pretty fast. Or you'd just have to stay till I did. How's that?"

"Well, who knows?" She had a way of looping strange suggestions into her conversation. He found himself wishing she weren't married. He decided to change the subject. "So—you knew the man we buried?"

"He was my uncle. I'm related to everybody. He was a pretty great old guy. Yeah. He was. You and Pastor Tim did a good job. I appreciated it."

"All this praise is going to go to my head. But don't stop. Usually I feel like I should give it up and do something useful. Work for the railroad. Raise chickens. Repair cars. Of course, I'd be terrible at anything else."

"Oh, don't be silly! This is useful. How useful do you want to be?"

"Well, most people seem to get along without it."

"I know that. But it doesn't make them happy. I mean, what would life be without—well, people that just work, they're really miserable. I mean, not that you don't work, but you know what I mean?" Her eyes got a faraway, sad look. "They're miserable. What you do is so important. And then you can help them have that. See? Oh, I'm not saying it right."

"You're doing pretty well."

"So no more of this now! God. I'd give anything to do what you do."

James didn't know how he could ever thank this person enough for coming his way. Now, she was someone truly useful. He left the church that morning more inspired than he had been in a long time.

Buoyed up by Kris, his thoughts turned that evening to Kathy. Like most fools, he reflected later, he was assuming the world shifted in obedience to his moods. He walked over to her house and saw someone else's car parked outside. He turned around and trudged home. It was all the more galling because he didn't have a car he could park anywhere.

Chapter Twenty-Three

Tim's parishioners ceased dying, though he suspected they were only waiting for the holidays to be over. First Lutheran was, however, the scene of another death when a drunken teenager drove his snowmobile into its manger display and impaled himself on one of the reinforcing rods holding up the third wise man's camel. Fortunately, what church connections his family had were with the Assembly of God. The family wanted to sue First Lutheran for criminal negligence and McGrath agreed to handle the case. James ignored the affair as much as possible, as did Tim, and being related to McGrath seemed to win for James a kind of sympathy from the congregation, which he found himself resenting.

The temperature sank to twenty below zero and seemed likely to stay there until March. James engaged in a constant war with some anonymous helpful parishioners who dropped by the church to lower the thermostat after he had raised it for his lessons. Danny was delivering fuel oil around the clock and, growing careless on his farm chores, had two of his teeth kicked out by one of his cattle. Patty had to run the station alone and refused to stand outside for more than a minute at a time; one of their pumps stuck open one day and spilled sixty gallons of gas into the street before she noticed it. The Minnesota winter had begun to take its toll early.

It was snowing so frequently now that yard litter would not be noticed, nor would golf balls. Instead, each morning, McGrath found the burst remains of several water balloons strewn from his doorstep to the highway. The ice was there to stay and grew thicker and more ragged daily. Leaving the house was treacherous and backing the car out almost suicidal. Even Blackstone took a few falls. When, thought James, would the man have enough?

He began to worry about his father. Though it would be hard accurately to judge if McGrath were growing more cantankerous, he seemed so. But he often had a distracted air, which bothered James, and a blank inattention, which bothered him more. Always clean and invariably neat, he became compulsively fastidious and James never saw him anymore without his coat or with his tie loosened.

The bright spot amid this storm of winter's consequences was that it distracted James from his regular duties as an organist, which in the best of parishes grew onerous at Christmas. The swelling flock, responding to the call of American business, craved a religious atmosphere to season its celebrations, the more sentimental the better, and Tim was eager to give it to them.

Kathy was a distraction of a more pleasant sort. She and James had slipped back into their routine of easy, informal visiting and weekend dancing and drinking at the *Mudhole*. And, since she allowed him the use of her car, he was mobile again. He made several trips to Grand Forks to buy Christmas presents. The selection disappointed him but if he had been limited to shopping in New Culloden he would have had to give everybody windshield wipers or jugs of anti-freeze.

Beckett had planned a party at his home for Christmas night, because he thought it the single most depressing evening of the year, after the high hopes of the morning of surprise had been inevitably crushed. Everyone was pledged not to bring a gift, as Beckett felt gift giving was at the root of the all-engulfing Christmas despair. So James distributed his early, reluctantly omitting Ben from his list.

For Danny, he bought a copy of Jane Jacobs' *Cities and the Wealth of Nations*; for Patty, a scarf, decorated with a William Morris design. He gave Kathy a wooden necklace with beads of irregular size, made in Brazil.

Each of the three of them gave him a necktie, which he was tempted to take as a comment on his dullness.

Patty had said, "Consider it a contribution to your sartorial splendor. With a father like yours, you have a lot to live up to."

"At least they're all different."

"And, James, the wonderful thing about neckties is, if you don't like them, you can always use them to hang yourself."

He gave all of his students a pocket music dictionary. To Lori, he also gave a book of organ preludes with easy pedal parts. He had coaxed her into taking on the organ and he thought she might make a decent organist someday. If she weren't headed for college, she could have taken over from him in a year or so.

For Kris, his other special student, he had found a book of Bach for young pianists. When he gave it to her at their last lesson before the holidays, she was ecstatic and insisted on picking her way through the first piece. Then she said shyly, "I got something for you."

She had carried in a stack of packages with her and she slipped a thin one from the bottom. She said, "I didn't know if I'd have the courage to give it to you, so I carried in all these others, as though I had just done all this shopping. Pretty dumb, huh? Here. Merry Christmas."

"Can I open it?"

"Well, sure."

It was a framed reproduction of a page from a thirteenth century altar book, the beginning of the *Gloria in Excelsis*. It was exquisite. He wondered where she had found it, how long she had looked.

Kris was looking at him apprehensively. "Do you like it?"

"It's lovely. It really is."

"I wanted to show—you know, thanks for all your time. And you're not even charging me."

"That's because," he said, "you're paying me too much already."

"Oh, geez!" Her face turned bright red, and she waved her hand in front of it. "Well, anyway—I'm glad you like it. Um…I should go."

James got a sudden inspiration. "Kris. A bunch of us are having a party Christmas night. Why don't you come?"

Her eyes opened wide in amazement, as though she had never imagined being accepted as an equal by another human. "Oh, I couldn't—oh, thanks, but—I mean, I wouldn't know anybody or—"

"So what? You know me. And you know the Danielsons from the station, don't you?"

"Yeah, a little."

"So?"

She sighed deeply. "I really can't. I mean, there's my kids and—"

"Get a babysitter. And bring your husband."

"Oh, no. No. We don't—I mean, that's not the kind of thing. Look—I just can't. But thanks for asking. Really. I have to go. Merry Christmas. Oh, and thanks for the Bach. I'm going to play it everyday."

He wondered, not for the first time, what the rest of her life was like. And he didn't know how to convey to her the greatest gift she was giving him, the rarest a teacher can get: the joy of insight and accomplishment taking shape in a student.

He took home her gift and hung it on the wall of his room. Looking around, he realized it was almost the only thing he had acquired in New Culloden.

Christmas morning came. There were no services at First Lutheran, since the last pastor had discontinued them and Tim hadn't been able to arouse any interest in resuming them. They tended to get in the way of holiday festivities. James was glad of it, since he was sick of hearing Christmas carols.

He had saved his father's present for this morning. Over the years, his father had sent him a check each Christmas and he had sent a card. But dwelling in the same house seemed to call for some extra effort. Since a tree would have been going much farther into the season than his father would consider, James had kept the gift upstairs and he handed it to his father after breakfast.

He had bought him the Library of America edition of the writings of William James, hoping it might serve as a common ground between them. For his father, it would be a volume by an old Yankee, a philosopher of the democratic spirit; for James, it would be by a Yankee with an open mind, as far as the less quantifiable aspects of existence were concerned.

McGrath, to James' surprise, seemed genuinely pleased. But then the strangest grin appeared on his face. "I have something for you. For us, really. A family present. But you can open it."

It was a box three feet long. James couldn't imagine what was in it. Gardening tools, maybe. Oversized kitchen utensils. He unwrapped it carefully while McGrath continued grinning. It was a pair of shotguns, one of them chrome plated. McGrath picked it up eagerly.

"This one's yours. I thought you'd like the chrome. Twelve gauge. Stop anything. Just keep pumping and firing. Holds seven shells, plus one in the chamber. What do you think?"

"They're very nice. I guess. But what are we going to do with them?"

"They're for home defense. I thought you could keep yours in the downstairs closet. Or upstairs, if you like."

"Downstairs sounds good."

"Mine will be in my room or, if I'm in my office, I'll have it with me there. That way we'll be ready."

"For?"

"Anything."

So James spent Christmas day finding ways to watch his father unobtrusively. But McGrath did nothing out of the ordinary except peruse the James volume and occasionally read passages aloud. His father probably enjoyed the day much more than he did.

When it was time to leave for Beckett's, James said, "Would you like to come with me over to Ben's? I'm sure he wouldn't mind."

"You are, eh? I am, too, since he already invited me."

"Oh. So are you going?"

"No. I have to stay home, just in case."

"In case what?"

"Anything."

Anything. James wondered if his father's combativeness had swollen to such a degree that he expected the sun to smite him or the moon to descend upon him in wrath. Anything could happen, true enough. But, taken literally, that meant the chaos sleeping beneath all things might rise up at any moment. One had to worry then not only about the sun and moon but also about one's own head, hand, heart. James didn't think a twelve gauge was going to be enough.

Perhaps it was only a minor aberration, McGrath's own way of offsetting the cloying seasonal madness. The old man didn't lack eccentricities to begin with. One more couldn't be fatal. And he seemed peaceful and relaxed for most of the day.

It could be that something had pushed its way up in McGrath from the depths that everyone had in them, something that would disturb his surface life for a while then sink out of sight again. James wished he hadn't also bought quite so many boxes of shells. What will I do, he thought, if he really does flip his lid?

But the possibility of such a thing happening to his father, eccentricities notwithstanding, seemed so remote that James was able to banish his apprehensions. By the time he reached Beckett's, he was ready to party.

Patty met him at the door. "Ho, ho, ho," she said in a deep voice, patting her belly. "Merry Christmas, James. Ho, ho, ho. Ben asked me to be the ho-ho-hostess. Just between you and me, there's a real dearth of women at this party. Too bad for the more bumbling sex."

"Who's all here?"

"Very intimate group. To tell you the truth, *I* should have given this party. Ben has a pretty narrow circle. After you and me, there's only Danny and Kathy. Oh, and Tim—kind of a surprise, mystery guest. Makes me feel right at home. Or at work really. Just another day at the station."

The drinking was well advanced. Beckett seemed to look upon refilling glasses as the only proper behavior at social gatherings. James said, "Hey. What time did you guys start?"

"When we got here," said Kathy. "What kept you?"

"I thought I was on time."

Danny and Kathy shared the couch, Beckett was in his easy chair, and Tim had pulled a chair from the kitchen. James sat on the floor near Kathy.

"Young McGrath," said Beckett in greeting. "And where is your guardian?"

"Home. He wouldn't come. Actually, I'm a little worried about him."

"Hush. 'Tis the season to be jolly. Away with worry and woe. Besides, your noble parent despises this season, and I can't say I blame him. But come, fill your glass. Now where were we?"

Patty sat on the arm of Beckett's chair and said, "I want to hear more of what Tim was saying. He was opening up a new perspective for me."

Tim reddened, glanced at James, and stammered, "I was just saying that one of the strangest times for me was at Communion sometimes. A lot of women wear these plunging necklines and it's all I can do—"

"Not to take a bite out of their boobs?" offered Patty.

Tim got redder. "Not to look, OK? It's pretty awkward."

Kathy said, "They trust you. It's a compliment. Anyway, a look won't kill you. Or them either. You could give them a wink and see if anything lights up."

Beckett said, "Women are merciless, that's a fact. Present company excluded, of course—well, at least you, Kathy,"

"Hey!"

"But," he continued, "if I'm not mistaken, in the middle ages, the clergy were sometimes thought of as a third sex. Didn't have to worry about them, you see."

"I'll bet nobody worried," said Kathy. "And I'll bet the clergy thought that up."

"No," said James, "there's something to that. Look—Tim, don't you ever feel, well, neither here nor there, as though you're not doing anything—"

"Manly?" said Patty.

James shrugged. "Something like that. I know I do."

"James," said Kathy. "You're ridiculous."

"Maybe I'm not putting it very well. Do you know what I mean, Tim?"

"Yeah, I guess. Useless maybe, like a fifth wheel. I don't know if sex enters into it."

"Gender," said Patty, "We're talking about gender. Do you or do you not feel genderless or extra-genderly or uncommonly gendery?"

"What have you got in your glass?" said Danny. "More of that heavy-weight motor oil?"

"Ho, ho, ho. You don't know. Ho, ho, ho."

"You'll all have to excuse my wife. She's been driven mad by pregnancy."

And then they talked about pregnancy and education and books and parties past and travel and food and music. James enjoyed the low intensity Beckett's gathering had, compared to those his father hosted. The speed at which subjects shifted increased as the evening went on and Beckett went on pouring, sending Patty to the kitchen for more bottles.

"I love consumption," said Danny, pointing to his glass. "Of all sorts. That's why I'm proud of what I do. I help the human race consume our natural resources. That's why we're here, in my opinion. Nature doesn't abhor a vacuum. Nature loves a vacuum. This planet's a mistake. So we evolved to use everything up. Bring us in line with the other dead planets."

"You know," said Beckett, "that's extremely plausible. I think you're really on to something."

"I think you're really drunk," said Patty.

James, who had never heard Danny make less sense, said, "She's right. I hate to admit it, but she's right."

But Danny wasn't listening. His eyes were closed and his head had fallen back on the couch. Patty rescued his glass and looked at him lovingly. She said, "And did you notice? Only four drinks. He has those four drinks once a year, at Christmas, and falls asleep every time. The man has a built-in limit. But that's Danny for you."

"I can think of times in my life when that would have been very useful," said James.

"Who can't?" said Kathy. She giggled. "Tim maybe. By the way, where is Tim?"

Patty and James looked around. They couldn't see him anywhere. "Maybe he's in the bathroom," said James.

"Nope," said Patty. "I've been going in and out of there like a yo-yo. Not presently occupied."

James said, "Maybe the earth swallowed him. God, that makes me envious. There've been so many times I've wished for that. You know, the earth just opens up and it—swallows you. And there you are. And then you're not. And you've just been—swallowed."

The two women looked at each other and collapsed in laughter. "God!" said Patty. "And they call us the weaker sex!"

James held up his finger in correction. "Fair sex." He put his head in Kathy's lap. "Fair sex. Oh, so fair."

She ran her fingers through his hair. "Poor baby."

Patty rose and put Danny's glass on the table. "If you two can tear yourselves apart, help me get my husband to the car."

"Hey," said James, pointing at her, "how come you're so steady on your feet?"

"Oh, no alcohol for me. Don't want to drive my interior companion nuts."

He gestured at the bottles. "Then who—"

"Well," she said, "there's you—"

"And me," said Kathy.

"And Tim."

"Wherever he is."

"Yes, and then Ben."

"Well, where's Ben?" said James. "Did he disappear, too?"

But Beckett hadn't moved. He had fallen asleep in his chair. Hearing his name, he awoke. He said, "Oh, dear. Is this really the twentieth century?"

James asked, "Were you hoping you'd sleep through it?"

"I had this beautiful dream. I was working in a scriptorium in some old monastery. And I was just putting the finishing touches on the loveliest manuscript."

"Sorry to disappoint you, Ben."

"Alas. Is there no consolation for an old man?"

"Well," said Patty, "you can outdrink my husband. Also, we think we've lost Tim. Is that enough consolation?"

"Lost Tim. How extraordinary. Why, no. There he is." Beckett pointed into the kitchen. Somehow Tim had managed to roll under the table. His head was wedged between the rungs of a chair. "Did no one observe him as he got himself into that position?"

"I was in the bathroom," said Patty. "I don't know what their excuse is."

"Not lost after all. My, that's a relief." Beckett fell asleep again.

Kathy stood up. "When the host passes out twice, the well-mannered guest departs. Let's wake up Danny. James and I will take Tim home in my car. I don't think he'll be able to walk. Wouldn't do to have the Lutheran minister freeze to death in a drunken stupor."

Kathy and James managed to rouse and hoist Danny while Patty started her car. After seeing her off, they returned for Tim, but there was no rousing him. They dragged him from under the table, then lifted him to his feet.

James seemed to himself to be watching a choppily edited movie. First he was here, then he was there. As they maneuvered Tim toward the door, he seemed to be functioning, but he wasn't sure how. Kathy didn't seem drunk, though James would have conceded he wasn't the best judge at that moment, but she did have a wild gleam in her eye.

When they made it to her car, she said, "Wouldn't do either to have the poor boy seen in this condition, would it?"

James agreed.

"Let's put him in the trunk."

So they dumped him in the trunk. Then James was sitting in the front seat, smiling to himself. Kathy wasn't there but the motor was running. Then they were driving.

He began to come to a little. He had the pleasure of watching her fingering the necklace he had given her. Then the car was turning very oddly. He heard her say, "Whoops."

They fishtailed around a corner and slid into a snow bank. The engine roared but the car wouldn't move.

"Shit." Kathy got out to examine their plight. "It's not too bad. You'll have to push."

James got out and found himself knee deep in snow. He pushed helplessly on the rear of the car. He thought he could hear Tim crying for help. Kathy joined him. "C'mon. Push. Here's your chance to establish your masculine credentials. C'mon. *Move, you motherfucker!*"

And the car moved. It was like magic. He would have to remember that: move, you motherfucker.

They pitched forward as the tires took hold. The car rolled away from them and they fell into the snow. James felt victorious, powerful. Kathy was spitting snow out of her mouth.

"We've got to get up. It's in gear."

His mind was slow to make the connection but, once it had, he was able to get his body moving faster than Kathy. The car was gaining speed. He tried to run but the road was icy and he was soon on his back, sliding down the gentle slope that the car was taking at a much faster pace. Kathy, more sure footed, ran by him.

She managed to catch up with it. What a wonderful, many talented woman she was. Running sideways, she managed to get the driver's door open. Then she lost her footing and her arm went up in the air like a signal of triumph or ultimate distress. She slid under the car. James wondered how he would explain this to the police.

But she rolled free. The car continued on, out of their power now. James hoped Tim was comfortable.

It was heading for Einar Ekdahl's house. It was heading there at a pretty good clip. James tried to estimate its speed, but he had never been very good at this. Somehow, everything began to seem hysterically funny. Kathy was running again and he thought she must be reacting irrationally because there was no hope of catching the car. They should have asked Patty to drive them all home.

He thought maybe the car would bury itself in Einar's yard but it didn't. He thought it might lodge itself harmlessly against one of the chopped off flagpoles, and it was a close thing, but it didn't. Then he thought it might miss the house entirely. But it didn't.

It struck the corner of Ekdahl's bedroom at ramming speed. The house seemed to frown a little and open its mouth, as the roof tilted slightly and a hole gaped around the car. The bedroom light, which had not shone through the boarded up windows, surrounded the car like a set of gleaming gold teeth.

Kathy caught up with it. James admired her presence of mind. She turned off the engine. He thought he should join her.

Einar Ekdahl walked slowly from his front door. He was wearing a winter coat and boots over his pajamas. Kathy was talking to him and gesturing apologetically, but he didn't say a word. He began to pick up fragments of wood and pile them neatly beneath his boarded up windows. His wife was peeking out the new opening in the bedroom.

James was not the first observer to arrive on the scene. Such a drama could not go unwitnessed in New Culloden. The surrounding houses were lit up and several interested, if neither helpful nor particularly sympathetic, bystanders had gathered. James pushed his way through them.

Ekdahl finished gathering up the remains of his corner. He went to his garage and brought out two sheets of plywood. Kathy got in and started the car. As it lurched into reverse, the trunk sprang open. She stopped. The crowd moved closer. Tim sat up. He said, with slurred tongue, "What the fuck is going on?"

No one told him.

He looked around at the faces peering at him, thought about life for a moment, then sank back into the trunk. James saw Kathy resting her head on the wheel, but he couldn't imagine what she was thinking. Probably something about the futility of despair. He walked over to the trunk and looked inside. "Are you okay, Tim?"

"Close the trunk," said Tim. "Unless you want to find a jack handle and beat me to death first."

James nodded. "Right." He closed it. Kathy backed out further.

Einar began to nail the plywood over the hole. James thought he should say something. "Einar—"

"It's nothing. I'm going to build, you know, we always intended to get a new place."

"Good idea."

Einar sighed. "Winter won't last forever, you know, everything will change come spring."

It was freezing. James shivered. Kathy was waiting for him.

And it seemed to him then that Ekdahl, safe in bed on Christmas night, had simply had the misfortune to be in the way of someone else's difficulties, as James himself so often had. One life was making sense, and another life was making a kind of sense, then they met and there was an accident. Sometimes it was yours, sometimes someone else's. James didn't think being on either side felt very good. He touched Einar's shoulder.

Einar didn't seem to notice. He kept on hammering mechanically. James thought he was probably getting good at it. He joined Kathy in the car. She said, "We're all staying at my place. It's time for this night to end."

She backed out through the crowd which was still watching Einar at work, perhaps admiring, perhaps only distracted.

At Kathy's house, they got Tim out of the trunk. She told him he could sleep on her couch.

"What will people think?" he said.

"Somehow I don't think that's going to be an issue."

Tim was asleep soon after they laid him down. She covered him with a blanket, then led James to her bedroom. Him too she gently guided to her bed. She kissed him. She said, "You didn't really think I was giving you a necktie for Christmas, did you? Things, things. Here's my real present." She kissed him deeply and they undressed, Kathy doing most of the work

James was in a daze. She had picked a moment when sleeping with her was further from his thoughts than it had ever been. But he wasn't going to argue.

All she had on was her necklace. It was like another, titillating part of her as she stroked and licked him. She fondled him gently. "Third sex, huh? I don't know, James, you look pretty standard issue male to me."

He laughed. "Thanks. I needed that."

"How about this?" She mounted him and he slid inside her.

"Oh, yeah," he gasped.

She slipped off her necklace, then, grinning, she put it around his neck. Her strong hands leaned on his chest.

James had a rational thought. "Shouldn't we—I mean, isn't there something—"

"Taken care of long ago. No more little ones from this woman."

"What do you mean?"

"Do you want to discuss my medical history or do you want to fuck?"

In the circumstances, it wasn't much of a question. He reached for her head to pull her close to him.

"Right answer, James. You finally got one right."

And the next day she was gone.

They parted after breakfast. They drove Tim home, returned to her house together, ate like contented lovers, she drove him home, and without a word she left town.

James had never felt so tormented and confused. She left when they were distant, she left when they were close. She left. And maybe that was it: she just left. James was no more relevant to what she did than anyone or anything else. She did what she wanted. He had never realized the depths of power in that phrase, power to intimidate, power to exclude, power to erase.

What she did had nothing to do with him. Devastating thought. He moped around the house for days. The temperature went to thirty below zero.

On New Year's Eve, McGrath and Beckett always got together to reminisce. The Danielsons had invited James out for the night and Patty had promised a more varied crowd, but James wasn't in the mood. He was going to celebrate by staying home and feeling sorry for himself.

He noticed it was taking his father forever to be ready. McGrath was cursing in his bedroom. He called for James. A little apprehensively, James said, "What's wrong?"

"I cannot get this tie tied properly. It must be the light in here. It's making me late. See what you can do."

"It looks fine to me."

"I was not trying to meet your standards but my own. And I wasn't asking for your opinion but for your help. However, if you can't provide any, I'll have to manage."

"Okay, okay. It was just a comment. Let's see it."

He tried to tie it to his father's satisfaction. He lost count of how many times he tried. He felt uncomfortable with his hands so close to his father's body, but as far as he could tell there was nothing wrong with his efforts. His father grew restive, James grew nervous. He could not satisfy the old man. McGrath tore the tie from his hands. "Oh, I'll have to do it."

He knotted it quickly. James couldn't tell that it was any different than those he had tied. McGrath said, "You see? Does that seem so difficult?"

"It looks fine."

"It looks fine *now*. You've never been able to do anything. I don't know what you think about your life. I don't see how you can fritter it away the way you do."

James stared at him. What had brought this on? McGrath was ranting about careers and values and James was suddenly afire with his old rebellion against a world of argument and money and aggression. He fought back. "Well, maybe I don't give a fuck about things like that."

His father slapped him across his face. James was silent, glaring. McGrath said, "Watch your mouth. If your mother were alive, she wouldn't stand for that." It was probably the worst thing he could think of to say to James.

McGrath turned away and went for his coat. James followed, unable to think of a word or action in response, followed like a scolded boy.

"Did you put some extra straw in Blackstone's dog house?"

James cleared his throat, not willing to trust his voice. "What straw?"

"What straw. Excellent. It's below zero. He's out at night. He needs a place to go, What straw."

"I didn't know."

"Do I have to do everything? Well, you'll have to keep him in. Do you think you can handle that? When it's midnight, you don't let him out as you would normally do. Will that be too hard for you?"

James said quietly, "I'll remember."

"We'll see."

McGrath left. James decided to get drunk. Midnight came and Blackstone began to whine.

"Not tonight," said James. "We all have to make these little adjustments."

Blackstone kept whining. James knew exactly how he felt.

That Sunday, after the service, Tim came to the organ to speak to him. "Patty said I should console you. I'm afraid I'm not very good at it, but I thought I'd give it a shot."

"Console me for what?" How about: everything.

"You know. Kathy. Always taking off like nobody cared she'd be gone."

"Oh, yeah. Well, I guess she does."

"I dated her for a while, did you know? Seemed like we were always fighting."

"About what?"

"Usually my life."

James said, "Sounds familiar."

"She always thought everything I cared about was trivial or stupid. So I got tired of defending myself and just backed up a little. You know, I like her a lot."

"Why didn't you just win the argument?"

"With Kathy? You've got to be kidding."

James smiled for what seemed the first time in a long time. "I guess so."

"Anyway, that's my consolation. It's just Kathy."

James didn't find the failures of others, or the realities of others, very consoling.

Chapter Twenty-Four

As winter hung on, New Culloden sank into an anxious passivity, an irritable steadiness, a tense calm. Everyone counted the days until the mercury would rise, the ice and snow melt, and life begin again. Even Einar Ekdahl was without projects and schemes. James heard them say, 'We're through January' and then 'We're almost through February', and it seemed to him that the town had become most itself. This was what the life around him was fashioned for: surviving winter. It was hardly a vision to lift the heart and enflame the spirit.

Not his, anyway. If it had not been for his students, he was sure he would have put his Christmas neckties to use by now.

He was doing a lot of reading. He had given up on Dante, stuck in the *Purgatorio*, which seemed fitting. He was working on Theodore Pliever's *Stalingrad* and a biography of Thomas Eakins.

There was a brouhaha at First Lutheran, which mildly amused him, when Tim Franklin, attempting to get back into the congregation's good graces after his Christmas escapade, had painted the inside of the church in red, white, and blue stripes.

"And," said James, when he told Danny about it, "it wasn't even a very neat job."

"He did this on his own?"

"Didn't check with a soul. I didn't even know about it until I walked in on Sunday morning. I think some of the council members want to assassinate him."

"A clear case of cabin fever," said Danny. "All he needs is some warm weather and a chance to get outside. Of course, that won't help the church."

"No."

"By the way, James., I love that book you gave me for Christmas, about cities and economics. You know, the woman's absolutely right. Look at us: a typical rural area. And basically we're nothing but a third world country. We ship out raw materials and everything we use we have to buy from somewhere else. Whether it's Cleveland or Tokyo doesn't make much difference. Doesn't give us much to say in our own destiny."

"Well, that doesn't make us unique."

"No. But I for one would like some say. I'll have to choose my next career more wisely."

"Next? I thought you were the king of contentment."

"Oh, by and large, I am. But I get tired of spending my days with petroleum products and wet animals. And I don't want to still be pumping gas when I'm sixty-two. On the other hand, I don't want to wash dishes in Arkansas either."

"That's wise. So?"

"Back to school maybe. I was thinking of going into accounting."

"You're really serious?"

"Yeah. What do you think about it?"

"Good luck, if you want that. I don't think I could take going back to school. And accounting doesn't really fire my imagination."

"If it fills my bank account, amigo, I'll be satisfied."

Patty walked in. "Ho, ho, ho, James."

"Then, too," said Danny, "there's the matter of psychiatric care for my wife."

She stuck her tongue out at him.

After wasting as much time as he could at the station, James walked over to Beckett's. He had an hour before his lessons began, and he had spent the time since Christmas avoiding being alone. But spring was on its way. If the snow had not begun melting yet, the afternoon sun was decidedly warmer. On occasion, slush reappeared, a strange harbinger of better days.

Beckett shouted for James to enter. He was scribbling at his table. "Ah. I was just thinking about you. Pour yourself some coffee."

James sat across from him. "What about me?"

"Not you so much as Kathy. But you come together in my thoughts."

"Oh." Mine, too, thought James.

Beckett studied him. "Miss her, don't you?"

"It shows, huh? I thought I was hiding it so well."

"Not from the old and wise. I won't be foolish enough to offer you any advice. Love is pretty far out of the reach of wisdom."

"So I've heard."

"We were quite close once. If you don't mind my telling you that."

"I heard that, too," said James. "Seems like she went with everybody."

Beckett nodded. "She did. But no one ever seemed to—" He searched for a phrase.

James said, "Touch her? Understand her? Mean anything to her? All of the above?"

"I wouldn't be quite that harsh. But she won't be possessed. She makes quite sure of that."

"Yeah."

"Still, she could make an old heart rise. Not to speak of another organ."

"Why, Ben. You're blushing."

"Am I? I thought I was over such things. Perhaps one never is." He doodled on his paper. "At any rate, you two had just come to mind. I'm making a new poem out of the titles she gave her sculptures."

"You know, they're pretty good."

"Oh, yes. They are. And I love the titles. I'm calling this: *Given by a Lady*. Still a collection but a bit of an extension for me. Rather unique. Of course, one would have to know her work to appreciate it."

James looked over at Ben's papers. "You must have hundreds there. What did you do? Get her to sit down and tell you all of them?

Beckett cleared his throat and blushed again. "Oh, you may as well know. I'm actually the one who makes them up."

"Ben, you never cease to amaze me."

Beckett shrugged shyly. "It's hard to break these habits."

"Creation? Or deception?"

"Ah. Now I could make a very clever reply to that, to the effect that they amount to the same thing. But I was speaking of creation. In fact—" He stood up, considered a moment, then beckoned James to follow him. "Come with me."

He went into his living room and shuffled through a large stack of folders atop one of his book cases. "Ah. Here they are. Now this is the whole truth: phone numbers are not everything to me. I dabble in various things. And I was wondering the other day if you'd be interested in setting some of my texts to music. What do you think?"

"I'm not much of a composer." He wanted to ask: what's the point?

Beckett said, "It's a way of being together. Art ought to be good for that at least. What else do you have to do?"

"Not that much, if you put it that way."

"So?"

"So let's see them."

Beckett selected two sheets of paper from his folder. "These should do. I think of them as minimalist fables of inspiration."

James read them.

The first one was called "The Horse":

> There was a horse
> with one leg shorter
> than the other three.
> But his stable boy loved him.
> His stable boy believed in him.
> He became a champion.

The second one was called "The Boxer":

> There was a fighter
> who was blind in one eye.
> Everyone thought he was finished.
> But he won the title bout.

"Inspires me," said James.

"I was thinking of something for solo baritone with a simple accompaniment. Or maybe something a little more complicated for guitar and flute."

"I suppose I could work something up. If you're serious."

"Serious. Now there's a word to conjure with. But what in heaven or hell would answer? Let's not say serious. Just compulsively playful."

"Good enough. I'll see what I can do."

"Good."

Old Ben. He puzzled James as much as anyone did. James felt flattered at being shown his playthings, which he had noticed were rarely shared with anyone else. But something about Beckett made him feel trivialized, kidded into insignificance or into only a private significance that was closed off, something to giggle over. Beckett seemed energized by his presence, always eager to talk, but much as James liked him, he had come to realize that something like the opposite was true for him. He often left Beckett's feeling tired and drained. He wondered what Kathy would make of that. Kathy.

Screw Kathy.

He walked away with Beckett's fables in his pocket. This was true enough: he had little else to do. Today he didn't even have Lori or Kris to look forward to. It was beginner's day. He supposed if any of his students were really challenging him he would only disappoint them.

With a little more time to kill, he took the long way round to First Lutheran, cutting through his father's woods. He had not been through them since he walked Kathy home at Thanksgiving. He remembered being impressed by them when he first arrived. By now he had come to take them for granted. Perhaps he needed to work at appreciating his surroundings more. That would certainly be Kathy's advice. She could be right about that much.

A pile of cans and bottles caught his eye. He was in a far corner of the woods, near the riverbank. It was fresh garbage, if garbage could be called fresh, since there was no snow on it. He thought that, with the spring, the assault of litter was beginning again, but he wondered why it was in such an unobtrusive spot.

He came closer to examine it, as pointless as that seemed. Then he recognized the ingredients and remains from some of his recent meals with his father. He picked up a stick to poke it. No doubt about it. This was their garbage and no one else's. He saw now a well worn trail leading towards the house.

So this was why the old coot insisted on disposing of the garbage himself. He was probably too cheap to pay the village to carry it away or, more likely, had squabbled with them about it. And now he was too humiliated to mention it.

James poked further, then walked along the riverbank, probing in the snow. There must have been several years' worth here, half buried, half carelessly exposed. Or maybe McGrath had ceased to care enough to bury it.

He peered down the slope. He couldn't believe he had never noticed this before. There was an immense amount of refuse here. He raised his feet and looked at his boots. They were slimy and discolored. He was ankle deep in rotting food, and who knew how far down it went?

About to turn away, he saw something caught on a tree stump half way down the slope. It was a piece of fabric, faded almost beyond recognition. Almost. He remembered that dress. His mother had looked beautiful in it. He felt a chill and a burning at the same time. He started down, slipping in the snow and the muck beneath it.

He pulled at the fabric, and it tore. But he dug in the snow and found it. Her dress. He dug further. There were more of her clothes.

Somewhere here there would be all of them. And her brushes and her bags and her pictures and her vases and her books and her quilts and her jewelry and everything she had ever left as a sign of her dwelling on earth.

Somewhere here there would be her piano, rotten now, beyond music, broken up methodically, no doubt, for easier transport by a single determined, or only dense, man. It would have to be done alone. Who would want witnesses for this?

That night, he could not look at his father in his unwrinkled three-piece suit. He should have thrown his discovery in the old man's face. But he knew how far he would pierce that ferocious incomprehension. Not at all.

He couldn't mention it. He was ashamed that he couldn't. He was ashamed that he had seen it.

Spring did come to New Culloden shortly after James' discovery. He thought of the snow melting in the woods, but he couldn't make himself go back there.

As though God were trying to prove that life was not all hopeless and evil mystery, he received word that his car was repaired. It was like getting a message from another planet. He had no idea how to respond to it.

He never worked on Beckett's songs. He had never felt so alone.

PART FIVE

sweet is the calm

Chapter Twenty-Five

Kathy returned with the warm weather.

She drove into town in the middle of the night, as she always did. She wanted to settle and arrange herself before she had to meet anyone.

It was a balmy night. She threw open the windows and doors of her house and lay on her bed, listening to the curtains catch the wind. She loved the fresh, damp breezes of spring.

At first light, she got dressed and checked her refrigerator and cupboards to see what she would need. She looked at the door to her workroom. But she was through with that, tired of all that junk. She was going back to making pots. Or doing nothing. Or something else. It didn't matter. She was tired of her house, too. It had belonged to her mother and she stayed in it as a matter of convenience. Her daughter had been there for a time. A short time.

There was less and less to keep her in the area. Though her old friends took her absences for granted, they had become more and more frequent. She was accepted here, but you could be accepted anywhere. Acceptance was up to you.

She went out for a walk. She had started to rise earlier, drink less. She was tired of poisoning her system. For the last month, at a friend's house in Arizona, she had been walking five miles before breakfast. She headed out the highway for the cemetery road, turning at McGrath's. James' car was parked next to the garage. She was pleased for him that he had it back and a little surprised that he was still around. James, the lost one. There seemed even less for James here than for her.

The gravel road was soft from the spring thaw. There was no dust, it was too early in the year for mosquitoes, and too early in the morning for most people. The world was at its freshest, and she could taste the moist sweetness of life. Her solitude was spoiled a little by the sight of a parked car up the road. It was facing her and the driver's door was standing open. It was one of the sheriff's cars. She searched the fields for the sight of a man. He had probably stopped to pee or watch some deer. She couldn't see anyone.

But as she came closer, she saw something beneath the door of the car. Bare legs. She smiled at the thought of an early morning sexual adventure on county time and wondered if she should intrude on it. She knew a couple of the deputies. But the legs looked limp, awkward. She stopped, squinted at them, then started to run. They didn't move as she approached.

It was one of the deputies she knew, viciously beaten, naked, and handcuffed to the steering wheel. He was wheezing and blood was running from his mouth and his scalp. She tried to raise his head gently but he moaned in agony. His wrists were raw.

The radio was smashed. There was nothing to cover him with. She didn't hesitate or dawdle helplessly but started running back to McGrath's. It was about a mile and a half.

A third of the way there she could barely breathe and she cursed her body and lax habits. She was running as fast as she could. It was taking forever. She saw Madison coming out of his door. He was looking at the sky. She tried to yell but could barely make a sound. So she kept running.

Madison started to come down the drive with his dog. She was almost at the highway. He saw her and stopped, puzzled. She waved at him and pointed up the road, kept coming until she stood by him, doubling up with a pain in her side.

"Kathy. What is it?"

She was gasping horribly, like a sick animal. She pointed again. "Sheriff's deputy. All beat up, handcuffed. We've got to help him."

Madison took it in quickly. "We'll take my car. Open the garage and get in it. I'll call the sheriff, then come back with my first aid kit. And some bolt cutters."

She nodded. She straightened up and walked toward the garage. Her legs were cramping. She felt faint and nauseous from her run. Blackstone followed her. She patted his head.

McGrath was out quickly. He chained Blackstone in the yard, and they sped down the driveway.

Kathy had caught her breath. She said, "Welcome back to the quiet life of New Culloden."

"Whoever said that?"

"I think of it that way. When I'm away."

"That's *why* you think of it that way."

She thought she had brought the emergency to the right man, efficient, capable, steady, and she reflected on what it would have been like to present James with such a challenge.

McGrath cut the chain on the handcuffs while Kathy held the deputy. McGrath got a blanket from his car to cover him. They examined his wounds. He had some teeth missing.

"I don't think there's much we can do," said McGrath. "Clean the blood off perhaps."

She worked at it, but they weren't there very long until the sheriff's car pulled up, followed by an ambulance.

They took away the deputy and questioned Kathy but she couldn't tell them very much. McGrath waited for her.

He took her back to his house for coffee. Waiting for it to perk, she said she'd like to wake James. "By all means," said McGrath.

She went upstairs and sat on his bed. He looked younger asleep, washed clean. She wondered how things were going for him. She put her hand on his stomach and shook him. He blinked, opened his eyes wide, started to speak, blinked. She leaned over him. "Been hibernating, lover? I have."

He sat up. "What are you doing here—back—here?"

"I just got back in town. But you'll have to get dressed and come downstairs for the rest of the story." She kissed him on the forehead. "Look sharp."

James pulled on his robe and shuffled to his bathroom. He was having a hard time assimilating her appearance. He went downstairs without bothering to dress.

McGrath looked at him with parental disappointment. "Ready for anything, eh? I never see you this early and now I'm happy I don't."

Drop dead, thought James.

Kathy said, "I was just thinking what it would have been like if I'd met James coming out of the house." McGrath snorted.

The both of you, thought James.

"So," he said. "What's the big adventure?"

Kathy told him while his father nodded smugly, as though some point in dispute between them were being settled in his favor.

James said, "Why would anybody do something like that?"

McGrath snorted again. "*How* is more the question. What was that deputy doing? Sleeping? He ought to be fired."

"Madison."

McGrath ignored her. "But *why*?! Are you serious? You're looking at the human norm, my boy. Every minute something like that does *not* take place is a hard-won victory for civilization. Sheriff's department! What's the use? There aren't enough of them. Never will be, never could be. If we're not all formed by the law, nothing will keep us down. We all have to make the choice for order. It appears that more and more of us are failing to do that. The rest of us have to expect things like this. We have to be ready. Why, indeed!"

The two men did not so much glare at each other as stare through each other in incomprehension. Kathy sensed some twisted bond of hatred between them. It was time for James to be gone. Long past.

James drank his coffee. Now that she was before him, his wanting her was giving place to the hurt she had caused him. He wondered how to begin again with her, if he could. It would have to be sometime other than this morning.

She said, "I'd better go. Thanks for the coffee. And thanks for the help."

McGrath nodded once, quickly, imperiously. James said, wanting her as much as ever now that she was leaving, "I'll walk you to the door."

She smiled at him. At the door, he said, "I'm glad you're back. Let's do something tonight." Then, weakened by sleep and surprise, he blurted out, "I always hate it when you pick up and leave. It really hurts."

Poor James, she thought. She wanted to tell him: and you never have the sense to go. But she said, "Come over tonight."

He nodded. The rasping whine of an airplane engine burst over them, the screen door shook in Kathy's hand, and a dark shape swooped across the yard.

"A little low, wasn't he?" said Kathy.

"You get used to it."

Chapter Twenty-Six

She let him make love to her. And there had always been so much desire and confusion brewing in him when they parted that he found a greater gift in the lying next to her, their passion spent, the evening stretching ahead of them in the calm of their satisfaction, their fragile union. They lay on her bed without dressing, drank the wine he had brought, talked quietly. She told him of her friend in Arizona and he felt privileged in glimpsing for the first time her life away from New Culloden.

There wasn't much to tell on his part. New Culloden had endured another winter. He wanted to tell her about his discovery of his mother's things. But it lay in him like some alien thing he could not rid himself of. He had been a guilty witness of something he could not even imagine taking place. Without wanting it, he bore the stain of discovery, was shamed by implication. And maybe something like this was why Kathy never spoke of her past. He gained some peace for himself by thinking that.

As midnight approached, he wondered if she would ask him to stay the night. But she finished her wine, kissed him, rose, and said, "I'll walk you home."

Still, after this evening, he could live with that.

They heard distant shots as they stepped outside. Three quick, dull blasts. Then another.

"What's that?" said James.

"Maybe just some of the boys thawing out with spring. But after this morning I'm a little spooked."

"Yeah. What a thing."

"I've seen worse. But it's never pretty."

Have you? thought James. Where? He pondered a moment, then said, "Would you really have regretted asking me for help, instead of my father? Do you think I'd be that helpless?"

"Oh, James." She put her arm through his. "Madison's just so efficient. He doesn't get rattled. First-aid response isn't really your thing, now is it?"

"I guess not."

"Look: I'm spending the evening with you. Now I would consider that a pretty fair compliment. Accept it."

I will, thought James. It's rare enough.

They walked in silence, enjoying their movement, their closeness. It was a chilly night, and by the time they reached McGrath's they were shivering a little.

"Let me give you a jacket to wear home," said James. "Unless you'd consider staying."

She looked up at him with, he hoped, some pleasure. She said, "Not tonight. First night back, lots to do. But I'm not ruling it out forever."

"So how about a jacket?"

"Oh, I'll be fine."

"Don't you think you've been heroic enough for one day?"

"Okay, James. Rescue me from the cold. Fetch a jacket."

"My big moment. God, I've waited for this all day."

Coming up the driveway, an unwelcome memory rose in him of the night Blackstone had attacked him. He could not bear the thought of looking small in front of Kathy again. He stiffened, anticipating the leap of the black hell hound.

"What's wrong?" she said.

"I was just thinking about—well, about our dog."

"Oh." She nodded. "Well, it looks like we're safe. We're almost at the house."

"He's probably still inside. Watch out when I open the door. He comes out like a rocket."

The house was dark. James wondered if his father had gone to bed early, exhausted from his morning adventure. He got the door open and fumbled for the light switch, expecting Blackstone to come flying at him.

The lights went on. A shotgun barrel was pointing into his face. He leaped back, knocking Kathy outside. "Jesus Christ!"

It was McGrath. Kathy peered around the door. She laughed. "It's OK, Madison. If you feel that way about it, I'll marry him. But only at gunpoint."

McGrath lowered his weapon. James didn't think he was in a joking mood. McGrath said, "What's the idea of sneaking in this way?"

James said, "We weren't sneaking. Well—I was trying to be quiet because I didn't want to get mauled by that dog."

"Dog?"

"Yeah. Blackstone, you know. The dog."

"Blackstone?"

James and Kathy exchanged glances. James said slowly, "What's with the gun?"

McGrath rubbed his eyes. "I was dozing. I thought I heard shots. Very close."

"So did we," said Kathy. "But it was hard to tell where they were coming from."

McGrath looked confused. "What were you saying about Blackstone?"

James began, "Well, I just didn't want—"

McGrath silenced him with an irritated wave of his hand. "I haven't seen him. He wasn't outside?"

James couldn't resist asking, "Didn't you let him out at midnight?"

"The last time I saw him," said Kathy, "was when you chained him up this morning. When you came out to help me."

McGrath looked at James with disgust. "So the dog's been chained up all day. Not fed either, I assume. Can I depend on you for nothing?"

James was flabbergasted. "Me? Me? He's your dog. What's the matter with you?"

"Of course. I should do everything. Has it never occurred to you that I might be busy? In fact, I believe we discussed this once. Yes! We did."

"Busy? You were busy today? Doing what? Pissing more people off? Or were you scheduled to lecture the sheriff's department on what morons they are?"

McGrath's eyes widened. He was unused to rebellion this close to home. "It seems to me my activities can be of little concern to you. Please be so good as to go unchain that dog. Kathy, you may step in for a drink, if you like." He turned and walked away.

James flushed with anger. Kathy put her hand on his arm. She whispered, "Something's wrong. I've never seen Madison like this."

Looks pretty normal to me, thought James.

She continued, "Go ahead. Let the dog loose. I'll go in. Something's bothering him. It's not you."

He took a deep breath. "Okay."

But nothing was going to calm him down. He never relished his father's humiliating comments, least of all in front of Kathy. Damn his father and damn his father's dog.

He tried to control himself a little as he felt his way in the pitch-dark yard. Above and beyond his anger, he was spooked by McGrath being armed, not to mention dangerous and devious. He could probably blow James' head off without blinking and get himself a suspended sentence, if not an acquittal. Better hurry and find the dog. James wished Blackstone were some other color besides black. Phosphorescent orange, maybe. He might be a little easier to see.

The worthless thing must be asleep or James was sure he would have been attacked by now. Or he was pissed off, like everybody else.

He bumped into the dog house. No one home.

It occurred to James that this might be a fool's errand. His father was just coming out of a nap when they arrived. The old coot had probably both fed and released the dog long ago and it had just slipped his mind. At this moment, Blackstone was probably hot in pursuit of female flesh, or fur, while James was stumbling around in the dark trying to satisfy the whims of the dog's master.

Next thing you know, he thought, he'll want to chain me up.

Well, he would be as methodical as possible before reporting back to McGrath. He felt on the ground for the stake that anchored the chain. He pulled on the chain. It came easily, as though it were attached to nothing, until he got the slack out, then it went taut, as though it were attached to concrete. He stared at the chain in his hands, bewildered. From where he was, the chain went up.

His flesh crawled with fear. He walked forward, following the chain until it was out of his reach. It went up into one of the trees. It seemed to be looped over a branch. Unless Blackstone can fly, he thought, he's probably long gone and some kids were fooling with the chain.

He peered into the branches, moving under the tree. He bumped hard into something and screamed with fright. It moved away. James was frozen. Then it collided with him again, soft, slimy. He flailed at it and stumbled backwards, panting in terror. He ran for the house. He didn't look back, too focused and too afraid.

He tore open the door and threw himself inside, losing his balance, catching himself against the wall. He looked at his hands, streaked, blood red, and shouted inarticulately. Kathy came running. She stopped dead when she saw him, put her hand over her mouth. "Oh, my God. Oh, my God."

James was shaking. If he could have shaken his hands loose from his arms, he would have. He looked down at himself. There were blotches of blood, dark slime, all over him. What had he met? His stomach turned and he retched once. He doubled over and vomited.

"What's happening to you?" she shouted. She was holding his shoulders. He vomited again.

McGrath was there. "Get him turned around," he ordered. "Set him here." He studied James for a moment. "This isn't your blood."

James shook his head. "I bumped against something. Something. Out there."

McGrath rose slowly. And James would think later that he already knew, he knew without being told and without having to look, because he came back and went outside with a flashlight and not the shotgun, he knew but he had to go and look anyway. And James would think: there was something admirable in McGrath.

Kathy got some rags and wet washcloths and started cleaning James up. His hands couldn't stop shaking. They heard McGrath bellow, angrily, hopelessly. Kathy held his hand and looked out the door. McGrath came back in. He was more of a mess than James. Without a word, he moved past them, stepping deliberately, returned with a blanket, and went outside again.

James stood up. Kathy opened the door. McGrath carried in his burden, covered in the blanket. He set it down under the coat rack.

"They shot off his legs. Those were the shots we heard. They slit his throat, hung him up. Disemboweled—" His voice cracked. "Disemboweled him." He was trying to list facts, make a report, wrest order from the madness. "His eyes were—" McGrath's voice was hollow. He looked at the floor and tried to clear his throat. Tears fell clumsily from his eyes. "His—"

Kathy moaned, "Oh, no." She put her head against McGrath's chest and hugged him He pushed her away. She went to James and he put his arm around her. He felt faint, sick. He felt guilty.

McGrath looked at the blanket. He said quietly, to himself, "Now why did I bring him here? I have to bury him. No. I'll do it in the morning. But he liked to be outside at night. Why did I bring him here?"

He stooped to lift his beloved dog, straightened, then swayed a little.

"I'll help," said James.

McGrath shrieked, "No!" Then he said quietly, "I'm sorry. I want—I'll do it."

They waited for McGrath to come back. Then Kathy went out to look for him. She returned quickly and said, "It's alright. He's just sitting out there. Let's get you cleaned up."

Kathy stayed the night. She lay on the sofa in the living room. James sat on the floor with his back against it, her arm across his chest. They slept fitfully. When the room lightened, James rose. He pulled a blanket over Kathy. He went to the kitchen and looked out the window.

McGrath was sitting on some straw, his back against the dog house. The blanket he had taken out the night before was over his legs. He was cradling Blackstone. His lips were moving.

Chapter Twenty-Seven

It had no connection with anything. That was the most horrifying thing about it. It meant nothing, neither revenge nor taunt nor calculation for profit. It was cold and meaningless. It could have been done to anybody.

The sheriff's department caught them two days later. They were two young escaped prisoners from downstate, headed for the Canadian border. They confessed to some thefts, beating the deputy, mutilating several animals. It had nothing to do with McGrath, with anything he had ever said or done or stood for. But once done, it had everything to do with him.

Now McGrath could have asked, in his turn, why anybody would do such a thing. James never knew if he formulated that question to himself or if he answered it glibly. James would not have dared to formulate it for him.

How it came about did not bear thinking either. James kept waiting for his father to throw the dog's immobility at him. But McGrath did not. He spoke very little. He seemed very composed when he did.

But now he slept for most of the day. At night he was in his office over the garage or prowling the yard. It was as though he had taken over the life of Blackstone. He failed to walk uptown for his mail. James carried it home, but it just piled up on the kitchen table.

James missed his father's iron routine. His own life now appeared more regular than McGrath's, and this unnerved him. The earth might as well have been slipping beneath his feet. He wondered how long this would last, what he could do about it. He supposed: nothing at all.

The weather was warm and wet. Spring was coming early, regardless of what humanity was up to. New Culloden took on a shaggy, wild look as Einar Ekdahl was too busy this year to beat back the wilderness. The rodeo was arriving soon, and he was printing and distributing posters. In his spare time, he was out working on the shell of the building that was to be the New Culloden Mall. It was acquiring a decidedly home-made look.

James neglected his own mowing because he didn't want to wake his father. It was also becoming dangerous to be about the yard during the day, as the pilot was buzzing them lower and lower, intoxicated by the delirium of spring. The thought of losing his head to a propeller did not please James. Moreover, the pilot had given up any pretense of attempting to stop his spray at the tree line and, when he roared through the McGrath yard, he left thick clouds of chemical death.

Though he was neither a lawyer nor a property owner, it yet seemed to James that this was a ridiculous way to live. He decided to try negotiating with their aerial foe.

But he thought he needed a neutral emissary. Ekdahl was out because no one in New Culloden was neutral about Ekdahl. James was not even sure Danny was neutral enough. So one night at the *Mudhole*, he sent Kathy over to talk to the man before he was too far into his evening stupor. He watched her do most of the talking. She shrugged, came back. He asked her how she had done.

She shook her head. "Forget it. Think of another plan. Maybe he'll drink himself to death. Tough it out until then."

"C'mon. What did he say? I can compromise. Maybe my dad won't have to know. What's he want?"

"He wants you to go fuck yourself. Happy? Still willing to meet him half way?"

"Did you tell him my dad's—well, that he's a little disturbed since—well, you know. Did you tell him?"

"Same answer, James."

Kathy had not been willing to spend much time at the McGrath place since the night they had found Blackstone. James had spent a few nights with her but then had become worried about his father roaming the property alone all night. He thought he should at least be available. In case of what, he could not have said. Anything, he supposed. Anything.

He dropped her off that night and walked home alone. She was no longer offering to accompany him and he couldn't blame her for that. She had begun to seem distant, willfully distant now, as though she were stepping back cautiously from something unknown but clearly harmful. He couldn't blame her for that either.

There were no lights on in McGrath's office. James entered the house and flipped on one light after another. He didn't trust the dark. As he hit the living room switch, a great roar came out of the window at him, as though a bomb had gone off. Shards of glass covered him, flew by his ears, danced in the light.

It seemed to take him forever to assimilate this data, communicate with his limbs, take shelter near the floor.

Another blast came from the shattered window and the light was gone. It had not been a bomb. Someone was shooting at him He heard a metallic sound, quick footsteps. He cowered on the floor. Right, he thought, negotiate. Now that drunken lunatic has come back to blow us away. Then he thought of his Christmas present, his chrome twelve gauge shotgun, standing ready in the downstairs closet. For home defense.

He supposed this was the time for it. He crawled to the closet, as though he knew what he was doing. He kept waiting for another shot, the last thing he would hear, but none came. The shotgun was leaning against the wall, just inside the closet door. Three boxes of shells were stacked next to it. James sat on the closet floor, trying to figure out how to load it.

He thought: I have to wound him because I don't want to go to jail for killing him. But since I've never fired this, I have no idea how to control it. Aim low, I'll have to aim low. Anyway, my father is a lawyer.

He thought: who am I kidding? He stood the gun up again, unloaded and not to be loaded, as far as he was concerned. He thought: but my father is out there.

Of course. His father was out there. Of course. No one had come to kill them.

It was his father that was doing the shooting. James crawled back to the door, took a deep breath, threw it open, and was about to yell: it's me, it's James, it's alright.

But suppose his father knew that. Suppose his father were deliberately shooting at him. Unpalatable as the thought was, it was more unpalatable to present himself as a target. This doubt silenced him, thus leaving the door swinging open noisily, his own body framed by it, and no word of explanation or identification shouted to protect it.

And so, he found himself thinking, as another blast tore the door off its hinges, if he wants to kill me *or* if he only thinks I'm an intruder, I've just chosen my own death. The optimum choice would have been to announce myself, hoping it was all a mistake. More merciless, comfortless knowledge.

He dove out the door, picked himself up and ran for his car. He heard more blasts behind him, felt a rush of power at his side, like the wake of a splendid runner leaving him in the dust, heard the tires of his car blow.

He kept running and made it to the other side of his car. He lay on the ground. Various fluids were running out of his engine from the countless holes McGrath's fire was putting into it.

Once he decided to identify himself, it took him some time to collect his voice. Finally he shouted, "Dad! It's me!"

"Where are you?" McGrath sounded concerned, anxious.

Relief. His father wasn't gunning for him. "Behind my car. It's me. Don't shoot."

"Keep quiet!"

His father ran out of the darkness and crouched next to him, his back against the car, reloading his weapon with shells he was pulling from his pockets. "Someone in the house," he whispered. "I thought he ran this way."

"It was *me*," whispered James, wondering why he was whispering.

"You were in the house?"

"Yes."

"I'm glad I fired, then. He must have been waiting for you. I suppose you didn't have time to grab your gun."

"You fired at *me*. There wasn't anybody else in the house. You were firing at me."

"Don't be absurd." McGrath raised his head above the hood. "I don't see anyone. You stay here. I'll make a sweep of the yard. If it's clean, we'll check out the house. But keep your eye on the door and holler if you see anything. Can you do that? James? Can you do that?"

"Can I stay here and watch the door? I think I can do that. I'd love to do that."

"Good." McGrath disappeared again.

There was a kind of consolation in knowing his father felt he was protecting him. Or was it a deeper, more vicious attack, perverting even the eye's casual glance, to look at your son and see *someone else*, someone you must destroy?

He stood up, forgetting his lunatic pledge to watch the door. He regarded his car, his poor, ruined car. His poor father. His own poor self. But when McGrath returned, they must search the house, only to find nothing.

James had a few minor cuts. McGrath dressed them. McGrath showed James how to load his shotgun. They sat up until dawn, drinking coffee. McGrath told stories about his army days.

He looked tired, old, frail. The animated talk coming out of him seemed to issue from someone else, it was too large and healthy for him, as though the devils had moved in and, having feasted upon him, had used him up and now had to use their own fierce voices. James felt madness in the kitchen that night and, at dawn, knew why God should be thanked for the light.

He felt grateful for a kind of steadiness that came over things then. McGrath, seeming more himself, began to fret over the cleaning and the planning of repairs. Unlike Ekdahl, he wasn't one to live with temporary patches. But James stopped him before he could run out to arrange for a new window. "Look, dad. It can wait a day. Why don't you get some sleep? I'll finish up here. I'll rig something up. I know where I can get some plywood."

To his amazement, McGrath agreed, as though his son had said something sensible.

Chapter Twenty-Eight

James drove his father's car out to where Ekdahl was working on the mall. He had never been out to see it up close, preferring to stay uninvolved in this particular project. He knew it was a pipe-dream, but he was not prepared for what he saw.

What construction had been done so far had been done by a pair of Ekdahl's cousins, who did small building jobs in the area. They were happy enough, in their spare time, to do whatever Ekdahl wanted. But what he wanted changed constantly as his fantasies revealed to him ever new horizons.

To the original potato warehouse structure, only half finished, Ekdahl had added, as the money became available to him, three small wings. These existed now only as wooden skeletons. The entire complex had an open-ended air, and not only because of the lack of sides. It had retained the eternal promise of absolute chaos, no option had been closed off by sensible choice, incongruous parts could continue to be added forever.

No work was in progress when James drove up. Ekdahl was scurrying around, climbing ladders, taking measurements, setting up signs: 'big store—expensive'; 'big store—cheap'; 'hobby stores'; 'clothing stores'; 'trees and fountains'; 'people eating snacks'; 'people talking politics'; 'children on playground equipment'. Ekdahl wasn't building a mall. He was building a world, a world shaped by a vision of commerce, of people gathering together to buy things. He could imagine no sweeter dawn than the fluorescent lights flickering on in a department store.

All he needed were the things for people to buy, the people to buy them, the money to buy them with, and the jobs that would provide the money, which he was hoping the mall would create. The building itself was Einar Ekdahl's Big Bang and he was counting on everything else to be ignited into being by it.

He waved to James and showed him his newest sign: 'ice cream—yum'. "Where do you think it should go? Of course it could go anywhere and, you know, none of this has to be for certain. We can change it around, there's lots of possibilities."

James looked around. "Next to 'children on playground equipment' would be good. Then, too, if you put it next to 'people talking politics', it might cool them off a little, keep them in a good mood."

Ekdahl's face brightened happily. "Wonderful! Wonderful! Keep them in a good mood. That's what we want. That's where it'll go. I'm glad you're on the staff."

"Right. Say, Einar, I need a sheet of plywood. Could you let me have one? I'll give it back. I'm not going to cut it up or anything. I just need it—to cover something for a day or so."

"Sure, sure. There's a pile of them over there. Take all you need. We've got everything on hold here, you know, these things don't go up in a day."

"Yeah. Well, thanks." James felt it would be awkward to run off after begging a favor from Ekdahl, especially one granted so graciously. He hung around and let himself be shown the mall's progress. Ekdahl ran back and forth, shifting signs constantly.

At last, there was little more that could be said about the empty shell. James asked, as a kind of final summing up, "So how's the rodeo? Just about ready to start? It's in two days, right?"

Ekdahl cleared his throat. "You know, there are always problems with these things, you know, nothing ever runs as smoothly as people think. Little wrinkles."

"What wrinkles? They're coming, aren't they?"

"Oh, sure, sure. They started setting up yesterday. Just a few wrinkles."

"What wrinkles?"

Ekdahl looked at the sky, seeming to wonder what could be beyond it, what mystery that so complicated things. "Well, you know, I took some kids out there, a promotional, you know, a promotional thing. I wanted them to look at the animals, you know, it would get them interested, they'd bring their parents, the stands would be filled."

James said apprehensively, "Yeah. So?"

"People can get hurt around these things, you know, you have to expect that. They get bruised, they break their necks, they get cut up."

"Einar. One of the kids you took out there broke his neck?"

"Yes, well, her neck, you know, accidents happen."

"My God."

"Oh, no harm done, no harm done. In a few months she'll be walking, you know. I'm not saying she won't limp."

"But that's awful."

"You know, you have to expect it. Of course, hospitals, you know, they want their money."

"Well, there's insurance—right?"

Ekdahl sighed. "Their insurance covers their people."

"No. We have insurance. I arranged it, remember? I gave you the bill." James frowned. "Einar, I gave you the bill."

"These things are never simple, you know, you have to cut corners. Everyone does it all the time."

"Not that corner!"

Ekdahl shrugged.

James said, "So what's going to happen?"

Ekdahl shrugged again. He started rearranging signs.

James got his plywood and drove home. He was happy that his name had not been on any of the documents connected with the rodeo. It was not the noblest or most compassionate thought he might have had, but it still made him happy.

His father came around to watch him nail up the plywood. McGrath had his shotgun over his shoulder, but he seemed relaxed. James told him about the incident at the rodeo. Some months ago, he would not have done this. But he was at his wit's end with Ekdahl. And something in him wanted to be close to his father.

McGrath was jubilant. "Did you get the name? Of the girl, the girl. No? Never mind. That's no problem. And the fool didn't—unbelievable!" He sprinted back to his office.

Some months ago, McGrath's reaction would have disgusted James. But he was glad to see some of McGrath's normal fire come back into him. Having seen him so grief stricken at the slaughter of his dog, James had worried about his health. And there had been something embarrassing about such naked suffering, something James would rather not see in his father, something too touching beneath and above their differences, something that issued too much of a claim. James preferred the old, indomitable, immovable McGrath, the McGrath with no claims on his sympathy.

His father returned smiling. He had his jacket off, his vest open, his sleeves rolled up. Ekdahl's misfortune had called him back from whatever unholy places he had been haunting. Maybe, thought James, we all pay for each other's lives one way or another. That's how it is, and that's all it is, and there's nothing to be done about it. He drove in the last nail and smiled at his father.

McGrath said, "It's a little crooked."

James sighed, opened his mouth to say something like: it's only temporary. Then the plane came upon them, trailing its cloud of malice. James ducked as the noise and smoke enveloped him. He looked up. McGrath was gone.

He could see the plane turning over the northern tree line and heading down on them again. He ran around the corner of the house, into the backyard. McGrath was striding out of the garage with his shotgun.

"Dad!"

The plane dipped and buzzed over them. The racket of its engine and the rush of its body terrified James. He threw himself to the ground. He heard McGrath fire.

"Dad!"

"Get in the house!"

"How about you?"

"Get in the house!"

It was coming again. They could hear its whine coming up from the river. McGrath set his feet and waited for it to appear over the trees. It seemed to burst from their top branches, drop lower, fill the sky. McGrath fired, pumped, fired, pumped fired. The plane, unscathed, continued on.

James stood up. His father was running for a better position, but he tripped over the stake of Blackstone's chain. The he rose on one knee and fired twice at the doghouse. Its wood splintered. James shouted and McGrath swung the barrel around at him, firing. Some bark flew off a tree next to him. "Jesus Christ! Dad!"

The plane was returning. McGrath stood up, reloaded.

He started firing again before James could see it. He followed it as it came straight over him, pivoted, and continued firing until his magazine was empty. He slapped his pockets for shells. He looked at the sky, the garage, at James. He gripped the shotgun like a club, hefted it.

James heard the plane's motor cough.

And he never knew if McGrath had hit it or if some mechanical problem, unrelated to human passion and stress, had happened at this moment to unravel its consequences. James never knew if McGrath had hit it or if it had clipped some power lines or if God had reached down in wrath to rid the world of a nuisance.

But it was in flames when it returned. It was dripping fire, shedding its skin as it came over them. McGrath threw down his weapon. Something was burning on the garage roof. James watched the plane climb out of their clearing, climb high, gloriously alight, then level off and head away.

McGrath was holding his head, staggering.

The plane was a fireball, descending like a meteor. With narrowing choices, the pilot was heading for his home, not to arrive, not to be saved, not to relive the day, but only to make the gesture.

The garage was afire. McGrath sank to his knees, pitched over. James ran to him, turned him on his back. Then he ran for the house to call an ambulance.

He heard a far-off explosion. He hoped someone else would call the fire department. The garage was gone before the ambulance arrived and James didn't bother to wait for the fire department.

When they got McGrath to the hospital, one of the nurses told him the pilot had overshot his runway and crashed into Ekdahl's mall. Ekdahl had left moments before the crash to buy some pennants and streamers. Both the mall and the McGrath garage had burned to the ground.

Chapter Twenty-Nine

The pilot, still alive, barely alive, was rushed to a hospital in Fargo, North Dakota, as the girl with the broken neck had been. He died in two days.

No one mentioned any evidence of the plane being fired upon. No one gave any indication of knowing its last flight was the personal vendetta of a maniac. James decided his father had missed with every shot. After all, he had missed James every time he shot at him.

So James, willing enough to accept the sympathy offered him, went along with the common deception. Given the state of general ignorance, he wondered why he didn't get more sympathy.

Einar Ekdahl had not yet absorbed what had happened to him. James heard he was stringing up pennants around the smoldering remains of his mall. James decided he could simply put up one more oversized sign: 'mall', and save himself a lot of trouble.

The girl with the broken neck was said to have an excellent chance of full recovery. Everyone in the hospital said it was a lucky break, for her, if not for Ekdahl. This did not quell the wrath of her parents. They would be seeing Einar Ekdahl and the New Culloden City Council in court. They would not, however, be represented by Madison McGrath. James thought that might increase their chances of success.

McGrath had not regained consciousness. The doctors said he had had a stroke. James didn't find this very enlightening, as his father might have predicted. Everything seemed to be working to prove one or another of his father's points. James found this neither enlightening nor consoling. It didn't do McGrath much good either.

Or maybe it did. McGrath's face had settled into a smirk which James could not believe was involuntary. He even asked one of the doctors about it. The man looked at him as though he were crazy.

Unless he was busy with lessons, James sat in the Carlsburg hospital day and night. One of the nurses remarked upon his devotion. This surprised James. He sat there feeling cursed.

He seemed to be waiting for his father to wake up and present him with some decision. McGrath had managed to chain him to this place more firmly than ever. The life he was living, the life around him, seemed intolerable. Again, he reflected, he had dallied and played and wasted time. Now he was trapped by a man who despised everything about him, a man who would decide neither to live nor to die.

It was more oppressive weight his father had tossed upon him, the weight of his own helpless life, and James could see no way out from under it.

Late one night, sleepless, he was pacing the hospital corridor. From one of the darkened rooms, he heard, "Ho, ho, ho."

He grinned despite himself and peeked in. "Patty, what are you doing here?"

"Giving birth, James, giving birth. We have a new, eight hour old baby girl. I'm surprised you didn't hear me screaming earlier."

He came in and took a chair near her bed. "I must have been gone. I go back and forth for my lessons."

"How's your dad?"

"The same. Still unconscious."

"That's too bad. He was quite a guy."

Is, is, he wanted to say. *He's not dead yet.*

The anger he felt at her shocked him. He took a deep breath. He said, "Apparently they just don't know how these things go."

"I guess not." Her eyes wandered. She seemed a little dreamy.

"I'd better go and let you rest."

"That's a pretty standard hospital exit line. Can't you think of anything more creative?"

He smiled at her unquenchable sarcasm. And Patty had gotten along with his father much better than he had. He thought of his father and friendships, his father and women, more mysteries. He said, "Sorry. I guess I'm anxious to get back to my dad."

She nodded, as though she understood. James wished he did. She said, "Come back and see me, as long as you're here. I'm still pretty far out of it. One thing about hospitals: the drugs are great."

James returned to his father's room. The drugs weren't great enough to help McGrath. James supposed even drugs needed a little co-operation from the patient. Perhaps he was seeing the perfection of Madison McGrath here: unapproachable, incommunicative, uncooperative to the end.

McGrath had at last reached an inner, perverse independence so imposing that it reduced everyone around him to slaves. But the tubes and the needles in him seemed like a kind of torture, the disguised malice of servants. In the morning, James asked the doctor what would happen if he pulled them out.

The doctor frowned. "With this particular patient? Medically, it would mean the end. Speaking more broadly, you'd probably be locked up and, if Minnesota ever brought back the death penalty, you'd be executed, which would undoubtedly please the deceased."

"Didn't like my father much, did you?"

"Let's say he made my life difficult. Did you like him?"

James shrugged. He could have said: let's say he made my life difficult, too.

Later in the morning, his student Kris came in, carrying a rose in a slender vase. She said, "I was in town and I heard about your dad. I thought you'd be here. I brought you this to cheer you up."

"Did you know my dad?"

"Not really. But I know how you must feel."

No, you don't, he thought. You're too nice.

Kathy came in to see him after lunch. She had been down to see Patty. James had not seen much of her, but he was tired of fretting over what was and what was not going on in Kathy's mind and heart. She stood by McGrath's side, gripped his hand. James knew she at least had liked him.

She pulled up a chair next to James, squeezed his hand as well. He could still confide in her. He said, "Tell me. I want to know what you think. Is this my fault?"

She looked disturbed, worried. "Is what your fault?"

"This. What happened to my dad. Do you think I brought it on?"

She shook her head slowly, baffled. "How could this be your fault?"

"I don't know. Just being around, I guess. All the stuff I did with Einar. He hated that. He really hated that. And—well, everything."

"That's stupid. No. Don't even think that. It's worse than stupid. It's con- ceited. It's smug. Who gave you power over life and death? Well?"

"I guess you're right."

But his father had not only hated his work with Ekdahl. His father had hated every choice he made and everything he did.

He sat there alone, after she left, thinking he must leave soon for his lessons. He had spent all the time in the room silently, never being able to think of anything to say. He realized he was humming to himself, humming hymn tunes. McGrath, if he could hear them, was probably in agony.

So be it. That was what James was. The old man could take it or leave it. Hate it or not. James left.

Madison McGrath thought he heard the regular, resounding stamp of a column of marching men. They were crossing a bridge. He was preparing some dynamite to blow up the dam that had formed Lake Culloden. He wanted to do it without de- stroying the bridge. It was of some value to him. By the rude bridge that arched the flood, their flag to April's breeze unfurled, there once the embattled farmers stood, and fired the shot heard round the world.

He heard the drums beating and the fifes playing their silly, brave tunes: *The Rights of Man, La Belle Catherine, The Rakes of Mallow, Yankee Doodle.* He saw the line of doomed redcoats stepping out across a green meadow under a bright American sun. He took a deep breath. The man next to him broke ranks and ran. McGrath steadied himself with a snarl of contempt. The redcoats opened fire…

There was a call waiting for James at the church to return to the hospital imme- diately. Tim said he would cancel all his lessons that day. James rushed back. His fa- ther was dead. After all his pointless waiting, his confused vigil, he had missed the end. A blood clot had formed in McGrath and killed him.

The doctor said, "With strokes, we never know. A thing like this sometimes happens."

Not to my father, thought James.

But it had. It seemed incomprehensible that McGrath's proud and tenacious discipline could be strangled, that his orderly days could be disrupted by his own blood, that his body could turn on him. It seemed incomprehensible that his orneriness alone could not keep him alive.

He walked down to Patty's room. She was sitting up. He sat close to her bed in the chair.

"James. What is it?"

"He's dead."

"Oh, no." She swung her legs off the bed and reached out to take his hands.

He looked down at her short, stubby fingers. The flesh was smooth, unwrinkled. It seemed marvelous to him, pure.

He got up and sat next to her on the bed, so he could touch something living. His body seemed to be deflating or falling and he needed something to keep him close. She put her arm around him.

"Oh, James. I'm so sorry."

He closed his eyes. McGrath was like a mountain. You may be indifferent to it, it may inconvenience you. But when it trembles, when it crumbles, all things shift and change, the world flattens, the wind shrieks through you. The mountain gone, you think you can see forever and now you realize how little you understood about anything.

Chapter Thirty

As the death of Madison McGrath made no sense, so there was no sensible way to bury him, no adequate or pertinent rite, no way of summing up. The best that could be done had perhaps already been done when his office had gone up in flames, when one of his antagonists had perished, when another had been ruined.

Anything James or New Culloden could do to observe his passing would be beside the point, in every sense. But the dead are at the mercy of the living. James insisted that a funeral be held at First Lutheran, though he more than anyone knew what his father would say about this. Because he knew.

Tim was willing enough to preside at McGrath's funeral, but he balked when James said he wanted to be the organist. "James, this is your dad's funeral. I don't think it's a good idea for you to play. You're the chief mourner. Somebody else will be happy to fill in."

"Listen. We're having it here *because* I want to play. Understand? Do you think my dad would care about any of this?"

"That's not what I'm saying. It's you I'm thinking about."

"Then think. I don't intend to sit there and listen to the shit these people consider music. This is my show and I'm playing. That's final."

"Well, I can't say no, but—"

"That's right. You can't say no. You never do. And you're not going to say no to me."

Tim held up his hands in surrender. "Okay, okay."

They would walk in singing *The Battle Hymn of the Republic*, which was the only thing in the hymnal that might bear some relation to McGrath's life. But they would recess to Luther's *A Mighty Fortress*, the Lutheran church's own battle hymn, an emblem of James' life and every way it differed from McGrath's. They would carry his father out of the church and lower him into the earth. He would be under the earth and James would still be walking upon it.

He asked Danny and Becket to be pallbearers but after that he was stumped. Beckett chose the other four from some of the older county activists who at one time or another had found themselves on McGrath's side in some legislative battle.

On the day of the funeral, James was surprised at how full the church was. His father had seemed too solitary and superior a figure to merit much popular affection. But everyone may have had their own reasons for coming, as he had his.

He thought Tim's painting of the church in red, white, and blue stripes was an appropriate preparation for this day, both comical and belligerent.

Since McGrath was a veteran, the American Legion post had turned out in their mismatched, hopelessly tight uniforms, and the coffin was draped with a large

American flag. McGrath had seen more combat than all of them put together, but he had never joined the Legion. He considered them little better than fascists. James wondered if they too were now laying a claim to McGrath when he was no longer able to dispute it.

The Carlsburg funeral director had given McGrath the usual look of the self-satisfied dead. He had made him look heavier. He had made him look ghoulishly happy. James looked closely at the face before he went up to the organ. Something had oozed from the corners of McGrath's mouth. He took out his handkerchief and wiped it away.

Something about it, the shoddiness of overlooking a detail, an untidiness at this particular moment, the distortion of his father's lean face, turned him into a proud son. He remembered that his father, unsurprisingly, had despised the Carlsburg funeral director. He went looking for him, as he thought McGrath might.

He was in a crowd outside the church, smoking and laughing. James slipped through the people who were still entering. As he came near, he heard the man say, "…only an old crab…"

He stopped, then turned around and went back inside. He couldn't be sure they were talking about McGrath, but, if they were, he was incapable of facing down their scorn. His father could have. His father had made a life of doing just that. But he had not. There was no use thinking he ever would. He walked up the aisle, ignoring the eyes that were trying to catch his.

McGrath's death had been a victory of the senseless and stupid. He sat down at the organ to make what sense he could of it. This sad organ was to him, he supposed, what he had been to his father: inadequate, hopeless, far less than reason could justly expect. His mouth tightened. Hopeless as it was, these people were going to hear what could be done with it.

He looked out at the congregation. To all of them, he was the son of the deceased; to many of them, he was their regular organist. This was his place. He was an unquestionable part of it. And all the ceremonies of the day were as familiar to this aging community as the rising and the setting of the sun. This was how burials were ordered. As his fingers touched the keys, few of them would suspect, and none of them would say, that James was defying the man in the coffin.

There is a mood expected at funerals, a fragment of emotion allotted to them from the crude resources of mass marketed culture, a mood of quiet tones and sentimentality. Freed by the intimidating power of the bereaved, James was at last in a position to ignore it.

He improvised a prelude from a medley of Welsh hymns: *Cwm Rhondda, Bryn Calfaria, St. Denio, Hyfrydol, Ar hyd y nos, Ebeneezer.* He used as much volume as his instrument could provide. He liked their strength, their bravery, their elaborate ornamentation. They overcame sorrow and defeat by delighting in their song of it. He liked their melancholy defiance.

As the congregation joined in the entrance hymn, and the coffin was taken to the steps of the altar, and everyone listened, responded, sat, and stood to Tim's directions, disciplined by the occasion, James saw that it mattered very little what anyone had come here feeling. The service was forcing them to be what they were intended to be in this place and at this time. Even McGrath, even though he would have hated it.

He didn't hear much of Tim's sermon. He was thinking of the first time he had seen his father on the day he had retreated to New Culloden, coming down the cemetery road with Blackstone, looking so easily professional, comfortable, commanding. They would go down that road today and throw him into the ground and there was nothing McGrath could do about it. There never was.

Tim was saying something about civic affairs, professional life, community service. James supposed this was standard consolation for the death of men like McGrath. But there was no victory in that, at best it was only consolation.

He looked at the coffin, then at the organ. It was what came through them that bore the hope, what leaped out of these earthly vessels that gave the victory, some moments of transcendence. He didn't know if he would say that anything like that had come out of his father. But maybe he wasn't the best judge.

Then neither was his father of him.

James had asked Lori to sing following the sermon, since he had expected Tim to do justice to neither his father nor the Christian faith. He had her sing an eleventh century Easter hymn, and he accompanied her softly and sparingly, letting the pure voice drift up and down the languid, mesmerizing chant.

She sang:

> Death and life have contended
> In that combat stupendous;
> The prince of life, who died,
> Reigns immortal.

This had nothing and everything to do with him, his father, and their lives. It was the kind of victory he was looking for.

When they sang the last hymn and carried McGrath out, James, as the only relative, should have been at the head of the procession. But no one else could have done what he was about to do. He let the last chord of Luther's hymn drift for a moment, then he hit the low pedal note of *Sine Nomine*, following it with the leap to the high inverted G-major chord. He would have had them sing it but he had wanted them to cover McGrath with their voices and so needed to provide more familiar hymns. But he wanted it played here. And he wasn't unhappy to be doing it alone.

That great beginning was a summons to judgment and glory. And the text was both a yearning for and a bestowal of that glory, as well as a diminution of the individual. It put everyone in their place. But the place was better than any they could imagine for themselves. Here was a large and stately order at the edge of death. Perhaps only James glimpsed it. The strange, driving tune, played without words, probably meant little enough to the people there, to the funeral director irritated at the enforced wait, to Tim exasperated by his willfulness, least of all to his father at any time, past, present, or future. But it was James' own ending and it was a kind of restitution.

He let himself be taken then to the graveside, endured the mumbling of the last words, the ragged firing of the Legion's rifles, the presentation of the flag. The organ was still playing in his head. He thought: I won. He looked at the coffin for the last time.

No. Death had won. But he had contended.

He had to take his turn then as the principal guest at the funeral lunch. Tim sat with him, as did Beckett, Danny, Patty, and Kathy. Kris squeezed his shoulder as she passed him. Einar Ekdahl went by, looking dazed. He was being guided by his wife. Neither spoke to him.

James had to shake many hands and look into many faces attempting to express something to him, of sympathy, of community, of memory. Most of the transactions were silent, ambiguous, searching without finding, offering the unknown, but well enough meant.

He thought how speechless and confused they all were at death, how helpless. And he saw how what he had done had, for a moment, given them a voice, shown them an order, given them what help could be given. Beckett said to him, "The music was magnificent. You gave him a splendid tribute."

But, to James, it still felt most like revenge.

PART SIX

*a yet more
glorious day*

Chapter Thirty-One

James still walked uptown for the mail. He gave his lessons. He played at the Sunday service. He stopped at the station to talk with Danny. New Culloden had never buzzed with activity, at least during his time there, but it seemed a lesser place now. It seemed, as it had during the winter, a little more itself without McGrath.

And without Ekdahl. The mayor, so reliable a presence on his lawn mower, was rarely seen anymore, except when he was haunting the site of his mall. The lawns he had kept so neat were overgrown and wild. Even the cemetery was looking shabby, and the city council was receiving complaints. A motion was made, seconded, and passed to buy more up-to-date mowing equipment.

There was talk of asking Ekdahl to resign. But he had run unopposed in the last five elections. The council decided to let him serve out his four years and discuss the issue again when the term ended.

People seemed more pleasant now to James. Danny's theory was that they somehow credited him with removing both his father and Ekdahl from their lives and were thankful for it. Or that they looked upon what had happened as a final defeat of something they had never understood and so extended to James the sympathy given to alien survivors who no longer posed a threat.

"You don't think they're just trying to be nice?" asked James.

Danny raised his eyebrows. "This is possible, too."

James could not have said how he had expected the town to react to what was, after all, only one more death in a community that had seen many. They must be used to these things, however unexpected or spectacular; must be used to going on. That James expected anything else suggested to him that he was taking it harder than he thought.

He had expected the sun to fall, the earth to quake, the people to panic. They did panic, in a sense, if heavy drinking and wild driving were signs of panic. But they had always done this, for their own reasons. And the face of the earth was shifting, but only because Ekdahl no longer mowed the grass.

James felt suspended in time. He moved through his days like a sleepwalker.

His father had only provided a place for him to come; he had been no part of his reasons for coming. But, with him gone, James could see no point in staying. But had there ever been a point? And what had McGrath to do with that?

As though in rebuttal to James' ruminations, he received word from a lawyer in Carlsburg about the terms of his father's will. The entire estate was to be liquidated, with the money to go to the American Civil Liberties Union. James was assured he could retain any personal items of the deceased. As if I'd want them, he thought. He had all that he could ever want from his father.

But the notification intensified his feeling of suspension. He could carry on with his daily tasks, but now he would have to go, to other lodgings in New Culloden if nowhere else. Put that way, he saw how little he wanted to stay.

He visited the garbage heap that held his mother's things one day, when he had nothing else to do. He thought of searching through it, to verify his suspicions, to carry something away. But he didn't have the heart. This was where the things had come. This was where he would leave them.

Then the direction he was waiting for fell upon him. Spending another blank evening in his father's living room, he received a telephone call.

"James McGrath?" It was a woman's voice.

"Yes."

"I've talked to you before. About a year ago. My name's Pastor Johnson and we were looking for an organist."

"Yes. I remember."

"We're *still* looking. No one's worked out. And—this was the oddest thing—someone recommended you, and then I remembered we had talked before. You weren't interested then but I thought I'd give you another try. Actually, it was a seminary classmate of mine who recommended you. She said to tell you hello. From Stephanie."

"Well. Hello." The woman laughed pleasantly. James continued, "How is she? And—her husband?"

"Both fine. They just moved. Someplace in Texas. Talk about a culture shock. Can you *imagine*? *Texas*?"

"No, I can't."

"So, James McGrath. Would you be interested in the position?"

"I guess—I would. Very interested."

The terms were the same his friend had explained to him a year ago. He would come down for an audition but, after all the trouble they had had, it would be only a formality. He would begin as an interim until September. If they liked him—

He would make sure they liked him. They were offering him his life back. He would kill for them if necessary.

"When's the earliest you can start?" she asked finally.

"I can drive there in six or seven hours."

"Whoa! Give us a week to get ready! Let's say a week from tomorrow. Be here first thing in the morning, I'll have the worship committee here, we'll talk, you'll start. We're sick of looking."

"Well, I'll be there."

"Well, we'll be waiting."

Well.

Stephanie. He wished now he had answered her letter. Apparently it hadn't bothered her. Maybe she was still trying to work off the guilt. Then thank God for guilt.

He was leaving. He had someplace to go, therefore he was leaving. It was as simple as that. He walked over to Kathy's in the morning to share the news. He found her packing boxes.

"What's up?" he asked.

"Getting rid of my stuff. Stuff! What an appropriate word. Stuff. It makes me feel like a turkey—stuffed. All this crap. Ooh, how did I ever stand it?"

"Why?"

"I'm going." She stopped fussing with her package and looked at him. "I'm going. For good. There's nothing for me here." She gave him her wise smile. "You should go, too. You haven't been happy here, James. Even before Madison died. You know it. So do it."

"I am. That's what I came to tell you." He told her about his phone call, described the position, what he had heard of the church.

Her attention wandered. She was full of her own eagerness. "Back to the rat race, huh? Well, best of luck."

This struck him as a little flippant after what they had been to one another. Or she had been to him. He had to admit that he never knew what he had been to Kathy. Inviting her to come with him had crossed his mind. He said, "So. Where are you off to?"

"Simple things. I'm sick of all this crap."

"Okay. But where? Say, geographically."

"I heard from my husband again. My long lost lover. He lives in Montana."

"You're going back to him? You know, somebody told me he was dead." Her *lover*. That hurt. Her lover.

"Who told you that?"

"I don't know. Danny, I think."

"Danny's like everybody else around here. What they don't see doesn't exist. Let me tell you: my husband lives so primitively it's a wonder he still uses words. No wonder no one notices him. He lives in a little shack, no running water. He told me he's stopped believing in electricity."

"What—does that mean?"

"Something about spirituality and vibrations. I can't wait to talk to him about it."

"Well, don't forget to pack your candles. How'd he get in touch with you? Carrier pigeon? Smoke signals?"

"He's literate, James. He's just pulled out of it all. He lives the simple life, real life. I really envy him sometimes."

"Oh, yeah. Sounds great."

She ignored him. "Listen: if you want my piano now, it's yours. Take it away. I'm finished with all this."

He thought of his mother's piano then, and because he had to tell someone, and because he had told her so much, he told Kathy about what he had found that wet spring afternoon.

Once he started, he was a little sorry he had. She didn't seem to be paying attention. But she said, "Really? Everything? It was all out there?"

He nodded. He thought, for a moment, she was going to come to him and hold him. But she looked away. Perhaps it would have been too much of a claim on her, something not simple, something she could not leave behind with her furniture.

She said, "Did you ever ask Madison about it?"

"I never could."

"Right. And now you never can."

James thought of what counted as an explanation for his father and decided that Kathy wasn't as smart as she thought she was. He shrugged. "Yeah. Well, listen. Best of luck to you, too."

They shook hands. He thought she tried to feign warmth. Nothing seemed very simple to him then, including Kathy.

A few days later, he walked by her empty house and met Beckett, carrying out her tools and the remains of her junk sculptures, loading them into his car.

"Need a hand, Ben?"

"Almost finished but I thank you, sir."

"You inherited some of her stuff, I see."

"Yes. You know, I put so much thought into these contraptions of hers that I hate to see them thrown away. And our lovely friend may drift back this way sometime."

"She says she's gone for good. Back to the simple life. Sounds like a voyage into hell, if you ask me."

Ben nodded. "Not my ideal either, but I sympathize with the impulse. At any rate, I'm going to store her things. It never pays to put too much faith in the future. It has a way of coming up behind you. Especially where Kathy's concerned."

For the first time, his coming departure came upon James with the force of reality. His own future was dividing him from others. Whatever happened to Kathy, James would not be there to find out. And he thought he could guarantee Ben that he, for one, would never drift back.

Chapter Thirty-Two

Tim took his leaving rather well, considering how short the notice was. James knew that looking for a new organist would be no picnic.

They were sitting in the Sunday School room Tim used during the week as an office. Behind Tim were fifteen identical posters saying: God made only one of me. In some cases, James thought, that was an act of mercy, in others an admission of failure. There must be a positive note in it somewhere, but he couldn't find it.

"Anyway," he sighed, "it wasn't something I could turn down."

"No," said Tim. "Please. Don't feel bad. We always knew you'd go some day."

Did you? thought James. So why didn't I? He said, "Maybe Lori can fill in for a while, until one of the veterans agrees to come back. Work on their guilt. But Lori's really progressed."

"Maybe she can fill in for more than a while."

"Well, until she goes back to school."

"But she's not. Didn't she tell you? Decided to stay home. She's working at the grocery store. I think she's going to get married."

"Oh, man. You're kidding me. With her talent?"

Tim smiled. "What do you have against marriage, James?"

"Nothing. It's waste that I'm against."

"Maybe she doesn't see it that way."

"But maybe it is that way, whether she sees it or not. Maybe somebody should get her to see it that way."

Tim shrugged. "She said she'd had enough school."

James had noticed lately Lori's indifference. "Enough for what?"

"Just enough."

"Well, then, lucky you. If she'll do it."

"Oh, I think she'll agree to play. Bang out a hymn or two. What's the problem?"

And Tim would be getting a musician far more docile and far less headstrong than James. Tim was probably giving thanks for his luck. They each looked away, fidgeting slightly, as though the dissolution of their partnership left them nothing more to talk about. James said, "How about you? Are you going to stay here forever?"

"For the foreseeable future. It's hard for me to think of leaving. I kind of like them all."

"The council get over your paint job?"

"They get over everything. That's the great thing about them."

James didn't know if he would put it in quite that way.

Tim continued, "And I was talking to Mayor Ekdahl. Boy, nothing gets him down. He wants to build a youth center, maybe a hotel for conventions. Wouldn't that be great?"

"Tim. C'mon."

"No, no. He's serious. And we really need something for the kids."

"Right. Well, it looks like you've found your niche."

"Could be, James. Could be."

After he left Tim, he had nothing left to do in New Culloden but pack. Pastor Johnson had called again, offering him the use of a small house the church owned. It had once been the parsonage, but she preferred to live in her own apartment.

"How do I rate all this?" James had asked. "You know, you people haven't even heard me."

"I trust Stephanie's judgment. And don't feel overprivileged. The house isn't that great. And we can always boot you out after the summer."

"Not if I can help it."

"That's the spirit."

What seemed to him an overwhelming gift was to them a matter of their own convenience. It was probably a trick of perspective, the same starvation that had made Grand Forks look so splendid. He would have to get used to taking things for granted again. He couldn't wait.

The night before he left, Danny, Patty, and Ben gave him a going away party. They took him out to the lake to grill hot dogs and get mildly drunk.

"We didn't want to dazzle you with anything too splendid," said Patty. "Afraid you'd change your mind and stay. Then we'd look like fools. Something I do *not* enjoy."

"No chance," said James. "Besides, I like hot dogs."

It was a beautiful, cloudless evening. The lake was still, shining with the setting sun's reflections. Most of the early visitors to the lake had gone home. It was still a little cool to swim. They had the beach to themselves. They ate, drank, sat together on the sand. The sky darkened, revealing its treasure of stars. A full, silver moon rose.

Danny sighed. "And so ends another chapter in the saga of New Culloden. The sands shift. The story goes on. Endless changes."

"Slight cosmetic changes," said Patty. "Mostly it's more of the same."

"Dearest, you're insulting our guest."

"No, I'm not. Why do you think he's leaving, bozo? But, okay, we'll admit we're going to miss you, James."

"Think of all you've given the community," said Beckett. "That wonderful music."

"You guys," said James, "never darkened the door of that church the whole time I was here."

"We didn't want to embarrass you," said Patty. "Make you nervous. We're very considerate people."

"It's the thought that counts," said Beckett.

Danny said, "Forgive us, James, for we have sinned. That's why we're giving you this party. Now you know the truth."

"I insist on enjoying it anyway. And you're all full of shit."

Lightning bugs had come out. Beckett went off to trap some.

"I think Ben's collecting bugs now," said Patty. "I guess there's enough stuff in the world to keep anybody busy. If you're loony enough."

"I'll go help him," said Danny. "If I drink any more, I'll pass out. I really hate that."

"Don't get lost," called Patty. She turned to James, slyly arching her eyebrows. "Alone at last."

He threw some sand on her. "Don't get any ideas."

She lay on her back, looking up at the moon. It seemed a time for confidences, whispers, confessions. But James didn't have any he wanted to give. He knew she envied him leaving.

He said, "So where's your little one?"

"With my parents for the night. They're tickled to have her."

"Finally told them, huh?"

"Yeah. Well, what could we do? You know what they said? They already knew it. How's that for a joke?"

"Why didn't they say anything?"

"My mom said she didn't want to bring it up in case I was only getting fat. Parents are very strange creatures."

"Amen," said James. Amen. He asked, "What do you think? Are you guys ever going to get out of this place?"

She sat up, looked down at her feet, shook her head. "Danny won't ever leave."

"He said he was going back to school."

"He says a lot. So. Why don't you take me with you?"

"You don't really mean that."

She sighed. "Oh, half." She paused, laughed. "*My* half. How about yours?"

"I'm not sure I have room in my car. For a new mother, you know. All that kid stuff."

She laughed again. "No, James, you missed your chance. Here I am and here I will stay. Ho, ho, ho, as the saying goes."

Beckett and Danny returned. They finished the beer and it was time to leave. This would be the last time James would see Patty and Danny. He would avoid the station when he left in the morning, avoid the lingering goodbyes.

He and Beckett watched them drive away.

"Ben, I wanted to ask you something."

"This must be the moment for it."

"Yeah." James began walking toward the lake. Beckett followed him.

James said, "My dad's funeral. I arranged it, you know. He wouldn't have wanted it. Especially not in a church."

"That isn't news."

"And—I felt a little malicious. I did. As though I was beating him finally. That's why I did it."

"That's not exactly news either."

"Ben, you're not being much help."

"In other words, you're wondering if I think that was really your motive and, if I do, do I think you're a vile person. I can't see that it matters much either way. You aren't going to change what happened. And, no, I don't think you're a vile person, or at least no more vile than most."

"I'm not sure what I'm wondering."

"Then you simply feel vaguely—let's say ill at ease. Perhaps you only wanted to mention it."

"I don't know. Maybe."

"Young McGrath, most of us who are worth anything are our own most severe judges. Think of it democratically. That would please your father. The funeral was your vote. The way he lived his life was his vote. That's all. Someday they'll be voting on you and me."

"True enough."

"Did you ever consider that that particular ceremony, a funeral, is nothing more than a victory of order over chaos? You could, you know, see it as the ultimate capitulation to your father."

"That, I think, is stretching it."

"Well, it's a thought." Beckett put his hand on James' shoulder. "You have your life, your gifts. He had his. You didn't get along. You and your father are not as unusual as you imagine. Or as he imagined."

"I'll try to keep that in mind."

"A deflating thought, but a helpful one."

They turned back to their cars. In the sky, above the trees, the Northern Lights were dancing.

"My God," said Beckett, "look at that."

It was as though some unearthly magician had harnessed the power of heaven and was creating mountains of soft light out of nothing. They reached high into the night, shifted, disappeared, soared again.

If they could stand like this with such glory about them, or spend evenings together like this one, or share their days moment by rich moment, who would yearn for anything, who would be restless? If you could stop time at the right moment, with the right people, you would never ache.

But you never could. James said, "I suppose I ought to admit to somebody that I'll miss you guys."

"I daresay you will. And be assured the feeling will be mutual."

"I think I still have some of your books."

"Oh? Which ones?"

"To tell you the truth, I don't remember. I guess I got stuck in them."

"Keep them. A little memento. I won't miss them. Things, you know."

"As Kathy would say."

Beckett sighed. "Kathy. Yes."

James looked at the old man. He had finally come to seem very wise to James, wise and tender. He said, "You're hoping she'll come back, aren't you?"

"An old man's fancy. Do you know that Yeats poem? 'An aged man is but a paltry thing' and so on. 'Unless soul clap its hands and sing', something like that.

Art, you know, not nature. The way to the eternal. Most of the time I agree with him. But there are nights when I think he was talking through his hat. Then again, perhaps that only proves him right."

"Greet her for me if she shows up. Goodbye, Ben."

"Goodbye. And Godspeed."

They drove to their separate homes, James for the last time. Godspeed. Yes.

Chapter Thirty-Three

McGrath's gunfire had not done as much damage to his car as James had feared. The mending of the radiator and the replacement of the oil filter, tasks well within the competence of the local mechanics, made it fit for the road again. But he would have walked to get where he was going.

He loaded the car in the morning and locked McGrath's house for the last time. Anything he might have wanted had burned in the garage anyway. The American Civil Liberties Union could have the lot, with his blessings. McGrath would have pointed out the blessings were not his to give. So.

He took a last look at the grounds, objective, unemotional, too confused and too full to grasp. He got in the car. Before he could turn the key, another car pulled into the driveway behind him and stopped. It was Kris. She ran to his car and he got out.

She was panting, breathless. "Oh, I'm so glad I caught you. I had to see you. One more time."

"You almost missed me." He pointed through his windows. "All loaded up. I was just backing out."

She nodded, gulped. "Here. I wanted you to have this. I wanted to get you something. But I didn't have the time. Then I thought of this. I thought it would mean something more. I mean, to me. For you to have it." She pushed Bach's *Well Tempered Clavier* into his arms, the book she had brought with her so shyly and hopefully when she had first come to him.

"Oh, Kris. I can't take this."

"Yes. Yes, you can. I want you to have it."

"But this—it's like your dream."

"Oh! I'm not giving up. Don't worry about that! And, well, if it is, then I want to give you a little of it. Of my dream. To show you—well, here. I wrote in it."

He opened the front cover. She had written:

For all you've given me. Love, Kris.

He felt the unintended brutality of departure then, its thoughtlessness and selfishness. He looked down at the book, speechless. It was almost as though she had sacrificed a child. But he hadn't asked her to. This was a gift.

She said, "I had a hard time figuring out what to write. I mean, I had to put something down. I couldn't put any more. Didn't want to leave that kind of evidence loose."

"Kris—"

"I thought—well, *you* can play this stuff. And I know you like it. And that when you did you'd think of. Well. Me." She cleared her throat. "That you'd think of me. Knowing that will make me happy."

"I—"

She put her fingers on his lips quickly. "Sh, sh. You gave me something I always wanted. Whenever I'm snowed, I can look at my piano books and—I feel clean. It's like—there's more to me than just a cook or a cleaner."

"It takes you away from yourself."

"Yeah. Well, no. That's what they say about those romantic novels. This is bigger and better. It's this wonderful world, all this music. But I'm learning it so it's part of me, part of my world. So that's a little more wonderful."

He put the book under his arm. He would almost have to build a shrine for it to do it justice. He looked down at his wonderful student, bewildered again by the mystery of human beings.

She raised her head and searched his face. She said, "I'm really sad that you're going." Her voice was husky. One small tear fell from each of her eyes. "But good luck. Have the *best* luck." She kissed his cheek and ran to her car. She didn't look back.

He placed her book carefully in the back seat, sat in his car, and stared out through the windshield. He supposed nothing was ever finished, or finished very well. But it was time for him not to look back.

He backed the car out slowly, checked for rampaging trucks, and pulled into the highway. In his rearview mirror he saw Einar Ekdahl walking toward him. He put the car in reverse, backing down the highway until he was even with the mayor.

But Ekdahl hadn't seen him. He was tying streamers from one tree to another all along the highway. James honked his horn.

Ekdahl waved and approached him. "The location was all wrong, you know, location is everything. We have to put the mall here, where people can see it. Of course, we'll have to tear down all these houses, you know, the churches, everything, but I think people will make allowances. Don't you? I think they'll have enough civic spirit for that, you know, it's for the good of the town. I'm just marking out the boundaries." Far behind him, James could see his wife rolling up the streamers, going door to door apologizing to elderly men and women who didn't know what she was talking about.

Einar slapped the roof of the car. "I'd love to talk, you know, but there's so much to do."

James said, "Goodbye, Einar."

He drove away then, dropped off his father's keys at the Carlsburg lawyer's office, and headed south. He would follow U.S. 59 to where it crossed the Interstate, then follow the path of all Minnesota roads into Minneapolis. One little town after another dropped behind him, and soon they would grow larger and then he wouldn't be able to tell where one stopped and another began.

But while they were still tiny, with one grain elevator, one gas station, one or two churches, one or two bars, no school at all and only gravel for their roads, he entered one that greeted him with this sign:

> IF YOU LIVED HERE,
> YOU'D BE HOME ALREADY.

He entered it, and he left it, perhaps at a slightly higher speed. He wasn't tempted. He didn't look back.

ACKNOWLEDGMENTS

This writing took so long to reach its final shape that I can no longer be sure of remembering everyone who had a look at it. Thanks to all who bothered and who continued to like me, or at least tolerate me, anyway. Please continue, even though my memory failed you.

Mary Carol Strug always smiles, says positive things, and allows space for all my creations, as I do for hers, and thus we display one of the secrets of a long marriage. Peter Geisendorfer-Lindgren said reading this was like listening to me talk nonstop for hours. Carolyn Strug blurted out, as each new character appeared, that it was only another version of myself, which I admit I was not always glad to hear. Gary Halverson, after reading the earliest version, has continued to ask me about it for years, somehow always managing to imply that publishing it would be a bad idea. Melissa Stueve was disappointed with the lack of romantic resolutions. Sally Nelson walked into my kitchen and beat me on the head with the manuscript because she hated what happened to the dog.

Sylvia Ruud, both the first and the last of all my readers, hated what happened to the dog, too, but she still edited, designed, and produced this book, thus providing its handsome look and its very reality. This will be the fifth work we've done together, and none would exist without her partnership. We sometimes wonder why it took us so long to get started.

www.ingramcontent.com/pod-product-compliance
Lightning Source LLC
Chambersburg PA
CBHW051148030726
47504CB00004B/1099